FUNNYBONE

A memoir by Frankie Funnybone

(Edited by John Gradwell)

Volume 1 – 1915-39 and 1945-51

To my inspiration – Bill Bradbury

From your friend

[signature]

Published in 2012 by FeedARead Publishing

This novel is entirely a work of fiction. Although certain characters may be loosely based on historical figures, events portrayed in the book are the work of the author's imagination.

A CIP catalogue record for this title is available from the British Library.

john.gradwell@hotmail.co.uk

www.johngradwell.com

Cover design by Iva Polansky

WHAT THEY SAID

Reviews of Funnybone on writers' website
www.YouWriteOn.com include

"Certainly the most original and entertaining read I've come across on YWO. I loved Frankie's voice and think his character comes across really well."

Kate Braithwaite, award-winning novelist

"Of all the pieces on YWO this is probably the closest to being of a professional, publishable standard. It reminded me of Brass ... which was written by my Dad."

Sebastian Roach

Other YouWriteOn reviewers said:

"Fantastic read ... leaves you wanting to read more which I will if it's published."

"I have scored this the highest I have scored anything so far ... and I don't usually choose humorous fiction."

"I am a huge fan of P.G. Wodehouse and now I am a fan of Frankie too."

"I thoroughly enjoyed this and laughed like a drain all the way through."

Frankie Funnybone rocks!

See these and other reviews at www.johngradwell.com

For Carole

PROLOGUE

Now that I've reached my ninety-seventh year I've decided I might as well come clean about all the sense and nonsense that's been written about me these last eight decades. And there's been more than a bit of both.

For instance, was it true that I played a crucial role in British foreign policy leading up to the Second World War? Yes it was.

Did I persuade my old mate Dapper Dave *(Edward VIII)* to give up the throne for the woman he loved? Undoubtedly, who wouldn't?

Was I the one who told Bernie Winters he had a future in comedy? No I flamin' well wasn't, but I can confirm that there's still a bounty - in guineas - on the culprit's head.

However, this volume is not just one long catalogue of my many triumphs on the international stage. It's also a history of the British entertainment scene, from the halls, through variety, films and telly to the blogosphere and Twitternet where I now have a whole new legion of followers *(they call themselves Boners)*.

From Formby and Flanagan, through Forsyth and Feldman, up to French and Flintoff; I can see them all like it was yesterday. Yes, my mind's as clear as it *(n)*ever was.

Where was I? Oh aye, as I said now that I've reached the grand old age of ninety-six, I might as well tell the whole truth and nothing but the truth about all I've got up to. This includes the dramatic wooing of my beloved Nancy, our action-packed elopement and a thrilling flight from her dad's goons – it's definitely a tale not to be missed.

Sadly Nancy passed on a few years ago and it is to my shame that I can finally own up to one or two extra-marital liaisons of which I'm in no way proud *(in particular, those steamy entanglements with the three Graces – Fields, Kelly and Slick)*.

So you'll just have to take me and my story warts an' all. Everything's in my own words too but the dunce who's editing this memoir keeps shoving his oar in. He reckons that if I've got me facts wrong he'll correct them with brackets and italics and whatnot. So, if you see any just ignore 'em because, take it from me, the accuracy rate in this book is 100 per cent *(34.86 per cent actually)*.

Incidentally this editor clot – whose name escapes me – had the brass neck to write a radio show about me a few years ago. Packed full of lies it was too *(it wasn't)* but luckily no bugger ever listened to it and the clown with a mangled moniker who played me *(Peter Serafinowicz)* has never been heard of since.

The only thing this editor idiot managed to get right was my famous catchphrase, "I've come on me bike," which is definitely not a double entendre so it's all right to let the nippers browse through this *(not advisable, mums)*.

As I gaze back down into that long, dark tunnel of time, I realise I've lived through the reigns of four monarchs, one of whom became a good pal, another who was best man at my wedding and one who was a very intimate acquaintance if you get my meaning. I'll not mention which of the four this was – you'll have to wait for the second volume of my memoirs *(1952-68)* for more about that little secret.

Anyroad, enjoy the book and see you next time, *(statistically unlikely)* you daft lot.

Frankie Funnybone,
Wisteria Home for the Terminally Bewildered,
Morecambe, Lancashire, June 2012.

PART ONE – 1915-39

Chapter One: Flexi to Funny

I never knew my father. You see, I was born in November 1915, nine months after Mum had tearfully waved her devoted husband Leslie off to the Western Front – and found immediate comfort in the arms of an illegal bookmaker called Pobjoy. She never saw him again ... or her winnings for that matter.

Thankfully, Mum was reunited with Leslie, who managed to beat the odds and stay more or less alive until Armistice Day. I'd love to tell you how he did it but, apart from seven words, Les Thirkettle hardly ever mentioned his experiences during the Great War. Those words, spoken to me on my ninth birthday when I asked him what life was really like in the trenches, were, "Plenty racket and nowhere proper to shit." We left it at that.

Times were hard for the Thirkettle family nearly a century ago. But, in case you think my childhood was one long catalogue of misery, let me say that on the up side I lived in a house full of servants. On the down side, most of them were members of my family. Dad was the chief groom and later mechanic, Mum worked as a scullery maid and my eldest sister Rose was a tub thumper. The rest of my siblings were pie wallopers, dolly bashers and goat nappers – everyday household jobs that sadly have all but disappeared in our helter-skelter dash to modernity. From the ages of seven to twelve I was a slutch slinger, which says it all really. *(It is fairly certain that, in his present imbecilic state, Frankie has made up many of these occupations).*

We all lived and worked at the mansion home of Butterthwaite's first family, the Protheroes. Great-grandad Caleb Protheroe had founded the cotton spinning dynasty in the 1850s and at the turn of the 20th century it was the town's main employer, with five mills.

By the 1920s, when I was growing up, head of the family was Joshua, a permanently angry cove who loved nothing better than sacking employees when they were fifteen seconds late arriving at Protheroe Mills. His infamous pocket watch was on public display until 1968 when long-haired anarchists blew it up, along with the rest of that organ of the fascist state, Butterthwaite Library and Museum.

Joshua had a son, Robert, and four daughters, the youngest of which, Nancy, was a couple of months my junior. When she knew her Dad was otherwise engaged, selling cloth or ducking maidservants, Nancy would sneak below stairs and we'd play marbles, shove ha'penny and rugby league together.

Those were carefree days but, even then, I harboured a suspicion that things could not go on as they were. And I was proved right. During a particularly subterranean scrummage we were interrupted by Nancy's mother, Agatha, who fainted clean away when she saw our tangled limbs.

After that the servants' quarters were out of bounds to Nancy and a short time later, aged thirteen, she was shipped off to finishing school somewhere or other in Europe. Our eager limbs would not entwine again for another seven years.

I could have pined away but, to tell you the truth, I had other fish to fry by then. For one thing I'd become so skilled at fettling the slutch pails that after school I was free to explore the surrounding countryside with my old buddies Stinker and Stonker from St Barnabas C of E School. Many's the time our merry threesome would while away the twilight hours playing hopscotch and fleeing from the local perverts.

During our weekly family all-in wrestling bouts - try organising those today without Social Services kicking the front door down - Dad noticed what Nancy had already

11

found out; that my limbs were extraordinarily supple. This gave him an idea.

"Just tek a look at him, Minnie," he panted admiringly to Mum, as my left leg disappeared behind his right ear. "I reckon it's about time Ma dragged Jackie Slack around these parts to have a dekko at our bendy bouncer."

Les hadn't gone prematurely gaga. You see, his widowed mother Molly lived with us after Joshua had given her a grace and favour job terrifying the local rat population. But, before she became a rodent botherer, Granny Thirkettle had appeared on the halls as The Blackburn Barn Owl. *(Mary 'Molly' Thirkettle, nee Puddock, 1854-1932, was indeed a noted music hall star of the 1880s to early 1900s. It was widely said that what she lacked in talent she made up for in raw sexual allure).*

Granny's old agent, Jack Slack, was still knocking around so one evening Dad smuggled him into the cellar at Protheroe Hall to watch me turn myself inside out and back to front.

"Ever seen owt like that, Jack Slack?" my admiring Gran quizzed her erstwhile mentor. Jack drew thoughtfully on his briar and admitted it had been many a long year since he had clapped eyes on such a phenomenon. Within days he had secured my first professional engagement at Preston Playhouse and for the next three years I was Francis Flexibones, Butterthwaite's Bendiest Boy. The curtain had gone up on my show business career.

If this were one of them modern misery memoirs, I'd give you chapter and verse on boring midnight journeys home spent unwinding - literally as it turned out - in the back seat of Jack Slack's Bentley. I might also mention bust-ups with Joshua over my increasingly erratic time-keeping and regular therapeutic visits to Mr Gordon-Bennett, osteopath to the stars. But I've had too long a life to dwell on childhood matters so I'll bring the early part of my story to a close with the tale of how I came by my famous catchphrase.

By now I was 16, no longer all that bendy and therefore not much use to Jack Slack, who'd garaged the Bentley and made me cycle to engagements. I didn't mind the new travel arrangements as journeys in Jack's limo had become increasingly hazardous. It was easy enough to fight off his wandering hands but the fact he steered the car with one knee while turning his attentions to me in the back became too much to bear.

All that, plus the realisation that Jack and I appeared to have the 90-10 per cent turn-agent split the wrong way round, made me decide to knock things on the head. I had just two more bookings as Francis Flexibones to fulfil – which was good. The first happened to be at The Liverpool Empire - which wasn't.

At this point it might be useful to explain exactly what the act entailed because I'll guarantee none of you under seventy will have seen a rubber man or boy in action. *(None at all, apart from the millions who watch Britain's Got Talent).* What would happen is that I'd wrap both ankles behind my ears and roll around the stage like a broken rocking chair, gurning on that the wind had changed and I'd be stuck like this for ever. A proper cue for laughter!

However, during my penultimate turn as Francis Flexibones, when the time came to stop rolling around, I found that I couldn't. That breeze I'd been bangin' on about must have changed because I was well and truly stuck. Even more upsetting, my screams of pain were treated either as part of the act or a huge source of amusement by those in the audience who'd twigged my dilemma. So my howls of agony led to echoing gales of mirth from all the Scousers present. The more I screamed the more they screamed.

Of course my main worry was that I wouldn't be able to cycle home to east Lancashire and my machine would stay on Merseyside for ever – more than likely propped up on two bricks. But groans of, "I've come on me bike," were, typically for that part of the world, taken as some sordid code. "You'd never hit it from that angle," was one of the more acceptable comments.

Luckily there was an orthopaedic surgeon in the house - Harley Street it turned out when the bastard's bumper bill arrived. He managed to free me using a coat hanger, two Smarties tubes and a large tin of dubbin fished out of her handbag by a woman on the front row - nobody ever thought to ask. *(Not for the first time Frankie is mistaken. Smarties were only introduced by H.I. Rowntree and Co in 1937. The cardboard tubes he mentions would most likely have contained powerful horse tranquilisers).*

This story must have done the rounds in double quick time because next week at the Bradford Alhambra the audience at my severely curtailed final bendy performance put up the cry, "What have you come on?" I had no option but to yell in reply, "I've come on me bike," and a comedy legend was born. I was ready for the big time.

Chapter Two: The Two Franks

It's often said, mainly by that soft gang whose members included Morecambe, Cooper, Monkhouse and Howerd, that you faced the roughest crowd of all at the Glasgow Empire. To escape from that place with your life and a decent share of limbs was reckoned some sort of triumph; the showbiz equivalent of Rorke's Drift with VCs *(Variety Clubs)* all round. What complete and utter hogwash! I always found the Jockos, as my old mucker Greavsie wittily calls them, a joy to be among. As long as you didn't mention religion, football, strong drink and the English you could, as I did on more than one occasion, have them eating out of your hand. Claim a line of descent from William Wallace, close friendship with Sir Harry Lauder and an abiding love of battered salt cake and they'd award you freedom of the city.

No, the old Empire with its rows of faded slashed seats disappearing heavenwards was a joy to play and definitely not the comedian's graveyard of legend. That particular dubious honour, I'm still here to tell you, goes to The Grand Theatre in Bolton.

If that seems a bit rum then don't just take it from me. Listen to Charlie Naughton of the Crazy Gang who estimated, "Some of them buggers was madder than us".

Or hang on to the words of poor Arthur Lucan, Old Mother Riley in proper money, who was chased, petticoats billowing, by a slavering mob along Deansgate.

"I thought me time had come, Frankie," Artie confided in me. "Ooooh I really did; tell him, Kitty!"

And then there's Frank Randle who reckoned ... but we'll get to Randle in good time.

That's because as usual I'm racing ahead of myself here. I should have mentioned that we're already up to a warm and muggy Saturday night in late June 1935 and, at just nineteen, I was second on the bill in Bolton. Great stuff eh?

Young Frankie, with his new moustache thickening nicely, has already hit the big time, I hear you say. Well, I can't hear a thing any more but you get my drift.

What I've not explained is that it was Wakes Week – holidays to you. In normal circumstances there wouldn't even have been a show because the entire town traditionally packed its collective bucket and spade into its cardboard suitcase and left for the seaside in steam trains and charabancs.

However, because so many Bolton lads had been banned from entering Blackpool again, the Grand management in their wisdom decided there'd be enough of an audience to stage one show with new acts on the cheap. With that sort of logic what could possibly go wrong? *(There is absolutely no record of Blackpool having banned Bolton lads; indeed anecdotal evidence suggests the seaside landladies were remarkably fond of them).*

Personally I wouldn't have booked Mad Hettie Twot to open proceedings. I reckon anyone whose main claim to fame is that she can turn her head inside out is asking for trouble and trouble is what she duly got. Poor old Hettie was last seen being carried out of the building on a gate, head apparently the wrong way out, although it was difficult to tell as, ironically, Hettie was hardly one of nature's head-turners.

Then it was time for Jimmy Binns, the bony balloon-bender from Burnley, to do his stuff. His attempts to get in with the mob didn't fare much better. After he confided to them that the heckling had started as he was driving in through Tonge Moor the witty riposte came, namely, "Sod off back up Tonge Moor then, you long streak of piss."

That was when the fighting started, the Hunger Hill boys against the Daubhill Crew and no quarter asked or given. There was total mayhem for ten minutes after which they all shook hands, sat down and prepared to welcome the next turn – Jimmy Binns having departed in haste as the first rabbit punch connected with its target. *(As a proud Boltonian I resent these unwarranted slurs on a fine and peaceable town. I'll kick Frankie's backside next time I see him).*

Unfortunately for me the next turn was Frank Randle. At that time Randle wasn't widely known and hadn't perfected the elaborate pranks that made him famous. Bombarding Blackpool with toilet rolls from a plane, putting quick-dry cement into the mayor's three-cornered hat and peeing into a tea urn - from the adjoining room - were not yet part of Randle folklore. His status in the business, however, was already legendary. A madman, totally without fear who was about to face the most difficult crowd around. I'll let one distinguished critic describe what happened next.

"A drum roll and then silence for maybe ten seconds. Think of it, complete stillness in that bear pit. Then from the wings the most extraordinary sight. A tatterdemalion in an ill-fitting suit shambled on and proceeded to harangue and challenge the audience, opening with, 'Call yourself a crowd. I've seen more people in me landlady's bed of a mornin' than in this s**t-heap.' And, do you know what, the Grand crowd, far from appearing disconcerted, positively embraced the demotic demon. This notoriously hard-to-please audience was eating out of the mad imp's hand – and would doubtless have continued to do so until, characteristically, thirty riotous minutes in, he went just that tiny step too far. Following his jutting, strutting challenge to the effect that, 'I'll take you all on, every last one of you,' Randle only survived because each man and not a few of the ladies were so intent on fighting each other for the signal honour of punching out the Lord of Misrule's lights. Sensing a chance to bring the act to an appropriate crescendo, Randle used the already well-worn stratagem of hurling his false teeth into the audience – with one significant adaptation which spurred the crowd to greater

heights of frenzy. This time his detached dentures remained clamped around the obligatory bottle of beer, in this case a flagon of Magee Marshall's Crown Ale. Unfailingly, Frank stuck to the local brew.

Osbert Jardine, Hall Our Yesterdays, Tamara Press, 1959.

What Sir Osbert neglected to mention in his entertaining memoir was that, as he bundled past me in the wings, Randle flashed his gummy letterbox grin and said, "I've warmed 'em up right good for thee, Frankie."

The mad sod *had* warmed 'em up all right. A selection of Bolton's finest were coming to the boil and looked like they were about to explode – all over poor little nineteen-year-old me. So I reasoned I had no choice but to meet them head-on, just as Randle had.

The chairman, a feeble specimen, just had time to announce me and duck back into his bunker before they launched all they had at the stage. From the wings I watched as plant pots, walking sticks, a Yorkshire terrier called Dustin and, somewhat inevitably, Frank Randle's false chompers cascaded down on the boards.

When I was sure the storm had subsided I stepped out from behind the curtain, stood among the debris and inquired, "Anyone here mislaid one or two items?" Thankfully that worked a treat on them and when I went on to reveal that the hideous crone furiously knitting on the front row - I'm not kidding either - was Miss Wigan 1927 they were all mine.

I say all but there was one fellow five rows back who caught my eye because he never even looked at the stage. This chap, who wore a muffler round the bottom half of his face, seemed more interested in the crowd around him than in my act. His eyes darted this way and that and his fists were continually clenching as if he expected trouble.

But there were few ructions of the sort that had seen off Hettie and Jimmy. In fact the only hairy moment came at what was usually the strongest part of my act. When I asked how they thought I had travelled to the theatre that night, one wag yelled, "In a cow's arse" to gales of laughter and I sensed I could be losing them. But a short explanation as to how I'd arrived at the theatre on a two-wheeled velocipede brought them back into my orbit and the act ended in considerable applause. *(It appears Frankie is not just boasting here. A contemporary report by Owd Gawker in the Bolton Evening Chronicle records that he was 'a copper-bottomed success' on his Grand debut).*

Walking offstage, with cheers swirling round the rafters, I half-expected to be collared by our friend in the muffler. I reckoned he was one of those stage-door Johnnies, or pests as we call them in the business. But, as he was nowhere to be seen, I hurried to share my euphoria with, in the absence of a friend or a loved one, the maniac in our two-man dressing room.

However, when I burst in shouting, "You'll never guess what, Frank," Randle was already snoring in an armchair, head thrown right back and with an upturned bottle of beer lodged at an angle in his toothless mouth. I carefully removed the empty bottle in case it throttled the mad bugger – that would have been true poetic justice – and gently replaced his false teeth which I'd managed to retrieve from the stage.

I was in the middle of scraping off the last layer of make-up when there was a knock at the door and a small, heavy-set chap in a homburg and camel-hair coat bowled in. As this cove closed the door behind him, Randle opened one eye and said, "Eddie."

"Frank," replied the stranger and, satisfied, Randle resumed his slumbers.

This bloke came straight at me hand outstretched and in a Cockney accent introduced himself as, "Eddie Star, theatrical agent."

"Frankie Funnybone, pacifier of mutinous crowds," I replied.

Eddie Star carefully removed his hat and sat down in my armchair. "Wotcher, Frankie," he chuckled, "I saw how you handled yourself out there. Very impressive!"

He glanced around at the Spartan surroundings and wrinkled his bulbous nose in disgust.

"You don't represent ...?" I said, pointing at the dozing Randle.

Eddie Star looked genuinely alarmed as he replied, "Christ almighty, Tosh, what do you take me for? I never go lookin' for trouble and, as you might have noticed, that fellow kippin' over there is trouble with a capital T."

Well, few could disagree with that and, while I made a pot of tea and gave him first run at the ginger nuts, Eddie Star reeled off an impressive list of names he had on his books. When he'd done he leaned back with a satisfied smile.

"And who represents you at the moment, son?" he asked.

"Well, I was handled by Jack Slack."

"Yeah, I've heard that happened to a few people."

"But for the last couple of years I've tended to just do it myself."

"We can't have that, old son," said Eddie.

He took a minute to look me up and down, as if he were about to send me for slaughter.

"What are you, Tosh, five-eleven?"

"And a half."

"That's good," said Eddie, smiling. "Audiences don't mind someone who'll fill the stage. We'll give you a proper haircut, shave off the soup strainer and you'll be ready for civilisation. You're coming in with me."

Crikey, two major accomplishments in one night and me only nineteen. First I've tamed Bolton Grand. Then I've done no more than got onto the books of a showbiz legend, who rarely ventured beyond the Home Counties. Although I played it cool with Eddie, I already knew that, not only did he have a client list that read like the Royal Variety Show line-up in a good year, but also numbered among his pals the Prince of Wales, Winston Churchill and Gracie Fields.

Frankie Funnybone, Butterthwaite's erstwhile bendiest boy, was about to go hob-nobbing with the quality – and Gracie Fields. *(As we'll see later, Frankie's unnecessary and unfeeling dismissal of Gracie means he is once again allowing personal preferences to get in the way of objective assessment. Silly old bugger!)*

With all that in mind it didn't take long to sort out the financial details to both our satisfactions. Eddie was about to take his leave when we became aware of a rumbling in the background and the light fittings began to swing back and forth alarmingly.

"Blimey, I didn't know they'd built an underground rail system in this part of the world," said Eddie, perplexed.

"That's no train," I told him. "It's the crowd. And they're turning even uglier."

Judging that they'd behaved themselves for far too long during the interval, the Grand mob had lurched into aggressive restlessness, making the whole building shake, never to my mind, a hopeful sign. At that moment the top of the bill bobbed his head nervously round the door. This sad article was Archie Shields, the Basingstoke Baritone, who volunteered hopefully, "Er, I'd say they sound an appreciative crowd, Frankie. What?"

The baritone's whine jolted Randle back to consciousness. He fixed Archie with an unsteady stare and informed him, "They'll eat thee alive, tha gormless warbling wanker," before subsiding back to sleep.

Archie's features turned the colour of baking powder as Randle's warning sent him staggering back against the trembling door frame.

"They do appear a trifle boisterous," he croaked, as the sound of splintering furniture drifted through the walls.

"Never let 'em smell the fear, Archie," I counselled with a comforting grin, while slamming the door on him.

Moved by my compassion, Eddie invited me to share a drink. What he actually did was pass me a note to avoid alerting Randle that alcohol was on offer.

"Share a drink? I'd rather have one of my very own," I replied as waggishly as one could by semaphore, before we sneaked out by the stage door to the accompaniment of Frank Randle snoring and Archie Shields screaming.

It was Eddie's intention, he later informed me as we marked our new alliance with pints of dark mild in the Old Three Crowns, that I should make London my operational base.

"Don't get me wrong, old son," Eddie explained. "You already seem the equal of Frank Randle and I know they love a typical northern lad round here. But I'd care to wager that Randle will be stuck in these parts for ever while, for you, The London Palladium beckons. More beer?"

He was as good as his word too was Eddie. Within a few weeks I was indeed playing the Palladium, meeting the Prince of Wales and starting the most important relationship of my life. But all that's for later. First there was Butterthwaite to take my leave of.

Chapter Three: The Leaving of Butterthwaite

It's an odd thing but I'm now considered more of a Butterthwaite fixture than when I first started my glittering career. These days, as you know, I'm an inmate of this grim old folk's prison – Cold Tits the women in here call it. However, until not long ago, I was a much beloved feature of the town, having moved back with Nancy when I retired from the stage in 1990.

Yet it was different when I was growing up because then I fell between two stools. I was considered a bit posh by the Butterthwaite lads I went to school with because I lived up at Protheroe Hall. On the other hand the quality took delight in looking down their turned-up noses on the likes of us below stairs. Not that either scenario particularly bothered me. I've always been a bit harum scarum if you get my meaning. In fact I'm still a real handful as young Ricky Hatton will testify. (*Frankie's all but bedridden. An arthritic tortoise can move faster*). OK, so Myrtle Leach knocked me over in the morning room yesterday but it was a low blow from a cunning woman and I was up at the count of eight – well on one knee anyway which must signify something at my age.

Anyhow it was a different story in the 1920s and 30s. I'd smash the living daylights out of any schoolboy rival who tried to get one over on me. Then, when their dads or big brothers marched up to the hall to duff me over, my Dad would repeat the process on them. What a team! Old Les didn't say much but he was hard as nails and took great pride in looking after the family.

Course, you couldn't go around knocking the collective blocks off Master Robert and his plummy pals when they felt the urge to go below stairs and taunt our family. But I soon became adept at returning any piss taken - and with interest. For instance, Robert would often dig his pal Edmund - you'll discover a bit more about him later on, unless I forget - in the ribs and announce, "I say, Edders, what's the jolly difference between a bucket of slutch and young Thirkettle here."

Edmund would profess himself absolutely baffled, what, and Robert would reply, "Only the bucket," to considerable hilarity – most of it his own.

Usually I'd let them have their fun before replying something like, "Very good, Master Robert, you should be on the stage." Just as the warm glow of self-satisfaction began to sweep over Joshua's eldest, I'd puncture his triumph with, "It leaves at five twenty-five - be on it."

Now you'll have heard that one a thousand times before but in the 1930s it was brand new. How do I know? Because it was me that made it up, then and there! If you think that's romancing I actually copyrighted it and, what's more, there's a bloke at the European Patents Office in The Hague, wherever that is, who'll confirm all I've said. So there! *(This is patent nonsense).*

Phew, where was I? Oh yes, Master Robert was harmless enough for all his bluster, something that couldn't be said for his explosive dad. While Robert had adopted many of the landed gentry's ways after his spells at Rugby and Oxford, his old man, who had rarely strayed from the North, was still as down-to-earth as ever – a real, solid gold, dyed in the wool, salt of the earth tosser!

I'd never got on with Joshua since I became Butterthwaite's bendiest boy and, in his view, neglected my work at the hall. I strongly suspect he'd have slung me out long before, had it not been for his appreciation of Les's capabilities. Joshua realised that if I went then so would the best groom and mechanic the hall had ever had. So there was an uneasy truce, ironically until the day I took my leave.

I'd gone upstairs to tell Joshua I'd be out of his hair within the week when, passing the doors of the great drawing room, I heard the unmistakable sound of a defenceless piano being clubbed to death. This could mean only one thing – Nancy was at home.

I peeped in and there she was, dressed simply but fetchingly in a white blouse twinned with jodhpurs and managing to make a Chopin fugue sound like Any Old Iron. I was about to sneak off and do my ears a favour when Nancy noticed I was gawping and beckoned me in with a smile. Since the tag team act all those years ago, our paths rarely crossed but when they did there was still an easy intimacy between us.

She pointed to the unfortunate instrument. "What do you reckon to the old Joanna bashing, Franco? Something else huh?"

"I couldn't have put it better, Nance. I thought someone was throttling a badger in here."

"Cheeky blighter! Are you aware that Daddy's shelled out oodles for me to sound like this."

"And it's been worth every last penny."

She stared gravely at me before we burst out laughing at the same moment. Nancy slammed the lid of the baby grand shut and got up from the stool, revealing that she was now not far short of my height. I noticed she wasn't wearing any shoes either. No make-up, no footwear, no jewellery. She looked sensational.

"You always give me a laugh, Frankie, I really don't see enough of you," said Nancy, lighting up a Craven A.

Well, what do you say when the lord of the manor's daughter reveals you're her particular favourite? "You're not bad yourself?" "Play us another one?" "Let's run off together?"

I snapped out of my daydream – after all nothing could come of it – and replied, "Well you won't be seeing much more of me either."

Nancy suddenly stopped laughing. "You're leaving us?"

When I told her all about The Grand, Eddie Star and the London contract, she whistled, expelling a storm cloud of smoke.

"Bound for the big time eh, Franco. I always knew you'd do it. You don't need a good pianist do you?"

"Yeah, do you know where I could find one?"

Nancy made a move towards me and I half hoped we might be in for a repeat of our legendary wrestling manoeuvres. But she contented herself with a friendly punch under my heart before turning and stalking over to the huge French windows. Gazing out on to the lawn, she gathered her long wavy blonde hair into a ponytail and fastened it with an elastic band. Then she said quietly, "I suppose you've heard I'm to be married?"

Sadly I was only too aware that Nancy had become betrothed to Robert's big drip of a pal, Edmund. However, I affected unconcern.

"Yes I had heard that," I replied. "When is the happy event?"

"I'm not pregnant, you fathead."

She always had a knack of catching me on the hop and, at this, I became proper flustered.

"Listen, Nancy, forgive me I wasn't being funny or anything."

"Oh yes you were, Franco," she said screaming with laughter. "Happy event, that's a hoot. Edmund's never laid so much as a perfumed glove on me. Ha ha ha."

Once again, her reaction made me uncomfortable and forced me into asking, "If he's such a joke then why are you going out with him?"

She stopped laughing and turned angrily to me. "He's not a joke and I'm not going out with him."

"But I thought you said ..."

"I'm not going out with him. I'm marrying him. It was all decided some time ago." And she started laughing again but this time as if she didn't find it at all funny.

26

I was about to ask how she really felt about the situation but the sudden arrival of Joshua and his bodyguard Maurice Lake put the mockers on that. Meanwhile Nancy continued to laugh mirthlessly while her Dad glared in angry bemusement.

"What's all this racket about? Is he bothering you?"

Joshua glowered at me while my mind worked overtime trying to imagine him sitting on the toilet.

"It isn't Frank who's bothering me, Daddy dear. In fact ..." Nancy left the sentence hanging and turned back towards the window. Predictably this further enraged Joshua.

"Running round the place half-naked," he shouted, looking daggers at yours truly.

Nancy coolly turned back to Joshua and murmured, "Oh, Frankie looks quite respectable."

"Not him you, you flamin' ..."

"Flamin' what, Daddy? Trollop?"

Blimey this was worse than Bolton Grand. At least there you could see what was about to hit you. I decided my old oil on troubled waters routine was needed more than ever.

"I'm sorry, sir," I said, "I only came up here to tell you that I'll be leaving your employment at the earliest convenience."

"Oh aye," replied Joshua, looking me up and down with contempt. "Off to jail are you?"

"No, sir, London."

"How you getting there - on yer bike? Ha, ha, ha."

"Very good, sir. You should be on the stage."

That wiped the smile off Joshua's face. He looked at me, eyes narrowed.

"You want to watch yourself in London. A cheeky chappy can come to a bad end down there eh, Lake."

Joshua turned to his bodyguard who kept an admirably poker face as he replied, "Judging from his recent appearance in Bolton, sir, it sounds as if he can look after himself."

"That's as may be," countered Joshua, "but remember Bolton's brimming over with half-wits. They're a fair bit sharper down south."

Nancy looked at her dad in amusement. "I'd back Frankie against any toffee-nosed softy," she drawled, blowing out a challenging plume of smoke.

"Frankie! Frankie!" Joshua spat. "How long's this little mutual admiration society been going?" He glared at me. "Do you realise, funny man, she's engaged to be married?"

"Yeah and she's not all that keen on getting hitched to some toffee-nosed softy with no lead in his pencil."

That, at least, was what I wanted to say. What actually came out was, "Yes, sir, and I hope they'll be very happy."

"And everyone'll be a great deal happier when you're not around. Take a week's pay in hand and get your arse out of here today."

Well, I wasn't anticipating a tribute etched on vellum and an onyx carriage clock but this display of ingratitude was a bit much, even for Joshua. I was just about to bloomin' well say so too before Nancy – ever so sweetly – did it for me.

"Daddy dear, Frank's worked here man and boy. He's devoted his life to the Protheroe family and you can't even bring yourself to wish him well on his great adventure. Shame on you, Daddy!"

Even though it's three-quarters of a century ago, I can still visualise Joshua hopping from one foot to the other, looking like a mongrel that had been thoroughly whipped. Of course, had it been me not Nancy who'd reacted like that, I'd have been bouncing off the walls on the end of Lake's boot. But the stroppy old bugger always listened when his darling daughter spoke.

Joshua took a deep breath and said through clenched teeth, "Yeah OK, all the best." And, catching Nancy's disapproving eye, he added to these heartfelt words with what sounded like the announcement of a school half-holiday, namely, "And up the Thirkettle family."

It was too good to miss. "And up yours too, sir," I replied extending my palm. Joshua, eyes on fire, had no choice but to accept the handshake before a delighted Nancy hustled me past the smirking Lake and out through the French windows.

Nancy linked my arm as we strolled down the endless front lawn towards the stables.

"I don't suppose you'll be coming to the wedding," she said wistfully.

"I don't suppose I'll be invited."

"You would if I had any say in it."

"But you don't so I won't."

Nancy shrugged and, with a quick glance at the house, pulled my head down towards hers and kissed me. It was a proper smacker too, which left me with the tantalising taste of a tongue coated in peppermints and Craven A. I was flabbergasted and totally uncertain how to react before she pushed me away.

"I'll not walk on the gravel," she sniffed. "I've no shoes on. Give my regards to Les." And, without looking back, she skipped towards the house and out of my life for ever – or so I thought.

I was still struggling to make sense of what had just happened as I wandered into the stable cum garage where my Dad was underneath the Alvis, with only a pair of overalled legs visible. His assistant, an unprepossessing youth called Cain Trotter, was lounging by the work-bench trying to look as if he was about to do something useful without chopping off both his arms. Cain was roughly my age and it's fair to say that he and I had never been best pals.

"I'd heard," Cain began, "that you was shittin' bricks on Sat'day at The Grand."

"Really, Cain? I'm so glad you paid good money to see me shit bricks."

"I didn't," he replied. "It was my Uncle Clarence. He was in th'audience, throwing stuff. He said you was crap."

I weighed up whether I should have a go at flattening Cain but decided against it as he was a full head taller than me and uncommonly handy with a monkey wrench. So I used another weapon.

"I'm so thrilled to hear your Uncle Clarence had been let out for the day ... without his keeper." I smiled at Cain who scowled at me and hit back with an even lower blow.

"At least I know who my family are," he replied with a nod which seemed to say that was the end of the matter.

I wasn't about to let that one pass, big as he was. But, before I could splatter him all over the garage walls, a sudden small whirlwind left Cain lying on the floor, nose streaming with blood.

"Now then, Cain," soothed Les, bending over him. "Go and get that crimson schnozzle seen to, there's a good lad."

And he ushered Cain away in such a caring manner you'd never have guessed it was he who had drawn blood.

I put my arm round Les and said, "He's a gobbin, Dad. Don't listen to him."

Les smiled at me and replied, "I never listen to people like that, son."

I nodded approvingly, even though I figured that Les must have listened to Cain and understood exactly what he meant. However, if he wanted that to be the end of it then it was fine by me. But Les hadn't quite finished and he properly unsettled me by adding, "It don't matter where you came from, you've allus been my son and you allus will be."

I was about to protest that there'd never been any shadow of doubt on the question when Les held his hand up.

"Don't say nothin' for a moment, son." Les paused, breathed deeply and forced another smile. "The war, it were a strange time right enough and we all got up to a lot of odd business, me more than most. That's how I managed to get through it. So I won't hear things against anyone else who ... did what they had to."

Well, what a turn-up! If Les had ever suspected that I might not be the fruit of his loins he'd kept flippin' quiet about it. Yet here he was, telling me in not so many words, that he'd known all the time about my mother and the bookie. I wondered if he also knew that Mum's romantic rebound time was better measured on a stopwatch than a calendar ... but I decided to leave things as they were. Instead I planted a kiss on the top of Les's salt and pepper thatch and he looked at me tearfully.

"You have a good life in London, son. I might just come and take a look at you when you're settled if that's no significant trouble to yourself."

"Jesus, Les, this isn't Great Expectations. You're my Dad and you can come and stay with me any time."

Les looked pleased as Punch. "Thanks, son. And you knock 'em dead at The Palladium, just like you did in Bolton Sat'day just gone."

"You heard about that did you?"

"Heard about it! I were there. Fifth row."

Aha! The identity of the mystery man in the muffler was solved, making me feel ever so guilty. Les had been there looking after me even while I'd forgotten his existence. If one of those yahoos had taken so much as one threatening pace towards me Les would have put him to sleep and then calmly taken the others apart. I put my arms round that big barrel chest and hugged him.

"You should have come backstage, you daft ha'porth."

"No, no, 'sides I'd brought the Alvis down and I had to get it back without Joshua twigging."

Les wriggled uncomfortably out of the embrace, grabbed my shoulders, looked me in the eye and said, "I might not be down there in London, son but I'll always be around for you. We all will."

I hugged him again but I knew this was a turning point. I was leaving the comfort of Butterthwaite and for what? If I'd known then that my future would include walk-on parts for the heir to the throne and his brother, two future prime ministers and the most famous spy ring we've ever had, well I'd have turned round ... and caught an even earlier train to the capital!

Chapter Four: Jimmy and the Prince

London's a rum old place and always has been in my estimation. On the one hand it covers a few hundred thousand square miles or whatever and, even in the Thirties, was home to eight million souls. On the other, everyone you - or more particularly I - needed to know was concentrated around a few square yards of Soho. Just forget about all the factories making food, furniture and fancies either side of the new routes that were shooting west out of the capital. And we can ignore the sprawling industrial centres springing up towards the east, manufacturing cars, trucks and buses too. Instead I'm concentrating on the one place that mattered. The London Palladium.

Eddie Star had been as good as his word. He'd installed me at the Regent Palace Hotel in Piccadilly with the promise of a small flat of my own in Fulham when the present tenant could be persuaded to leave. In the first couple of weeks he'd also got me spots at the Hackney Empire, the Grand in Clapham and the Golders Green Hippodrome. All well and good and I think I can safely say I didn't disappoint anyone. But then, a fortnight after I'd moved south, Eddie secured me a week's booking that was to change my life in so many ways. Bottom of the bill at The Palladium.

Now, I reckon you might just be thinking London Palladium - good, bottom of the bill - not so flamin' hot. Yet the fact was that, unique among variety venues in the Thirties, bottom of the bill at The Palladium could become top of the bill, in the space of a few minutes. These amazing promotion prospects owed less to the quality of your act – although I like to think that my potential was spotted very early – than to the mob of maniacs who made The Palladium their own throughout that decade, The Crazy Gang.

It's true they weren't everyone's cup of tea, particularly Frank Randle's – then again I'm not sure he'd ever had a cup of tea. Randle once told me that he reckoned the Gang would get eaten alive if they ventured north of Oxford and I have to admit some of their wordplay was pretty lame even for those times. Moreover, when Bud Flanagan and Ches Allen started to sing, matters could quickly take a turn for all points mawkish.

But The Crazy Gang had something that other comics could only dream about. Being masters of the physical stuff, they made it appear, even while the theatre was apparently coming down around everyone's ears, that the audience was in on it all. That's where I come back to how bottom of the bill could rise to the top in record time.

The first occasion it happened to me went like this. I'd finished my spot to mild applause, having fired off one or two "I've come on me bikes" and even slipping a Randle-inspired "Geroff me foot" in there, figuring that nobody would know or care who Frank was down those parts. I was back in the dressing room, congratulating myself for being well shy of the mayhem when, uh-oh, in popped Charlie Naughton and Teddy Knox. For anyone not totally familiar with The Crazy Gang line-up, Teddy was the one with the spiv's moustache who spoke as though he'd just inhaled a wasp's nest and Charlie, my favourite among all of them, was impish and bald, a squashed version, if this were possible, of W.C. Fields.

Without a by your leave, they grabbed me, one arm each and pulled me towards the door.

"Don't fight it, Frankie," counselled Teddy. "I did and look where it got me, arm in arm with a fella."

Charlie was more conciliatory. "We've not lost anyone yet, old son; mislaid a couple, mind," he said as they propelled me towards the stage. "But if you do come to any harm, contact our insurers. Here's their card." He'd handed me the joker.

The five minutes after I was announced as Funky Frannybone were a blur. I remember at one point being in a sack and then a wheelbarrow. I was also suspended by my ankles from the circle rail before crawling round the stage blindfolded, braying like a donkey. Finally reprieved, I stood panting in the wings while Charlie informed me, "You're a gamecock and no mistake about it."

He then recalled how Beryl Formby had threatened all six of the Gang with slow agonising deaths if they so much as laid a madcap finger on her precious George.

"And did you lay a finger on him?" I asked.

"Did we bollocks," Charlie replied. "First rule of show-business, son. You don't go up against Beryl." *(The career of George Formby, one of the biggest stars of stage and screen from the 1930s to the 1950s, was kept determinedly on track by his formidable wife, Beryl).*

"You know, I can see Beryl's point," I told Charlie slightly testily. "I mean, it's no thanks to you lot that I got through all this unscathed."

"Got through it unscathed! I like your use of the old past tense," said Charlie giving his bald dome a rub before stepping back in shock.

"Hey is that your ten bob note on the floor?" he yelled.

OK, so not one of you clever lot would have fallen for it; but allow me to add that it was chaos in that place. There was even more pandemonium when I bent over and, with what I'm told was a classic drop-kick, Charlie launched me across stage and into the orchestra pit. The first violinist must have been in on it because when I landed in his lap all he said was, "Mind the syrup" and raised a pair of sad eyebrows. Instinctively I grabbed at his hair and it came away in my hands – a wig. Further merry mayhem ensued and I was wondering how I could crawl away unnoticed and gently expire when I saw a face in the audience which made me forget about everything else. It was my face. Only kidding, I couldn't resist that old chestnut. *(Which, coincidentally, is what Frankie's face does resemble nowadays).*

What I actually saw was a face I thought was already part of my past. It belonged to Nancy who was laughing fit to wet herself and waving madly at me. Taking her lead, so was the whole row she was on. It was that kind of night.

I scrambled out of the orchestra pit, not before remembering to hand back the first violinist's syrup. And, while the Gang were busy persecuting third on the bill, Wally Simple – from memory he was naked apart from his pants, socks and flat cap – I sneaked off the stage to hearty applause.

Back in my dressing room I was hardly aware of how bruised and battered I'd become chasing the laughs. All I could think of was Nancy. She was on her own as far as I could make out and – unless she'd developed an unlikely crush on Charlie Naughton – was here to see me. But if she was in the theatre then I was sure that Lake and his chums would not be far behind. Joshua wasn't about to let his little sweet pea loose around London without a bunch of burly chaperones. I needed to take great care.

So preoccupied was I with Nancy's unexpected appearance that I forgot to take my curtain call. I'm told nobody missed me as everyone was concentrating on how, when or even whether, Wally Simple would ever get down from there. I opened my dressing room door just as the Gang flowed past, chortling and bouncing each other off the walls.

"You're a real sport, Frankie. We'll not forget this, old fellow," drawled Ches Allen, stopping and patting me on the shoulder.

"My eye, but you are a trouper," affirmed Jimmy Nervo, poking me in the eye.

As my sight slowly returned to normal and the Crazies melted away I saw to my utter joy that Nancy had appeared at the far end of the corridor. What would I say to her?

How would she be? However, just at that point, someone grabbed me from behind and started to drag me away from her.

"I didn't do anything, you've got to believe me," I squealed, convinced Lake and his bruisers were about to set about giving my poor old noggin a damn good floggin'.

"You're being a bit hard on yourself," said a familiar voice.

"Eddie, thank god, I've never been so glad to see a Cockney," I burbled, hugging my agent.

"I hope you still feel the same after I've pocketed my commission," he chuckled. "Now let's go."

"I'm not going anywhere." I glanced back at Nancy who was carefully keeping her distance.

"Oh yes you are," said Eddie pushing me towards the stage door. "You're off to see someone very important."

"I'm already seeing someone important."

"Not half as important as this cove, I do assure you."

As Eddie pushed open the stage door, dragging me behind him, I managed to signal to Nancy that she should follow us before we were outside, tearing around corners and up back alleys. I could swear that we careered along the same street in different directions and I began to wonder why Eddie was so worried about Nancy tracking us, not yet realising that his concerns lay in an entirely different direction. We finally emerged in front of the great white ocean liner that was the new Broadcasting House.

"Eddie, you rascal," I said, "have you got me on the wireless?"

"Blimey, Tosh, not with that accent," he replied. "It's enough to give Jolly Johnny Reith a blue fit. Nah, we're over there."

He steered me across Portland Place and through the imposing triumphal arched entrance of the Langham Hotel. Glancing back, I couldn't immediately spot Nancy but just hoped she'd stayed on our trail. Then it was two stairs at a time up to the first floor suites where the quality could usually be found. Who was up there waiting to greet me? My money was on Ivor Novello or maybe even Noel Coward. Either way I was already resigned to being darlinged to death.

When we came to a pair of forbidding black oak doors, Eddie put his hand on my shoulders and looked me anxiously up and down. Then he took out a handkerchief, licked it and began wiping the side of my nose.

"Jesus, Eddie," I said, wriggling free, "you could be my mother."

"You do say the nicest things, Tosh. Now in you go and mind your Northern manners."

He knocked and I could just make out a vague muttering as if someone was in the middle of talking to himself and had forgotten the gist of what he was saying. That was the cue for Eddie to open one of the double doors, shove me inside and follow a couple of paces behind.

The room was not well-lit and it took a moment or two to get my bearings. When I'd located them, I saw a well-groomed, medium-sized cove in a smart light grey suit standing in the centre of this vast salon. He was gazing into the middle distance as if waiting for a bus that would never come.

A few yards away, on an enormous chaise longue was a figure very familiar to me. It was my old pal, the comedian Jimmy Jewell no less, dressed in an expensive looking double-breasted suit and open-necked shirt. Jimmy took absolutely no notice of my sudden appearance.

Eddie stepped up beside me and bowed to the well-dressed chap.

"Frankie Funnybone, sir, as you requested."

In a squeaky voice, this bird replied, "Thank you so much, Edwin. I take it you were not followed by our friends."

"Not to my knowledge, sir," said Eddie backing out and bowing at the same while I gazed in amazement, mouthing the name "Edwin Star?" to him. I hadn't seen that one coming.

"Please make yourself at home, Mr Funnybone," muttered the dapper fellow as the door closed behind Eddie.

Only when I got a bit nearer did I realise with a jolt that this chap, speaking like a ventriloquist out of the side of his mouth and glancing anxiously at the oblivious Jimmy Jewell, was the world's most eligible bachelor. Yes, right here in front of me, was our own Prince of Wales, months before he became King and a year-and-a-half before he managed to ... well you've probably heard the story.

We shook hands and, with that familiar lop-sided smile, he said, "I hope you've recovered. The boys did rather give you what-for, what?"

I was staggered. "You were at The Palladium, sir?"

He nodded and replied, "At a discreet distance from the merriment. After all, The Crazy Gang are our favourites, what?"

The Prince glanced once again at Jimmy who continued to ignore him - a bit dangerous I reckoned as it doesn't do to get the royals' backs up. I mean, look what happened to poor old Wat Tyler. *(Leader of The Peasants' Revolt who, in 1381, was run through by the Lord Mayor of London as he talked to Richard II and then had his head stuck on a pole.)* To save Jimmy from himself I decided to draw him into the conversation.

"How's it goin', Jim?" I shouted.

In my defence the room was poorly lit but I'd have been in a right pickle if my accent hadn't saved me. For, when the character on the chaise longue turned to face me I saw that, despite the centre parting and vacant look, it wasn't Jimmy Jewell at all but was ... well at that point I could not be sure what I was looking at. Man, woman or a little bit of both.

This character weighed me up, turned to the Prince and barked, "Hey, Dave, who's dis putz? And what in goddammit is a Goan gym?"

Well, whatever else, he or she was unmistakeably fluent in American.

The heir to the throne hopped nervously from one foot to the other.

"Mr Funnybone, forgive me for I have neglected my duties. This is Wallis."

That didn't help much and neither did Wallis's confident sashay towards us nor the subsequent question.

"So I repeat, Dave, who's de Limey?"

"Er, don't you recall, dearest. He's the comedian from the theatre tonight. You know, Frankie Funnybone."

Wallis looked me up and down with what appeared to be a practised eye, grinned and said, "Haw, haw, dem crazy guys sure cleaned your clock, buddy."

The Prince frowned and whispered even more markedly out of the side of his mouth, "Darling, please, ditch the demotic. At least in public."

Wallis looked annoyed, muttering "demotic schmenotic." And then wondrously her face broke into a smile and her accent switched to a delicate New England tinkle which left no gender doubts. Offering a perfumed hand she said, "Mr Funnybone how delightful to meet you. Drink?"

Still in shock, I said I'd take a gin and tonic thanks and off Wallis toddled to the drinks cabinet.

Meanwhile, something seemed to be troubling the Prince. Beckoning me closer, he glanced around nervously and whispered, "I need your advice."

Aha we're getting down to it, I thought. I'm not just here because he thinks my act deserved an award for Best Performance by Man Dragged Round in a Sack by

Lunatics. Although quite what a nineteen-year-old fresh from the sticks could teach the heir to the throne wasn't at all clear. So what he said next surprised me.

"It's my image, Frankie. I'm rather concerned about ... well, what my people think of me."

I could have kicked off by telling him that his image would soon be on every postage stamp in the land, now that his grumpy old man was on the point of pegging out. But I made do with blank incomprehension and the comment, "Sorry, sir, I don't really understand."

The Prince tugged thoughtfully at his cuffs before replying, "The thing is, Frankie, you're a man of the world. People think you're what Wallis over there would call 'a regular guy'."

"I suppose so but ..."

"You see, I'd like folk – the people – to think that I wasn't just some kind of terrible stuffed shirt. Eh, what!"

"I'm sure they don't think that, sir," I replied, in truth not knowing what the people thought of him, if they even considered him at all. But when the heir to the throne wants your advice, do what I do and flannel for all you're worth.

"I mean, sir," I told the Prince, "they admire your war record, your ambassadorial visits abroad and most of all your many leg-ov ... achievements." I glanced at Wallis but she wasn't listening.

"That's all very well," the Prince replied, "but I'd appreciate it if you were to put it around in your coterie so to speak that, well, that I'm a regular kind of fellow too. Get them on my side if you will."

The Prince smiled contentedly, as if saying what he said had been some kind of great achievement.

Well, if I could get into the next monarch's good books by telling all and sundry he had a passion for The Crazy Gang and dodgy-looking Yanks, then it was fine by me. One thing did strike me however.

41

"Look, sir, it might help our cause if I could mention Glenys." I nodded towards the figure by the drinks cabinet.

"It's Wallis for pity's sake!" he wailed.

"Forgive me, sir. Wallis."

The Prince appeared worried. "I'm not entirely certain," he began, "that the world is quite ready for ... Wallis."

"They might be if you encourage her to, well, be herself."

At this the Prince looked even more alarmed, glanced at Wallis and hissed, "Be herself! You mean a foul-mouthed colonial with distressing tendencies?"

If what happened at that moment hadn't happened, the conversation could well have veered off into very dangerous territory indeed. However, what did happen was that a man walked straight out of the wall. This bird, a hard looking, well-built military type, must have been there all the time; I just hadn't noticed him what with one thing and another.

But I saw him now as he moved quickly and silently to the double doors, drawing a blackjack from inside his dinner jacket. It appeared that someone was in for a pasting and I was relieved it wasn't to be me. I was considerably less relieved when the bodyguard threw open the doors and into the room tumbled Nancy.

The Prince looked thunderstruck, as if having stunning-looking female strangers fall at his feet was completely outside his experience.

"Good lord," was all he could find to say.

Wallis, on the other hand, had plenty to get off her chest.

"So this is what the Special Branch uses to spy on us," she drawled as Nancy was dragged to her feet by the bodyguard. "Take the Limey bitch out back, Johnson, and put one behind her ear."

Even though I was unsure about what Nancy could expect behind her ear, it didn't sound too promising and I

42

felt it prudent to intervene on her behalf. So I appealed directly to the Prince.

"Actually, sir, she's nothing to do with Special Branch."

"Give her the bum's rush anyway, Johnson." Wallis was running this show and definitely disinclined to let up. I needed to explain the situation pretty sharpish.

"The thing is, sir - and madam - she's, well the fact is that Nancy here and I are to be married. In fact we've eloped."

It was a lie made up on the spur of the moment but, if you'd thrown a switch, the atmosphere could not have changed more thoroughly. Wallis's steely sepulchral features broke into a huge delighted smile.

"Sweet fuckin' Jesus how romantic is that," she yelled. "Get your pretty ass over here, honey."

Then she dashed across the room, elbowed Johnson out of the way and ushered Nancy to the chaise longue.

Over the next half hour Nancy, who let's face it was not unused to loving attention, was smothered in the stuff. It seemed that Wallis Simpson, once and soon to be twice divorced, had had her romantic instincts stirred and nothing would stop her demonstrating the fact. The Prince did try to muscle in but was quickly reduced to a walk-on role.

For her part, Nancy told a story which more or less coincided with what I'd said – and then considerably embellished the tale. Apparently not only had we eloped but her spurned fiancé Edmund and furious Dad were on our trail along with a dangerous gang of hired rapscallions.

"The Crazy Gang, what," said the Prince in the only stab at humour I ever heard him make.

"Button it, meathead," was the response from Wallis who immediately went back to pumping Nancy about Edmund's many inadequacies.

"British men, ha! Chinless fuckin' wonders the lot of 'em."

"Present company excepted, dearest, surely," whined the Prince.

"Whaddevuhh," bellowed Wallis who was already ordering Johnson to bring the royal car round the back of the hotel and transport Nancy and myself to safety.

"Hey, lover boy," she yelled at me. "Which hotel you at?"

"Oh, er, The Dorchester, ma'am."

I'm not sure why I told such an outrageous lie but it seemed to fit in with the general tenor of the evening so far.

Wallis turned back to Johnson. "Ring down to Forsythe and tell him to get these lovebirds to The Dorchester, lickety fuckin' split."

As Johnson picked up the white pearl-handled phone Wallis came back over to Nancy and held both her hands.

"Aw, honey, you godda go now. But come back and see us real soon why doncha." And turning to the Prince she finished off with, "Hey, Dave, ain't this the most romantic thing you ever hoid?"

The Prince looked gravely at me and said, "I am sure you'll follow your conscience in the matter of the woman you love."

"I certainly will, sir," I replied, having not the foggiest what he was blathering about.

"And please remember the matter of which we spoke," he added.

Oh god, I had completely forgotten about my task of making the Prince of Wales, known to his close pals as Dapper Dave, a man of the people. I decided to start that very instant with Nancy who was backing away towards the double doors, managing to bow and curtsey at the same time.

"Nancy stop that!" I ordered sharply. "They're just regular people. The last thing they want is folk bowing and scraping to them."

The Prince held up his forefinger and said, "Let her be for just a moment, there's a good chap."

I could see that I'd have my work cut out.

As Nancy and I flew excitedly down the stairs to reception, we could not have imagined what fate had in store for the odd couple we'd just left behind. Within a few months everyone in Britain would find out what our American cousins and fellow Europeans had known for months from their magazines - copies of which regularly arrived on our shores with great big holes cut in them where the juicy stories should be.

But for now the knowledge of their affair, not to mention abdication and disgrace, were matters for the future. As was their vital part in our own dramatic start to married life ... but we'll get to that in good time. For the moment all that mattered was that the royal driver, ordered to spirit us away, was waiting at the hotel's service entrance.

As the Rolls pulled out into Portland Place I tapped the driver on the shoulder and told him we weren't bound for The Dorchester but just down the road to The Regent Palace.

"I know, Mr Johnson already guessed as much," he replied. Cheeky sod!

As we pulled up a minute later in Piccadilly I told the driver to transport Miss Protheroe to wherever she was staying. However, at this Nancy looked miffed and replied mischievously, "But, darling, you can't have forgotten our engagement already."

"Nancy, listen, all that back there was a bit of fun but if your old fellow got wind of this he'd have my skin."

"Don't be such a spoilsport, Frankie."

"Yeah, be a man for Christ's sake." This was from the driver.

"Who asked you, big ears?"

"Sorry for speaking out of turn, sir," he said, "but I reckon someone who lasted five minutes with The Crazy Gang should fear nothing else."

Nancy wrinkled her nose in appreciation at the driver and turned to me. "There you go, you're famous. Come on." And she dragged me out of the car and into the hotel.

I reckon she only stopped jabbering about the Prince and Wallis after we'd been in my room about half an hour and by then I was so sick of hearing about them I seriously considered issuing her with marching orders.

But then something truly wonderful happened. I still can't explain how it began but we found ourselves wrestling just like we'd done years before - apart from the small difference that our clothes appeared to be falling off as we grappled. It wasn't long before the floor was littered with our kit and we were both totally in the nip. Ninety seconds or so later I realised that I'd just lost my virginity.

Now I don't know where sex education is up to these days but back when I was a lad the teacher would hand each of us a cigarette card showing the stoat family along with a copy of The Old Testament and we'd be told to get on with it.

Due to these gaps in my sexual knowledge I genuinely imagined that I'd broken my duck four months earlier with Sandra Tomlinson's sister Jean in the gloom of Les's garage among old cycles and other odds and sods. However, when Nancy got down to business, I quickly worked out that what I'd actually done on that earlier occasion with Jean Tomlinson, albeit in a spectacular piece of irony, was literally to come on my bike. At that point I couldn't be sure which bits of the bike I'd ... but all would become clear some months later.

However, there were no such ambiguities in my coupling with Nancy. In fact, as she heaved herself off me and fired up a Craven A, I was bold enough to ask, "Er, how was it for you, dear?"

"Well," she said, releasing a blue cloud, "the one thing I can say is that it's a step up from anything Edmund has managed."

She was kidding of course - I think - and, after a respectable interval, we resumed relations with a great deal more gusto on my part, if you get my drift.

Later on, as we lay under the eiderdown together, I weighed up whether to ask Nancy where and from whom she'd picked up such a catalogue of interesting moves. But I didn't and, in fact, I never mentioned it at all during her lifetime, the right thing to do in my opinion as a lady is entitled to her secrets. Besides there were more pressing matters on my mind such as getting her out of the hotel without Joshua's goons noticing us and taking things out on my napper. It was clear though that Nancy had other preoccupations.

"You realise what this means don't you, Franco."

"Er, is it that we're going straight to hell?" She was chapel you see.

Nancy stared at me oddly. "You're going on your own then, you chump. No, I mean about you and me. Us."

It was out before I could stop it. "Nancy, there is no us. That was all make-believe for Prince Charming. You're getting married to Edmund. Remember?"

Oh dear, it had all been going so well, too well as it turned out. With an almighty squawk, she set about me with her fists, a hairbrush and one of my spats.

"We've just made love and all you can talk about is Edmund." Thwack. "What kind of man are you?" Shtunk. "And I thought you were different." Kerplop. That last bit was me subsiding like a burst blancmange.

I held my hands up in feeble surrender. "Nancy, please, I didn't think you cared."

"Cared! I've never been able to stop bloody caring," she roared, launching the hairbrush across the room. "That's been my problem. And now, just as I think we've

47

consummated our love, you go and smash everything."
Nancy tumbled in a heap beside me sobbing her heart out.

Crikey, what did she just say? Was it what I thought I'd heard? I tapped her heaving, naked shoulders.

"Nance, did you just say you loved me?"

Her muffled reply sounded something like, "If I did I must be mad."

"No, you're not mad, well if you are so am I. Oh, Nancy, please I didn't think I was in your league."

She looked up at me red-eyed and shook her head. "Franco, it's true you aren't in my league. You're a confidante of the heir to throne for goodness sake."

"That means nothing, Nancy. The only thing that matters is you're willing to give me another chance. Please allow me the opportunity to demonstrate how much I've always loved you."

My appeal straight from the heart so disarmed Nancy that I began to wonder if another bout of mattress mambo could be in the offing. But, after flinging her arms joyously around me, Nancy gazed soulfully into my eyes and said, "Have you any gaspers, darling?"

"You know I don't. Smoking is a filthy habit."

"Look who's talking after what you've just been up to."

I was about to protest but she grinned, gave me a quick kiss on the nose and jumped up from the bed.

"I'll see if I can get some from the desk," Nancy said as she pulled on her dress and grabbed her handbag. "I'll be a couple of minutes. Keep everything nice and warm for me."

I lay back down and I have to confess, after all the excitement with mad comedians, royalty and whatnot, that I dropped off. I must have dozed for ten minutes and would have gone on longer but for a delicate tap on the door.

"Hold on, darling," I stage-whispered groggily while pulling a dressing gown around me. "You've been a heck of a ..."

I opened the door and flew straight back across the room, banging my head on the floor. Following me in at close range was Joshua's bodyguard Maurice Lake, seemingly about to repeat the smack on the nose that had decked me. A large bony fist was poised over me but thankfully it didn't fall. Instead Lake hissed, "I like you."

"Jesus, I'm glad you don't hate me."

"You make me laugh." Lake stared at me grimly. "So I'm not going to tell Jumpin' Joshua where I found his beloved daughter."

"Where is she? What have you done to her?"

Lake ignored me and moved round the room gathering up Nancy's things. When he'd finished he looked down at me again.

"Now you listen," he said. "Miss Nancy is engaged to the honourable Edmund double-barrelled shotgun. That's her look-out but it's the way it is and how it's going to remain. So I don't want to see you around again. If I do set eyes on you, I'll knock your stupid nose through the back of your stupid head."

Lake opened the door and took a last look at me.

"I enjoyed the show though," he said. "You should stay down here in London and get accustomed to the big time. That's my advice"

Then he closed the door behind him, leaving me to gingerly ascertain if my stupid nose still belonged to my stupid face. And to begin planning how I'd win Nancy back.

Chapter Five: Brian O'Reilly

"And don't forget to use your return ticket before the end of the month, sir."

Colin 'Stinker' Stanworth, a lad I'd known twenty years and who gained his moniker after being pulled half-dead from the slime-filled canal - by me - glanced disinterestedly up from under the shiny peak of his dark blue London Midland and Scottish cap, as he clipped my ticket.

"I sortainly will do that, sir," I replied, congratulating myself as I took leave of Stinker that the first small part of my mission had been accomplished. I had arrived back in Butterthwaite incognito. Oh, and I wouldn't be using that return ticket at the end of the month either. Or the accent!

More than three quarters of a year had passed since I'd lain bleeding on the hotel bedroom floor while Lake bundled together Nancy's things and warned me to stay out of her life for ever. At first I'd ignored his threats and tried to get in touch with Nancy using various subterfuges. There had been coded letters, phone calls in a variety of voices and even a desperate and frankly farcical attempt at semaphore using the good offices of my sister, Beryl. I had no way of knowing if the messages had got through to Nancy but, in any event, none had led to a response and sadly I began to accept that the youngest Miss Protheroe was destined never to become a Funnybone.

Again I was fortunate to have other distractions. Under the supervision of Eddie Star, my career was really starting to take off and I'd played halls as far away as Bristol and Nottingham to a satisfying level of critical acclaim.

"Frankie has touched the nation's funnybone," was one typical review. *("This clown's patter stinks the place out," was another)*. At the same time I was still a fixture at The Palladium, such a regular in fact that even The Crazy Gang began to lay off me.

"You're not the new boy any more, Frankie," Jimmy Nervo told me over a couple of late pints. "And far as I'm concerned you're one of us." High praise indeed, although it didn't stop them stuffing me into a hamper every other night.

Minor inconveniences like those aside, life was good with only one small but significant cloud on the horizon. I was being pursued amorously - and it has to be said rather vigorously - by one of the world's most celebrated movie stars. This would have been no drawback at all had my lovelorn pursuer been say Greta Garbo or Carole Lombard – or, let's face it, even Rin Tin Tin. The problem arose because the film siren on my trail was Gracie Fields.

Now believe it or not, until she became an out-and-out pest, I had a lot of time for Our Gracie. She'd proved to everyone that a northern accent and gormless demeanour was no bar to success in the south, thereby blazing a trail for George Formby and a score of other bumpkins who struggled to find their arses with both hands. I also knew that Gracie's personal life was far from idyllic so I could understand why she needed a shoulder to cry on.

Because of all that, I'd been friendly and encouraging in our many soul-searching late-night sessions at the Horse and Groom in Soho and therefore it should not have been such a surprise that, during one of my sympathetic moments, Gracie made a grab for me. Yet frankly I don't know who was more startled; me or the drunk sitting at the end of the bar on whose lap I landed as I shot out of Gracie's grasp. I wasn't too interested in finding out either as I made the sharpest of exits.

But setbacks like that didn't daunt Our Gracie; in fact they spurred Rochdale's very own on to greater heights of amorousness and so began an awkward couple of months where it seemed I couldn't turn round without hearing Gracie's siren cry of, "Frankee, Frankee, let's hankee pankee." *(At the time Gracie Fields, 1898-1979, was*

51

indeed a major film star and, as such, unlikely to need the ministrations of such an unlikely lover. Typically Frankie is, once again, inflating his own importance.)

To escape Gracie's clutches I decided to remove myself from the field, for a weekend at least, by inviting my Dad down to London for the first time. It was mid-July, a fortnight before the wedding of the century and Les along with the rest of my family had been slaving away preparing for the big day.

I figured Joshua must have had a brainstorm allowing Les to travel south at such a crucial time but maybe he thought it was a price worth paying to ensure two hundred miles remained between me and his beloved daughter. Whatever, he needn't have worried as I'd all but resigned myself to Nancy marrying her Nancy Boy. My Dad's visit, however, threw everything up into the air again.

I met Les at Euston on Saturday evening and we rushed straight over to The Palladium where I'd got him the best seat in the house. He adored The Crazy Gang and loved my part in their madness, especially the bit on the trapeze where I ruffled his hair on the way past.

The following day we took a river boat trip up to Hampton Court, got lost in the maze and ended up having to kick our way out; two northern lads enjoying themselves in time-honoured fashion. The image was slightly dented by Les's insistence on tea at a Lyons Corner House in The Strand. But it was his weekend and, as we relaxed over the Battenburg and Earl Grey, the last thing on my mind was that Les would drop a bombshell.

We'd been discussing my brother Ronnie's promotion to the new post of footman, established in response to Joshua's knighthood in the last New Years Honours list. It must have been one elevation too much for the old King who'd cashed in his chips just three weeks afterwards with, as everyone found out much later, a spot of narcotic assistance from the royal quack. *(Frankie is blunt but correct. The ailing King was despatched with a lethal overdose of morphine from his physician Lord Dawson of Penn so the death could be reported immediately in The Times).*

"Footman's an ideal job for our Ronnie," I told Les. "He's always been a nosey little rubber-necker and now all the gossip will fall straight into his lap."

"Funny you should say that," said Les drawing deeply on his briar, "He was in the box seat while Joshua - Sir Joshua begging his pardon - and Miss Nancy had their latest blazing row."

"What was that about? Joshua wants the wedding guests to bring their own sandwiches?"

Les chuckled. "Far from it, son. While Joshua usually has short arms and deep pockets, he's pushing the boat out on this one and no expense spared. That's why he wanted it in the magazine – only Miss Nancy put her foot down."

Apparently the old skinflint was planning to show the world he'd suddenly become Sir Barnaby Bountiful and what better way to do that than publicise the lavish wedding plans in the pages of Lancashire Living magazine. He'd set everything up and the reporter and photographer were all ready to head Protheroewards – only for Nancy to shoot down his strategy in flames.

"According to our Ronnie she was spittin' spanners," Les told me through a blizzard of cake crumbs. "Said she wouldn't go on show like a prize heifer; she'd be damned if she'd let the world know her business. Her words of course."

I brushed bits of Battenburg off my lapels and smiled. "Good old Nancy. She'll never change."

"You're right there, son. But I've not told you the strangest thing. She kept banging on about this character that nobody's ever heard of. She said it about ten times and our Ronnie thought she'd gone bloomin' mad. It certainly drove her dad crackers."

Frankly, by this time I was getting fed up with the Nancy wedding pantomime and secretly wished that Les would talk about something - anything - else. But then again, had he done so, he would never have dropped his bombshell and the rest of my life would have been very different.

So it was more for form's sake than much else that I asked about this strange phrase of Nancy's - and was told it sounded a lot like, "Dapper Dave's pal wouldn't let this happen."

I sat bolt upright, scattering a plate of fancies across the lino.

"You sure she said that?"

"Didn't I just tell you," Les replied testily. "In fact she no more than kept on saying it. Now give this young wench a lift clearing up all your clutter."

I helped the scuttling waitress gather up the cakes and broken crockery before turning back to Les.

"Does Nancy know that the new footman is my brother?"

"Course she does!" Les's chest swelled. "Miss Nancy's always taken a considerable interest in our family."

He could say that again and in my view she was still taking a considerable interest in our family - particularly me! For what else could her reference to Dapper Dave's pal be other than a coded message for yours truly to rescue her? Incidentally the real Dapper Dave, now six months into his brief reign, was already demonstrating the qualities which would propel him rapidly towards the door marked 'Unsuitable royalty, this way out'. But more about him later.

As Les banged on proudly about how my mother, brothers and sisters were working their fingers to the bone to ensure an absurdly wealthy family's nuptials went off like a sky rocket, I was already anticipating a different scenario for a fortnight's time. One that needed very careful planning.

Next day, after I'd seen Les off on his train I travelled down to Brighton on a mission. Unlike most of the passengers boarding at Victoria, I wasn't interested in catching a spot of mid-season sun or stuffing myself stupid on chips and ale, splendid pastimes though both were.

No, my mission was to track down Clifford Holliday among whoopee cushions and plastic dog turds. You see, when he wasn't in demand on both sides of the Atlantic as a top make-up artist, Cliff helped out in the novelty shop run by his wife Ivy just the other side of Marine Parade. I was in luck too for when I arrived Cliff was behind the counter showing two young lads a toy monkey that kept farting as you pushed it up and down its stick. It was an odd scene as, with his owlish specs, red nose and moustache, Cliff looked for all the world like he was wearing one of his own disguises. Perhaps he was.

"What do you think, boys?" Cliff asked enthusiastically as the lads' heads bobbed up and down in time with the monkey's movements. "Every house should have one, eh?"

"Depends whether or not it's a monkey house," I interrupted.

Cliff looked at me in delight. "Frankie Funnybone, as I live and breathe. What's the story, matey?"

"Well first off, Cliff, I reckon these lads'd rather be feeding the slots on the West Pier," I said, slipping each of them a bob and watching as they helter-skeltered out of the shop.

Cliff blinked at me through his comedy specs. "Thanks, Frankie. Remind me to come round and do my business all over your front parlour some time."

I smiled and patted him on the shoulder. "Never mind about toys like that, Cliff. I'm giving you the chance to make a real monkey out of someone." And for the next ten minutes I outlined exactly what I wanted with Cliff making detailed notes and the odd comment.

"Think you can do that?" I asked when he'd snapped his notebook shut.

Cliff snorted derisively. "Do it! Who do you think turned Charlie Laughton into Henry the Eighth?"

"Oh, it was you who stuck a silly beard and funny hat on him! Good work!"

Cliff puffed out his chest in defiance and I half expected his bow-tie to start spinning madly.

"All right then," he continued, "who do you reckon helped turn Karloff into Frankenstein's monster?"

Well, we'd all seen the film and I had to admit that the transformation was impressive. My admiration for Cliff's work only increased four days later when I returned to the south coast to try out the finished disguise in the back of his shop.

"Thing is," explained Cliff as he teased the folds of rubber around my head, "it's a look that's easy to put on and get off in a trice."

"You could have fooled me," I said as he fussed around, arranging wisps of fake hair here and false teeth there – but he was later proved dead right. Finally Cliff stepped back in satisfaction and steered me to a full-length mirror in the corner of his cluttered sitting room. "Take a good look at someone else," he said proudly.

I did – and nearly fell over. In place of the craggily handsome young athlete who'd strode confidently into the shop half an hour before, there slouched a decrepit creature with a bald head, rimless specs and mis-shapen teeth. I swear I even looked as if I had bad breath.

"See how a new forehead alters the whole shape of your face," said Cliff proudly. "Why your own mother wouldn't recognise you."

And nor did Mum a week later, giving me a pitying look as I shuffled past her on the driveway up to Protheroe Hall a few minutes after my old pal Stinker had waved me on my merry way from the station. I knew I was on really firm ground when my 14-year-old brother Thomas, who was with Mum, started to giggle and point at this exotic apparition and promptly received one of her haymakers for his cheek.

The disguise had also come through with flying colours on the way up to the hall when I passed Jean Tomlinson sweating as she shoved a giant pram laden with a pair of prop forwards in the making. Tweaking the twins' bulging cheeks, I comforted myself that with what I now knew they couldn't possibly be mine – unless Jean had gone for a spin on my bike straight afterwards. I wished her good day and she shuffled off none the wiser.

If my own mother and brother didn't recognise me then it was unlikely that Sir Joshua would. And nor did he, being as he was far too busy swanking around on the gravel outside the hall like he owned the place *(which he did)*.

Joshua was conducting one of his regular inspections of the domestic staff, which included most of my family, none of whom even glanced at me. The new knight did look in my direction but he obviously mistook me for one of the many forelock-tugging tradesmen filling the hall with their wares – not that my forelock was visible at that moment.

While Joshua continued to plague the servants, one of them, a good-looking woman in her late twenties, auburn hair scraped back into a bun, detached herself from the group and hurried over to me. She introduced herself as Mary Cunliffe, Sir Joshua's new secretary and housekeeper, to whom I explained I was Brian O'Reilly, correspondent of High Society magazine, here to photograph and interview the blushing bride-to-be.

Mary glanced sadly at Joshua and said, "I'm afraid, Mr O'Reilly, that Miss Protheroe is adamant that she will not be interviewed by the Press."

She couldn't help stealing another look at Joshua and, aye aye, his stealthy returning glance suggested something a touch more intimate than dictation at 180 words a minute might be happening behind that locked office door.

Joshua must have overheard part of my tale because he broke off from bonding with the staff to shout, "You might as well bugger off back to the bogs because she's not having it."

Well, a knighthood hadn't magically made the old goat any less ignorant and it was with some relish that I vowed to let the new Lady Agatha know all about Sir Joshua and Mary Cunliffe and let's see who'd be pushing who around then.

But for now I confined myself to telling the master that maybe just a bit of County Mayo blarney would persuade the young mistress to open up. Joshua shook his head in exasperation and washed his hands of the matter.

"I don't think it's any good at all asking, I really don't," squeaked Mary Cunliffe as she led me round the side of the hall and into the drawing room through the huge pair of French windows.

"Maybe you're right an' all, Miss but the thing is you might pass on to the young lady that we have a mutual acquaintance."

Mary regarded me suspiciously. "And who might that be?"

"Why sure it's a fella who says he met Miss Nancy at Lady Esther Pargeter's ball last summer, a mister David Mallon, such a snappy dresser he's known by one and all as Dapper Dave."

Mary Cunliffe's mouth dropped open. "I wondered who Dapper Dave was," she said.

"Miss, I'm not surprised you've heard of him. He's known the length of the kingdom, so he is."

"You don't mean he and Miss Nancy are ..."

The possibility was obviously too awful for Mary to articulate out loud so I came to her rescue with reassurance.

"Ah sure I'm sure they're just good pals. Now run along and tell Miss Nancy I'm here, there's a good girl."

And run along Mary Cunliffe did, leaving me to kick my heels in the very drawing room where Nancy had murdered that tune nearly a year ago. As I sat on the piano stool, idly reflecting on all that had happened in the intervening months, who should mince past the doorway but the new footman himself, my brother Ronnie. After doing a double-take worthy of Jimmy Jewell - the real one - Ronnie demonstrated exactly how a footman can put both feet in it.

"You're not allowed in here," he spluttered. "You should be at the tradesman's entrance. Now shift your arse or I'll call Mr Lake to deal with you."

For one brief moment I thought Ronnie had recognised me and was having a joke, such was his confidence that I was where I shouldn't have been. But sadly not. He was behaving as if he hadn't the brains he was born with – in other words as bleedin' usual.

I got up slowly from the stool and approached my brother. The fact that I felt sorry for him over his pathetic attempt to assert his new authority didn't stop me from having some mischief.

"Ah, sir, I'll be on me way to the tradesman's entrance right now, so I will. Just do something for me would ye. Point His Excellency in that direction when he asks where his old chum Brian O'Reilly's got to."

The self-satisfied grin slid straight off Ronnie's thin face and you could almost see the swagger drain out of him.

"You're a guest of Sir Joshua?" he mumbled. "I'm so sorry I didn't realise."

Eyes narrowed, I stuck my face directly into Ronnie's. "Here's a wee tip for you, sonny. Treat every one who comes here as a valued guest. Every last visitor. You understand that?"

Ronnie gulped and nodded. His eyes then filled with panic as Mary Cunliffe walked into the room.

"Ah, Missy," I boomed as Ronnie squirmed, "I must tell you something about this young feller here."

Waiting for the blow to fall, Ronnie cut a miserable figure as I added, "He's looked after me royally so he has."

Mary looked uncertainly at my brother who, in turn, stared stupidly at me.

"Well," she said, "he's new to the job but he seems a willing learner. Haven't you anything to attend to?"

This was addressed to Ronnie who was still gawping at me and no doubt trying to work out why I hadn't tossed him to the lions. He finally pulled himself together and, with mumbled and bowed thanks, departed arse-first.

I smiled at Mary. "Let's hope he is a good learner," I said. "Now lead on, Miss. For I would bet - if I were indeed a betting man - that the young lady is keen to talk to me."

Indeed the young lady was. More than keen as she all but drop-kicked Mary Cunliffe out of the dressing room which adjoined her bedroom. When Nancy was sure we were on our own she turned to me with an urgent question.

"Am I right that you have a message from Frank?"

Maybe it was the Irish in me, but I wasn't going to miss a chance for further devilry. I slowly took out a notebook from inside my jacket and gazed confidently round the room.

"Ah sure we'll get to that in good time, Miss. First I'd like your views on the Indian question."

Nancy's eyes widened in disbelief. "The Indian question! Hang the Indian question. And hang the Mahatma too for that matter."

Blimey it could have been her dad speaking or even my old mate Winston himself. I made a mental note to attend to her political education before she became the first Mrs Funnybone.

Nancy glared at me. She looked magnificent but I could see she was anxious and unsure.

"Well, what about it. Have you a message from Frank?"

"Indeed I have, Miss. Mr Thirkettle seemed anxious I should convey it to you personally."

"Then why are you blathering on about the sub-continent? Come on, man, out with it."

I beckoned her to come closer and, despite all instincts, Nancy leaned her ear towards my mis-shapen mouth.

"He says," I paused for full effect, "Mr Thirkettle says ... would you mind coming on his bike?"

Nancy jumped back as if she had been electrocuted, possibly because the final seven words were uttered in the unmistakeable voice of Frankie Funnybone. For a moment she must have thought Brian O'Reilly was messing her about but, as her mouth fell open, I knew that the truth had revealed itself. Still gawping, Nancy signalled me to stay exactly where I was and moved to open the sitting room door.

"Mary," she called and I heard the eager-to-please patter of dainty feet. "Mary, I don't want to be disturbed for an hour. Is that clear?"

The housekeeper had appeared at the open door and was straining to look over Nancy's shoulder at me.

"Er, as you wish, Miss but ..."

"Mr O'Reilly needs to take down my particulars at once. Understand?"

"Yes, Miss," answered Mary and, before she'd finished speaking, the door had been slammed in her face. Nancy turned to me and began to unbutton her snow white blouse. "Right, buster," she purred as the garment slid to the floor, "prove you are who you claim you are."

Although I say it myself, I think I put Nancy's mind at rest on the question of my identity. To emphasise the point, I performed once with my disguise on and, when Nancy became hysterical - with laughter - I removed it and clambered on board for the second house. Old Cliff was dead right; the whole shebang was much easier to get on and off than it looked. A good thing too because, as the smoky trails of Nancy's post-coital Craven A drifted around us, we were jolted back to reality by the sound of Joshua's approach up the stairs. We knew immediately it was him as each heavy footstep sounded as if it were crushing a domestic.

Immediately Nancy was on her feet, sprinting to unlock the door and frantically doing up her buttons as she went, I jammed the rubber bald pate over my sweaty locks, inserted the false teeth and as Joshua burst in I was pointing my camera at Nancy.

"Ah, sir, 'tis good that you're here for I'm almost finished with your fine girl."

My words didn't make much sense but Joshua wasn't listening anyway. I don't know what had spooked him; maybe he had heard our laughter. Whatever, he had a good snoop around the room and looked me up and down suspiciously before grunting that we'd talk downstairs. Turning to go, he brushed against Mary Cunliffe who had arrived to see what the fuss was about and I was sure their eyes met again as the door closed behind them.

I told Nancy as much.

"Ye know your oul fella's got a crush on young Mary there, don't ye?"

"Franco, why are you talking to me in an Irish accent?"

"Ah sorry, Nance. Lost in the role and all that, call it a showbiz thing. But it's still true. Your Dad is sweet on Mary Cunliffe."

Nancy dismissed a jet of smoke from between her lips. "If Mummy finds out she'll cut off his credentials with a ceremonial sword and feed them to the regimental goat."

"Now that would be worth a picture," I replied, pointing the camera and capturing her framed by milky sunlight streaming into the room. It was the only shot I ever took when there was actually film in the camera and I still have the beautiful photograph which looks as if it was taken yesterday.

It's on the desk beside me as I write and last week one of the care home staff asked if it was my grand-daughter. I told her that it was.

Before I left all that remained was to outline the laughably simple plan I'd dreamed up for our elopement. The following night, a Thursday, Nancy would visit me at seven o'clock in my hotel to look at contact prints, whatever the hell they were. Before anyone got wind of what was happening we would be beyond Joshua's grasp.

So it was with the feeling of a job well done that I strutted downstairs only to run straight into the old tyrant. I managed to steady myself and put up some small talk about how I'd like to photograph the wedding and would that be all right with him?

Apparently it was, as long as I didn't damn well get under the feet of the official photographer or allow the guests to trip over my confounded carcass. I assured him he was safe on both counts and turned to go. But Sir Joshua wasn't finished and ordered me to follow him into the drawing room where Edmund sat disconsolately alone by the piano.

"Ask him your damn fool questions an' all," snapped Joshua slamming the door behind him.

Edmund looked up somewhat surprised and it occurred to me that, had I not lived here for twenty years, I would not know this was the middle son of the seventh Lord Welbeck. Joshua, displaying his usual social graces, had not introduced us.

"Would you play us something, sir, on the old Joanna," I asked Edmund.

Nancy's intended studied the piano as though unaware of what he'd been sitting next to.

"Oh, I'm afraid I don't play the piano," Edmund told me sadly. "I don't play anything." He paused before adding, "In fact, the truth is, I don't really do very much at all."

Do you know, at that point I actually felt sorry for the man whose bride-to-be I was about to steal. So I took out my notebook and made a great show of interviewing Edmund for the magazine, taking down his views on subjects as diverse as fox-hunting - bally good - and Socialism - bally not so bally good. I pretended to take his picture too. Well I wasn't going as far as to waste valuable film on such a noodle!

But, sadly for him, what he'd said was true. Apart from attending a posh school and spending bundles of his aristocratic Dad's bally tin, Edmund had accomplished absolutely nothing in his twenty-three years. It was somewhat sad really, made all the more poignant by his final comment. As I tucked the fountain pen back into my jacket pocket, Edmund looked at me glumly and came out with something I've never forgotten.

"Do you know, Mr O'Reilly," he said very definitely. "I can't wait for the war to begin."

That threw me and no mistake. "War? Sure we want no more of that business after the last hoo-hah."

Edmund shrugged. "It's coming whether we want it or not and when it does I'll be ready to serve and to sacrifice. It's what our family does."

It was said with such simple resolve that I almost warmed to Master Edmund. He was right too, not just about the coming conflict but also about his sacrificial role in it. I was reminded of this moment at Salerno seven years later as I watched the sea gently draw his broken body into her embrace. I've often wished I could have waded in and saved his remains for the Welbeck family vault. But that wouldn't have looked at all appropriate, what with me dressed in full German storm trooper's uniform and keen not to arouse suspicion among my Kameraden. Especially as it looked like it was my fault he'd been shot. However that story's for another time. *(Frankie discusses this ambivalent – and frankly disgraceful episode – at length in his special volume of wartime memories 'The Fighting Funnybones' to be published soon).*

Meanwhile hostilities were about to begin on a different front sooner than Edmund or anyone else could have envisaged.

****

I spent most of the next day in my room at the Station Hotel in a state of high anxiety. To try to calm myself I went over and over our getaway plan. It was beautiful in its duplicity because everything pointed to London as our destination; train tickets left for just long enough on the saloon bar; my scheduled appearance tomorrow night at The London Palladium and the very public booking of a suite at The Dorchester for the entire weekend.

Meanwhile, ha, ha, ha, Nancy and I would actually be fleeing northwards on The Royal Scot like Richard Hannay and Madeleine Carroll. *(Frankie really ought to get his facts in order. His reference to Alfred Hitchcock's 1935 film, The 39 Steps, is largely correct. But, to be consistent, he should have referred to Pamela, the name of the character portrayed by Ms Carroll. Hannay was, of course, played by Robert Donat).*

But, as seven approached, I became even more uneasy. What if Nancy had had second thoughts? Maybe she'd start to feel sorry for Edmund. I certainly did after our conversation. Or perhaps Lake would arrive and finish the facial reconstruction he'd started in The Regent Palace. By the time I was ready to go down and meet Nancy I'd packed and repacked my suitcase half a dozen times and was in a fine old state – with good reason as it turned out.

Coming downstairs into the bar, suitcase in hand and a raincoat over my arm, I was actually beginning to relax, a feeling that lasted just a few seconds. It was fortunate that I was only halfway down when the outer door of the bar flew open and in stepped Nancy. She glanced immediately up at me in sheer panic, spun round and said loudly, "For goodness sake, Daddy, don't be so clumsy."

Before Sir Joshua had finished protesting that he hadn't damn well stepped on his daughter's confounded heels, I was already back up the stairs, clawing in my coat pocket for the room key. Blimey, what had happened, I wondered as I quickly locked the door behind me and weighed up the window as a means of escape. Surely Joshua and his jackals would be pounding on the door in a few seconds time.

Now it's a fact that you can only have a theatre audience eating out of your hand if you stay sharp and it took me just a few moments to rationalise what had - and had not - happened. If Joshua had suspected any funny business then he and his merry men would have been here earlier – and significantly minus his darling daughter. He wouldn't want her to witness me being kicked from here to next Thursday. Certainly something had gone very wrong but it might not be too late to fix it. I peeled off my jacket, lifted the rubber disguise and wiped away the sweat that was cascading from my actual forehead. I needed a credible plan and quick.

Two minutes later I strolled as nonchalantly as humanly possible down the stairs to the saloon, this time minus suitcase. Seeing Joshua shouting the odds at the bar to Nancy's squirming embarrassment, I affected extreme surprise.

"To be sure, sir and miss. Why I wasn't expecting you tonight."

"If I'm paying for these snaps I'm damn well going to look at them first," growled Joshua.

I gazed calmly as I could at him, aware that every eye in the crowded bar was on me, before replying, "Oh, did Miss Nancy not get my message?"

"What damned message?"

I explained that I'd phoned earlier to inform Nancy that a technical problem meant the contact prints were not ready. Unfortunately I'd been unable to get through to her but someone from the garage had answered and promised to pass on the news.

"I think I spoke to some feller called Dane or maybe Lane."

"Cain Trotter," barked Joshua.

"I think that's the chap, sir."

"The idiot. I'll get Lake to take a crop to his useless hide."

Well, the prospect of Cain on the wrong end of a thrashing was just the ticket for me but, seeing Nancy's rebuking stare, I was forced into a plea of mitigation for the clumsy clot.

"Ah don't be too hard on the feller, sir. Maybe I didn't explain meself all that well. Now how's about you and Miss Nancy taking a drink with me? Celia, whatever these fine people are having."

I'd like to report that the next half hour was a relaxing one filled with idle chit-chat and bonhomie. In reality, while I surreptitiously checked my watch every thirty seconds and Nancy stared glumly into her port and lemon, Joshua held forth at length on the inadequacies of the town's tradesmen, many of whom, judging from the resentful sidelong looks, were keeping him company in this very bar.

However, the lord of the manor's tirade had its uses. While he thundered on about chiselling and short-changing, I was able to plan my back-up strategy. Accordingly, when Joshua finally gave everyone a break and went to the toilet, I let Nancy know what I had in mind.

As all eyes were still on us, I couldn't break into easy intimacy so, after a few platitudes, I merely said, "I'll telephone you at six tomorrow, Miss. Then you'll know exactly when your prints will come."

Trying gamely not to laugh, Nancy was about to reply when Joshua lurched back into view. The entire clientele braced itself for another onslaught but Sir Josh seemed to have exhausted his store of bile and, at Nancy's suggestion, they left soon afterwards. I promptly bought drinks all round by way of apology.

The following day I decided I had to get out and about, if for nothing else but to clear my head and formulate the plan in detail. With a knapsack containing a flask and sandwiches provided by Celia the landlady, I set off on foot and was soon bouncing along the moorland ridge that loomed over Butterthwaite to the south.

As it was a Friday morning I'd reckoned to have the wide open spaces to myself but soon I realised this would not be the case. I lost count of the number of shabbily dressed men in stained coats, collar-less shirts and greasy flat caps who I passed. Many seemed to be shambling along aimlessly in small groups but, judging from their pinched and shifty looks, others were obviously up there to trap game. They watched me go by with suspicion and, although I couldn't do it out loud, I silently wished them good luck in their pursuit of rabbits for the pot. The latest depression in the textile industry was obviously biting deeper than I'd ever known.

Reflecting on all that, I scrambled up Butternose Tor and found myself alone at the summit, monarch of all I surveyed. Spread out below was the town with its five Protheroe mills stretching away east along the valley. And to the west on the facing slopes, where smoke from his mill chimneys seldom reached, stood Joshua's - and for that matter my - family home. It was a grey-stone Gothic pile which from up here looked like a particularly ugly municipal library, built and maintained through the efforts of men like those I'd just passed. People such as my own family.

Ah well, nobody ever claimed things in this world were fair but perhaps my actions the following day would bring some sunshine into those men's lives. Indeed my brainwave came as I mused on whether Joshua's well-stocked trout stream would provide richer pickings for unemployed workers than the odd coney on largely barren moorland. My eyes followed the meanderings of this stream where it flowed past the main gate and was culverted under the start of the drive, which cut through the beech plantation and up towards the house.

So far so familiar but as I gazed at the drive's mid-point I noticed something I'd forgotten long ago – the path from the old house which veered off to the left and ended a quarter of a mile away at a long disused gate.

You see, in 1864 old Caleb Protheroe had bought a fine medium-sized early Georgian property with extensive grounds from a merchant who'd been cleaned out by unwise speculation in railway shares. Caleb had promptly flattened the house and raised the present towering monstrosity. He'd also had a grand new entrance gate built nearer the town to show everyone exactly what he was about, which left that overgrown path and gateway without a purpose. Maybe it was time to bring it back into use. From this old track the main drive skirted a private chapel where the wedding ceremony was to take place, and wound past the stables where right now Les would be working his fingers to the bone. In all my years of living there I'd never noticed how close the chapel and stables were to each other. Hmmm.

I must have sat there a good hour making notes and weighing up distances while nibbling Celia's potted meat sarnies. I would have probably stayed longer too but, noticing a much darker tinge on clouds far away to the west, I decided to pack up as I didn't fancy a soaking. It was a shrewd move too because by the time I was climbing the stile back on to Antcliffe Road those distant clouds had arrived to ruin what had been a pleasant late spring day and when I burst into the Station Hotel bar I was half-soaked.

The phone call to Nancy at six o'clock went smoothly; nobody listening in could surely have suspected my talk of missing photographs hid the code that would help liberate us both. When I say nobody, I was thinking of somebody eavesdropping at the telephone exchange or a nosey parker on another phone at the hall. What I did not have in mind was someone in the bar with an ear for my business. And that someone being Maurice Lake!

I hadn't encountered the prick since he'd punched out my lights in London and stolen Nancy so when I turned and saw him lounging at a table in the corner, my fingers automatically flew up to my nose. That giveaway was bad enough but what made things worse, much worse, was that Lake held in his hand a large photograph – of me!

I had half a mind to run for it but something - possibly the fact I was still in one piece - persuaded me that things could not be quite as bad as they seemed. I therefore approached his table with caution, sniffing as I went.

"Caught a cold, Irish?"

"I got a bit wet this afternoon, sir."

Lake weighed me up for a few seconds before replying, "You want to be careful. You could catch your death. Like this chap's about to."

He held the picture in front of my face. It was a Frankie Funnybone publicity photo, and it took all my concentration not to whip out a pen and sign it as I'd done to hundreds before.

"That feller looks a proper rascal. Who is he?"

"Do they not teach you Irish to read," replied Lake, evidently auditioning to replace Sir Joshua as the villain in the hall's Christmas panto. I believe that this year they were doing Macbeth.

I squinted at the picture and gave my opinion. "Ah yes. I see it now. Frankie Funny...bone. Don't know the chap."

Lake studied me while I squirmed internally. Finally he stood up.

"You let me know if you see him around these parts," he said, finally handing me the photograph. I told him that yes I surely would and turned towards the bar, thinking Lake would do the decent thing and leave. Instead he joined me at the counter.

"I will take a drink," he said, even though I hadn't offered him one, "should that be all right with you."

I couldn't exactly tell him I'd rather sup with Benito Mussolini so I had no alternative but to buy the man a pint.

"So what part of the Emerald Isle threw you up then?"

His question was delivered ever so casually but there was no disguising its menace. I needed to be extra careful.

"Ah, sure you wouldn't have heard of it."

"Try me."

"Well, I'm from a little place called Westport.

"Isn't that in County Mayo?"

"You're dead right there, sir."

Lake smiled in a way that suggested he didn't generally have much use for smiles and for one glorious moment I thought the interrogation was over. But his next comment showed that snares were still being set.

"Yes, Westport, I know it well. What's that mountain nearby? Place of pilgrimage I'm told."

Don't let anyone, especially my old teachers, tell you that Francis Thirkettle never did his homework.

"If you know the place so well, sir, then I've no need to tell you that the mountain you speak of is The Reek or Croagh Patrick as you've more probably heard it called." And god bless The Encyclopaedia Britannica.

71

Lake nodded and I could tell he was beginning to think I was who I said I was.

"That's the one."

"Indeed it is, sir. In fact on Reek Sunday every July you'll catch the pilgrims, hundreds of 'em, clambering up barefoot."

"And do you do that?"

I smiled and shook my head. "Ah sure the last time I went up The Reek barefoot I was just fourteen. These days if I want to cut my old tootsies to ribbons I'll stick 'em in the bacon slicer thank you very much. With apologies to old St Patrick an' all his snakes."

You have to agree it was an impressive performance. Understated yet authoritative as Sir Osbert Jardine would no doubt have put it. It was, therefore, with no little inward annoyance I greeted the fact that Lake was not about to let up.

"So what did you get up to in the war?" he asked.

It was time to seize the bull by the horns. I put an arm around Lake and, with my smile never wavering, said, "I lost too many fuckin' good pals to go blabbin' about it to some prick who probably never got nearer the action than Aldershot barracks."

The moment before I pulled my hand away I felt Lake's back muscles go rigid. I picked up my pint and took a long draught before resuming the tirade.

"I joined the 2nd Connaughts in 1915 and I could still give you the name and number of my company sergeant major, the devil take him. Now fuck off, sir, unless you'd rather take it outside."

Of course I'd be completely scuppered if that did happen. Lake would knock off my disguise shortly before knocking off my block. But I'd calculated correctly. The tougher you are with these characters the more they respect you – and leave you alone. Lake's eyes blazed briefly before he nodded sheepishly.

"I'm sorry, Mr O'Reilly, I was not questioning your bravery."

He made as if to go but turned back towards me, stood to attention and saluted.

"For the record, sir, I was at Gallipoli. 1st Battalion, the Lancashires."

It was my turn to salute. "Then you, more than anyone, will know why I don't want to talk about it."

Lake nodded and left the bar. I had more than three-quarters of my beer left, which I downed in one before ordering another. And another. And another.

Chapter Six: We've Gone on Me Bike

"Good day to ye, their worships ... sure 'tis a fine old time for a ceilidh, His Excellency and Mrs Excellency... ah, Your Grace, nice to see ye to see ye nice."

Yes, the birds were singing, wedding bells were ringing, and with profuse apologies to Irish readers, I was adding my own peculiar splashes of colour to the merry tableau. More exactly I was by the Protheroe family chapel's lych gate - thatched wouldn't ye know it - 'photographing' the guests as they got out of their cars, cabs and carriages.

And, had I bothered to put any film in my camera what a fascinating story those pictures would have told. On one hand we had the local gentry backing the bride's side; families headed by pan-scrubbed, centre-parted, self-made gents who looked like they couldn't wait to set about spilling beef gravy and old ale down the fronts of their morning suits. And supporting the groom we had a gang of aristocrats and minor royals, whose languid, effortlessly easy manners masked the fact that they knew they'd arrived among some very serious money.

How had I managed to become the official wedding photographer? That's easy, I hadn't. Dennis Sloan, the man hired for the job, was fifty yards away by the chapel door, smiling falsely and sweating freely as he chivvied into photographable groups, people who didn't take kindly to the lower orders pushing them around. The arrangement suited us both. Dennis could get on with what he'd been contracted to do while I'd promised him use of any or all of my snaps. That meant I could get myself into position to carry out the devilishly cunning plan to which I'd put the final touches the previous evening.

Following the potentially disastrous encounter with Lake and my submission to the medicinal qualities of best bitter, I'd made a phone call then staggered off in the direction of The Carders Arms, a pub at the rougher east end of town where I reckoned the person I was meeting would be more at home.

As our rendezvous was not for another half hour and the beer had made me peckish, I whiled my time away in a sweaty, steamy chip shop queue behind a gaggle of tipsy mill girls discussing tomorrow's nuptials. Their views interested me because a) I'd been at school with most of them and b) if it had anything to do with me, what they were speculating about was not going to happen.

"She's a right lucky so-and-so," volunteered Alice Wright, the prettiest of this band. "What I wouldn't do for a wedding like that."

"What you wouldn't do for five Woodbines," cracked Lizzie Hopkirk and the queue exploded into mirth.

"Well I'm not so sure." This came from a large, earnest-looking girl I didn't recognise.

Lizzie, confirming her status as St Barnabas's sharpest ex-pupil (female) snapped back, "Sorry, Al, I'm doing you down. I should have said *ten* Woodbines."

There followed a short but lively discussion on the relative frequencies at which the under-garments of Alice Wright and Lizzie Hopkirk were discarded in pursuit of romantic fulfilment. I'd give it you chapter and verse but the thing is, I want this memoir published and not festering for years in the Lord Chamberlain's bottom drawer. *(As usual Frankie is talking nonsense. The Lord Chamberlain's role as ...)* All right, all right I am aware that the LC hasn't been a censor since 1968. Back in your fridge!

"No," intervened the girl I didn't recognise, bringing the cat fight to a sudden end. "I mean I'm not sure she's that lucky. Have you seen the honourable Edmund? I don't know what Miss Nancy is thinking of."

It was Sandra Tomlinson's turn to stick in her two pennorth. "She's thinking of what he's hiding in his pocket."

"You've got to be talking about his wallet." This was Lizzie again. "Because there don't look owt else in there."

The cackling commenced again and Alice, who stood at the rear end of the coven turned to me, shook her blonde Shirley Temple curls and said with a heart-melting grin, "Sorry about all that, dad. We're not usually this naughty."

I was relieved she hadn't recognised me and rushed to put her mind at ease. "Ah sure I'm not sure what you lovely ladies are on about."

Cue more appreciative howls before Lizzie cemented her status as my all-time favourite among the Old Barnabessians by telling the queue, "Anyway, I reckon she'd have been better off with Franny Thirkettle. He's not doing too bad for himself is he."

It took all the self-control I had not to step across the chippy and hug her. My self-esteem soared ... until Sandra Tomlinson opened her big fat gob again.

"Yeah well," she said, "maybe she'll have a word with our Jean first – if she doesn't want to end up with someone who's finished before he's started."

Damn the cheeky mare, her lumpy, frumpy sister too - I only kissed her out of kindness - and her podgy stodgy twins, whoever they belonged to! Was nothing sacred? My appetite totally shot to pieces, I slipped unnoticed out of the squawking queue and across the road to The Carders.

I might have known he'd be early. On his own in one corner of the public bar among the crib players and shove ha'penny merchants sat Les. You'd guessed it was him I was meeting hadn't you? Of course *he* hadn't yet guessed it was me he was meeting and, after I'd stood him a pint of best, he reluctantly agreed to follow me into the snug, glancing at his pocket watch as he went.

"I'm sorry, Mr O'Reilly," Les said firmly. "Can you get your business over with sharpish? You see I'm due up and around very early."

My little verbal sally, "Why is there something happening tomorrow, Mr Thirkettle?" had Les shaking his head in exasperation. So, as I could see he was in no mood for levity, I got straight down to it.

"Only kidding, sir. Can I put a quick proposal to you?"

"If it is quick."

"Very well, it is this ..." and at that point I abandoned Hibernia's lilt in favour of my own broad vowels. "Dad, I want you to help Nancy and me elope."

By the time I'd peeled Les off the ceiling, sat him down with a double scotch and persuaded him that I wasn't planning a kidnap, he'd become somewhat taken with the idea. The fact that I'd added that it was what Nancy and I wanted more than anything else in the world did my cause no harm either. Indeed, as I sketched out the plan, Les even suggested a couple of refinements of his own.

Ten minutes later it was all done and dusted and Les was free to head for his bed. He grabbed his old flat cap, stood up and held out his hand.

"I wouldn't go anywhere near this if I thought it wasn't best for the both of you," he said earnestly.

Hugging him, I replied, "I know, Dad, and I wouldn't want you to either. What's more I promise my plan sees to it nobody will connect you to anything."

Les shrugged. "I'm not fussed either way, son. For all I care, Sir Joshua can go and ..."

I raised a warning hand. "Remember, Dad, it's not just you. The whole family could suffer."

He had to concede I was right and assured me that nobody would notice him slip away from the chapel after completing his duties as usher.

And nor did anyone see him the next day, apart from me, looking on in admiration as, with a perfect trailing leg technique, Les Thirkettle, fifty-something of this parish, effortlessly hurdled the church-yard wall and sprinted off up the drive.

By this time the last of the guests had left their eternal images in Dennis Sloan's magic box and made their way into the chapel. I calculated there were a few more minutes for me to get my thoughts in order before the final two actors in the drama were due on stage. My watch showed five to three and it was surely the bride's prerogative to be at least ten minutes late. In which case, someone should have informed her Dad.

For, at exactly two minutes to three, I was startled to hear the sound of wheels, horses' hooves and jingling tack and turned to see Sir Joshua staring nervously at the rumps of my oldest girlfriends, Bess and Dolly. The two carriage horses, done out in ridiculous purple plumes, were between the shafts of the open topped landau, freshly re-painted by Les in the family's colours, including the Protheroe crest, a bullwhip crossed with a man-trap - I made that last bit up.

Next to Joshua on the padded driver's seat was Nancy who, despite her obvious agitation, looked radiant in a flouncing snow white dress of tuille, organza and a load of other bridal nonsense I can't be bothered to spell out – because there wasn't going to be a bride.

Joshua would not have thanked me for drawing attention to his nerves as he took great pains to hide what Les and I had known for years – that for all his bluster and bravado, the dark knight was scared stiff of horses. The fact that he was pathologically determined not to show his fear and give his daughter this most traditional start to her big day would work to my advantage.

The carriage clattered to a halt and I fished a handful of sugar lumps out of my pocket for Bess and Dolly which they accepted excitedly from me as they had done a thousand times before. Evidently they had no problems seeing through my disguise. As I shovelled sugar into the horses, Joshua stared at me in surprise and exasperation.

"Where the devil is young Powell?" he demanded.

Wilfred Powell, a cousin of mine who had just started duties under Les in the stables, was supposed to greet the carriage in his fine new huntsman's rig and take hold of the halter to ensure the bride-to-be and the grouch-that-already-was didn't break their necks as they alighted. However, it hadn't taken much - one of my white fivers actually - to persuade young Wilf that he should make himself scarce.

"Ah Master Wilfred got taken short but you'll have no worries, sir. Brian O'Reilly at your service."

"What do you damn well know about horses?"

Goodness he was nervous so I gave the knife a quick twist.

"Ah you'll have no fears at all, sir. What I'm saying is name me the Irish lad who doesn't have a way with the gee-gees."

Joshua looked as if he was about to protest that he wasn't damn well scared but decided not to draw attention to his fear. He made a huge effort to relax as I put on a show of photography and even attempted something very loosely resembling a smile. I fervently hoped it would be the last to crack his joyless mug for some considerable time.

While Joshua was pulling his face into unfamiliar shapes Nancy was becoming noticeably more nervous so I decided the time to act had arrived.

Ever so casually I suggested to Joshua that the carriage could be turned round so we'd have the chapel in the background and an atmospheric addition to the wedding album. Glancing testily at his infamous pocket watch, Joshua reluctantly agreed and I gently tugged Bess and Dolly this way and that until the carriage faced the main drive.

Instinct told me I didn't have much more time and I could see that even Dennis Sloan by the chapel door was getting restless. So, after quickly clicking the camera shutter a few times, I asked Joshua if he'd mind if I climbed up next to Nancy and took the most beautiful portrait of her with the chapel in the background. Oh, and would he be so kind as to hold the horses while I did so?

As I'd expected, he wasn't keen at all so I added, off-handedly, "Course, if you'd rather not mess with these beasts I'll quite understand."

Now listen, Sir Joshua Protheroe wasn't having accusations of funk chucked at him. He bounded off the carriage seat and was beside me before you could say, 'It's a stampede'. I handed him the halter and clambered up next to Nancy, my camera tucked under my left arm.

It was important, I told Nancy, that she should hold the reins in a particular manner which I would demonstrate. Speed was really of the essence now because out of the corner of my eye I saw Dennis with Nancy's brother Robert striding down the path to see what was holding things up. In for a penny! I picked up the reins, shouted at Nancy to hold them, "like this," and urged the horses forward.

Stunned, Joshua dropped the halter and leapt backwards as the carriage shot off. It was with the most profound pleasure that I looked back and saw of Nancy's Dad only his legs pointing skywards, the rest of him having disappeared over the churchyard wall. I sort of hoped the fall hadn't quite killed the old rogue and, wouldn't you know, nor had it. For, just before the carriage reached a bend in the drive and disappeared into the woods, I heard him bellow, "Give the reins to Nancy, you fool."

It suited me to let him think he had a runaway vehicle on his hands and not a runaway daughter.

Glancing at Nancy who seemed to be enjoying her flight through the forest, I shouted. "You OK?"

Her eyes gleamed. "Never better, Franco," she yelled. "I'd be even happier if we were in a fast car. We'll not get very far on this heap of junk."

"That's handy because we're not going very far on this heap of junk," I shouted back. "Take off your shoes."

"What?"

"Take your shoes off and leave them on the seat."

Nancy shrugged and bent down to remove her shoes while I brought the carriage to a halt at the point where the drive intersected with the start of the rutted grass track which led down to the old house's main gate. As we stopped, a small figure stepped out of the trees and began to fuss the horses with gifts of more sugar. This was my 14-year-old brother Tommy, the same little blighter who'd giggled at me a couple of days ago and received a winger from Mum for his cheek. He was holding a pair of lady's riding boots.

I leapt down and swung Nancy from the landau before grabbing the boots from Tommy and urging Nancy to put them on. Tommy, meanwhile, was already up on the carriage with the reins in his hands. He grinned down at me and I noticed one of his front teeth was missing. But apparently it was my appearance that proved ripe for comment.

"Your disguise, Franny," snorted Tommy, "it's a big improvement."

I was much too on edge to banter with him but I managed a quick, "Leave the jokes to me, Tom, there's a good little lad," before getting down to brass tacks.

"Just remember to drop one of Miss Nancy's shoes before the bend. Leave the carriage by the old gate and, whatever you do, don't get caught."

Tommy shook his head and spoke as if being addressed by an imbecile.

"Yeah, it's not as if I'd ever played hide and seek in those woods. You truly are a comedian, Franny. Good luck."

He snapped the reins and the horses disappeared down the old track, the landau bouncing along behind. When Nancy had pulled the boots on and tucked her dress into her knickers - an oddly stirring sight - we set off at a good lick up through the trees towards the stables.

We'd left the drive not a moment too soon either as seconds later there was a rush and the Bentley tore past. I glanced back and just caught sight of a thunder-faced Joshua in the passenger seat. The car screeched to a halt - someone had obviously spotted Nancy's shoe - reversed slightly and moved off very carefully down the undulating old track. The plan was working like a dream.

After a few seconds scurrying through the wood I stopped Nancy and spun her round to face me.

"You're sure about this?" I asked her. "There's still time to say I abducted you."

"I'll show you how sure I am," Nancy replied without hesitation, tugging at her undergarments.

Well, I wouldn't normally turn down a spot of open-air fun but there's a time and place for everything and this was neither. I put my hand on hers.

"You've convinced me. Come on."

A minute more of dodging roots and ducking low branches saw us at the edge of the wood where it met the sloping lawn. To our right, about a hundred yards away in front of the house was a giant marquee. I could clearly see servants in black scurrying in between the two like lines of ants. To the left was the stable block, our destination.

"You ready?" I asked. She nodded and we sprinted across the short expanse of lawn, Nancy moving surprisingly gracefully in her unconventional gear. We dashed across the gravel path and shot into the stables through a side entrance. Rushing past the stalls, Nancy paused a moment to stroke her favourite Cleveland Bay, Bouncer, before we tumbled through the internal linking door and into the garage.

Without the cars and carriage the place looked more cavernous than usual and our footsteps echoed up to the eaves. Crouching in the corner, Les was lovingly tightening a wheel nut on his double-seater Norton CSI. With a twinge of guilty déjà vu I realised he was on the exact spot where I'd nearly, but not quite, broken my duck with Jean Tomlinson and given the old pushbike a re-spray.

Les looked up and grinned before asking, "Are you sure that you both still want to do this? It's a big step and there'll be no going back."

Nancy and I glanced at each other and nodded in unison.

"Right," said Les struggling to his feet, "let's get you going."

"Nobody is going anywhere."

The voice came from behind me and I had no need to spin round theatrically to know that it belonged to Lake. Nonetheless I spun round theatrically and came face to face with my nemesis who, having closed the door behind him, was leaning against it, smiling smugly and shaking his head.

"There's no record of a Brian O'Reilly from Westport joining the 2nd Connaughts in 1915," he informed me. "Either you were a conchie or you're hiding another secret under that stupid disguise ... Mr Funnybone!" Lake made as if to tear at my false bonce but Les stepped in between us.

"Look, Maurice," he said, carefully wiping his oily hands on a rag. "It's what they both want. You wouldn't deny them happiness."

"Happiness!" said Lake shaking his head as if this were the oddest concept he'd ever had to consider. "What about the happiness of all those people in the chapel? Of the poor booby sucking his thumb at the altar?"

Nancy shifted uncomfortably so I put my arm round her.

"And what about the happiness of the man who pays my wages? Aye and yours too, Les."

"He'll get over it," said Les. "And besides you can't stop them. I'll make sure of that."

"Is that so?" replied Lake, "Then we'd better do something about it."

83

And from under his coat he pulled out an evil looking dagger with a six-inch blade.

Les stumbled back in horror and cried, "You can't use that, man?"

"Want to bet," growled Lake, approaching me and Nancy, who to her credit never flinched.

"Touch either of them and I'll kill you," Les screamed, pointing at him.

"Why would I hurt the apple of my employer's eye?" Lake said coolly and stepped past us to the motorbike. Before Les could move, Lake had brought the knife down hard once on each tyre. Then, as Les ran towards him, he picked up a hammer with his left hand and drove the claw deep into the side of the Norton's petrol tank.

Les's run skidded to a halt as the bodyguard brandished the shining blade at him. There was a moment's silence, punctuated by the last of the air escaping from the Norton's tyres and the tank pumping fuel onto the garage floor like a broken heart.

Les curled his lip. "You're a big man with that knife, Maurice," he said. "Let's see how tough you are without it."

"I was the regiment's middleweight champion," boasted Lake. "I'd tear you apart, you silly old fool."

Carefully removing his coat, Les threw it to me. "Put the blade down and prove it then," he challenged.

Lake didn't move for maybe ten seconds. Then he threw down the knife and rushed at Les.

You may recall the 'phantom' punch with which Muhammad Ali knocked out Sonny Liston to retain the world heavyweight title in 1965. I remember it because I was there on the front row, wildly celebrating with all the other famous faces and hangers-on. I can even remember catching Frank Sinatra's trilby after he'd thrown it in the air. I knew it was Sinatra's hat because his wig was still inside it.

But, close as I was to the action, I never saw the punch that floored Liston in the same way that, thirty years earlier, I didn't see the blow that turned out Maurice Lake's lights. Nor did Nancy and neither, for that matter, did Lake.

One moment he was advancing on the balls of his feet across the garage, head tucked into his shoulders, guard well up and an alarming glint in his eye. The next he was spark out and Les was flexing his knuckles in annoyance that it hadn't been a cleaner KO. *(Frankie's memory is playing him false here. Sinatra was present at an Ali-Liston fight but it was the first one, in the Miami Convention Centre on February 24th 1964 when Liston failed to rise off his stool for the seventh round).*

So completely was Lake flattened that I thought for an instant that the punch had killed him. However, my Dad's only worry was that Lake would come round before he'd been firmly chained to a cast iron heating pipe, which Les managed by means of a pair of handcuffs he produced from his jacket pocket.

"Don't ask," was his advice so we didn't. After Les had secured a still unconscious Lake, he checked the Norton and sighed in exasperation.

"You'll be going nowhere on this," he told us. "Both of you will have to travel on your pushbike."

"We'll hardly outrun a Bentley on that," I said but Les was insistent.

"Leave me to deal with the Bentley. Just get yourselves to the main gate and you'll be away, I promise."

Glancing round the garage, I spotted my sister Rosemary's old sit-up-and-beg bike.

"Could Nancy not use that?" I asked.

Les shook his head firmly. "No it's not roadworthy. Just take yours. Come on, son, you've been all over the show on it."

He was right of course. Riding a bike is a bit like, well, like riding a bike and, although I'd be carrying a passenger, I should be able to pull it off.

Les wiped his hands a final time, threw the rag on the floor and gave us our instructions. "Leave it exactly two minutes. Then ride across the lawn and down through the beech plantation to the main gate. But whatever you do, don't get onto the drive until you're well into the trees. You'll see what I'm on about."

Les grabbed Nancy and me by the shoulders and stared hard at us. "You two have a good life together. Promise."

"We promise," I said and hugged him. As all three of us were near to tears I pushed him away as playfully as I could. Les smiled through red-rimmed eyes and was then away out of the side door. I had no idea what he was planning but felt sure it would work.

Thirty seconds had limped by when Lake stirred, opened his eyes and began pulling violently at the handcuffs.

"You'll do yourself a mischief," I warned him. "Just wait a few minutes and somebody'll find you."

"I'll do you a mischief when I find you."

"Oh do shut up," said Nancy. "You tedious man."

But Lake would not be silenced. "I have my duty to do," he said as self-importantly as one could while manacled to a wall.

Nancy picked up Les's oily rag and walked over to Lake. I was worried he might grab her but he knew better than to lay a finger on the lord of the manor's girl. Nancy obviously had this in mind as she thrust her face right into his.

"Let's get this straight, buster," she told him. "Your duty will not include mentioning Les's part in this pantomime. If you do I shall write to my father and tell him you interfered with me. Is that clear?"

I looked at my watch. In just a minute we'd be gone. But still Lake wasn't finished. He drew himself as high as the handcuffs would allow and challenged Nancy to her face.

"How will I explain who knocked me out? Eh? Nobody's ever going to believe *he* did it," he spat pointing contemptuously at me. "It's just stupid and there's another urgle gurgle wurgle."

Those of you paying attention will remember that Nancy was holding an oily rag and Lake's final few sounds were made after she had stuffed it into his mouth.

"You can tell my Dad it was me who bashed you," she told him. "Come on, Franco, let's get that bike moving."

I dashed over to the double doors and pulled them open just wide enough to take the bike and peered out. There was no-one in the courtyard and through the small arch to my left I could see the lawn sloping away invitingly down to the beech plantation. When I turned back Nancy already had the bike pointing towards the door and was straddling the back wheel. But we had a problem. Lake was waving his arms around madly and his face had turned an alarming shade of puce. I hesitated and Nancy tore into me.

"He'll live for god's sake. It's time, Franco. Now!"

But I couldn't leave a man to choke, no matter who he was, so I ran over to Lake and pulled the rag from his mouth. It was only then that the folly of what I'd done became apparent.

Without warning and like a complete sneak, Lake produced a large monkey wrench and swung it at me. I managed to partially dodge the blow but even so it caught my right knee and I went down screaming – it bloomin' well hurt you know. I only just managed to wriggle away from a second blow before Lake took one himself, courtesy of Nancy's right boot which caught him full in the kisser.

Nancy supported my weight as I limped back to the bike but, hardly able to stand, it was clear that I would be pedalling nowhere in the near future.

"Damn Lake," I lamented. "We're scuppered."

"Nonsense," replied no-nonsense Nancy jumping onto the bike. "Get on."

And so it was that anyone lucky enough to have been in the courtyard at that moment would have witnessed a very odd sight indeed bursting through the double garage doors. A bride-not-to-be, dress tucked into her knickers and riding boots pumping up and down like pistons was crouched over the handlebars while on the seat behind her perched a limp specimen of humanity trying his utmost not to fall off.

After shooting through the side arch and out on to the lawn we did pick up an audience too. As we raced past the marquee, the servants all stopped to goggle at this extravagant sight and, never one to deny the populace a show, I ripped off my mask, waved and threw it towards them. I saw my mother's mouth fly open in amazement and the tray full of champagne glasses she'd been carrying crash to the ground.

Most other members of my family began to cheer as they realised that one of their own was sticking it to the man - as I believe the happenin' folk say these days. The exception was Ronnie who allowed his sense of duty to overcome notions of family loyalty. Luckily, as he bounded eagerly forward to intercept us, a strategically placed foot belonging to our sister Rose sent him sprawling to the turf as we shot past the marquee. I looked back to see Ronnie being smacked around the head by a demented Mary Cunliffe.

With only a hundred yards between us and the beech plantation I was convinced we were nearly home and hosed. Don't you often find though that things are never that simple?

"Look down there," Nancy yelled. "And hang on."

I glanced at the drive to the right of us and saw the Bentley had appeared round a bend and was racing to cut us off at the woods. By the time we were fifty yards from the trees, the car had almost drawn level with us and I could see Joshua - his features the colour and consistency of a prune - hanging out of the passenger window, shaking his fist.

"We'll not make it," I shouted to Nancy. "They'll get there before us."

But Nancy did not waver. "Les told us to head for the trees," she shouted, "and that's what we're doing."

And that's what we did, flying into the wood a couple of seconds after the Bentley had entered it.

"Mind the timber," I yelled as Nancy slalomed her way round the beeches that seemed to career at us from all sides. Then came the inevitable crash, followed by crunching, shattering and oaths yelled. The odd thing was, however, that as metal crumpled and people cried out in pain, anger and exasperation, we were still on the move.

Indeed, without slowing down appreciably, Nancy was already steering the bike out of the trees and on to the drive while I turned back to see what had happened. What I saw was that the Bentley's nose was buried in the trunk of a largish tree which had somehow fallen across the road. What a stroke of luck that was! While the car's radiator was bent double around the tree – more work for Les there – the occupants appeared uninjured including Sir Joshua, who in trying to scramble over the obstacle and shake his fist at the same time went arse over tip.

I really wished I still had my camera and had put some film in it but before regret could consume me, I noted that we were already out of the woods and racing down the drive towards the main gates which lay invitingly open as Les had promised. Why would they not be on such a joyous day?

I took one last sentimental look back at the old place ... and my blood froze. Not ten yards to our rear and gaining quickly was Lake on the other pushbike. How in heaven's name he'd escaped I never discovered but I did notice the handcuffs on his right wrist flapping wildly in and out of the bike's basket.

"Faster, Nancy," I shouted. "We've got company."

Nancy bent further over the handlebars and pumped her legs even harder. Yet it was no use. Lake was already upon us and grabbing the back of my jacket. I just managed to slip it off in time but this only delayed him for a moment. I tried not to look back but was nearly sick as the front wheel of Lake's bike appeared next to us, accompanied by a scream and a loud splash.

Fortunately for us, the rest of Lake's bike and crucially Lake himself were elsewhere; to be exact sitting next to each other on the bottom of the shallow stream which bisected the road.

"I wondered why Les didn't want us to take the other bike," I told Nancy, who was more concerned about getting us in once piece through the gateway. We shot into the lane outside the hall and Nancy kept going downhill until reaching a three-way junction, where we stopped to catch our breath. Turn left on to the main road and we'd continue downhill into Butterthwaite where we could surely pick up a cab. But Nancy had a different idea. She turned the bike to the right.

"That's uphill, Nance," I cried.

"Yes and it's precisely where they won't look first. Redwood Halt's only a couple of hundred yards up there and a train's due any minute."

That's my girl, everything under control. Well almost everything. After travelling just twenty yards uphill Nancy turned back to me, sweating like a pig.

"Blimey, Franco, what've you done to this bike?" she spluttered. "The bleedin' gears are really stiff."

So that's what had happened!

Chapter Seven: It's the Porridge

You'll doubtless be fascinated to hear that they had a fire drill at Cold Tits yesterday.

"Don't you worry, Frankie love," the auxiliary nurse cooed as she tried to shoo me outside to hear matron hurry through the register before another inmate dropped dead, "It's only an exercise."

"Then you won't mind if I stay in bed while you lot piss about," I told her and rolled over.

I mention the incident for two reasons. One because, on the pretext of keeping everyone safe and sound, they dragged me outside to freeze my nunchucks off. Some bits of me still haven't warmed up twenty-four hours later and if anyone out there knows where the European Court of Human Rights hangs out then get in touch, preferably via Morse Code so these care home Bolsheviks don't twig what's comin' to them.

Secondly *(and hopefully more to the point)* it shows just how the mighty have fallen. The whole sorry fire drill pantomime left me looking back longingly over seventy-odd years to the time when I could run the mile in four-and-a-quarter minutes, go seven-and-a-half rounds with Jack Dempsey and elope with the lord of the manor's daughter from under everyone's nose. *(Jack Dempsey, 1895-1983, was a fearsome American heavyweight boxing champion who would have killed Frankie just by looking at him)*

OK, I wasn't exactly a picture of glowing health as Nancy dragged me to the station on the back of my bicycle. But, by the time we'd chained the bike to railings on the Butterthwaite-bound platform and were dodging back across the track to catch a train going the other way, the worst effects of Lake's sneaky drum roll on my kneecap were wearing off and I could sit back to take stock of what we'd done.

What we'd done was get away with it – for now! And, as I gazed infatuatedly at Nancy who was coolly smoking a roll-up cadged from a travelling salesman in the next compartment, I was mightily glad we had. She looked a proper picture and I for one wasn't going to tell her that she still had her wedding dress tucked inside her knickers.

Neither was the conductor who, under the spell of her flickering eyelashes, went from spitting outrage over the fact we were ticketless on his train to offering to buy them for us himself – all in about ten seconds. His generosity was not needed as I had a store of cash in the money belt Les had insisted I wear. Good job too as we'd have been in a pickle if the cash had been in my jacket that Lake had snatched.

The contents of the money belt came in handy too when we got to Manchester, found Lewis's and kitted Nancy out in a less conspicuous outfit – although she did keep the wedding dress and boots and wore them specially for me every year on our anniversary.

The cash also easily covered a pleasant night in Midland Hotel luxury, with champagne, oysters and complimentary slippers thrown in, before we left the northern England smog behind the following morning.

What we also left behind, I found out later from Les and others, was a Protheroe Hall in absolute turmoil. At the sight of her youngest pedalling madly in pursuit of the cycle world speed record, Lady Agatha began to perspire before nearly expiring there and then. It took all the delicate ministrations of Sir Joshua, limping and bellowing his way up the grass slope from the bashed-up Bentley, to get his wife to damn well pull herself together or else. When he'd dispensed his clinical duties, Joshua turned to the aptly-named Lake who was squelching miserably back to the house after his unscheduled swim.

I'm grateful to the attentive lugholes of my second youngest sister Edwina for details of the following exchange.

"What do you mean Frankie got the drop on you?" Joshua yelled, glowering at the bodyguard's already panda-like shiner. "That character couldn't batter his way out of a bag of chips."

"It was a lucky punch, sir," replied Lake to the background of tittering from members of my family.

"Lucky! The bastard's pinched my daughter and you call that lucky?"

"I meant he caught me off guard, sir."

This provoked more Thirkettle merriment.

"Oh the little sneak did that all right," snarled Joshua. "In fact he made a right flamin' tater out of you. But do you know what, Lake, I don't believe your tale. There's only one man on this estate who could dump you on your arse like that and we both know who that is."

Apparently, Lake clenched his walnut-shaped fists and grimaced as if tiptoeing across the red hot embers of some existential inner turmoil – it won't shock you to know that Edwina later made a successful career in local journalism. Lake then turned a damp gaze on Joshua and replied, "It was all young Frankie's work, sir. You'll have my immediate resignation."

It turned out this was the last thing Joshua wanted when there were lovebirds to pursue so he ordered Lake to take a towel to himself, put together a team of fleet-footed bruisers and get on our trail pretty damn quick.

Another thing Joshua didn't appear to want was Les's head on a plate despite his strong suspicions that, if it was a Thirkettle who had cleaned Lake's clock, it certainly hadn't been yours truly. In any event, he couldn't prove a thing and passed over the opportunity to confront Les in front of the servants.

That reluctance may also have been because he had other matters to deal with. Wedding guests, sensing something was up, had begun to swarm out of the chapel and a flood of England's highest and mightiest was sweeping across the lawns towards Protheroe Hall. Again the nascent editorial and eavesdropping skills of my little sister must take the credit for a report of the following exchanges.

Lord Something Or Other to Baron Whatnot: "I say, this is damned poor form even among the commercial classes eh what, Whatnot."

Baron W to Lord SOO: "What else can one expect when one's got an ironmonger in Downing Street?"

LSOO: "Isn't Baldwin a Harrow man?"

BW (with a curl of the lip): "Exactly!" *(Stanley Baldwin, 1867-1947, a Conservative politician, served three terms as Prime Minister, the last from 1935-37).*

If most of the assembled Old Etonians were keeping their barbed comments among themselves this was patently not true of the seventh Earl of Welbeck. Edmund's pater gave as good as he got in an entertaining ding-dong with Joshua on the gravel in front of Protheroe Hall. The theme of his sermon appeared to echo his aristocratic chums and concern itself with Precisely What You'd Expect from Someone in Trade. The pair were only discouraged from coming to blows by Nancy's tomboy sister Imogen who pulled out a revolver and threatened to plug the first galoot to make an unwise move.

The only person to retain any equilibrium was Edmund who, said Edwina, seemed unsurprised and somehow relieved by everything that had happened. While his Dad banged on about horsewhipping, handcuffs and the stocks, the jilted bridegroom was heard to whisper to no-one in particular, "I never really considered that I was the one for her."

But the pantomime back at Protheroe was the last thing on the minds of Nancy and me as we made our escape. By the time Lake and his team had picked up the beginnings of our trail in Manchester, we were already on The Royal Scot, steaming through the Lake District well on our way to Scotland.

We weren't bound for Gretna Green either - that would have made matters a bit too easy for our pursuers. Instead we pushed on, with one train change, to a small village on the west coast, to start our fifteen-day qualification period. In those days, while you had to be twenty-one to get married in England, the legal age in Scotland was sixteen – which I'm pretty sure explains a lot but buggered if I can think what.

Anyhow, your eloping couple would put in marriage notice forms to the local registrar, in our case based in the ancient town of Ayr a few miles north. Then thumbs and anything else within reach would be twiddled for just over a fortnight until permission to get hitched arrived.

If we'd hung around in Gretna, Joshua would have been at our throats in a flash. But I calculated – rightly as it turned out – that once he'd seen that we weren't in the immediate Scottish Border area he'd reckon that we were hiding up in the Highlands as far away from England as possible.

So for nearly two weeks Nancy and I followed the proud tradition of serial killers, suicide bombers and countless other barmy sods, and kept ourselves to ourselves – mainly in the bedroom. Our desire for a solitary existence was aided and abetted by Mrs Fairbairn, the widowed landlady of the guest house, who told us more than once between sniffles that she loved nothing more than a fine romance.

Unfortunately, Mrs Fairbairn's one precondition for romance between her immaculately pressed cotton sheets was possession of a valid marriage licence, something Nancy and I neglected to mention we lacked.

This would not have been a problem but for the intervention of Lord Beaverbrook, confound him. He, you may recall, owned The Daily Express which in those days was Britain's best-selling newspaper. So when five-column pictures of yourself and your loved one appear in the Express under splash headlines like "Comic kidnaps tycoon's girl" and "£1,000 for information" it won't be long before your Presbyterian landlady is beating you with a broom while denouncing you as a moral-free fornicator – just before picking up the phone and claiming her reward. Luckily Nancy overheard Mrs Fairbairn betraying us to the Express news desk and, not for the first time that summer, we were on the run again.

It's a fact that in my business you're never too far from somebody you know so we headed for Edinburgh and the home of a ventriloquist pal, Gentleman Jocky Jardine. I say 'pal' but the truth was that Eddie Star had forced us into the same orbit by insisting that Jocky stayed at my place a couple of months previously when he'd done a week at the King's Theatre in Hammersmith.

I'd managed to tolerate his unsettling habit of constantly communicating through the medium of his doll, Wee Wullie, a foul-mouthed bairn in a soiled tam o'shanter. And yet, despite my previous hospitality, Jocky and Wullie did not seem pleased to see me.

"I might gi' yon hen's da' a call," Wullie informed the entire street even before we were across the threshold of Jocky's terrace house just off the Grassmarket, "after I gi' her one. Ha, ha!"

Jocky shrugged in a convincing show of embarrassment before informing us in the rolling tones of a Mid-Lothian family solicitor, "I'm afraid that, like everyone else north of the border, Wullie's been following your somewhat outrageous exploits in the Scottish Daily Express."

Even though I'd already endured a week of this nonsense, I'd forgotten quite how annoying it could be.

Nancy, on the other hand was enchanted, hooting in delight and patting Wullie on the head. So I merely glared in exasperation at the malevolent dwarf and his handler.

"Sorry if our antics have upset Wullie's delicate disposition," I told Jocky. "But perhaps you could remind him that he enjoyed my hospitality not too long ago."

"Preck," was all I got in return but at least we were allowed in. And, after a late tea of oatmeal bread, sardines and Dundee Cake, things began to look a little rosier, all the more so since Jocky had locked Wullie in a brightly coloured wooden box in the corner. However, this still did not prevent the doll from regularly interrupting our conversation. For instance when I asked Jocky how his act was going the muffled reply from the corner was, "It'd be a whole loat be'er wi'oot yon numpty." Ungrateful little tick.

Yet, even though all this was most annoying, I had to concede that Jocky was rather good, if clinically barmy. I mean, two competing voices in one body is not natural is it? *(No it's totally insane)*.

The big advantage of this set-up was that Jocky, being totally friendless for obvious reasons, never had a single visitor. This made his house the perfect bolt-hole and it would have remained that way had Nancy not decided what we really needed was a trip to the theatre.

It was our second night and I was enjoying a rare moment of peace, with Jocky and Wullie away offending other people on his week-long booking at the Empire Theatre. I even began to plan a spot of under-the-eiderdown activity to take the edge off Nancy's restlessness. But she had other plans.

"Come on, Franco, it'll be great to get out and smell the good air," she urged me.

"Good air, Nance! This town isn't known as Auld Reekie for nothing. Let's just lie low for another two days and we're home free."

That clinched it – we were going out first thing in the morning. Luckily the quid pro quo was another rehearsal for honeymoon night – as any agony aunt will confirm, you can't take a single chance on these things. By the time Jocky arrived home I was relaxed enough to open the large coloured box and pat Wullie indulgently on the tam o'shanter. He bit my finger.

Next day, before venturing out into the Athens of the North, I took the precaution of filling a large haversack with most of the items from our nice new suitcase.

"We won't need sandwiches," said Nancy.

"This isn't about foodstuffs, Nance. It's so we can make a quick getaway."

"You worry too much," she replied, shaking her head. Her opinion would have changed by the evening.

The last time Nancy and I went to Edinburgh in August was twenty years ago when the place was a bear pit. The Festival and Military Tattoo bring all kinds of hawkers, gawkers and show-offs out from behind the wainscot. In 1992 it took this elderly couple's best efforts to negotiate these obstacles without losing our minds and a sizeable chunk of our wealth.

Things were different in 1936. Oh, you'd have recognised the place right enough apart from all the buildings being blackened by soot and Arthur's Seat, the tallest of Edinburgh's volcanic hills only occasionally visible through a rolling blanket of smog.

But in those far-off August days there was no Festival or Tattoo and it was much easier to move around the place without being molested. We spent a pleasant day being deafened by the Castle's one o'clock gun, picnicking among the half-built follies on Calton Hill and visiting John Knox's House - he wasn't in - before a short stroll got us to The Empire Theatre for the first house at 6.30. Even I was totally relaxed by then – right until the moment we were grassed up by Wullie.

Nancy and I had settled into our central stalls seats, about five rows back, when up went the lights and on came the dancing girls; not a patch on the Palladium troupe I dismissively informed Nancy. They were followed by the second spot comic Neddy Lochead, a name unknown to me. A few minutes listening to his lame patter and I understood why.

But this Edinburgh first house, with its smattering of showbiz landladies, people on complimentary tickets and families with kids, quickly fell in love with Neddy and he departed on a wave of goodwill.

"They'll laugh at anything up here," I sniffed.

Nancy, however, was not listening and dug me in the ribs.

"Look," she said, excitedly pointing at the curtain which had begun to billow about like a galleon's mainsail. At first I didn't spot him – god only knows how the circle crowd were meant to – but then I noticed what Nancy had seen; Wullie's head was poking out from in between the curtains. He was doing nothing apart from glowering at the audience – but it was enough. As Wullie's gaze began to swing slowly this way and that, a few titters rose up from the stalls; then there were one or two self-conscious laughs; followed by full-throated guffaws. Before long the whole place was in uproar - over a doll's head for goodness sake!

"I'm obviously in the wrong game," I told Nancy.

"Sssh," she hissed. "You'll put Wullie off."

As the laughter started to subside we could make out Jocky's dry-as-dust tones inquiring, "And what are they like tonight our audience, Wullie?"

Wullie's head swung from side to side in a great exaggerated arc before turning back towards the curtain and announcing, "They're a reet aul' pile o' keech."

Uproar again, especially from the kids who evidently understood the meaning of the word 'keech' better than I did. Then Jocky, dressed in a dinner jacket and bow tie stepped out from behind the curtain and started to chide Wullie for insulting the ladies, gentlemen and children. From then on things settled down into the usual ventriloquist-dummy routine you'll have seen a hundred times, before something totally unexpected happened.

Jocky had just finished drinking a glass of water while Wullie belted out Scotland the Brave and was dabbing daintily at his mouth when Wullie's head shot forward. He appeared to be looking intently towards the back of the theatre before turning first to Jocky and finally fixing his gaze on Nancy and me. Then Wullie started to yell.

"They're o'er here, sir. Doon on the fifth row. Aye, shameless fornicators the pair of 'em."

Nancy's face was a mixture of puzzlement and indignation at this defamation by a lump of wood she'd regarded as a friend. I, however, was one step ahead of her. Glancing quickly towards the rear of the theatre I saw exactly who Wullie had been addressing. Luckily we were on the end of a row so I jumped up, grabbed the haversack and hauled Nancy to her feet.

"Franco, what on earth are you doing?" she spluttered through a mouthful of fruit.

"We're leaving. Unless you'd rather share that tangerine with your Dad."

Nancy spun round to see Sir Joshua and four burly figures skidding into our aisle. She threw the fruit down and we made a dash for the stage.

Luckily some bright spark, convinced Joshua and co were "the polis", tripped up the lead pursuer, Lake, and the rest tumbled over him to huge hoots of derisive laughter.

The pile-up gave Nancy and me time to clamber on to the stage to huge applause we'd done nothing to deserve. While I was desperately trying to weigh up in which direction the stage door lay, Lake was the first to hurdle on to the boards and, as he dived forward to grab me, I did the only sensible thing possible. I yanked Wullie's head from his body – the hateful object was attached to a long stout stick - and when Lake grabbed a handful of my jacket I smashed him across the knee with Wullie's head. More applause – this time much-deserved.

As Lake went down screaming in pain like a wounded buffalo, I was in a fine state, yelling how this was pay-back for the stables at Protheroe Hall, while Wullie urged me to, "mind ma heed, ya feckin' preck." I turned and grabbed a terrified Jocky.

"Och, please, Frankie," he whined, "I cannae control wee Wullie."

"Then keep a closer eye on him," I hissed and jammed a protesting Wullie's head stick-first down the front of Jocky's waistcoat. Then I spun the ventriloquist round and without ceremony kicked him into the rest of our pursuers scattering them off the stage like skittles, with Wullie still jabbering on and the audience going berserk. To this day I'm convinced that half of them thought it was all part of the act.

By now we were even more popular than Neddy Lochead but couldn't afford to hang around for curtain calls. After a quick bow, Nancy and I tore through the wings, straight through the startled dance troupe towards what I hoped was the stage door. Luckily I'd guessed right and we tumbled out into an alleyway where I was immediately presented with an autograph book by a lone female fan of indeterminate age.

"There's no time for that," yelled Nancy desperately pulling at my arm as I scribbled a suitably upbeat message - you must never disappoint your public.

"Now then, hen," I said as I handed back the book, "you'll tell them that nobody's come this way, won't you?"

"I can do better than tha', honey lamb," she replied flashing a smile which reminded me of a piano keyboard. Whereupon she took a large key out of her handbag and locked the stage door. Don't ask me how she'd got the key

101

or why she'd even want it - the mind can only boggle - but she'd bought us a few precious seconds.

Wishing her well, we raced down the alley to the front of the theatre where there was no-one about apart from a band of latecomers tumbling drunkenly out of a taxi - they'd missed the best part of the show that's for certain. As they got out of the cab on one side Nancy and I jumped in at the other and five minutes later, after a dash through light evening traffic, we were deposited by the ticket office at Waverley Station.

I sprinted to the nearest window and gasped, "What's the first train out of here?"

"First train to where, sir?"

"Anywhere."

The ticket seller weighed me up from under his green eye-shade before deciding I was a man with whom he could do business rather than someone who deserved locking up.

"Well, the Aberdeen Express, the last of the day I might add, leaves in exactly three-and-a-half minutes from platform seven.

"Right two first class singles on the Aberdeen Express. Here keep the change."

Luckily platform seven was only yards from the ticket office and we were through the barrier and up to the far end of the train with half a minute to spare. As the station master's whistle went I was contentedly leaning out of the carriage window when, through the steamy gloom, I spotted a commotion at the ticket barrier. Although it was one hundred and fifty yards away there was no doubt what was happening. Joshua and his men were piling through the barrier and on to the train.

"Quick, Nance, we're getting off," I cried as the train started to move. But, to my consternation, as we bounded back onto the platform, who should be still be standing next to the rear of the train but Lake. The mistrustful swine obviously thought we'd pull a stunt like this. We could clearly see Lake urging Joshua's people off and, as the train started to move slightly more quickly, the whole group, including Joshua, cascaded from it like Mack Sennett's Keystone Cops.

I looked at Nancy and asked her, "Are you ready for this?"

There was no need to explain what I was on about because she took a deep breath and nodded. By now Joshua's gang were dusting themselves down, ready for a stroll down the platform to claim their winnings. But we weren't quite ready to be the prizes.

"Right," I gulped. "One two three ... run."

To his damnable credit, Lake actually spotted what was about to happen and set off at a gallop towards us. But we too were already going like the clappers and, as the guard's van drew level with us, I scooped Nancy up onto the step, grabbed at the rail ... and tripped up. I barely managed to hold on with one arm as I half ran and was half dragged along the platform.

"Don't let go, Franco," screamed Nancy. "I'll get you on." But that was surely impossible as the train was speeding and she wasn't strong enough. Yet, just as the platform ran out and I felt my left arm was about to fly from its socket, a pair of huge confident hands shot out and hoisted me on to the guard's van.

I lay face-up on the step, breathing heavily. "Welcome aboard the Aberdeen Flyer, sir," said the guard, a red-bearded giant of a man in a fine-looking kilt and matching socks with green garter tabs. "Might I suggest that next time you catch the train when it's stationary. And kindly desist from looking up ma kilt."

I stood up, turned to Nancy and we burst out laughing and hugged each other. Receding into the distance, Lake was shaking his fist at us at the end of the platform. We all waved back, including the guard.

A touch under three hours later we were pulling into Aberdeen and, nothing against the Granite City, but if I'd had the casting vote we'd have been pulling straight out again on the last train to Glasgow which was due away ten minutes later.

However, after the day we'd had, Nancy was well and truly whacked and I wasn't feeling too bouncy either. What we needed was a late supper, a nice hot bath and a few hours kip, all of which, after I'd checked that the first express from Edinburgh arrived at seven in the morning, we found at a hotel just across the road.

Joshua, we reckoned correctly, would not risk trying to get there by car as overnight road travel in those days was not an attractive prospect even during the half-light of Highland summer nights. As long as we were up and away by six-thirty we could breakfast on the Glasgow train and then change for London at our leisure. At least that was the plan.

By now I was feeling rather pleased with myself, a state of affairs which persisted until next morning when I strolled with Nancy towards the Glasgow train, due out in ten minutes at 6.35. So pleased was I that, as the ticket man checked our singles to Glasgow at the barrier, I couldn't resist asking at which platform the express from Edinburgh would arrive. I wanted to imagine Joshua and his goons tearing around the station, offending the locals and, with any luck, falling foul of the local constabulary.

"The Edinburgh Express, you say? That would be platform nine just over there, sir. But you'll be well away tae Glasgow before that." And he handed us back our tickets. "On the other hand if it was the Edinburgh milk train you wanted a glimpse of."

Nancy and I had hardly gone three steps. We both stopped at the same time and turned slowly.

"What's that you say about the Edinburgh milk train?" I asked carefully, the panic rising slowly in my throat.

104

"Well I call it the milk train but it's simply the first of the day that ..."

"I don't care about its antecedents," I shouted. "What time does it arrive?"

The ticket collector looked most put out. "Why," he said sniffily, "it's already here."

He pointed down the platform and, sure enough, about a quarter of a mile away a train was rolling slowly into the station. I looked at Nancy and it was obvious she'd jumped through the same mental hoops as I had.

"My Dad's on that isn't he?"

"It's very likely."

"Then they'll be here before the Glasgow train leaves," she said. "Run for it!"

Gazing around in blind panic, my thoughts were dragged into focus by the station master's sudden shrill whistle. He was standing flag raised on the adjacent platform whose train began to move slowly.

"We'll soon be able to turn professional at this," I told Nancy as I sprinted with her across the platform, flinging open the nearest door and piling on to the moving train.

I turned to see the ticket collector waving urgently at us but his warnings, if that's what they were, became drowned in the hiss of steam and the metallic din of locomotive wheels.

Nancy, meanwhile, was smiling at me, despite all I'd put her through. "Where's our mystery tour bound for now, Franco?" she inquired.

"As many miles from Aberdeen and your Dad as is humanly possible."

****

Thirty-three miles to be exact. An hour after making what we hoped was our final dash to freedom, Nancy and I stood forlornly in front of a station which was very

105

definitely at the end of the line. We were in a pretty little country village called Ballater on the edge of a mountain range covered in mist.

"So we've landed in the middle of nowhere," said Nancy gazing around perplexed.

"Looks very much like it," I replied.

She voiced our predicament. "If we go back on the train they'll be waiting for us. And if we sit on our thumbs they're bound to arrive here."

"Looks very much that way."

"Is that all you can say, Franco?"

"Nance, I'm trying to think. What do you reckon your Dad would least expect us to do?"

"Fall sobbing into his loving arms? I can't speak for what I'd do."

"Be serious, please."

Nancy looked all around her before facing the dark grey mass of rugged hills stretching westwards into the distance.

"Go on a mountain walk?"

"Give the girl a coconut. So, come on, let's get back into the station."

"But I thought we were ...

I tapped the side of my nose. "Watch and learn, Nance. Watch and learn"

There followed a five-minute comical interlude which owed much to the movies of my dear old buddy Will Hay. Myself and the elderly ticket seller, whose name turned out to be Sandy Shaw, conducted an orderly shouting match about stopping-off points of trains to Aberdeen. The discussion reached such a pitch that none of the other people behind us in the short queue could have failed to hear about our plans to visit Banchory further back down the line. *(Will Hay, 1888-1949, was a popular stage and screen comedian of the 1930s and 40s. The catchphrase in his most famous film, Oh Mr Porter, was "The next train's gone," which makes no sense at all).*

106

Even after all that clowning, there was still just time to re-board the train on which we'd arrived. We got into an empty carriage whereupon Nancy slumped immediately down ready for a quick nap and was therefore surprised when I opened the door opposite the platform and beckoned her to follow me. Give the girl credit, she didn't think twice and seconds later we were on the gravel next to the train track but crucially hidden from the rest of the station.

After that it was a short sprint across a small sidings, through a gap in the wooden slatted fence and we were out of the station and away.

Away to where was another matter! The mist was slowly being burned off as we struck out westwards on what looked like a well-used road. My idea was that there would be someone along soon to give us a lift but all the traffic, such as it was, came the other way along the glen.

Two sleek shooting brakes, empty apart from the drivers, was the sum total of what passed us in the first three or so miles. Furthermore our predicament appeared to be mocked by the tranquillity of the scene. To our left the River Dee sparkled serenely in the mid-morning summer sunlight and, beyond that, even the Cairngorms appeared to look down benignly.

However, the mist had now gone and the sun was beating down with such a force that walking was becoming increasingly unpleasant. To set the seal on our discomfort there came the muffled sound of gunfire - the British aristocracy had launched its annual clearance from the Highlands of god's defenceless creatures.

Wiping her brow with a handkerchief, Nancy stopped and slumped down on to the heather.

"God I'm hot," she gasped, ripping her shoes off and waggling her now less than dainty feet.

Although I agreed that a rest was needed, I knew we could not afford to dawdle too long. The more I thought about it the less I was convinced that the Sandy Shaw pantomime would fool anyone. However, I tried not to look too worried.

"You look worried," said Nancy.

"Not at all," I replied. "I'll just fill this up."

I picked up a bottle I'd cannily placed in our haversack and went down to the river. At least the water was crystal clear – I didn't relish being poisoned on top of everything else. Filling the bottle, I surreptitiously scanned the route ahead. Without a map I could not be sure where it was taking us or even whether the road would just peter out as we headed into the mountains. However, if we went back I felt sure we'd run into Joshua and his desperadoes. What a pickle! I tried once more to mask my fears by telling Nancy to imagine the contents of the bottle were gin and lemonade. But by now she too looked thoroughly miserable.

"This is not exactly how I envisaged our life together you know," she complained.

"I know, darling. Me neither. But it won't be for long I promise."

Nancy turned away from me and said nothing for a moment before starting to put her shoes back on.

"Well," she said firmly, "we'll just have to keep right on to the end of the road as they say in these parts." What a girl!

Another hour's walking threw up a significant change of scenery. Well-kept farm fields and stone walls replaced moorland heather on either side of the road. The glen had widened out too and the scene appeared so much more welcoming that my spirits lifted. Someone would be along soon, I reasoned - and I was right. First it was one of the shooting brakes we'd seen earlier, whose driver totally ignored our waves and turned left into a narrow road about a hundred and fifty yards further on.

We watched resignedly as the car clattered across the river over a bright green iron bridge and came to halt before a group of two men and two women. Three were dressed in posh country gear while one of the women was in flowing silks more suited to the opera. With no apparent discussion about accepting lifts from strangers, all four quickly climbed into the vehicle and it moved off down a track parallel to the road we were on before disappearing round a corner.

I don't know what made me suspicious about the second car before it came round the bend into view. Maybe it was the sound of the engine struggling under a weight too great for it to manage. So, as Nancy prepared yet again to tuck her skirt into her knickers and play the damsel in distress, I grabbed hold of her and we tumbled together over the stone wall.

"For god's sake," she complained. "Not here."

"It's not a romantic move, Nance. I just don't like the sound of that vehicle."

"We'll never get a lift at this rate," she grumbled but I silenced her as the car had come to a halt virtually alongside where we were hiding. As the doors opened I swear Nancy was just about to pop up like Wullie's head through the curtain when a familiar and extremely unwelcome voice boomed out.

"I reckon you're talkin' out of your backside as usual, Lake."

Nancy stared open-mouthed at me and I signalled for her to remain silent.

"Trust me, sir," replied Lake. "The man in the village was most definite that this was the road they set out on."

"He was a gibbering yokel. I couldn't make out the half of what he said."

Lake remained resolutely calm. "Nevertheless, sir, he had no reason to lie and by my calculations this is roughly how far they could have walked in the time they've had."

And he started to sniff, so pronouncedly that Nancy and I could clearly hear it.

"Stop doing that, Lake," barked Sir Joshua. "Use a handkerchief like anyone else."

"I was sniffing the air, sir," Lake explained. "I thought I caught a whiff of ... well it was a whiff of your daughter."

I blame that old busybody Baden-Powell. Before he came along townies like Lake tended to misspend their youth by earnestly drinking and smoking themselves to death. But, after BP had dibbed his dobs you couldn't move for young chaps singing hearty songs, making bad plaster casts of dogs' paw prints and doing their utmost to keep their beastly hands to themselves. Oh and sniffing the air while successfully following every last trail that presented itself.

I leaned over and sniffed Nancy; her perfume was unmistakeably pungent and musky.

It was fortunate for us that Sir Joshua could not see a stick without grabbing the wrong end of it.

"Are you sayin' my daughter stinks, you cheeky sod?"

"No, sir, I meant ..."

"I know what you meant, you bleedin' oaf. Stop it off at once."

I couldn't resist having a peep through a small hole in the stone wall. Lake, head bowed, was limping across to the other side of the road and it was most gratifying to see Wullie's hard wooden head had done its work well. Lake gazed at the mountains and, as he turned back to Joshua, I whipped my head away from the hole. Then we heard an unfamiliar sound, a bit like someone opening and closing a latched door.

Lake's voice drew closer. "They won't have struck off into the hills yet, that's for sure, so they must be further on that way."

I stole another glance through the hole in the wall. Lake was pointing along the road in the direction which we'd been walking but it wasn't he who held my attention. Instead my goggling eyes were drawn to Sir Joshua who was expertly cocking a shotgun and levelling it at the sky. Where the hell had he got that and why did he have it? Things were about to get a whole lot worse too. I could see each of the other three members of the party - rough looking coves - were also holding and aiming shotguns.

They all looked like a particularly ill-disciplined firing squad, which brought to mind our own predicament. I closed my eyes and tried to stop breathing.

"Whichever way they're going we'll find 'em," said Joshua. "And when you lads do find 'em, I don't want guns going off anywhere near my daughter."

My relief lasted but a few seconds.

"On the other hand," added Joshua, "if you manage to corner the comedian on his own then anything, even a very nasty accident, goes."

Another voice piped up. "But, sir, won't the locals think gunshots are a bit suspicious?"

Joshua snorted. "It's the shooting season, you prick. Open your ears. They're massacring birds all over the fuckin' Highlands."

I gazed at Nancy and I could tell she was as shocked as I was. Neither of us had heard her Dad swear like that before. Or threaten to have me slaughtered. The only saving grace was that at least he didn't know we were behind the wall directly opposite.

"Anyhow put the weapons back in the boot while I have a slash over there."

Sure enough, Joshua was pointing straight at our hiding place and I shook my head in despair. We were done for.

"Hold on, sir," said Lake as Joshua strode towards us, unbuttoning his flies. "I can see an inn just up there. It might be a good place to gather our thoughts. And relieve ourselves."

Joshua stopped barely three feet away from us and turned back to Lake. To our relief, if not to his, he began to button up his trousers.

"Aye," he said "I suppose we could all do with a pint of whatever piss they drink round here."

And, no doubt holding on to that happy thought, they all piled back into the car and off it spluttered. A few seconds later, I peeped over the wall in time to see the vehicle veer right off the road towards the inn. Standing up, I realised I was shaking uncontrollably. Nancy put her arms around me.

"What are we to do?" She sounded beaten so I tried to appear resolute.

"Well, I'm not hanging around to see if your old man was joking. Either about shooting me or drowning both of us."

"But where can we go?" said Nancy looking around in bewilderment.

"As far away from here as we can. Come on."

Nancy and I climbed carefully over the wall and, when it was obvious Lake hadn't sneaked back to trap us, we dashed across the road, vaulting the wall opposite. Sprinting through a large field towards the iron bridge, we were observed benignly by a herd of long-horned Highland cattle.

Once across the bridge, we turned left down the rough road the shooting brake had travelled a few minutes earlier. It was only after we'd been trotting along briskly for about a minute that I looked up and saw to my horror that the inn where Joshua and his men were refreshing themselves was clearly visible to us a quarter of a mile away between a gap in the trees beyond the river and the main road.

If I'd turned right round I'd have seen another sight to give us further pause for thought but we'll come to that a little later. The fact was that right now if we could see where Joshua was then he would be able to see ...

Without even having to discuss the matter, Nancy and I veered off into the trees which turned out to be not much more than a copse. However, when we re-emerged into the open, we found ourselves on the slope of a small hillock, the folds of which shielded us from the inn.

"We'll keep on up here for a while. It must lead somewhere," I said without much confidence.

But we ploughed on and soon were high above a straight stretch of the rough track. And, about half a mile further on, the shooting brake we'd seen earlier was parked up and the driver leaning against the bonnet reading a newspaper.

"That's it," I cried.

"What's what?" replied Nancy.

"He'll get us out of here," I said pointing at the driver. "We hitch a ride and we're back in Aberdeen before you know it. Then after a quick ceremony Bob's your uncle and Joshua's your dad who can't do a damn thing about it because we'll be man and wife."

Nancy didn't look convinced and reckoned I might be gibbering out of sheer funk.

"The driver might not want to leave the other people," she reasoned.

"He will if I offer him enough bawbees. There's still about a hundred guineas in this belt. And if he doesn't agree I'll knock his block off and we'll pinch the car."

I expected another principled argument but all I got from Nancy was a shrug and the order to damn well get it over with. Sometimes she was too much of her father's daughter.

However, as we were about to set off down the hill, Nancy caught my arm and pointed to something that was happening on the ridge away to our right. Clearly silhouetted against the sky, two men appeared to be doing their best to strangle each other. Circling them were the figures of two women.

"It must be the people from the car," said Nancy looking puzzled.

"Good, we can tell the driver his passengers have murdered each other and so it'll be just fine to give us a lift."

But Nancy shook her head emphatically. "No we just cannot do that," she insisted.

"Nance, you know what they're like in Scotland," I countered in desperation. "It's probably one of their ancient customs. They half kill each other, break off for yet another wee dram and a short prayer then back to the fun."

Nancy studied the group. "They don't look as if they're about to take a break. Or that it's much fun. You must stop it."

I sighed and gazed longingly at the car. That way lay freedom and happily ever after. To our right was conflict and the risk that, while we delayed, Joshua would find us. There was only one rational course of action.

"I wish you weren't always so bloody good ... and bloody right," I moaned as we trotted full-throttle towards the throttlers.

"No you don't. That's why you love me," she smiled and to be fair she was spot-on.

As we got closer to the group it became clear that, although one of the protagonists was a full head shorter than his opponent, it was he who was the aggressor and it was all the other man could do to stay alive. Adding to the surreal nature of the scene the two females swooped in and out of the action like vultures. One was short and dumpy and wore a cloche-type hat which looked like an upturned flowerpot; the other, dressed in a silk blouse and well-cut slacks, was taller, bareheaded and stick thin and I couldn't shake off the notion that I'd met her somewhere before.

Dumpy was in the process of belting the bigger bloke with her handbag - as if he didn't already have enough problems - while Stick Insect was kicking out at the smaller

114

man and giving Dumpy the odd whack when she was within range.

We stopped about twenty yards away and gazed at the whirling tableau.

"How the heck am I supposed to sort that one out?" I demanded of Nancy. But she was taking absolutely no notice of me. Instead she gazed in wonderment at the group.

"Oh my godfathers," she said. "Would you listen to that."

At first I could only hear the smaller man yelling incoherently at his opponent. I caught the words "disgrace" "dishonour" and "strumpet" but that was about it. The women's voices were shriller and much clearer. Dumpy was shouting, "Leave him, Bertie, he's not worth it," before adding, rather confusingly, "Stove his bonce in."

But it was when I heard what the other woman was shouting that I understood what had given Nancy pause for thought. As she whirled around the group, her skinny limbs flying in all directions she was clearly yelling in an accent straight out of Hell's Kitchen. *(In those days a particularly unsavoury area of New York).*

"Take da palooka's goddam head off, Davy boy," she screamed. "Rip it clean away, an' I'll spit in da hole."

Uh-oh, it appeared that Dapper Dave and his moll were out and about again – and this time they'd brought the family.

"Do something for goodness sake," hissed Nancy, "or we'll be looking at two corpses and a 10-year-old on the throne."

"What do you want me to do, arrest them for treason?"

"No," said Nancy and I could see she'd had one of her brainwaves. "Be an authority figure, a schoolmaster!"

"What, sadistically thrash the royal family one by one? I suppose it might work."

"No, you idiot, act as though you're in charge - like a teacher does. This mob respond to stuff like that. Take it from me!"

"But, Nance," I whined, "I don't even know what schoolteachers say."

She glared at me with such intensity that the thought occurred that she, not me, should be sorting out this rabble. However, there was nothing for it so I took a deep breath, coughed and said as firmly as I could, "Er, time gentlemen, please!"

The King and his brawling brother quickly pushed each other apart and turned guiltily towards me. The women carried on bashing and kicking each other until I added, "That applies to you ladies as well."

Whereupon they too stopped what they were doing although not before Stick Insect, or Wallis Simpson as it undoubtedly was, took a last sneaky swipe at Elizabeth, Duchess of York.

Well I'd managed to get their attention all right but I was jiggered if I knew what came next. "Have you no homes to go to?" was hardly appropriate as they probably had a couple of dozen between them. I was half hoping that they'd all have a pop at me – that at least would have given new focus to their unruly behaviour. But, like the well brought-up Victorian children they'd all been – nearly all anyway – they stood patiently and waited for what I had to say.

So I decided to play up the schoolmaster role.

"Er, listen, er, Your Majesty, it doesn't look at all good that you and your brother are trying to kill each other in public and it's got to stop. Right now. Do you hear?"

I was beginning to worry that I'd gone a bit too far, especially for a 20-year-old but do you know what they all hung their heads in shame! I say 'all' ...

"Who'd ya think you're talkin' to, punk?" snapped Wallis. "This here is the King of jolly old England, ya Limey stumblebum."

Not for the first time I would imagine, the King looked at Wallis in apprehension as if the future was revealing itself to him in all its horror. Then he silenced her with a swift hand gesture and turned to me.

"I am genuinely sorry you had to see what you saw, Frankie, but believe it or not my brother and I were getting to grips with a matter of some constitutional significance."

At that Bertie snorted in exasperation, moved away from the group and lit a cigarette. I had to put my hand on Nancy's arm to stop her cadging one off him.

"That's all well and good, sir," I replied. "But where would we be if they carried on like that in Parliament eh?" Again they just gazed at me.

"OK, bad example but you get my drift."

"D-david, d-do you know this damned insolent fellow?" This was from Bertie who was obviously gearing up for the shout of, "Seconds out, round two!"

"Of course I do, Bertie. This is Frankie Funnybone, a fixture at the London Palladium."

"And soon to be starting a long run at Pentonville Prison!"

All of us spun round to look at who it was adding to the brains trust. What we saw was Sir Joshua and his merry men standing threateningly in a line, shotguns cocked at the ready.

"Who the d-devil are you, sir?" demanded Bertie. "And how dare you bring guns on to our land."

"Don't butt in, shortarse, and you'll come to no harm. It's him I've come for," said Joshua pointing at me.

Now it was the turn of the King to get stroppy.

"How dare you speak to my brother in that tone," he yelped, forgetting for a moment that the offended sibling had just been trying to murder him.

"You can shut it an' all, tiger, or I'll ram this weapon where the sun don't shine."

Never having seen anyone commit social suicide before, I watched in fascination while weighing up whether to tip Joshua the wink or let him carry on digging his coffin-sized hole. I was leaning in the direction of a touch more spade work when, seeing Nancy's discomfort, I realised what I must do.

"Er, Sir Joshua, I really wouldn't have a go at these people if I were you."

For the first time, Wallis appeared to agree with me.

"You wanna listen to him, you Limey asshole," she rasped.

But Sir Joshua, bless him, ploughed on with the finesse of a bullock fleeing the abattoir. He faced Wallis and spat, "Keep your foul mouth shut, madam."

"And I especially wouldn't have a go at her," was my follow-up piece of advice, sadly wasted on Joshua who turned to me and said, "I'll deal with you in a minute, lover boy."

It was left to Nancy to put her parent straight.

"Daddy, do you not recognise this man. Last time you were in his presence a couple of months ago he was tapping you on the shoulder with a large sword."

"Yeah and next time he'll take your stoopid fuckin' head right off, ya prize palooka."

No points for guessing from between whose gleaming white teeth this little gem emerged.

The penny finally dropped with a terrifying suddenness as did Sir Joshua and his four minions - to their knees. Gazing up like a stricken owl, Joshua beseeched the King, "Sire, forgive me," before prostrating himself at Dave's feet.

That did it for Nancy. "For goodness sake, Daddy, get up," she snapped. "These people don't want to see you grovel."

I've almost no need to tell you what happened next, have I? The King glanced doubtfully at Nancy, looked down his nose at the five figures snogging the heather in front of him and put his hand on her arm.

"Let's leave them there for just a touch longer," he smiled.

When all was said and done, I thought Joshua and his crew got off pretty lightly after their treasonable behaviour. These days an armed band of desperadoes would have been shot to bits before they got within miles of any royal party.

But back then there was no such thing as security, at least not at places where the royals thought they could swan about in perfect safety. So, after a jolly good ticking off, Joshua and co were despatched, minus weaponry and with tails firmly between legs. Even then Nancy's Dad couldn't help taking liberties. As he slunk away he turned back to the King and said, "I realise you've not yet been blessed with the gift of children, sire."

The King looked puzzled as if he were making various mental calculations and Wallis's eyes narrowed dangerously. Even Lake stole a nervous glance at the other three men.

However, Joshua bulldozed on. "But I know that you are a doting uncle." At that Liz's eyelids nearly shot through the top of her head and it was Bertie's turn to look dangerously at Joshua.

By now the King had had enough. "Get to the point, man. We'll be here all night."

"Well what I was thinking, Your Majesty, is, er, would you be in a position to order my daughter to come with me."

The King looked at Nancy. "Do you want to go with him?"

"Not likely."

The King nodded and told Joshua, "You heard her. Now clear off my land or I'll have our gamekeepers thrash the living daylights out of you."

"Yeah," chuckled Wallis, "you sure don't wanna be grabbed by the ghillies. Haw, haw, haw."

It was a rare moment of light relief during which even Bertie struggled to suppress a smile. However, any ice that had been broken by Sir Joshua's galumphing performance returned with a cold vengeance when he and his gang had disappeared from sight. With co-ordinated sniffs, Bertie and his wife stalked off towards the car followed by the rest of us.

Wallis absolutely insisted that Nancy should travel with her so the King of jolly old England was abandoned by the side of the road with only me for company.

"I'm sure they'll send another car for you, sir," I told him.

The King shrugged. "To tell you the truth, Frankie, I'd rather walk. Clears the old noggin, what!"

And off we strode, the King deep in thought and occasionally rubbing his neck. Ten minutes later the green bridge we'd fled across an hour or so before came into view beyond which lay what I hadn't noticed before – a fairy tale turreted castle peeping out between the trees.

"Is that thing real?" I asked the King.

"I'll say it is," he replied.

"Then I'll wager it belongs to you, sir."

The King smiled. "Yes, I like to think it's an integral part of who I am and I think it always will be. *(At least up to the point where, after abdicating, he flogged it off along with Sandringham to his brother for a tidy sum).*

Of course you'll think me an idiot for not twigging where I was before now. Balmoral! I mean, where else in the Highlands would you find the royal family out and about trying to murder each other?

For no particular reason I told the King, "There's a pub in my town - Butterthwaite - called The Balmoral."

He looked at me intently before asking, "Really? Nice place?"

"No, it's a shithole."

Now, as far as I knew, King Edward VIII had no responsibility whatsoever for what went on at the Balmoral in Butterthwaite but, all the same, I glanced nervously as he digested this information - and then burst out laughing. He clapped me on the back and for the next few minutes waxed lyrical about the common herd he'd met during tours of the coalfields, cotton mills and shipyards.

"First-rate chaps," was his assessment. This professed enthusiasm for all things proletarian was only halted as we strolled across the vast lawn to the castle.

What stopped the King in his tracks was the sight of Bertie and Liz supervising a couple of minions who were hurriedly loading a car boot up with all their clobber. Bertie glanced briefly in our direction before pointedly turning his back on us and climbing into the car's front passenger seat. I was near enough to notice that sitting behind him was his eldest daughter who looked very much as if she'd been crying. I would not be this close to her again for another sixteen years when coincidentally she would also be in tears. *(More than a coincidence surely)*.

The younger girl, who couldn't have been more than five or six, capered about happily doing handstands against the castle wall. Only the Duchess of York stared straight at us, pointed at the King, and said, "Just don't even think about it!"

As Dapper Dave bowed his head in embarrassment, she ordered the younger daughter to stop flashing her knickers and within half a minute they were in the car and away down the drive.

The King gazed sadly after the vehicle, sighed and showed me into the castle where a flunkey whose name was McWhirter or something similar took me up to the apartments that had hurriedly been prepared for me and Nancy. And what preparations! Closing the bedroom door behind me, I saw Nancy was stretched out seductively on the huge bed in her birthday suit.

"Look, Frankie, an actual four-poster," she said, adding with a smile full of mischief, "I've never done it in one of these before."

Five minutes later – blame it on the excitement of the day – and she had.

To say we were treated royally for the rest of the afternoon and evening would be an understatement. The King was otherwise engaged with urgent phone calls – Winston Churchill, Baldwin and someone with the initials AH, were mentioned – so Wallis took it upon herself to behave like a perfect lady.

She gave us a tour of the castle and its grounds and in her New England persona even outlined detailed plans to carry on David's Dad's work and smarten up the south gardens – all without giving too much of an impression that they would be round the place much longer.

Later in the evening Nancy and I were invited into the King's apartments for an informal dinner of corned beef hash and beetroot followed by a punishing couple of hours tasting whisky from the distillery down the road. This left the King and I *(a musical by Richard Rogers and Oscar Hammerstein II – sorry I appear to have momentarily lost concentration)* on our own after the ladies had excused themselves.

Dapper Dave leaned back in his armchair and examined the malt in his glass by the light of a dim standard lamp. We hadn't spoken for five minutes and I was beginning to plan my getaway when he piped up, "Frankie, this whole business is such a terrible mess. What am I to do?"

I was so legless that I could as easily have told him that the correct course of action was to ski bare-arsed down

Mount Lochnagar with Wallis balanced on his head. However, I took a deep breath, concentrated my remaining faculty and slurred, "You must follow your heart, sir."

He nodded and repeated, "Follow my heart? Yes, what a very good idea." Then he looked me in the eye and added, "Do you follow your heart, Frankie?"

"That's what all the palaver with Nancy's Dad was about. You remember, the groveller."

"Indeed, you were attempting to escape his clutches."

"Yes, but things didn't really work out as intended," I sighed. "And no doubt he'll pop up when we try to get married next time."

The King sat up suddenly. "That's it," he cried. "We will damn well have a wedding after all."

"Ah but, sir, think of the constitutional implications ..."

"Not my wedding, Frankie. Yours! You'll be married tomorrow in the great ballroom here. I take it you find no just cause or impediment to that course of action?"

"Er no ... but is it allowed?"

"Allowed," he thundered. "Anything's allowed. I'm the King, dammit! Er, I trust you have the correct paperwork?"

Well, yes I did as a matter of fact. The 15-day limit had passed so we were free to get it done. Besides you don't argue with the monarch – or anybody really who's just necked a shed load of the best malt.

The King scrambled unsteadily to his feet and manhandled me to the door.

"Go and tell your bride-to-be she's on her own tonight," he slurred. "After all, we can't have anything improper going on the night before your nuptials."

This from one of the libertines of Europe, a character who didn't think once before hopping into bed with another man's wife.

Nevertheless I followed his orders or at least I would have done had Nancy not been snoring like a Gloucester

Old Spot. Obediently I slipped into the room next door and passed out on the bed.

When I awoke with a mouth like the bottom of a slate-hanger's nail bag, it was mid-morning and at first I thought the previous night had been a very odd dream. But, peeping into Nancy's bedroom, it was immediately apparent that matters had been all too real. Nancy was being fussed over by two ladies in waiting; one was doing her hair and the other stretching a tape measure across her shoulders. Nancy looked up through a curtain of hair rollers as I staggered in.

"Don't you know it's unlucky to see the bride before a wedding," she said with a grin.

"So you've been told you're getting married?"

"Yes, Wallis is tremendously excited. She's given me one of her suits and Catriona here is measuring me up so she can let it out."

"You do realise that your wedding dress is still in the haversack."

She smiled shyly at me. "That dress was for Edmund. You deserve something a lot more special."

"Aw, how nice."

"I know. Now bugger off before they set the dogs on you. And don't forget to have a shave."

Seeing as we thought we'd be getting hitched in a poky little room at Ayr town hall, the great ballroom at Balmoral wasn't a bad substitute. And, instead of a couple of gawpers off the street to be our witnesses, we had the King of England and his consort to sign the marriage certificate presented to them by the registrar who had been dragged in from Braemar by royal command.

With all that done and dusted and the ring from my money belt firmly on Nancy's finger, the registrar told me, "You may now kiss the bride."

I looked at Nancy in her smart suit and pillbox hat and it was all I could do to stop myself ravishing her there and then. That babe was well hot – she'd really got it goin' on!

(It has come to our attention that an American student on gap year experience at the Wisteria Home in Morecambe has been exerting undue influence on the more suggestible residents).

Smokin'!

I wasn't the only one with ideas either. As we finished our smooch, David decided to make his move.

"Noblesse oblige and all that," he drawled as he grabbed Nancy with practised hands. And goodness knows what might have happened had Wallis not crowned him with her handbag, telling him to, "Keep the mitts where we can all fuckin' see 'em, lover boy."

The incident had no lasting effect on proceedings; indeed after a pleasant wedding banquet on the lawn, which included champagne and Fort William smoked salmon, Wallis informed us we could stay as long as we liked. But I declined politely, arguing that honeymooners needed to get away on their own.

The King nodded in agreement and ordered the chauffeur to bring the car to the front. As Nancy went to collect her gear he drew me to one side and whispered, "I've been thinking about what you said last night."

"I can't remember what I said last night."

"You told me to follow my heart. It is sound advice."

"You mean you're going to ..."

"I shall do whatever I must to ensure my relationship with Wallis Simpson stays strong. Thank you, Frankie."

Crikey, I didn't like the sound of this. The King was about to risk everything – on the say-so of a music hall comedian. I could see that going down well in the country.

I tried a frantic bit of backsliding. "Er, I'm grateful for your thanks, sir, but you must remember that you have a duty to your subjects as well."

"I'm sure my subjects, such as those at the Balmoral in Butterthwaite, would want me to be happy."

He'd obviously never been near the Balmoral in Butterthwaite at chucking-out time - which, come to think of it, was any time - but I could see he was not for turning. So I tried to limit the damage.

"It is your decision of course, sir. However, given my rather lowly status, I'd strongly suggest you keep my name out of the public domain to avoid headlines like 'King Gets a Spot of Funny Advice.' You might also think about not mentioning our wedding. It could detract from your own, er, position."

The King looked at me and said with half a smile, "You should be in the diplomatic corps, Frankie." Then he nodded, adding, "It will be as if you were never here."

As we took our leave of this odd couple for the second time in a year I had no way of knowing that, apart from one rather exasperated phone call, we would never speak to or meet them again.

I glanced back out of the car's rear window and gave a final tentative wave before the two figures moved out of my vision for ever. Then it was across the iron bridge and a right turn towards Ballater.

"Look, Franco," said Nancy after we'd been travelling for less than a minute. "There's that wall where we hid from my Dad yesterday – before we were rescued by the King of jolly old England."

"That reminds me," I mused, "I could do with a shower."

Chapter Eight: Winnie the Brickie

It is truly sad that the mere mention of Churchill these days evokes one response only. People, regardless of age, gender or class, will smirk guiltily before rolling their eyes, wobbling their heads and repeating, "Oh yus" in an extremely silly voice. Bloody hilarious! Even the bloke who said all political careers end in failure can't have envisaged that the reputation of our foremost statesman would be dragged down to the level of a nodding dog who flogs insurance in the breaks during Countdown.

To redress the balance somewhat let me tell you that I first met Winston Leonard Spencer Churchill before he was a cuddly toy and even before he became the Greatest Living Englishman who saved all our bacon. This was in his darkest days during the mid-1930s when, to people at either end of the political spectrum - and most of those in between - Winston couldn't put a foot right without sticking it firmly into his mouth.

Of all his contemporaries the previously mentioned Stanley Baldwin had it about spot-on. In May 1936 Baldwin said:

"... when Winston was born lots of fairies swooped down on his cradle with gifts – imagination, eloquence, industry, ability and then came a fairy who said, 'No one person has a right to so many gifts,' picked him up and gave him such a shake and twist that with all these gifts he was denied judgement and wisdom. And that is why while we delight to listen to him in this House we do not take his advice."

In my estimation that's not a bad summary at all. For a Harrow man. About another Harrow man. However, on reflection, it hasn't really redressed the balance that much away from the idea of a nodding dog.

Perhaps it would help if I were to hold up my hand and admit that I was partly responsible for the great man committing one of his most notorious political blunders. What happened was that, on a dark December night at Chartwell, Winston had been hammering the Johnny Walker Red Label and yours truly was floundering in his wake when I made the mistake of mentioning our royal wedding ... but as usual I'm racing ahead of myself.

Before that load of drunken buffoonery we must deal with the train of events which links Eddie Star, a randy Rotherham landlady and, first off, a spot of alcohol-fuelled malarkey with Denis Compton.

"The trouble with you, Compo," I said as I picked up a champagne bottle, "is that you're not unorthodox enough. Now watch and learn."

The setting was the Royal Grand Hotel, the time minutes after a fine post-performance supper and the dramatis personae were myself, various members of the great and good and young Compton.

In September 1936 Denis was a fresh-faced whipper-snapper who was on the MCC ground staff at Lord's and had just made his debut for the Gunners. *(Better known as a cricketing legend Denis Compton, 1918-1997, scored on his first game for Arsenal against Derby County).* Denis had drifted into my orbit because he was fond of the odd night out at the Palladium and, being a confident young fellow, came backstage and introduced himself one time after the show. Although there were three years between us, we'd quickly become great pals. Such great pals that I soon felt able to pass on some of my vast store of cricketing knowledge.

"Oh, I know you get your head right over the ball when you play a cover drive," I told him. "And don't think I've not noticed how you step away perfectly to leg just before you execute the square cut but I'll tell you this, young

Denis," I paused to take in vital fluid from my brandy glass, "you're not much cop on the sweep."

Denis ran his fingers through that soon-to-be-famous black Brylcremed mop of his and glared at me as if I'd just said his great aunt was on the game.

"But Wally Hammond says that the sweep to leg is my best shot," he replied irritably.

"What does bloody Hammond know about batting?" I countered. (*Walter Hammond 1903-65 played for England in 85 test matches between 1927 and 1947 in which he scored 7,249 runs. His obituary in Wisden Cricketers' Almanack described him as one of the best four batsmen who ever lived).*

"And furthermore did I mention anything about the leg sweep?" Compo looked puzzled as well as angry. I now had his full attention as I expanded on my thesis.

"No, not the leg sweep, dear boy. I'm talking about the reverse sweep."

"What the devil's that when it's at home?" he replied petulantly.

"I'll show you what that is. Here, we'll use this bottle as a club."

After he'd weighed up the champagne bottle, Compo reckoned it to be just a touch on the heavy side for a cricket bat. So we popped it open and spent an enjoyable twenty minutes getting it to exactly the perfect weight, which happily coincided with the moment it became empty.

Then I pushed our table to one side, picked up the bottle, lobbed Denis a pomegranate from the fruit trolley and told him to do his worst.

Now any of you with the first idea about cricket will know that a pomegranate is the ideal piece of fruit with which to bowl a fast in-swinging Yorker. And Compo didn't disappoint, pinging down a real toe-crusher of a delivery. But I was ready for it and sent the pomegranate soaring to the far corner of the dining room where it landed with a satisfying thud on Hutch's grand piano. In fact it nearly brained Lady Mountbatten, who was stretched out seductively on top of it, miming along to Any Old Iron. (*Leslie Hutchinson, 1900-1969, known as Hutch, was a West Indian cabaret star of the 1930s who was rumoured to have had a scandalous affair with Edwina, the wife of Lord Louis Mountbatten*).

Compo gazed at the scene in complete and utter amazement. "I didn't know you were left-handed," he spluttered.

"I'm not. What you witnessed there, my young friend, was the reverse sweep. Now you try it."

Denis, being Denis, soon got the hang of it and spent an enjoyable ten minutes despatching chunks of fruit to all parts. The session soon developed into an impromptu match, diners against the waiters with Hutch as umpire and Lady Mountbatten showing first class glove work behind the timbers.

It had the potential to develop into the very first night-day fixture too until the officious maitre d' stuck his oar in and put an end to the fun with our mob poised to chase a target of 159 on Duckworth-Lewis calculations.

So, a bit of harmless late-night fun that had no lasting consequences. Wrong! One of the diners – and I have my suspicions about the shifty cove I'd placed down at deep backward square – ratted on Denis. Not to Middlesex, who probably wouldn't have minded the youngster sharpening up his batsmanship at all hours but to the Arsenal, who took a less sanguine view about one of their rising stars drinking till god knows when during the football season.

When the Gunners management complained to Eddie Star that one of their brightest boys was being corrupted by one of his I was in for it and no mistake.

The following day Eddie pulled me into his plush suite of offices round the corner from the Palladium, gave me the mother and father of all bollockings and said that as a punishment he was sending me on the road for a couple of months. I protested that Denis Compton wasn't exactly a snow white innocent in the late-night shenanighans stakes – as his subsequent career would prove – but Eddie was having none of it.

"Listen, Tosh, you've upset the powers-that-be and now you'll have to suffer. It won't do you any harm to play the provinces either. A man can get too comfortable in London. And that means I'll have Nancy all to myself for a few weeks."

I've just read that bit back and it doesn't sound too good, does it? But there is an innocent explanation. Nancy, inspired by a chance meeting with George Formby's redoubtable wife, Beryl, had decided that she too fancied a future in showbiz management.

"I need some sort of career," she argued one morning over the marmalade.

"You need to get my tea on the table," I nearly joked before thinking better of it. She'd have killed me. Besides Nancy was right; everybody needs something to keep them active.

Eddie, who had no trouble with Nancy's ambitions, hired her on the spot and began teaching her the ropes, an education that would go on as I continued my own further north.

Incidentally, before we ignore him for twelve years, Denis Compton was forbidden to use the reverse sweep by Middlesex. He'd been caught demonstrating it to the apprentices on the practice ground at Lord's behind the stand which now bears his name.

However, I have it on good authority – from no less than my old mate Eddie Paynter, the Lancashire and England batsman – that Compo pulled off the reverse sweep in an innings of 63 at Old Trafford the following summer. Later in the bar Denis told Eddie that he'd dedicated the shot to me but pledged never to use it again as he was uncommonly fond of his front teeth.

I, on the other hand, was uncommonly fond of living in London, playing The Palladium and Home Counties halls. The truth was that with just a few "ay oops" and "nethens" a comic could get away with being what passed for an archetypal northerner in these parts. Yes, I'd become complacent.

Now, thanks to Compo and Eddie, I was faced with having to sharpen myself up back among actual northerners and the prospect wasn't inviting. Oh, I've nothing against my own folk; I am one of them after all. But it's because I'm one of them that I know what demanding audiences they can be.

And, sure enough, in the following few weeks as I trawled the halls of Lancashire, I found just how difficult things had become for me. Every night was a battle against violence, hostility, resentment and indifference – and that was just from the other acts *(boom, flamin' boom)* wanting to take the "Palladium show pony" down a peg or two.

The audiences weren't much better either. I barely escaped serious harm in Barrow, where they threw rivets at me, Wigan where the missiles were lumps of coal, Blackpool (sticks of rock), Bury (black puddings) and inevitably Bolton (other Boltonians).

Yet, for all that, I sensed that in a strange way the North West crowds cared about me; they just wanted to keep me on my toes. Things changed, however, when I crossed the Pennines.

Oh, I was relieved Yorkshire folk were much too 'careful' to waste valuable local produce on me, especially in Sheffield where they make sharp knives. But, while they didn't throw things if they didn't like you, they didn't seem to do much of 'owt else either.

My act, which by now I'd really sharpened up to Sheffield steel standards, was met with stony indifference by forge men, textile workers and farmers all over the three Ridings. And things looked to have reached the bottom of the barrel among the coal miners of Rotherham and district.

I was nearing the end of a dispiriting first week of a fortnight's booking as second spot comedian at the town's Regent Theatre. In those days, the second spot man acted much like a compere. You'd introduce the other acts, sing a couple of songs and keep the audience on their mettle with a string of top-notch gags.

Only all I got, especially during the first house, were rows and rows of pit-blackened faces staring up at me in bemusement and pity. Over that week I came to appreciate that perhaps our pal Neddy Lochead, north of the border, had done a better job than I first thought.

By Friday I'd tried everything bar starting a dialogue with the audience. So I tried that.

"Good evening, sir, what's your name and what do you do?"

"Isaac, pitman."

"Is that shorthand for something?"

There was no response to what I thought was a pretty impressive off-the-cuff joke.

"Very good. And you, sir?"

"Saul, collier." Pause.

"What about your good self?"

"Emmanuel, pitman." Longer pause.

"And you over there, sir. Perhaps you could tell me a bit about yourself."

"Dennis, collier." Even longer pause.

"Well, Mrs Pitman and Mrs Collier *have* been working overtime." Tumbleweed.

At this low point an older man on the front row stood up to considerable cheers from his workmates. Pausing to light his pipe, this chap fixed me with a keen pair of eyes and said, "Yon poster thing out theer."

"The bill, yes what about it, sir?"

"It says that tha's live from t'Palladium."

"That's right."

The man gave a few considered puffs on his briar before adding, "Thing is, I don't notice much signs o' life." Lots of laughter.

"Leave the funny lines to me, sir."

"All reyt. Gi' us a nod when tha's ready t'start." Gales of mirth.

Even though matters were slipping quickly out of my control, I should not have been insane enough to utter the words that appear on headstones in every comedians' graveyard. These were, "Perhaps you think you could do better."

The old chap knocked the pipe out on his boot heel, shoved it into his pocket and, with a spryness that belied his appearance, vaulted up on to the stage next to me. He did this to enormous cheers which became even louder when, from nowhere, he produced a pair of spoons.

I was about to crack a joke about how this old man looked ready for his supper but he saved me from myself by launching into his act. And what an act! He bashed those spoons against every bit of his whirling body, from his apex to his anus as we say in the business.

The audience, zombies a couple of minutes before, joined in with gusto and we had the odd sight of rough, tough colliers square-dancing with each other in the aisles. It was pandemonium on stilts and, when the old fellow finished his spoon dance, the place went even wilder. So I decided to grab some of his thunder.

"Ladies and gents," I boomed, "let's hear it for ... what do they call you, dad?

"Percy, shot firer."

"Everyone give it up for Sir Percy shot firer extraordinaire. Master of the King's spoons." Mad applause.

Percy leaned over and whispered in my ear, "What's thy name son?"

He obviously hadn't been concentrating earlier but I told him anyway, which led to a touching moment. He raised my right arm in the manner of a boxing referee and shouted, "Reet, lads, let's show *our* thanks to young Frankie Funnybone here."

At first I thought it was a gag and they'd all stare at me blankly like they had before. But Percy, to give him his due, was a man with clout because they went berserk again.

There are times when you just have to stop scheming and go with whatever is happening. I made a couple of modest bows, waved back enthusiastically and quickly introduced the next act, the juggler, Jimmy Juggles. Obviously wanting to mine the goodwill that was flooding all over the theatre, Jimmy bounded on shouting, "Who wants to see my balls?" Stony silence.

Later, after the curtain call, I jumped down into the auditorium to shake Percy's hand. He and his coal dust-encrusted mates clapped me on the back, wished me well and reckoned I was the best act they'd seen here in a long time. Crikey, I wondered, how did the others fare?

On the way back to my dressing room up in the attic, I ran into Jimmy skipping down the stairs with an energy belying his years. Despite the lack of enthusiasm for his act, he too seemed pleased with how things had gone.

"At least they were interested enough to boo me," was his rationale and, after what I'd seen, I couldn't fault it.

I thought he might want to celebrate being loudly barracked before we walked back to our shared digs but he shook his head vehemently at my suggestion of a pint.

"Hot date, Frankie boy," he said with a wink. "You wouldn't want to keep this tasty little dish waiting, take it from me." And he dashed off, knotting his tie as if he were tucking a bib into his shirt front.

"Best of luck then, Jim," I shouted at his retreating back, trying to disguise the envy in my voice. I mean, here he was going on fifty and no oil painting and yet looking forward to a gourmet night of love whereas I was barely twenty-one and facing an evening of not much. Moreover I was missing Nancy terribly.

When I finally got to my dressing room up in the eaves I was feeling thoroughly sorry for myself and dawdled while scraping off the five and nine. *(Stage make-up. Five is ivory and nine is brick red)*.

By the time I was more or less a recognisable human colour again the last stage door fan had long since departed. I consoled myself that at least there'd be a nice hot meal back at my digs in Reservoir Street.

I'm sure there is a more miserable pastime than pounding the cobbles in Rotherham on a mid-winter Friday night. It's just that nobody's mentioned it to me. To cheer myself up I imagined what Nancy was up to at that very moment but the thought that she could be enjoying herself without her loving husband made me even more morose.

My mood changed dramatically, however, when I let myself into the digs as it was immediately obvious there were burglars on the premises, doing terrible things to my poor landlady, judging from the awful screams and moans coming out of her kitchen. I knew there were some ruffians knocking around but, bloody hell, I draw the line at torturing an elderly woman.

Pausing at the kitchen door for a second, I remembered how Les had always told me to stick up for folk less strong than myself. That gave me the necessary resolve so in I piled.

What greeted me as I burst into the kitchen was a scene more degraded than any I could have imagined. My poor landlady, Mrs Swineford, was stretched helplessly face down across her kitchen table and to her rear – doing unspeakable things to her rear was ... Jimmy Juggles!

Blimey, talk about a hot date; she hadn't even got her teeth in. She'd also kept her cardigan and slippers on – well you can't be too careful this weather – and Jimmy's shirt tails were flapping around all over the place.

To make matters even worse, they were whispering sweet nothings to each other. Sweet nothings like, "Don't let up, love, I'm nearly there," and, "Never fear, Elsie, I'm a marathon man not a sprinter." As I might have mentioned, a truly sickening scene.

As neither had yet spotted me, I tried to creep out but landladies have a sixth sense about these things.

"Oh, Mr Funnybone," she gasped, turning to look at me while Jimmy ploughed on, "I'm ever so sorry ..."

"Think nothing of it, madam," I mumbled, counting the black and white squares on the cracked floor lino as I backed out towards the doorway.

"... but I've done you sprouts instead o' cabbage. Hope you don't mind. Oooh bloody 'ell, Jimmy, keep it there."

I assured her that, when all was said and done, greens were greens. Then I snatched the meal out of the oven as quickly as possible and left them to it.

Munching unenthusiastically in the front parlour, I wondered if I could feel any more wretched. The only consolation was that the racket had died down.

A couple of minutes later Jimmy Juggles swaggered into the parlour, adjusting his silver sleeve garters and looking mighty pleased with himself.

He grinned at me and said, "Enjoy your sprouts?"

"Tremendous. How was the crumpet?"

"Sorry about that but at least you can tell your kids you saw the master in action."

"Yeah, and perhaps I could give you a call next time my great-grandmother's on heat."

That wiped the big fat smile off his stupid mug.

"Elsie's a mature woman," he protested. "She's not that old."

"She's ninety-six," I whispered. "And not a young-looking ninety-six. She didn't even have her teeth in for pity's sake."

"That was at my request," grinned Jimmy, "if you get my meaning."

"Oh for god's sake, no more please."

I felt sick but I became a whole lot more nauseous after Jimmy dropped his bombshell.

"Anyway, however old she is," he explained, "you'll have her to yourself next week."

I gagged in horror as Jimmy revealed that his agent had sent a message telling him to move his backside sharpish up to Stockton-on-Tees where he was an emergency fill-in at The Georgian Theatre. So I'd be alone in the house with Elsie.

"It'll be on a plate for you, son," Jimmy chuckled. "Like the sprouts."

"And about as appetising. At least you're here until Sunday. Oh my god, Jimmy, please say you're here until Sunday!"

"Sorry, old son, I'm off first thing. They have Saturday matinees up in that part of the world."

This was far worse than I'd imagined and it threw me into desperation. "But you can't let The Regent down," I pleaded. "Think of those poor upturned blackened faces. Who will they boo?"

Jimmy smiled. "Teddy Butterfingers is filling in for me. He'll be in Rotherham by tomorrow afternoon."

I never imagined that I'd greet the imminent arrival of a comedy juggler with such enthusiasm.

"Teddy Butterfingers! Oh good old Teddy. Thank goodness. How is he with the, er, slightly more mature lady?"

At this point Jimmy played his trump card.

"Christ, Frankie, he's not staying here. Teddy thinks altogether too much of himself for that. No, he wouldn't be seen dead in crumpet digs."

This got worse with every second.

"Crumpet digs! Is that what this place is?"

"Of course. What you think the CD scratched onto the gatepost stands for – corps diplomatique? Did you imagine you were staying at the French Embassy?"

"The only crumpet I've seen round here is in packets marked ... oh good evening once again, Mrs Swineford."

The landlady shuffled into the room, buttoning up her cardy.

"What's that about crumpets, Mr Funnybone? You still peckish? I could whistle you up something hot in no time."

"No, no, Mrs Swineford, please don't whistle, even though I note you do now have your teeth in. Or exert yourself in any way. The sprouts were, er, totally ... satisfying. Excuse me."

As I took the stairs two at a time I heard Jimmy mumble something to which the landlady gave a huge belly laugh.

Though I had a restless night, I was up earlier than ever the following morning. Even then she nearly collared me. As I opened the front door ever so delicately there was a noise and a shout from the top of the stairs.

"Got to go out, Mrs S. See you later. Much later." I shouted back, drowning out her call and disappearing out into the driving rain before I could be manhandled to the floor.

When kids of today complain there's nothing to do just refer them to me and I'll take them back to a wet, cold Saturday in December 1936.

To be fair, Rotherham was no better or worse than most depression-hit northern industrial towns but in my current state it seemed the most miserable in the world. I was soon snoozing in the only cinema that wasn't showing a kids' matinee and letting folk in for a couple of jam jars but even this had its disadvantages.

The downside of being sheltered from the elements was being suddenly jolted awake by a 20ft-high image of Gracie Fields bearing down on me, Singing as she Went, which did my delicate state no good at all. By the time afternoon had arrived I don't think I've ever been so relieved.

By the time the second house was over I'd never been so alarmed. The prospect of trying to wriggle out of a scrum-down with my landlady was looming inexorably. To put off the terrible moment I persuaded Teddy, a podgy little dandy who obviously enjoyed the good life, to join me in a pint or two.

He was good company too and told me a really funny tale about an epic drinking contest between Frank Randle and Sid Field at the Palace Theatre in Burnley. (*Sid Field, 1904-50, was a well-regarded Birmingham-born comedian who by the age of 13 was addicted to alcohol given to him by his mother to cure his stage fright. His most famous character was the spiv Slasher Green*).

In return, I told Teddy about the time I'd smashed a thug's knee with a foul-mouthed dummy's wooden head before saving the King from being strangled by the Duke of York and getting married at Balmoral with the randy royal as my best man.

I'm not entirely sure he believed me yet he was considerate enough to smile in all the right places. But all too soon it was chucking-out time and Teddy revealed his fastidious side by refusing the offer of a nightcap back at my digs.

"No offence, Frankie old boy, but I'll get back to my nice country hotel for a last drinkie-poo if it's all the same to you."

"Fine, Teddy. I'll tag along if you don't mind."

Teddy breathed in sharply and shook his head – never a good sign from car mechanics or jugglers.

"I don't know about that," he said. "Hellaby's a way out of town and you'd have to get a cab back. Besides they're a bit funny about guests so I don't tend to push it. See you on Monday morning."

And with that he skipped off, leaving me to a lonely walk back. On the way I stopped at a chippy whose Saturday night rowdiness and bawdy behaviour I could easily put up with if it meant missing out on the landlady's meal – and her favours.

It had finally stopped raining and, as I guzzled chips in a bus shelter, I figured that if I walked back to my digs via the scenic route, Mrs Swineford would have succumbed to exhaustion after her epic exertions the previous night.

An hour later things were looking promising as I let myself in as quietly as I could. There was no light on in the parlour and all I had to do was hare up those stairs in front of me, shove the wardrobe up against the bedroom door and start saying my prayers.

I might have made it too but for the inevitable creaky floorboard on the fourth stair – a staple of showbiz landladies everywhere. Out of the kitchen she shot like a V2 Rocket and, fair play to her, she had made an effort. Gone were the slippers and cardigan, to be replaced by a low cut white blouse with frills and a tight plaid skirt. Her teeth were firmly in situ as well.

Crikey, in my half-cut and lonely state she actually didn't look that bad. I'd really have to keep on my toes.

"You've been a while," she said. "Another two minutes and I'd have been in bed."

I reflected that, for a comedian, my timing was rubbish.

"Never mind," she cooed. "Come and have your meal. We all need something hot inside us when it gets to this hour."

"Haaaaaa." That was the sound people like me make in the absence of ability to form words.

"Are you all right, love?"

"I don't feel entirely well, Mrs Swineford."

"Call me Elsie, my darling. We've no side round these parts. Come on we'll soon have you right as ninepence."

She guided me into the kitchen, closing the door behind her, and beckoned me to sit at the table. Which I did.

"You know," I said, "I'm not sure I could face all those sprouts."

"Don't worry, poppet" she said opening the oven door, "I've done you cabbage."

She stationed herself opposite me as I toyed over my plate. Even if I'd fancied the cabbage – and I didn't – there was no more room inside me, after the bellyful of fish, chips and scraps. Yet to keep her at bay I had no real choice but to try to eat.

Elsie nodded approvingly at my efforts. Then, out of the blue, she said, "I don't normally go to The Regent."

Small talk was fine by me and I responded with, "Oh you should, it's quite an experience."

"You're probably right. I mean one of my dear friends, Marjorie Forshaw, also has a guest house. Well, she was round here after she'd been to the early show."

"And did your friend Mrs Forshaw enjoy the show?"

"Oh very much. Especially when you were on stage. She said you were ... magnificent!"

Have you ever been about to swallow a forkful of beef and cowheel pie when an eleven-stone woman lands in your lap? If not, allow me to advise you it's not an experience I'd recommend.

The next bit was shaping up to be even less pretty when to my surprise - and considerable relief - the kitchen door flew open. My joy was quickly curtailed, however, when I saw our late-night intruder was Nancy.

Don't get me wrong. Up to two minutes previously if you'd told me that my wife was all set to arrive I'd have been overjoyed. What tempered my delight was the fact I was staring at Nancy over Mrs Swineford's left shoulder while the landlady writhed away on top of me. I gazed beseechingly at Nancy and, thank the lord, her grim expression turned into a grin. She winked and said, "Is this woman bothering you, sir?"

Elsie, totally immersed in my impending seduction, was brutally jolted back into the real world. She turned to Nancy and barked, "Who the heck are you, lady? How did you get in? And what gives you the right to interrupt our pleasure?"

"In that order," replied Nancy ever so coolly, "I'm this unfortunate man's agent, the front door was on the latch, oh, and I also double up as his Missus."

The landlady jumped to her feet as if she'd been electrocuted and slapped my face.

"And don't try any such thing again, you naughty boy," she sniffed, ostentatiously straightening her wispy blonde hair. "Honestly, show folk these days!"

I tried to keep a straight face as Nancy demonstrated how Eddie Star's training had paid off by laying down the law to Mrs Swineford. Keep your mucky old paws off the turns or I'll stop sending them round to this dump *and* I'll put the word round other agencies as well, seemed to sum up her message. Oh, and only boil your sprouts for ten minutes not two-and-a-half hours. Well, amen to that as well.

After she'd dried her tears, Elsie swore blind that what Nancy had seen was a terrible misunderstanding which would never happen again. She even insisted that we share her double bed that night, adding quickly that she'd be in the spare room.

Maybe I was giddy about my lucky escape because I took advantage of Mrs Swineford's kind offer to become reacquainted with Nancy. In fact by the morning we were both absolutely reacquainted to bits and slept in late. Then began a day of surprises.

The first was that, feeling I had served my penance, Nancy had utilised her new skills to extract me without penalty from next week's booking at The Regent. The second surprise was Nancy throwing open the landlady's grimy bedroom curtains to reveal a bottle green two-seater MG sports car sitting outside the digs. I noticed it was attracting the attention of admiring urchins who'd hardly ever seen a car, let alone one of this style.

With a shouted goodbye to Mrs S, who was uncharacteristically nowhere to be seen, I threw my suitcase into the small car boot and we roared away for ever from Reservoir Street.

As she drove, Nancy explained that her mother had arrived unannounced at our rented flat in Fulham – without the knowledge of her husband – eager to re-establish contact with her favourite daughter and no hard feelings.

Lady Agatha was also keen to give Nancy a fistful of white fivers as a late wedding present. This would more than cover the price of the car and provide a deposit on a decent-sized terrace house in Earls Court – Nancy had already been out scouting.

So, things were looking up – but sadly not for everyone. A Daily Express tucked down between the car seats revealed that the matter of the King was well and truly in the open and appeared to be approaching its endgame.

Nancy glanced at me while I read. "Your best man's doing his utmost to make a pig's ear of things isn't he?"

I couldn't disagree.

She added, "To make things worse there's a rumour going around that milady's been seen in the company of Von Ribbentrop."

"The German Ambassador and Wallis? I said, shaking my head in disbelief. "That's terrible! I hope the poor sod realises what he's in for."

Nancy laughed dutifully and, keeping a careful eye on the road, pointed out that if true the matter would become even more political than it was now.

I nodded and said, "No wonder Baldwin's going bonkers. It says here that Winston Churchill's weighing in an' all."

Nancy glanced at me in an odd way. "That reminds me," she said. "Churchill was on the phone yesterday morning. He wanted to speak to you."

"To me! What about?"

"Well I'd guess it's not to discuss the price of haddock. Maybe something to do with our mutual friend."

Putting the newspaper down, I tried to remember if I'd even met Churchill before. I managed to recall one brief handshake after a show at the Palladium but that was about it. He and I didn't exactly move in the same circles. In fact I struggled to imagine in which circles Winston Churchill moved these days. I recalled that he'd been in the Cabinet a few times for one party or the other but equally I also knew that he was now a sad case with a glittering political career firmly behind him. Maybe kicking up a stink about Baldwin's treatment of the King was his one final bid for attention.

By the next morning I'd totally forgotten about Churchill mainly because I was forced, by Nancy, to concentrate on assessing a pleasant five bedroom terrace in Earl's Court. It needed one or two repairs but the price of just over a thousand pounds, Nancy assured me, was a bargain and well within what we could afford.

We were back in our Fulham flat and just about to have lunch when the phone rang. It was Winston Churchill and in those soon-to-be-familiar sonorous tones he ordered me immediately into his presence.

"It's a bit awkward at the moment," I told him.

"Do you want to serve your country, sir?"

"How do you mean?"

"I'll explain when we meet this afternoon."

"At the Commons?"

"No, at Chartwell."

"Where?"

"Chartwell! Take the train to Sevenoaks and pick up a cab." The line went dead.

"I've been summoned to the Churchill residence," I told Nancy as I came back into the dining room. "Can you possibly do without me for another day or two?"

"I've managed for the last few months," was her off-hand reply so I went to pack an overnight bag.

A couple of hours later I was in a taxi on my way to Chartwell, Churchill's home in Kent. At Sevenoaks Station I'd been concerned that the cabbies wouldn't know where I was on about but I needn't have worried.

"Thing to remember about Winnie," said my driver as we roared down shady lanes between high hawthorn hedges, "is that he's fine until the sun goes down. Then you've got to watch yourself."

"How do you mean?"

He glanced into his driving mirror and added with a gap-toothed grin, "I won't spoil the surprise."

I was still mulling over this little mystery as we pulled up in front of an impressive red-brick mansion peeping out from between high beech trees. Although smaller than Protheroe Hall, it was ten times more attractive and I could see that a lot of work had gone into it recently. Like Protheroe, it looked a place that would be brimming with servants but, to my surprise, continued ringing of the doorbell produced no response. Eventually I gave up and strolled round to the back of the house.

Nobody was there either, apart from a little fat brickie making a dog's mess of putting up a low wall at the far end of the magnificent stone terrace. But what took my breath away was the view. Even in the falling dusk of a winter afternoon it was stunning. The lawns, framed by beech and oak, sloped away towards a series of lakes and thereafter the vista widened to take in miles and miles of undulating Kentish Weald.

I drew in a deep breath of sharp clean air and realised this was the first time in months I wasn't filling my lungs with smoke and soot.

I strolled over to the little fat brickie who hadn't yet seen me. His wall, I noted, did not look at all straight.

"I think you need a spirit level, chum," I told him. "Oh, and have you seen the owner of this hovel?"

The figure put down his trowel, turned to me and said in an unmistakeable growl, "Mr Funnybone, welcome to my 'hovel'. Should I ever require advice on building from a comedian then I shall know upon whom to call."

Well, fair enough I suppose – though I still didn't think the wall was straight. Nevertheless, I shook hands with Winston Churchill, who stood up to reveal he was wearing a loose garment of indeterminate status.

"You're looking mighty well, sir" I told him. "Apart from the frock."

"It's a smock, Mr Funnybone. I wear it for painting as well."

"If you paint as badly as you lay bricks then you're not coming near our window frames. Now how about a cuppa."

You may consider that I was unduly cheeky to a soon-to-be-great man. Yet experience had taught me that the high and mighty expect characters like me to behave in a certain cavalier way and it doesn't do to disappoint them. Call it the court jester syndrome. Whatever the arguments, it seemed to work with Winston who clapped me on the back and told me that he was indeed ready for a drink.

When ever was he not? By the time we were settled into easy chairs by the huge dining room window watching

147

farm house lights twinkling across the Weald, we were already onto our second large shot of Johnny Walker Red Label and Winston had put the entertainment industry to rights.

I glanced at my watch remembering the cabbie's warning about what would happen when two hours were up. I sensed we were about to move on to weightier matters than Will Hay's false teeth and I was right.

"Do you know who's responsible for the state in which the world finds itself today?" Winston asked as he jabbed threateningly at me with the burning end of his hand-rolled Romeo y Julieta. I was about to finger Wilson, Keppel and Betty, when it became clear that my opinion was not required.

Fakirs," he thundered. "Damned Middle Temple fakirs."

"Mind the language, sir," I protested, "there may be ladies listening."

I needn't have worried as it turned out that there was no-one else at Chartwell. The housekeeper was having a night-off and Winston's missus, Clemmie, had gone up to London to deal once more with their problem child Randolph.

Of course this was long before I'd got to know Randolph. That happened during the infamous yard of ale fiasco at Cleveleys in 1945, an incident for which I blamed myself and, somewhat uncharitably, so did Randy.

Anyhow, getting back to his altogether weightier Dad, Winston was banging on about this little Indian, Gandhi, who he clearly couldn't abide because the cheeky wee chappy wanted his country to be independent.

Now, while you and I might consider that a fair ambition, to Winston it was a short step down from imperial high treason. I didn't help matters by pointing out that the Mahatma had made quite an impression among the mill workers when he'd visited my patch some years before. Indeed, I couldn't help smiling as I recalled

Joshua's apoplexy as a skinny Indian in a loincloth calmly began to lecture him on how everyone might benefit if he treated his mill hands with a touch more compassion.

However, my Gandhi story was interpreted by Winston as gross insolence from a young pup. To calm him down I asked what he was writing these days as I was aware he did a spot of scribbling now and again. *(Winston Churchill made his living from writing. As well as innumerable newspaper articles, he wrote 43 books and won the Nobel Prize for Literature in 1953).*

But my innocent inquiry led to another rant about the second subject obsessing him at this time.

"I am approaching the conclusion of my magnum opus on John Duke," he informed me grandly.

"John who?"

"My esteemed ancestor John Churchill, the first Duke of Marlborough."

Although I was already starting to feel ever so slightly befuddled, I definitely knew something about this cove.

"The Duke of Marlborough? Didn't he suffocate in a barrel of tits?"

Churchill glowered at me as though I'd just pissed into his upturned hat.

"That, sir, was the Duke of Clarence. And he drowned. In a butt of Malmsey wine."

"If you say so, Winston."

"I do say so, young man and furthermore ..."

Winston's eyes misted over as he began banging on nineteen to the dozen about his famous ancestor's set-tos with the French King Louis the Fourteenth. Soon he was at full throttle.

"John Duke shtood shteadfasht," - I'll stop that malarkey right now, you'll just have to imagine it - "against a tyrant who menaced the whole of Europe. Now, as the continent again finds itself in thrall to a new and even more malevolent despot, it must surely fall to another Churchill to fulfil his manifest destiny and ..."

I must have nodded off for a second because the next thing whisky was swilling all over my lap.

"Ow shit," I shouted. "I've spilled me bleedin' drink."

"... stand firm in the face of tyranny ..."

"You've not got a dishcloth have you, Winston?"

"... to protect the English-speaking ..."

"Any old pot rag'll do."

He dismissed me upstairs with an impatient wave and I grabbed my overnight bag from the hall on the way up. After changing my trousers in the bathroom and dumping my bag in one of the bedrooms, I stopped as I passed Winston's study.

His desk was tidier than I'd expected but on a large table in the corner were three mountains of documents. I sneaked in and pulled out the top paper in one of the piles. It was headed "Political and Economic Implications of the Treaty of Rastatt, 1714", and evidently a key part of his great work.

I made a mental note to order a dozen copies as light reading for each member of my family. (*Marlborough: His Life and Times by Winston S. Churchill was published in four volumes between 1933 and 1938, with a combined sale of 42,000*).

When I got back downstairs I noticed Winston had not been idle. On the dining table was a large stew pot and a tureen of vegetables both of which looked as if they'd been cooked some time before. Nevertheless as we sat down at the table I realised I hadn't eaten since lunch-time and tackled the stew and dumplings with gusto. Inevitably it was washed down with a pleasant vintage port.

I recalled that Winston had been in full flow when my clumsiness had interrupted him.

"What were you saying about Europe's descent into tyranny and all?" I asked.

He glared at me. "It does not matter. You are here to speak of other things."

So finally we were getting down to the purpose of my visit. About time too. Winston put down his knife and fork and committed arson on another airship-sized cigar.

"They inform me you are *moderately* acquainted with my *very* good friend the King?"

"I suppose you could say that."

"I just did. I want to know what you say."

"Well, OK, yes, I do know him. In fact he was my ..."

Some people love the sound of their own voice a bit too much, don't they! Before I could elaborate on my links to the House of Windsor, Winston was slurring on about supporting Edward in his current troubles and then began talking wildly of forming a King's Party. This seemed to back up Baldwin's assertion about a lack of judgement. Even I, a mere comedian, knew that this would jigger up the constitution as royalty's not supposed to dabble in politics let alone have its own backers in the Commons.

Incidentally someone should point this out to the current lot, especially that jug-eared clown who talks to parsnips. *(Edward VIII himself was not above entering the realm of politics. He opposed League of Nations' sanctions on Italy after Mussolini had invaded Abyssinia in 1935).*

Ten minutes into his rant, Churchill paused for breath and I grabbed the opportunity to speak.

"Look, Winston," I told him, "you seem sure in your own mind what you're up to. So why don't I just toddle off upstairs and ...

"Stay where you are, sir. You are needed right here."

"Whatever for?"

"I wish to know about Wallis Simpson."

Apparently in all his social meetings with David when he was Prince of Wales and latterly King, Churchill had hardly exchanged two words with the Baltimore Bullet.

"I believe this woman may have led the King astray and I want to know if ... if there's a chance she'll be persuaded to do the right thing and ... disappear."

I had to choose my words rather carefully.

"Well, Winston," I began, "while I've only met the lady on two occasions, I can say with a degree of certainty that she won't be pushed around."

"She is a determined woman?"

"I should say so. And of course she's a Yank."

That set him off again. "My own dear mother was a 'Yank' as you so disrespectfully put it."

"Winston, I simply meant that, as an American, she isn't likely to bow down to pressure from the British establishment."

He puffed thoughtfully on his cigar. "Yes, I can see that," he conceded.

My confidence boosted, I then went too far with the assertion, "And you've forgotten something."

Winston leapt out of his seat, sparks flying everywhere. I thought he was going to set about me with the poker.

"Forgotten something," he roared. "I've forgotten more things than you'll ever know."

I paused to let the fact sink in that he was agreeing with me. Winston suddenly wore an expression of complete befuddlement and subsided back into his chair, looking every one of his sixty-two years.

"Explain yourself, sir," he mumbled.

I pointed out that, even if Wallis were amenable to being bribed to clear off, the King would never allow this to happen. The uncomfortable fact was that he loved the woman and any political, religious or constitutional manoeuvres would have to take that into account. Oh, and could I go to bed 'cos I was really cream-crackered.

Winston ordered me to stay exactly where I was and gave it to me with both barrels.

"I number the King amongst my dearest friends and I refuse to listen to a strolling player's opinions of him. You, sir, are here to give me information not advice. I will use my political experience, accumulated over forty years to decide how to proceed. You, sir, do not know the King."

It always ends like this, I mused. When two men have drunk more than they can reasonably hold it's generally time to see who can piss higher up the wall. Well, brace yourselves for my wee effort.

"Who was best man at your wedding, Winston?"

The question threw him and for a moment I thought he'd forgotten – it had been in 1908 after all. But then a smile crept over his face.

"My best man, and a very good man he is too, was Lord Hugh Cecil."

"Well-connected sort of cove is he?"

Churchill stared in complete amazement before informing me, "Linky is the son of the Marquis of Salisbury, three times Prime Minster of these islands. Is that 'well-connected' enough for you?"

"Not bad," I conceded. "Want to know who my best man was?"

Now, Winston Churchill had not been a politician for upwards of four decades without being able to sense an approaching elephant trap. He guessed immediately that I held some unnamed advantage and immediately began to cut his losses.

"I find this kind of talk distasteful," he mumbled unconvincingly. "Perhaps we should adjourn to bed after all. Help me up."

Approaching Winston's chair, I leaned over as if to assist him to his feet - and whispered a name into his ear. The force of the erupting Churchillian rage sent me staggering back into my own chair.

"You, sir, are a confounded mountebank!" he bawled.

"No I'm not! Actually I don't know what a mountebank is. But I'll bet you any money I'm not one."

"There is only one King's man in this house and it is not you, sir."

"All I'm telling you is that David, sorry King Edward VIII, was best man at my wedding this summer – at Balmoral too. Are you familiar with the old place?"

"Aaaaaaaargh!"

"Ring him up if you doubt me. If you don't have his telephone number, I could always ..." And I reached into my inside pocket.

Winston was out of his seat like the greyhound in trap two, scrabbling at the phone in the hall before I could move. A minute later I heard him mumble into the receiver so I strolled across. Bless him, he was already waffling.

" ... just to inform Your Majesty of my enduring loyalty in these your darkest days when the forces of ..."

He broke off and I could clearly make out exasperated tones on the other end of the line.

"Of course, sir, we shall talk tomorrow. Yes I will be back in London. There's just one more insignificant matter ..."

After he'd asked the question I leaned over the receiver to hear the King reply, "Well, yes I did act in that capacity but goodness knows how you've found out. And what damned business is it of yours anyway, Winston?"

And then from the background came those familiar dulcet tones, "Dave, geddoff that goddam phone right now and get your sorry ass back in here."

Churchill's befuddled expression turned into one of extreme alarm.

"Sir, are you being menaced in your own chamber? Shall I inform the security services?"

"I wouldn't do that, Winston, if I were you," I said and gently removed the receiver from his grasp.

"Goodnight, Your Majesty," I whispered into the phone. There was a croak at the other end.

"Frankie, is that you?"

"Yes, sir."

"I didn't know you were part of Winnie's set. Is the old fellow all right?"

I looked at Winston, doubled up in a chair by the telephone table, and assured the King everything was more or less normal for this time of night.

"I'll leave you now, sir," I said. "Good luck with ... everything."

"Thank you, Frankie, and especial thanks for ..."

I never found out why the King had reason to be particularly grateful to me because after a last, "shake your goddam butt and get back up ..." the line went dead.

Winston looked forlornly up at me and said, "I don't know about you but I need a drink."

It's hard to estimate but I'd guess we hammered the Johnny Walker bottle for another hour. The episode of the King's bedroom, which had sobered both of us up, was not referred to again.

Instead, Winston became maudlin and started to come out with stuff like, "I wish you were my son, Francis."

In my experience, this sort of rubbish is usually the preliminary to, "Me an' you against the world," and a pile of sawdust where the chairs once stood. Sure enough in the next breath he was ranting and raving at me, yelling that I wasn't fit to lace Arthur Askey's boots or Gracie Fields' corsets – the very thought!

Winston ended up pointing at me and shouting, "If you were my son I'd put poison in your whisky."

"And if you were my Dad," I replied coolly, "I'd drink it!"

Well, this tickled him no end and suddenly we were best mates again. When he'd finished scribbling something down on a notepad, we staggered off upstairs with no hard feelings.

When I staggered back down the same stairs at nine the following morning the house seemed to have taken on a new life. Winston was barking orders down on the phone, his housekeeper scurried in and out of the dining room laying out breakfast dishes on the sideboard and the chauffeur was busy out front polishing the Daimler.

I'd just settled down to tackle a steaming plate full of scrambled eggs and black pudding when Winston came in looking mighty pleased with himself. He began jabbing at a plate of kidneys while reporting lucidly and concisely about the threat of German re-armament. It was powerful stuff, all the more so when contrasted with his incoherent performance the night before. Apparently a contact in the Air Ministry was feeding him information about Britain's woefully unready state for conflict and he was using this to make mischief in Westminster. I know, I could hardly believe it either!

Later, as the chauffeur drove us up to London, Winston continued to fulminate about the easy ride Germany was being given. But the King was never mentioned again and I was relieved that the old fellow appeared to have purged all that nonsense out of his system.

Next morning Nancy dropped the Daily Express on to the breakfast table in front of me.

"I see your pal's been at it again," she said in such a way that indicated 'it' was not the most sensible thing to be 'at'.

I looked at the paper, half expecting to read that Dapper Dave had thrown in the towel but we'd have to wait another couple of days for that. Instead the front page was full of how Winston had made a complete ass of himself in the Commons the previous evening by banging on about forming a King's Party and endangering the constitution.

Nancy sighed and said, "This has been coming for a while. In fact I'll confidently predict that is the end of Winston Churchill's career in politics."

"You know what, darling," I replied, "I could not agree more!"

Chapter Nine: Brummie Nev

Did I ever mention that I was fluent in German? It's not swanking or anything. I'm just bringing the matter up because of something that happens later in this chapter. In the meantime, relax until I've managed to bring this story up to date.

First off, you'll probably already know that Winston survived his right royal balls-up. Not only that, by September 1938, when this memoir splutters into life again, he was cutting an altogether more substantial figure due, in no small part, to the matters I'll be detailing later on.

But for now let's leave Mr Churchill to his canvases, dodgy brick walls and knitted squares for little African children and take a closer look what was happening chez Thirkettle.

Our happy wee threesome was now firmly ensconced at the new place in Earls Court and we were even able to afford ... what was that? Oh, had I neglected to mention that we had a daughter? Yes, eight-and-a-half months after Nancy liberated me from Rotherham, little Julia came bawling and puking into our lives.

Actually, she was a lovely wee thing with perfect smooth skin and beautiful round cheeks which brought to mind a rather large pair of gob-stoppers. Whereas these days she looks like something someone put under the grill and forgot about.

And that reminds me, the ungrateful old trout hasn't visited me for days on end – it gets extremely lonely in this geriatrics' gulag, you know. (*Dame Julia Pennyfeather, nee Thirkettle, is a modern day saint and far too busy with vital charity work to bother with surly curmudgeons*).

Maybe I'd omitted to mention the sprog because my wife had been fiercely determined that Julia's arrival would not change our lives. Accordingly, a couple of months after the baby came along, Nancy was back directing my career as if she'd never been away. And, I know I'm biased, but she did have a real feel for it. In fact she could have written the handbook for these modern-day spin doctors and policy gonks.

If you doubt that, let me tell you she was the first one to really appreciate that the value of the Funnybone 'brand', as we must sadly call it, could be enhanced by the use of my famous catchphrase.

What had happened was that a train became derailed in the middle of nowhere and, of all people, who should be stuck on it but the Minister of Transport, old Hore-Belisha himself. In case you don't know, this was the cove who gave half his surname to a beacon of joy which has illuminated and 'saved' countless lives – and the other half to a big orange balloon next to a zebra crossing.

Of course, some of the papers had a field day with the tale yet it was Nancy alone who spotted its full potential. She got in touch with a chap she knew who worked at British Paramount News and suggested they sign off their report on the incident with, "Perhaps he should have listened to Frankie Funnybone and come on his bike."

The Paramount people, who saw themselves as risk-takers, bought the idea and for four days and nights, my famous catchphrase was repeated in cinemas and news theatres all round the country. Just try to buy publicity like that and see what it costs. *(It seems that Frankie's well-documented partiality to an off-colour gag has got the better of him once again. Leslie Hore-Belisha had been Minister of Transport from 1934-37 but was then Secretary of State for War. The unfortunate Transport Minister stuck on the de-railed train in September 1938 would have been Leslie Burgin, the Liberal MP for Luton).*

So, career-wise Nancy was flying high. Which is why she wasn't at all pleased when, just six months after Julia came along, she discovered she was pregnant again.

"You should have kept your confounded hands to yourself," she grumbled as we left the doctor's surgery after receiving the joyous news.

"I did keep my confounded hands - and everything else - to myself, for nearly six months," I replied calmly. "Might I add that your self-imposed abstinence from alcohol had just ended and, after seeing off a Wincarnis or four, you reckoned it would be a jolly idea if we ..."

"All right, all right," she snapped, her face reddening. "What's done is done so let's draw a line under the matter and move on." As I said before, a consummate spin-doctor.

However, before she finally got her ruler and crayons out to draw that line, Nancy was moved to proclaim in no uncertain terms, "Whatever happens, I'm not staying away from work for long this time."

Pretty rich, coming as it was from someone who had been dictating correspondence to a harassed temp while being wheeled into the delivery suite. But it was fine by me as I was confident we'd be able to cope. We already had a nursery maid, Jennifer, and then there were the ministrations of Nancy's mother, who seemed to arrive in the capital once a week laden with baby clothes and exotic food parcels.

I'm not sure if Lady Agatha thought we were both working for nothing but, whatever the situation, I was getting mightily fed up with peacocks' tongues in aspic.

Maybe Agatha was simply using the food parcels as a decoy to stop Sir Joshua smelling a rat. Perhaps she'd told him she was delivering roll-mop herrings and mussels in butter to the fallen women of Whitechapel. Who knows?

At any rate the ploy appeared to work because neither Agatha nor, more importantly, Nancy and I, were bothered by the old ratbag. So that was one less thing to worry about and I'd almost forgotten about my incendiary father-in-law when things took an unexpected and sinister turn.

I'd just finished a successful week at the new De La Warr Pavilion down there on the south coast. Apparently the locals had raised their plummy voices, demanding a change in the relentless self-improving diet of dramas by G.B. Shaw, J.B. Priestley and, almighty god help us all, T.S. Eliot.

The management, hearing these cries from the wilderness, had put together a variety extravaganza in which, if my memory's anything to go by, M.W. Miller was second on the bill - below me. *(If the official records are anything to go by, Max Miller was top of the bill with Frankie a good deal lower down than Solomon the Sword Swallower).*

The Pavilion suited me down to the ground because the new facilities were several cuts above what we were all used to and the grateful audience was largely respectful. So, by close of play on Saturday, I was feeling rather pleased with myself as I chiselled away at the five and nine; so pleased that I never heard him come in.

In fact the first time I realised that Maurice Lake had infiltrated my dressing room was when I heard the door click shut.

You may remember the last time I'd set eyes on Lake, he was waving a shotgun around like he was auditioning for the part of Wild Bill Hickock's considerably wilder brother. So, when I saw him leaning there, smug smile and all, I panicked.

"There's a bell under this table," I squeaked. "If I ring it the whole theatre will come to my aid. Audience and all. They adore me in Worthing."

Lake smiled and shook his head.

"Francis," he said, "the audience has gone home, the theatre people ring a bell for you, not you for them ... and we're in Bexhill on Sea."

"OK then, try anything and I'll scream the place down."

Lake's eyes narrowed. "I really wouldn't do that if I were you, Francis," he said quietly.

Blimey, there was no disguising the naked menace in that voice. Plus, if anything, he looked stronger and fitter than at our last encounter. Handy as I was, I'd have no chance in a rumpus.

"I'm warning you," I spluttered, "I can make a great deal of noise."

"Yes but why would you want to?"

"Why? Because at our last meeting you and your pals were pointing weapons at me and Nancy."

"Not at Nancy. Only you!"

Jesus Christ! I glanced shiftily at the window but it was closed and locked. I was trapped with a madman intent on revenge.

I had one more card left to play but luckily it was my trump. Subtlety!

"Look here, Maurice," I said. "You may think you're doing the lord of the manor's work but I'm here to tell you that Joshua is well and truly off his rocker. Even his daughter thinks so."

Lake took a determined step forward and I braced myself for a good hiding. But he stopped directly in front of me and said, "I'm not doing Joshua's work because I'm no longer employed by him."

I peeped feebly out from beneath my raised arm.

"So you've not come here to give me a pasting?"

"Why ever would you think that?"

"Well, maybe because I whacked you hard across the knee with a dummy's head, Les knocked you out cold and because of me you ended up taking an unscheduled bath in the stream. Very funny that was too. And then there was that time on the station platform ..."

"All right, all right," snapped Lake, suddenly looking a lot less smug. "So you bested me a few times. Fair play to you. But the plain fact is that I'm no longer comfortable working for a nutcase."

I studied Lake carefully. "So you agree that Joshua is barmy?"

He nodded and sat down in the spare armchair. For the next ten minutes he described what had happened after their gang was sent packing by the King up in Scotland two years before. Apparently they were barely away from the royal party before Joshua began to rant about how he'd nail me if it was the last thing he did.

"Nobody gets the drop on me in business or pleasure," was one of the more repeatable phrases he'd bellowed and even Lake, who'd seen all his moods, was shocked by the venom in him. Matters were not calmed by a couple of Joshua's entourage who egged him on to mount an armed raid on Balmoral and snatch Nancy away.

"I can't tell you how worried I was," said Lake, biting his lip. "Joshua was going crazy and these clowns he'd hired weren't exactly making things any better. It took all my powers of persuasion to get them back in the car and away from that place."

However, if Lake thought that was the end of it – and I'm not at all sure he did – things failed to improve when they were back at Protheroe Hall and for months Joshua made life hell for everyone. Matters only appeared to calm down when he heard he had a grandchild on the way but Lake was under the impression that he was merely biding his time.

There was a long silence and, thinking that he had finished his account, I poured Lake a large Scotch and had one myself. I couldn't pretend I'd ever liked him but I did reckon that he was an honest man. Which is why I shouldn't have come out with what I said next.

"Cheers, Maurice, for that information."

He nodded curtly and we both drank.

"So how much do you need?"

Lake's eyes blazed as he jumped up and grabbed me by the throat.

"You stupid little sod," he spat. "Do you think I've come here for your tin?"

"Oh, is that not what you want?" I squeaked.

He pushed me away angrily. "No, Francis. I don't need money but, if I did, I wouldn't come to you for it."

"Why are you here then?"

For the first time in about twenty minutes, Lake smiled. "I'm here, Francis," he said, "to tell you it's highly likely that Joshua is planning to have you killed."

It was a good job we'd not made too many inroads into the Scotch because boy was it needed now. Lake explained that he hadn't found out what he'd told me from Joshua – they were barely on speaking terms by then. However, one evening in the pub one of Lake's old Army buddies revealed that Joshua had approached him with the offer of a job.

"What kind of job?" I asked nervously.

"He wanted my oppo to make something disappear."

"That could mean anything."

"It could indeed and we don't have details as my pal walked away from the job because it sounded wrong."

"But, still, it could have been anything."

Lake shrugged and said, "You could be right. Maybe there is nothing for you to worry about after all."

I could tell there was a huge 'but' on the way.

"But, if you wanted me to speculate from what I've pieced together, then I'd say that at the very least you were in for a rather savage beating."

I drained my glass and poured another quickly. As I drank, I realised my teeth were chattering.

"You're saying that, right now, there's a gang of hoodlums on my trail?"

Lake shrugged again. "I can't say exactly what stage his plan's got to. All I will suggest is that you should take great care."

And, with that, he turned to go.

"Hold on," I cried. "You must know more than that."

He shook his head. "I told you I no longer work for Sir Joshua Protheroe."

I was forced to think on my feet. "OK, Maurice, look I have an idea. How about working as my bodyguard? I could pay you a lot more than Joshua ever did. Er, how much *was* that by the way?"

Lake smiled. "Even if I wanted to work for *you,*" and the way he said 'you' made me suspect that he wasn't altogether fussed about it, "I doubt I'd be much use. You see, the chap I spoke to in the pub had been trained in special operations. I wouldn't have stood a cat in hell's chance against him."

This was becoming far worse than I could have imagined – then Lake twisted the knife for the final time.

With another smile, he said, "Maybe you could persuade Les to look after you. After all he is a handy fellow. Like I said, take great care!"

And before I could protest again, Lake had closed the door behind him leaving me to tremble all on my own. Not for long though. He hadn't been gone for many seconds before I decided I needed to be out of that building as well.

Without removing the rest of my make-up, I quickly pulled on an overcoat, grabbed a bag and jammed my hat tightly down over my face. Then I got Arthur the caretaker to unlock the front doors and let me out there – god knows who could be lurking in the gloom outside the stage door.

I didn't dare risk going back to my hotel either but spent the night barricaded in a flea-trap B&B on the edge of town. I'd half-decided to nip around Beachy Head to Brighton and see if my old make-up buddy Clifford Holliday could turn me into Shirley Temple for a day or two. But in the end I caught the earliest train to London for an unscheduled appointment with Eddie Star.

Before revealing how I intended to stay in one piece, can I interest you in a bizarre postscript to the Maurice Lake story? I never saw the man again but did attend his funeral in the mid-Seventies by which time he'd become Sir Maurice and a pillar of society.

You see, after the war he teamed up with an old army pal – the handy lad from the pub for all I know – in a speculative venture. They'd had the idea of slicing potatoes very thinly and then frying them until they were, well, crisp. Lots of people were doing that by then but Lake's big idea was to flavour the crisps.

If he'd told me what he was planning I'd probably have built a comedy routine around it – but the laugh would have been on me because who these days has not heard of Lake's Crisps? (*Me for one*). Yes, I always think of Maurice whenever I try to keep down a bagful of his cowheel and trotter BSE specials.

Well, if the crisps weren't my cup of tea his advice was, and an hour after jumping on the train to Victoria I was sneaking off at West Norwood and into a cab on my way to Eddie Star's mansion in Richmond.

I'd like to report that my agent/manager was delighted to welcome one of his most valued clients but, opening the door in his silk dressing gown, he looked anything but pleased to see me.

I quickly waved aside his protests about the sanctity of showbiz Sundays and bundled him into the house. He was therefore forced to listen as I carefully detailed what Lake had told me and, surprisingly, did nothing to allay my fears.

"This does sound very serious, old son," he said, tugging at the end of his moustache. "Maybe we should get you out of the country for a time."

It sounded a decent idea, with one small drawback.

"Er, Eddie," I said, "aren't things on the continent a tiny bit hot at the moment?"

Eddie considered this – and smiled. "You're right," he conceded, "but funnily enough, through an old china of mine, I could get you on the bill in the one country where you'd think it was least possible. Trouble is, you'd need to be fluent in German."

I smiled for the first time in twelve hours. "Then it's to everyone's great good fortune that I am fluent in German."

It's possible you're unfamiliar with the Locarno exchanges in the mid-1920s, inspired by the pact that tried to bring Germany back into the international fold. *(The Locarno Treaty of 1925 between Germany, Britain and France was a move to guarantee borders in western Europe and normalise relations with the German Weimar Republic).*

And I'll bet old whatshisface has given you a dry-as-dust rundown of the Locarno Treaty and neglected to mention it was so popular that countless dance halls and ballrooms were named after it.

But another less-remembered effect was that schools were invited to send their best young scholars to meet children from Germany and, at the age of eleven I'd been chosen by St Barnabas's to stay a fortnight with the family of young Manfred Holzenbein in Wuppertaal.

Typically, when I got there, the peevish Teuton tick refused to speak a word of English so I was forced to pick up his ugly lingo pretty sharpish. It was then I found I had a real feel for the tongue and, in the following years, I stuck at it and became fluent.

I could see Eddie was impressed by my tale.

"If that's the case, Tosh," he told me, "then I'll have no problems getting you bookings all over southern Germany."

Eddie smiled to himself again and I half guessed what was coming.

"And maybe after that we'll send you to Madrid and Barcelona? Or how about I pack you off to Shanghai? You'll come to no harm there." *(At this point Spain was in the throes of some of the fiercest fighting in its civil war and China was desperately resisting invasion by the Japanese).*

I greeted Eddie's little jests with the thinnest of smiles because he did have a point. Uniquely in the 1930s, I was attempting to escape persecution by fleeing to Nazi Germany!

And, if I'd known exactly into what sort of inferno I'd be jumping from Joshua's frying pan, I might have paused a moment and taken whatever punishment the old scoundrel was planning for me. As it was, I leapt at the chance to evade my father-in-law's clutches.

I didn't want to worry Nancy in the condition she was in so I told her Eddie was sending me to test out new material in The Irish Free State and I had to leave immediately. She didn't sound too chuffed down the phone but was placated by Eddie's promise of the rising young comedian Terry Tripe to manage. *(She must have done a splendid job).*

That evening I slipped out of the country on a boat from Harwich to Hamburg.

Now you may think that trying to make Germans laugh would have a similar difficulty rating to those well-known northern pursuits of sawdust plaiting and treacle knitting. Yet as I blazed a trail across southern Germany – from Mannheim through Karlsruhe, Stuttgart and Augsburg – it became clear that my act was loved by the Boche.

Of course I adapted my famous catchphrase to their ears and my shout of, "Na, und jetzt wie bin ich gekommen?" was invariably answered with the rousing reply, "Mit dem Fahrrad! Ho, ho, ho."

Their favourite joke of all, though, was the one in which I would ask, "Was machen Sie, wenn ein Vogel auf ihrer Windschutzscheibe scheisst?" They were usually one step ahead of me as everyone really 'gets' comedy over there but that didn't prevent my answer "Ich wuerde ihn nie wieder einladen," from bringing down the house. *(Quite apart from the disgusting nature of this joke, Germans do not call young women 'birds', it is unlikely the term was in use by young British males at the time and the word 'windscreen' had yet to come into common parlance. Oh, and the German word 'Vogel' is masculine not feminine, so goodness knows what everyone was laughing at).*

The final stop on my month-long blitzkrieg of the German halls saw me pitch up at Munich's Fun Palace. As ever, I was treated like a Kaiser and put up at the Adelschloss Hotel - cruet included. And it was there that things began to go Titten vergrossern as they say in those parts.

I was unwinding with a very late cocktail in the Wolf's Lair bistro when, of all people, who should mince in but a very familiar figure; none other than my old mate Brummie Nev. I knew him as a bit of a prankster who managed to touch me for complimentary panto tickets every year – he was particularly fond of my Wishee-Washee. But I digress - you'll probably remember the coffin-faced old gimmer as The Right Honourable Neville Chamberlain, Prime Minister of Great Britain and all the rest of it. Oh, and can I remind you once again that this was late September 1938. In Munich.

Anyhow, old Nev traipsed in looking like the dog had crapped in his silk hat and started hammering on the bar, demanding a pint of Ansells Keg Mild in the broad Birmingham twang he used when he was off duty. I was weighing up whether to sneak off and leave him to his misery when he spotted me and made a beeline over.

"Now then, Nev, business or pleasure?" was all I could manage before he kicked off. It seems he was over on some dicey diplomatic bun-fight which wasn't going too well so he'd dodged security and nipped out of his own hotel for a quickie down the road.

"This jumped-up Jerry's pissin' rings round me," he wailed as I ordered him up a grosse stein of the local firewater. "He's mekkin' me look a royt knobber. I'm at me wits' end, I truly am. I mean, Francis, what would yow dow?"

"Yow dow, Nev? What's that, some kind of boat?"

Nev gazed at me slack-jawed. "No," he sobbed, "what would yow dow?" jabbing his bony finger into my chest.

"Oh, what would I do? OK, what did you say this German was called?"

"Adolf bleedin' 'itler. What kind of pissin' name's that, I ask yow."

Well, I could have replied it was exactly the name Winston kept banging on about a couple of years before at Chartwell. I didn't mention this because I knew Churchill and Nev weren't exactly big buddies. However, I could see Nev was out of ideas so I endeavoured to put him right.

"What you need, Nev, is a plan," I told him and, do you know, he perked up right away.

"A plan of course. That's what I need. Any suggestions, Francis?"

Before I could reply the barman stood to attention in front of us and clicked his heels. "Entschuldigen Sie, meine Herren," he barked, "aber wir schliessen gerade die Bar. Darf ich ihnen ein letztes Getraenk anbeiten?"

Nev's eyes narrowed and his hand slid towards whatever was in his inside pocket. "Is he 'avin a gow?" he asked.

"No, Nev," I explained. "All he said is the bar's shutting and do we want one for the road."

Eyes still like slits, Nev ordered two double rounds on the British taxpayer and continued pumping me for advice.

"Well, Nev," I began, "the first advice I'll pass on to you is something my old mucker Dr Crock, he of And The Crackpots fame, taught me a few years ago."

I could tell he wasn't exactly familiar with Crocky's oeuvre but he had the sense to listen when I said, "The good Doc always reckoned that when the horse is dead then it's best to stop flogging it."

A big fat tear rolled down Nev's cheek. "That unfortunate creature. Dead, yow say."

"Don't fret about the horse, Nev. Think of it as a kind of metaphor. It means don't dig yourself further into a hole."

Nev nodded and smiled for the first time that night. He even gave the barman a ten pfennig tip when he brought our drinks over.

Meanwhile, I was getting firmly into my stride.

"Shake hands with this Hitler bloke," I advised. "Tell him our two countries are united for ever in perpetual peace and harmony. Then get home and prepare for war. I reckon you've got a year at best."

Nev's smile disappeared. "War, Francis? I don't like the sound of that at all. What do yow reckon this preparation would entail."

I remembered what Churchill had told me in 1936 so I relayed it word for word to Nev.

"Triple the size of the RAF, put the armaments industries on full production, get me - er Winston - back at the Admiralty and push Lord Halifax off Westminster Bridge. That should do the trick."

You could see I'd struck a chord but something was still troubling him.

"That's all well and good, Francis," he said, "but I can't go home empty-handed. Oh no! The British public won't stand for it. And then there's the Press. Particularly Lord Beaverbrook."

Then hoist the old bully into the Cabinet an' all, I thought but kept my counsel on that matter. *(It turned out to be Churchill who, in 1940 appointed Beaverbrook as Minister of Aircraft Production and later Minister of Supply).*

171

"Perhaps you could ask Herr Hitler for a gift," I mused. "Something like, I don't know, a cut-glass decanter."

Nev looked doubtful. "So I turn up at London Aerodrome waving a wine jug around."

"I wouldn't exactly suggest waving it but show it to the masses. Hint that it's the first thing Germany has given us since the Black Death."

He nodded. "I think yow are definitely on to something, Francis, I really dow. But not a decanter. Mek me look a royt piss-head." He finished one stein of industrial-strength rocket fuel and dived immediately into the next.

I tried another suggestion. "OK then, how about mutual messages. Er, their mob might say thanks ever such a lot for coming and we could reply something like, 'we've very much enjoyed our visit and we hope you've appreciated this, er, piece of our time.'"

It was a throw-away line but Nev's eyes gleamed.

"Peace in our time, Francis. Now that would truly be something to which our international diplomatic efforts could aspire."

"Er no, what I actually said, Nev, you cloth-eared old ..."

But I didn't get any further as we were interrupted by two tough looking Jerry Johnnies. The taller of the pair, who had a shaven head and an evil-looking scar across the left cheek clicked his heels and bowed to Nev.

"Herr Chamberlain, why here you are," he rasped. "The Fuhrer is most concerned for your safety. Please accompany us back to the hotel. This instant!"

Nev's hand shot instinctively to his inside pocket but he must have thought better of it because he shrugged and got to his feet a bit unsteadily. As the smaller of the pair guided him into a bath-chair and wheeled him away, the duellist turned to me.

"You will forget all you have seen and heard here," he hissed, staring beadily into my eyes. "I repeat you will forget."

In retrospect, my reply, "I didn't realise I was talking to Helmut the Hapless Hypnotist," wasn't the wisest. Grabbing me by the throat, this charmer demonstrated why he was the last person in the world I should be tangling with before depositing me on my back behind the bar.

Now I don't know about you, but I was never too keen on being pushed - or thrown - about by Germans. Nor apparently was Nev who'd got his second wind judging by the struggle he was waging up from his bath-chair. I watched from the hotel's rear entrance as the British PM took a forward roll on to the cobbles and, while the Germans struggled to pick him up, I decided on a course of action.

Nobody was going to treat my mate Nev like that and it was up to me to see that fair play was observed. Parked just up the alley was a massive Mercedes staff car which was obviously going to ferry them all back to their hotel so I decided to tag along for the ride.

The boot of the Merc was so large that it could have easily accommodated Ivy Benson and her Band. Luckily that night they were elsewhere so I went unmolested after I'd jumped in and partially closed the lid. I was surprised, however, to find I had slightly less room than expected due to the presence of two large bundles wrapped tightly in a carpet-like material.

The night had suddenly turned cold; so cold in fact that I wished I had a bit of the carpet to wrap round me. However, I consoled myself that Nev's hotel could only be a few streets away, whereupon I could see the old fool safely to his bedroom. But, as I lay there, this relief quickly began to be assailed by a gnawing anxiety that I would be discovered in the boot and unmasked by the Germans as a complete idiot. A few more sobering moments of straight thinking led me to the conclusion that I should cut my losses and get out of the car with my last few shreds of dignity intact.

But, just as I was about to start banging and hollering for them to stop the vehicle, I caught a snatch of the two Germans' conversation. And, blow me down, if they weren't actually ripping the piss out of poor old Nev, who obviously didn't have a clue what they were on about. Even though their Bavarian accents were fairly impenetrable, I could clearly make out my duellist friend with the bad scar and even worse attitude saying to the Prime Minster, "Here is a nice little ride for you, Mr Walrus," and "Pray tell us, do you keep fish in that stupid hat of yours?" at which point his buddy fell about.

Things went on in this hilarious vein for a few minutes and I began to wonder if they referred to their dear leader as Mr Toothbrush. Somehow I reckoned not.

Yes, something definitely odd was going on, a point that had not escaped Nev as I suddenly heard him complain, "Oi, chum, this ain't the way back to my digs."

Curious, I managed to roll over, push up the boot lid and peep out. And what I saw astounded me. The city was already disappearing behind us. I could see the sodium yellow lights of Munich twinkling as we clattered along a highway between tall pine trees.

What's more, we were climbing and the air was becoming even chillier. Yet, even at that point, I consoled myself that we were in no danger. After all, Nev was here as the guest of the German leader and I was ... well, a bloke who got him the odd matinee ticket to Mother Goose.

I was still comforting myself with this thought when I realised that the Germans had stopped fielding Nev's questions about what was happening. In fact they were ignoring him completely and talking to each other. To his great credit Nev was having none of it and kept pestering the pair until they could stand it no longer and ... crack!

Even in the boot I felt the force of the slap which, as far as I could tell, had smashed Nev's head against the side window. I heard him cry out in pain and then shout angrily, "If I were a few years younger I'd give you a royt pasting, you Jerry bastard."

Say what you like about his policy of appeasement but I'm here to tell you that old Nev Chamberlain had guts to spare. Sadly, it didn't cut much ice with his hosts.

"But you are not a few years younger, Herr Chamberlain," said my pal. "On the contrary you are extremely old. In fact it would appear to my eyes that you are at death's door. Perhaps, we shall be doing you a favour."

Maybe it was dust from the carpets or it could have been the clear implication that Nev would not need a return ticket on this particular journey. Whatever, at that point I lost control and sneezed, very loudly.

The whole car suddenly fell silent and I felt it slow right down.

"Was that you, Karl?" demanded our duellist friend, in German.

"On the contrary, Erich. As you are aware, I am a very healthy specimen."

"If you did not sneeze then ..."

There was another explosive atishoo. Fortunately it came not from me but Nev.

"I'm going to catch my bleedin' death here," he complained, at which Karl and Erich began to laugh like drains. Good old Nev again. He must have twigged that I wasn't too far away, a point confirmed by his next comment.

"You're forgetting that my pal Frankie knows yow two jokers snatched me from the hotel."

"Correct, Herr Chamberlain," replied Erich. "That is why the Gestapo will be dealing with your foolish funny man right now."

"Ja," said Karl, putting his oar in. "And then we will be finally be rid of his terrible jokes. Did I mention, Erich, that I paid good Reichsmarks to see that fellow's very lame performance earlier this evening." Bleedin' sauce!

"Fear not," Erich told his stooge. "Herr Funnybone's farewell performance will have the secret police rolling in the aisles." They both burst out laughing while Nev took the opportunity to launch into another sneezing fit.

The car speeded up again and I could feel we were climbing higher into the mountains. This pair of comedians were not about to leave any traces.

After another ten minutes the car slowed down and turned sharply right. This was it, now or never. As the Mercedes slid to a halt I pushed up the boot lid, jumped out and quickly rolled away from the car.

Everything was pitch black – until Karl the driver switched on a powerful electric torch. To my dismay, in its light I could clearly see Nev being dragged from the car by Erich who forced him to kneel among the pine needles – and him in his best pinstripes too. This was happening about three feet from where I lay as still as the grave. Standing almost on top of me, Erich pulled out a pistol from inside his coat and examined it carefully. Nev gazed defiantly up at him.

"You're a royt pair of knobbers," he said, "I mean, what will Germany gain from killing the British Prime Minister?"

Erich paused in his examination of the pistol and looked down pityingly on Nev.

"Germany you say? On the contrary, Herr Chamberlain, no German would ever stoop to such a vile deed. Your murderers will be clearly identified as Czech extremists, intent on undermining the Sudeten Germans and their claims for independence."

That made as much sense to me as the Schleswig-Holstein Question. *(Famously understood by only three*

176

people; one mad, one dead and Lord Palmerston). However, I could see it struck a chord with Nev.

"That's clever," he acknowledged. "Very clever. And I'd back you to get away with it too ... if it wasn't for all those fellows over there." And he inclined his head in the opposite direction to where I lay.

I'd never had Nev down as a fan of the Tupenny Rush but his diversionary tactic came straight out of the Saturday afternoon cowboy films we'd all sat through as kids. And if it always worked for Hopalong Cassidy ...

As Donner and Blitzen turned to look in the direction Nev indicated, I knew I had to act quickly. Using those long-ago rugby league sessions with Nancy as an inspiration, I pushed forward and launched myself at Erich's legs, striking him perfectly. He collapsed like a pole-axed ox but, as he did so, the gun went off, there was a terrible scream and the light went out.

It can't have been much more than a second or two before Erich scrambled free from my grasp and found the torch but in those brief moments, I was sick with terror that I'd been complicit in killing our Prime Minister.

However, as the scene was illuminated again, I saw that thankfully this was not the case. Nev was still kneeling and breathing heavily, with his head bowed. About five yards away Karl lay on his back with the top of his head blown apart and a huge ugly hole where his right eye used to be. Served the bastard right for not recognising true comedy genius.

I was able to see all this because Erich had bent over to check his pal was actually dead. He then began urgently sweeping the torch all around the area and I realised he'd dropped the pistol. Scrambling quickly to my feet, I shouted, "Surely a tough Teuton like yourself doesn't need a gun to deal with a failed comedian."

The light from Erich's torch swung first towards Nev, who was still kneeling but thankfully breathing, and then into my eyes.

"I shall take great pleasure in breaking your stupid neck," he hissed, "with my own hands."

Without warning he lunged at me, which is precisely what I'd banked on.

"The quicker they come at you," Les had drummed into me during our weekly sparring sessions, "the easier they are to dodge." As Erich flew towards me I took one step to the right and he made a grab. This was a feint, however, as the German realised a fraction too late when I stepped smartly away to the left and snapped two quick rights into his face. As he tottered for a second I swung my left with all the force I could muster ... and landed a beauty. With a cry of pain, Erich spun around and fell to the ground.

Rather than retire to a neutral corner, I followed up with an attempted kick to his head – Les had never exactly worshipped at the Marquis of Queensberry's altar. However, the German had quickly stopped under-estimating the figure he'd tossed behind the hotel bar without a thought.

As I was about to make contact with the side of his head, he grabbed my boot and it was I who now went spinning through the air. I was up quicker than I expected as I actually landed on the car bonnet. Quickly rolling off, I dodged to the far side of the Mercedes and peeped around. The beam of the torch was urgently sweeping the area in which I'd fallen.

"As well as a cheat, you are a coward," shouted Erich disdainfully, all the time moving the beam around. He could have informed me that my Granny Thirkettle was Satan's Whore for all I cared. I would not rise to his bait – not, that is, until he forced me to.

I watched Erich stroll over to Nev and shine his torch on the kneeling figure.

"Pay attention, funny man, I'm sure Herr Chamberlain's neck will be even easier to break than yours" And he grabbed Nev around the throat.

To be honest, if I'd been sure Erich would leave me alone I'd have simply watched him put Nev out of his misery. There, I've said it. But, of course, once that deed had been done Erich wouldn't want me left around to tell inconvenient tales. Yet if I replied he'd know where I was immediately.

It was at this desperate point I recalled Jocky Jardine and the foul-mouthed Wullie. During the interminable afternoons we spent together during his stay with me in Fulham, my ventriloquist chum taught me one or two tricks of his trade, including projecting your voice – or throwing it as the non-cogniscenti would have it.

"Ach," complained Wullie as I'd taken my first faltering steps in the ventriloquial arts, "yer fuckin' great rubber cakehole's all o'er the shoap."

Our potty-mouthed puppet was right of course. As a stage ventriloquist I'd have been less use than a chocolate soup spoon but in a dark forest nobody can see your lips move. The trick, Jocky had drummed into me, was to speak somewhat quieter than your target expected – so he would think that you were further away. Well, it was time to put his teaching to the test.

I took a deep breath. "You can't break the Prime Minister's neck," I informed Erich from the back of my throat.

I knew immediately I'd been successful because the torch beam began to swing in all directions.

"Why ever not, Mr Comedian?" came Erich's reply and I noted with satisfaction that it contained a trace of bemusement.

"Nobody would believe Czech extremists could use such a method." Again the voice came from deep inside me and once more the beam flashed this way and that. The bit

179

about the Czechs was complete rubbish of course but it did give Erich a pause for thought.

"Then how do you suggest I get rid of our friend here?" he asked.

"I suggest that you don't. I suggest that we all come to an understanding."

"What kind of understanding?"

The torch beam was swinging frantically hither and thither and it was clear that Jocky's coaching was bearing fruit. But now I had to think really quickly.

"I suggest that you accept a large sum of money to leave us both alone. That way you could be across the border before anyone found out. And we would say nothing."

There was a moment's silence before Erich replied, "I take it you have the money about your person."

"Of course not," I said. "But you have our word – as English gentlemen – that it will be in your bank account by this time tomorrow."

I don't know if Erich was about to swallow this – it sounded pretty thin even to me – but, in any event, Nev's interjection strangled the whole enterprise at birth.

"I've worked hard for me flamin' tin," he grumbled, "an' no Jerry bastard's gerrin' his mitts on it."

"Christ, Nev, work with me will you," I shouted in exasperation – and immediately regretted my crucial mistake. The comment had not come from the back of my throat; the torch beam illuminating my face testified to that.

For a second, the beam actually moved away from me and I imagined I'd got away with it. But then, to my horror, I saw it was focused on a patch of ground between Erich and me, the patch of ground where his pistol lay.

By my reckoning it was equidistant from both of us but there was no way I would be second to it. The beam of the torch began to move violently up and down and it was obvious Erich had had the same idea.

However, I'd been quicker off the mark and must have been a fraction closer to the gun when disaster struck. In the darkness I failed to notice a prominent tree root and went crashing to the ground. Temporarily stunned, I gazed up and saw Erich, illuminated by his own torch light, stroll over to the weapon and pick it up.

That's it, we were done for. My last hope, the noise of what I thought was a car in the distance, faded as the wind whipped up and began to bend the pine trees as if great waves were rolling over them. I felt flecks of snow on the back of my neck and realised I was shivering with cold and fear.

"Stand to your feet please, Mr Comedian," said Erich in a soothing but sinister voice. He stood the torch on the ground so it illuminated the whole ghastly scene. This was it. I'd never see Nancy or my dear little Julia again. And our new baby would only know its Daddy through old photographs and playbills – plus the scores of tributes from my legion of admirers. I was cursing the moment Eddie Star walked into my dressing room in Bolton and reckoned that I'd do anything just to be taking a hammering from Joshua's thugs right now.

There was nothing for it. I stood up, Erich pointed the pistol at me and fired. I braced myself for the bullet tearing into me - but it didn't. Erich had missed, due entirely to Nev gamely throwing himself at the German and knocking him off balance.

I could see Erich on one knee and thought I might have a chance of taking him. But before I could move he pointed the gun at me again – why he didn't fire then I'll never know. Instead he stood up, swung round and levelled the weapon at the top of Nev's skull. There were gunshots, a human head exploded and a body slumped lifelessly to the ground.

History buffs among you will already have worked out whose head exploded. I don't know who looked more surprised; me or Erich as his brains tumbled out of his broken skull.

As he collapsed to the ground I stood perfectly still while a figure sprinted past me, stood over Erich and put two more bullets into him – one in each in eye. A moment later he shot out Karl's remaining eye to claim the set. Nothing like being sure, say I.

Then our saviour tucked his pistol into his belt, knelt down gently next to Nev and examined the old man's head. He sighed with relief, picked up the torch and walked over to me, shining the light in my face and carefully looking me up and down.

"Thank the lord," he said.

"Unless you're some kind of angel, I'd rather thank you," I told him.

"Thank me!" he snapped. "I deserve no thanks. My stupidity nearly led to the death of our PM." Again he shone the light on Nev.

"You sure you're OK, sir."

"Yeah," replied Nev, "but it's bleedin' brass monkeys out here."

Our rescuer dashed to the Mercedes, tore a blanket off the back seat and wrapped Nev in it. He helped the Prime Minister to his feet and supported him towards a small Volkswagen at the edge of the clearing. How he'd got so close without the German hearing the car, I'll never know.

When Nev was safely settled on the back seat, our rescuer walked back to the Mercedes, opened the boot and beckoned me over.

"Look," he said as he pulled back the carpets to reveal the bodies of two young men. "This pair would have been blamed for your deaths. They'd probably have been found a few miles away near the Swiss border. Cornered by the Gestapo or so the story would have gone."

I looked a bit closer at our saviour. His fair wavy hair framed a rather boyish, somewhat mischievous countenance. He looked more like an apple scrumper than a ruthless assassin .

"Who are you?" I said.

"The name's Frobisher," he replied, extending his right hand which I readily took. "I suppose I'm what you'd call a diplomat of sorts."

I smiled for the first time in goodness knows how long. "Well, your type of diplomacy was effective with old Erich there," I told him.

Frobisher smiled back. "You mean the duellist?"

For a moment I was nonplussed. "How did you know he had a duelling scar?"

Grinning again, Frobisher added, "No, I mean that when they find these two clowns it will appear as if they've killed each other in a duel. Of course it won't fool anybody as duellists don't generally shoot each other three or four times – bad form if nothing else. But no-one will be able to say anything tomorrow, or rather later today. Here, help me drag them into position."

I pulled Karl to within ten feet of Erich while Frobisher wiped the handle of his pistol and placed it in Karl's hand. Then he and I jumped into the VW at the edge of the clearing and within seconds we were speeding back towards Munich.

"With any luck nobody will have missed the PM and when he appears in the conference chamber tomorrow, Herr Hitler will just have to grin and bear it," said Frobisher in between humming the overture to HMS Pinafore.

"But why," I wondered, "does Hitler want dear old Nev dead?"

"He doesn't really," explained Frobisher. "Ideally Adolf would rather have Britain as an ally in the coming war against the Soviets. But he's sniffed the wind and realised that's not going to happen. So he's prepared to sweep us out of the way while he's ready and we're not before he's forced to deal with Uncle Joe Stalin. This little pantomime was meant to spark off a chain of events in which Britain would have had no choice but to go to war. What actually happened is going to make it a lot more difficult for Hitler. Eh, sir?"

Frobisher glanced back towards Nev who showed his teeth wolfishly as he smiled. "You said it, young 'un. I'm going make that bastard sing for his supper – or breakfast – later on. Let's see what did you say, Frankie, earlier on? Peace in our time."

"Actually, Nev, what I said was ..."

"That should do the trick," added Nev. "Course I'll get portrayed in many quarters as some sort of soft knobber but the important thing is we'll buy time to build up our armaments industry, triple the size of the RAF get Winston back and what was the other thing you suggested, Frankie?"

"Er, I forget," I said, trying to put out of my mind the image of Frobisher dunking Lord Halifax in the Thames.

Nev leaned back and began to chuckle, "I remember it now," he said. "You very bad boy."

As Nev continued guffawing, I quizzed Frobisher about the likely official impact of what had happened this evening.

"Nothing at all – officially" he said. "I mean, it won't exactly be all over the front page of the Daily Herald ..."

"But unofficially?"

"Well, certainly all the right people will hear about it."

"Including Winston?" I whispered as Nev continued to chuckle.

"Especially Winston," murmured Frobisher.

Figuring he might already have said too much, Frobisher clammed up for a while and concentrated on getting us back into Munich as quickly as possible. I thought Nev had dropped off to sleep but as we reached the outskirts of the city I heard him chuckling once more and repeating, "I've got the bastard now."

Without looking back, Frobisher said, "I'd get used to thinking of him as Herr Hitler, sir. I mean, you will be shaking hands with the bastard in a few hours."

Nev snorted. "Not that bastard. No, I've finally got one over on our Ozzie. God rest his soul."

"Who's he on about?" I wondered out loud.

"His brother Austen," explained Frobisher. "Foreign Sec in the Twenties. If you remember he got a load of credit, the Nobel Prize no less, for the Locarno Treaty."

"Well, it's funny you should say that," I replied and went on to tell him about the exchange scheme and how it led to my fluency in German.

Frobisher beamed. "Hear that, sir," he told Nev, "if it hadn't have been for your half-brother's work, young Frankie here would never have known what those murderers were up to. So I'd say, in effect, Austen saved your life tonight."

We heard no more chuckles from the back.

Fifteen minutes later the car pulled up outside the Adelschloss Hotel but as I made to get out Frobisher put his hand on my arm.

"That was impressive work back there," he said. "Maybe we'll use you another time."

"I doubt it. I don't plan to go near Germans ever again."

"You never know," chuckled Frobisher. "They might be planning to come and visit you. Have a long and happy life Mr Funnybone."

I got out and was about to shut the door when I had a real brainwave.

"There is something you could do, Mr Frobisher," I said. "You see, I'm in Germany because of problems with my wife's Dad."

"Not been letting him win at dominoes, eh?"

"No, I eloped with the apple of his eye."

"Ah well, love's young whatsitsname and all that. Who is your father-in-law?"

"Sir Joshua Protheroe."

"What did he get the knighthood for?"

"About five thousand guineas."

Frobisher burst out laughing and then I told him about the desperadoes on my trail. He stopped chuckling and shook his head in annoyance.

"Bloody amateurs," he grumbled. "You can set out for home as soon as you like. By the time you get back Sir Joshua will have been warned that if you are harmed then he and his scary gang will answer to me and my even scarier gang. After all you are now officially a national treasure."

"I've done nothing."

Frobisher shook his head vehemently. "On the contrary, you've given your country breathing space. It could prove vitally important in the long run."

"I was lucky," I replied. "Besides I'm a comedian not ... whatever you are."

Frobisher smiled again and said, "If you're a comedian then tell us a joke."

There could be only one, the joke that had captivated southern Germany for the last month. I coughed and glanced at Nev who by now was fast asleep.

"OK," I said. "What do you do if a bird shits on your windscreen?"

Frobisher grinned. "I don't know. What do you do if a bird shits on your windscreen?"

When I told him the punch-line, Frobisher went off into such fits of laughter that I thought he was having a heart attack.

"Priceless," was all he could splutter, before easing the VW shakily away from the kerb.

Indeed, when I met him again, in similar strained circumstances four years later, Frobisher briefly forgot about his troubles to whisper through parched and swollen lips, "Got that old windscreen clean yet?"

Chapter Ten: The Short Goodbye

Using my vast experience, I'd say that most showbiz memoirs tend, unsurprisingly, to put the shiniest gloss on a life. When things have gone well, make no mistake you'll hear about it in glorious detail. And, after misjudgements, crises or actual horrors, what usually emerges is in no way negative. On the contrary, show folk will claim to have learned valuable life lessons as we triumph over adversity – even though the original mess is usually down to our own stupidity.

You need look no further for an example of this sunny outlook than at the end of the previous chapter after my incredible survival in the forest outside Munich. Or later in this memoir when I see off another similarly murderous attack.

Yet, try as I might, I find it difficult to put any positive spin on the story of my mother and her death from cancer. I did consider leaving the matter out completely, arguing that readers like yourself opened this volume to be entertained and not clubbed around the head. Or maybe confine myself to one or two uplifting lines about how Mum bore her final struggle with cheerful stoicism, even though she didn't particularly.

But if I did that I'd be excluding a large part of what made me who I am. So those among you who can bear to, should plough on and readers who haven't the stomach for it, simply move to the next chapter where I discover penicillin and a cure for the common cold.

Eight months had passed since my outstanding bravery/incredible stupidity/ unbelievable luck in that south German forest and by May 1939 it was clear that, as predicted by himself, our Mr Walrus had indeed been made to look a right soft knobber by their Mr Toothbrush. Hitler's admittedly half-hearted endorsement of Nev's manifesto for perpetual peace was shown up for the worthless drivel it was when Germany had strong-armed its way into the rest of Czechoslovakia two months earlier.

Since then we hadn't needed Winston to remind us that war was inevitable and everyone's eyes remained eastwards, this time nervously focused on Poland.

Yet, despite the deteriorating international situation, I was preoccupied by things much closer to home – in fact, at home. Now two weeks overdue with our second child, Nancy had assumed the shape of one of the barrage balloons that were springing up above London's docks and parks – and with a temper big enough to match.

Nothing was right for her. Not the lovely weather which was apparently too damn sticky; the doctors who were treating her, no bleedin' idea; or even my own heroic attempts to make things better, too flamin' half-hearted. There was just no pleasing my wife and to tell you the truth, looking back over things I reckon this was the rockiest patch in our marriage. *(Even rockier apparently than when Nancy caught him canoodling with Janis Joplin at Altamont).*

So the only positive spin I can put on what happened to my mother is that it placed our little troubles into perspective.

I took the telephone call early on a Saturday and at first I couldn't make out who was on the other end, so subdued was the voice. It was, therefore, with some considerable shock that I belatedly realised I was talking to my Dad.

"It's your mother, son," he told me after I'd shooed everyone away. "She wants to see you."

Confound the man, we'd been through this I don't know how many times. Was his memory on the blink?

"Dad, don't you recall," I told him as patiently as I could. "You're both coming down in six weeks. I know it'll be Mum's first time here but don't worry we'll look after her."

There was a long silence on the other end of the line before Les answered carefully and without any apparent emotion, "I'm afraid six weeks might be too late, son."

Despite the fact that I was in my mid-twenties and a big boy now, the news that Mum was dying came as such a sudden, awful hammer blow, I thought I was about to have a heart attack. I staggered back, dropping the receiver and had to scrabble around for it to reassure Les that I'd not passed out.

Economical with his words as ever, he told me that Mum's 'trouble' had started a few months previously with a persistent stomach ache. She hadn't gone to the surgery immediately and by the time the quacks had finally diagnosed what it was, things had already gone too far.

"It would be good if you could see your way to visiting us," Les said simply and I fell over myself to assure him I'd be on my way as soon as possible.

When I told Nancy the grim news, whatever troubles we were facing vanished in a tearful embrace. She was typically practical in the matter of other arrangements too. I'd been due to round off a triumphant week at the Collins Music Hall in Islington that evening but Nancy assured me that she'd sort out a late replacement and virtually shoved me on to the train at Euston.

As the engine picked up speed through the northern suburbs, I fought back tears as I tried to come to terms with the fact that these were sights my mother would never see. I was also forced to confront the gnawing guilt of the son who's spent too much time away.

Don't get me wrong, I had seen Mum since Nancy's non-wedding day. Even though I'd never been near Protheroe Hall since then, she and Les had come to my show on the North Pier in Blackpool and the four of us had had a lively time staying at The Norbreck Hydro. But, imagining that she'd be around for ever, I could not deny that I'd neglected my mother.

This tearful, self-hating mood hardly lifted during the entire journey and I stepped down from the connection at Butterthwaite Station still furtively wiping my eyes. It was thus that I didn't immediately notice who was taking my ticket until I heard the greeting, "Franny! You're back!"

I looked up with a start and there, blocking my way, stood my old pal Colin 'Stinker' Stanworth in his smart blue London Midland and Scottish Railways uniform. The last time I came across him I'd had half a ton of rubber smothering my bonce and Mum was fit and well.

Stinker continued to greet me. "Well, well, the wanderer returns. Good to see you, old pal. I do hope you have a valid ticket."

By the time I'd extracted the proof from my inside pocket, Stinker had become more subdued.

"I'm sorry to hear your Mum's not well, Fran," he said, awkwardly shifting from one foot to the other.

"How do you know she's ill?"

"It's just that my mother was ... well, things do get around don't they."

I considered tearing into him for idly gossiping about such a tender subject but what would be the point?

"You're right, Col, things do have a habit of getting around," I said, patting him on the shoulder.

"I'll tell Jean I spoke to you," he shouted as I walked off.

I turned and shouted back through a curtain of steam, "Jean who?"

"Jean Tomlinson, as was," he yelled. "Did nobody tell you we were wed?"

Aha! The hideous twins I saw Jean pushing around three summers ago suddenly made perfect sense.

"Congratulations," I told him after retracing my steps and shaking his hand. "Any kids?"

"Yes," he said proudly. "Twins! Ralph and Ernest. They're three now."

Somehow even this news could not lift my spirits but I made a huge effort to appear interested.

"They sound delightful," I said, shaking his hand once more. "I really should carry a box of cigars around with me."

"I'll tell Jean I ran into you. She really likes your act."

"A girl with taste!"

"Yes, she always has a big smile whenever you're mentioned."

I was unsure how to take this piece of news but was comforted that at least Jean hadn't told her hubby about our messy encounter in the garage.

It was a pleasant early summer day so I decided to travel the mile or so from the station up to Protheroe Hall on foot. Given my current state of mind, I'd simply taken it for granted that Butterthwaite would be mired in depression, much as it was when I was last here three years before. But, to my surprise, the place appeared in rude health, positively buzzing in fact.

My walk took me past two of the five Protheroe mills from each of which there was an infernal clatter of looms. That racket, plus the mills' chimneys belching out the blackest smoke, indicated that they were in full production. Sir Joshua was growing richer in front of my eyes.

I walked on, hoping not to be recognised but fully expecting to be. So I was rather put out that not one passer-by spared me a second glance. Other matters to think about, I suppose.

Protheroe Hall too was showing more signs of life than I'd anticipated. As I strolled through the gates of the estate, past the stream where Lake took his bath, half a dozen servant girls scurried past in their short brown pleated skirts and bright yellow singlets, obviously on the way to play an evening rounders match.

I may have looked a bit closer at them than I should – just to ensure none were relatives, you understand –

because one of the girls turned round and stuck her tongue out at me before rushing to re-join her cackling coven. For some reason, the incident reminded me of Jean Tomlinson again.

The first person I saw as I approached the main building was my little brother Tommy who appeared from the stable block.

"Franny," he boomed, for Tommy was not so little any more. "You made it!"

He gave me a bear hug, during which I was astonished to discover that my youngest brother was a full head taller than me.

"Tommy," I told him, "you appear to have turned into Primo Carnera." *(Known as "The Ambling Alp", Primo Carnera, 1906-67, a 6ft 6in tall Italian boxer, was world heavyweight champion for a year until June 1934).*

Grinning, I aimed a shadow right-hander at his head and we ended up circling each other in mock battle until Tommy suddenly dropped his guard and grimaced.

"We shouldn't be doing this," he said and set off towards the hall.

I followed him on tiptoes so I could put my arm round his shoulder.

"I'm sure Mum wouldn't mind us having a jape," I consoled him, adding, "Does she know how ill she really is?"

Tommy looked down at me in surprise. "Of course not," he said. "How could we tell her that?"

I was mulling over how I would explain to Mum why I had suddenly come home to see her only six weeks before she was due to visit me, when who should appear round the corner of the main building but my Dad and Sir Joshua deep in conversation. Joshua was first to spot me followed closely by Les, doubtless alerted by his boss's sudden uncharacteristic silence.

"I'll speak to you later," I heard him tell Les before he disappeared into the house without a second glance in my direction. Meanwhile Les rushed over and embraced me warmly. I was comforted to discover that his overalls still had that distinctive smell, a mixture of diesel oil and horse manure.

"Oh, son, I'm so, so relieved that you're here," he told me, struggling to hold back his tears.

"I wouldn't be anywhere else, Dad. Despite our host's warm welcome."

Les stared at the front entrance through which Joshua had just disappeared.

"Don't judge him too harshly, Francis," he said. "Sir Joshua's been good to us since Minnie started with her ... trouble. He's given me as much time off as I want. I've appreciated that and I know your mother has too."

I could see Les was trying ever so hard to stop the tears coming but he couldn't manage it. Embracing this teak tough man sobbing his heart out, I gazed at Tommy who shrugged helplessly. Eventually Les shook himself gently free of my arms, took out a yellowish handkerchief, dabbed his eyes and blew his nose.

"You've not come here to see me carry on like a soft wench," he sniffed.

"Dad, for goodness sake, carry on how you like."

Les blew his nose again and tucked away the handkerchief.

"In fact you're not here to see me at all. Come on," he said and walked briskly up the front steps to the hall. I hesitated for a second, uneasy over encountering Joshua but much more, I had to admit shamefacedly, about seeing my mother. I wanted to be with her - I did truly - but not in the state I knew she was in. Nevertheless I followed Les.

Walking into the entrance hall was an unsettling experience, primarily because I could not remember ever coming into the building through the front door. I'd lived here twenty years so I must have used the main entrance sometimes. I just could not recall ever doing it.

Les led me off the main hall, through a nondescript door and into familiar territory. We were on a long dark corridor which ran to the back of the house and an entrance into the stables yard. Halfway along the corridor was a small door which hid the way down to our family's quarters. The stairs were a lot narrower than I remembered and my parents' bedroom, as Les ushered me in, seemed tiny.

"I'll let you talk to her on your own," he said.

"Please, Dad, I don't mind you staying," I responded quickly but he had already turned and was making his way slowly and painfully back up the narrow staircase.

Thankfully my mother was asleep so I had a few moments to get used to the changes in her before I painted on my smile. Her long grey hair spread across the stained pillow like sunbeams. I think whoever did this had meant to make her look peaceful and serene but to me the whole tableau was unsettling, as if she'd already been laid out. There was hardly any sunlight in the first place, the only natural illumination coming from a grille where the wall met the ceiling at ground level.

I could hardly help noticing that Mum had lost a lot of weight but was relieved it wasn't as much as I'd been fearing.

She opened her eyes and smiled when she saw it was me.

"You're here," she whispered.

I bent down and kissed her on the forehead.

"Yes, Mum, I'd heard you were a touch off-side so I thought I'd give you a bit of a tonic."

My mother smiled again but it was a sad smile and at that moment I knew that she had already guessed how poorly she was. With great effort she beckoned me to sit on the candlewick bedspread which I did as carefully as I could.

As I sat, I became aware of an unpleasant smell and immediately chided myself for even noticing it; the poor woman was bed-bound, for goodness sake. Yet the foul odour wasn't half as unsettling as what came next.

"Francis," my mother wheezed, "I have something to say. About your father."

"What about Les?"

She stared desperately at me.

"Not Leslie!" she gasped. "I want to talk about your father."

The moment I became aware of what she was saying, I was up off the bed as if electrocuted.

"Please, Mum," I insisted desperately. "I don't want to know."

"But Francis, I need to explain," she whispered between laboured breaths, "I must do it."

Oh, Jesus and Mary, this was her flamin' confession. Which I did not want to hear under any circumstances! I put my face close up to hers and said as soothingly as I could, "Look, Mother, there really is no need for this."

And I silenced her protests by holding up my hand.

"Les is my father and always has been ... as much as you're my Mum. Nothing else is important. I love you no matter what."

Again, apologies are in order because I am aware that this is extremely heavy going for a showbiz memoir. I'm also ready to wager that some of you are thinking, 'In just a minute he'll get his foot stuck in the chamber pot and hop around like a prick.' On past form it could easily have happened. But not this time.

Instead my mother continued to wrestle with her troubled and troubling conscience. Displaying heroic effort, she pushed herself up on to one elbow.

"Francis," she gasped, "can you forgive me?"

This came from a woman who'd brought up her family in all the right ways and given each of us everything she could. And she'd never laid a finger on me – unless I'd deserved it, which I frequently had.

By now I was almost pleading with her. "Mum, I would forgive you like a shot, if there was anything to forgive. But there isn't. You were ... you *are* a fantastic mother to me – to all of us – and there's an end to it. "

I silenced her wavering objections, adding, "Now stop this silly talk and let's make plans for when you come down to visit us. We'll have a boat trip down to see The Cutty Sark. Then a visit to the Greenwich Observatory. You'll be able to put your watch right there."

She smiled at my prattling, heaved a great sigh of relief and sank contentedly back down on to the bed. I returned her smile, hoping she hadn't noticed the film of tears that was obscuring my vision.

I had intended to get her reminiscing about my Granny Thirkettle's later-life eccentricities, including the time Gran had put linseed oil on her porridge. Or when she decided to give Ronnie's goldfish a bath.

"Blackburn Barn Owl," Mum would sigh when Les was out of earshot. "Blackburn barm-pot, more like."

But our fraught exchange had evidently exacted a heavy toll and her tired eyes were already closed.

An anxious ten-minute vigil followed, during which I thought she'd stopped breathing at least three times. When my fears finally subsided, I crept out, tiptoeing quickly up the stairs - straight into Sir Joshua. Now I found myself hoping that *he* couldn't see the tears in my eyes. I broke the awkward silence.

"All the mills seem to be working at full tilt."

Joshua smiled, and his permanently florid features took on an even more vivid crimson shade, a most unsettling sight.

"War's on its way," he said.

For a moment I thought I'd misheard him. "Sorry, what's on its way?"

"Conflict with Germany," he hissed, as if it were better that only he and I were party to this information. "And, not that it's any of your business, but I've signed up to a big War Office contract. Making webbing for the soldiers' uniforms."

"Oh, er, bully for you. What is webbing, by the way?"

He leaned over and whispered into my ear. "Webbing is the stuff that'll mek me a fuckin' fortune ... one which neither you nor she will ever see."

To be honest I was more shocked by the swearing than Joshua's faultless grammar or the plans to disinherit his daughter. However, I decided not to take him on, instead adopting an uncharacteristically humble demeanour.

"It's been good of you to treat Les so well," I said, "and allow me to stay here."

I trailed off into silence, aware that my thanks sounded false and rather hollow. After all, my father-in-law's hand had been somewhat forced by the threat of a visit from the diplomatic corps' violently non-diplomatic section.

Joshua must have been thinking along the same lines because he told me, "For a comic, you've got mixed up with a right rum bunch. But, think on, make sure no harm happens to that bairn or the new baby I'll come after you no matter who your new pals are."

Recalling that the bastard had been planning to have me slaughtered, I wasn't letting him have all his own way on this. I stood about a foot from Joshua, a position from which I was able to look down on him.

"Don't worry, Pops," I said and watched as his face turned a deeper crimson. "There's about as much chance of any bad stuff happening to our children as there is of anything nasty happening to me. And you know how unlikely that is, don't you. Stay healthy."

Well, what would we have done with his fortune anyway?

I won't claim to have exactly swaggered down the steps of Protheroe Hall but I did pause to reflect on a job well done and, for a moment, it was Lord Francis Thirkettle not Sir Joshua Bothersome who was master of all he surveyed. Then I remembered my mother and the triumphal mood evaporated.

I made my way slowly to the garage where my not-so-little-brother was busy drawing a tarpaulin over a vehicle in the far corner so I had a quick stroll around this place full of different memories.

There, for instance, was the pipe to which Les chained Lake and from where the bodyguard had smashed me across the knee with an adjustable spanner. Over there stood my bike, the very machine against which Jean Stanworth, nee Tomlinson, rested her backside as I gave a new twist to my famous catchphrase. And in the corner, still gleaming nearly three years on was the wedding landau in which Nancy and I had made our helter-skelter getaway while Joshua executed an acrobatic back-flip over the churchyard wall. Ah, happy days!

Tommy must have noticed me smiling because he abandoned the tarp and joined me next to the coach. At the same instant Les appeared in the doorway and within a few seconds we were a merry little threesome, remembering the great day.

"I could hear the Bentley clattering nearer all the time," Tommy told us as he recalled his fourteen-year-old whippersnapper self steering the carriage down the old hall path to throw Joshua and co off the scent.

"But I managed to jump off the landau and open the gate before they could catch me. Then I dodged into the woods and from there I could peep over the wall and watch them rushing around like rats on fire. They reminded me of The Keystone Cops."

The three of us laughed fit to burst as if we were watching it at the cinema then and there. Les even began pointing at a non-existent image on the far wall. Our laughter must have been so cathartic because, without any discernible break or change of emotion, we were suddenly sobbing and hugging each other.

I'd always taken considerable pride that I hadn't blubbed since I was a nipper yet this felt so right. Tommy was still trying his utmost to bottle up the tears but Les just let go and I loved him all the more for it.

"Don't worry, Dad, she's going to a better place," I said as I hugged him tightly. What did it matter that I didn't believe a pious word of it?

Les detached himself from my embrace and, with the sleeve of his overall, rubbed his eyes which were bloodshot and sad. He gazed at me beseechingly.

"What did she tell you, son?"

"Not much, Dad." I lied, figuring not for the first time that dishonesty was very much the best policy. "Just how pleased she was to see me. Tell you what, let's all three of us go to the pub and get plastered."

Which is just what we did.

Mum passed away in her sleep three nights later. Ever since I'd first spoken to her she'd drifted in and out of consciousness, sometimes heavily sedated to dull the pain and on other occasions too tired to do much else. I was therefore spared further death-bed confession attempts.

I would like nothing better than to report that Les bore his loss with quiet dignity. But the truth was that the poor man came apart at the seams like an old cushion.

Although he'd known for a while what was coming, Mum's death nearly crushed all the life out of him as well. Our Dad was in such a bad way that my brothers and sisters drew up a rota to keep watch by his bedside and I felt duty-bound to hang around and take my turn.

During Mum's illness Les had started sleeping in my old room so as not to disturb her and now he couldn't face returning to their bedroom. It was in that familiar small space that I found him late in the evening.

As I squeezed in - there was barely enough space for a bed and an armchair - my sister Rose got to her feet and we hugged. Over her shoulder I could see Les sound asleep, his mouth wide open.

"I put a sleeping draught in his Horlicks," she explained. "So there's no real need for you to stay."

"Maybe not but I reckon it's important that I do."

Rose smiled, patted my forearm and left us. Despite my noble bravado, I dreaded Les waking up; there was nothing I could say that would possibly comfort him. In the event, I needn't have worried. Rose had given him enough knockout drops to flatten a rhino so he stayed out for the count. Which was lucky because I too was asleep within five minutes of flopping down into the armchair.

Four hours later I was awakened by a rough shaking and found myself staring up at my brother Ronnie. It was the first time we'd met since, as Brian O'Reilly, I'd saved him from being sacked by Mary Cunliffe. You'd think he'd be eternally grateful but then you didn't know our Ronnie.

"Lounging there asleep doesn't make up for anything," he informed me prissily.

"And a very good evening to you, Ronald," I replied, getting to my feet and stretching. "I'm sorry I made a complete monkey out of you that time in front of Mary Cunliffe. To be sure, so I am."

"I'd forgotten all about it," he said in a throwaway tone which told me that every last humiliating detail was burned into his psyche. He hadn't finished either.

"I just meant," he added, "that it's a bit late to play the good son when you've not been around these parts for years." And he sat down in the armchair I'd vacated.

There was no way I wanted an argument which might wake Les so I simply told Ronnie, "I may have been away but he's still my Dad."

I could see that Ronnie was inwardly debating whether to respond with the obvious snide comment so I made his decision for him.

"And if you want to make anything more out of that remark then we can always go outside and settle things." He decided to button it.

Four days after mum died, Protheroe Hall came to a halt for her funeral. With Sir Joshua's permission, Tommy hitched up Bess and Dolly to an old cart he'd discovered rotting in an out-building behind the stables. He told me proudly that he'd had to evict a colony of mice before man-handling the vehicle from its long-time home into the garage.

However, Tommy's weeks of dedicated effort had led to a remarkable transformation. Gone were the splintered boards and wheels with half their spokes missing. In their place was a sleek, shiny vehicle, done out in the Protheroe livery and festooned with lilies adorning my mother's coffin. Tommy, in a smart black frock coat, sat proudly behind the horses, also plumed in black, and steered the vehicle towards the chapel. It was his own tribute to Mum and we all agreed there could have been none finer.

Following the carriage were members of our family, Rose supporting Les, and behind us was the rest of the hall staff and a few of Mum's old friends from the town. I walked alongside a wheezing, waddling Nancy who, despite my pleas, had arrived back at her birthplace the day before. Unsurprisingly, she'd been smothered with love and kisses from her mother and sisters and, moreover, had managed to avoid seeing her Dad until half an hour before the funeral when an attempt to speak to him had ended with Sir Joshua cutting her dead.

As we approached the chapel, I squeezed Nancy's arm.

"You OK?" I asked her.

"I'm fine," she replied with a tired smile. "I just wish the little blighter would use a couple of his kicks to force his way out of here."

"I didn't mean that," I told her, "I just reckon it's a bit off being snubbed by your father."

Nancy shrugged and said, "Franco, you've just lost your mother. At least I have a chance to get my Dad back – in the unlikely event I should ever want to."

I glanced over my shoulder to where, at a safe distance from the horses, a sober-suited Sir Joshua was bringing up the rear of the procession with Lady Agatha. For a moment I caught his eye and shook my head as if to say, "If you don't make up now it could be too late." He stared straight through me.

Two hours after Mum was laid to rest in the graveyard plot reserved for the estate's most loyal retainers, Nancy's waters broke. And, deep into the night, she was delivered of our first son, a 10lb 2oz giant. As her mother and sisters took turns in fussing the new arrival and carefully left an exhausted Nancy to her own thoughts, I noted that the happy family group was not quite complete. Of Joshua there was no sign whatsoever.

Chapter Eleven: The Day War Broke Out

The day war broke out I was ambling across Hyde Park, glumly wondering if I could manage to keep down a spot of lunch when who should I run into but my bosom buddy, Robb Wilton. This bout of mid-day Sunday gloom had been brought on by another old pal, Brummie Nev, who'd just been on the radio declaring war on Germany with all the passion of the one-armed, one-eyed bloke who whispered out the Housey Housey numbers on Southport Pier. *(Housey Housey was the original name for bingo).*

Even though it was a nice warm morning with a late summer haze about it, I hadn't been feeling too chipper anyway as I was still struggling to get over my mother's death three months before.

So Nev's tight-arsed delivery put the tin hat on it, reminding us all that, at the moment we needed someone to lead the nation into battle, he wasn't exactly Charlemagne ... or even Charlie Chester. It also brought back to me what had not happened over the previous year.

I mean, I wasn't expecting the Freedom of Westminster and its environs for saving the miserable old bugger's skin – after all I had to admit that Nev had saved mine too. But since September 1938 there hadn't been so much as a dicky bird from our Mr Walrus. No thank you letters, Christmas cards or even a postal order. I was hardly angling for a guided tour of 10 Downing Street and tea in the garden - but it would have been nice to be asked. And I'd have gone like a shot.

So I was in a less than sanguine mood when I nearly stepped on old Robb Wilton as he gazed out wistfully at the rowing boats on the Serpentine.

"Hello, Robb," I said as we shook hands, "you thinking of joining the Navy?"

"Not likely, Frankie," he wheezed in that much-loved bumbling Scouse lilt, "I get seasick when I run de bath. Besides the Missus would never let me."

"Don't talk to me about wives," I groaned. So he did.

"Speaking of the old lady, you'll never guess what she just said to me."

When Robb talked his arms had a tendency to wander all over the shop, as if he'd been freshly unwrapped; one minute they were smoothing down his wispy, unruly, grey hair, the next they were scratching his backside.

I looked him up and down and, being in no mood for guessing games, came straight out with it.

"Well, by the look of things I'd reckon your perceptive lady wife said something like, 'what good are you?' "

It was simple rough and tumble among two entertainers at the very top of their game. But, in the manner of bluff Yorkshiremen and no-nonsense Scots, I'd forgotten how thin-skinned Scousers could be.

It's my experience that the ones who say they don't give a tuppenny damn about what people think of them are invariably the most sensitive. So it proved with Robb who looked really hurt. He even paused in his windmill impression.

"My Missus would *never* say dat about me," he whined, "So I'll thank you not to repeat it." *(Robb Wilton, 1881-1957, was a Liverpool-born comedian famous in the 1940s for his catchphrase, "The day war broke out." It was usually followed by, "My Missus said to me ... what good are you?")*

What Robb's wife had actually said, he was keen to emphasise, was that Britain had declared war on Germany.

"That's right," I replied, eager to take the sting out of the situation. "The Brummster ... er, our esteemed Prime Minister's just been on the wireless, waving his pension book in a particularly threatening manner. Anyway what are you up to?"

Robb scratched his backside and told me he was looking for someone to make up a foursome at cards this afternoon.

"Cards," I said warily, "who's playing?

Robb looked at me innocently. "Well," he said, "there's me, Teddy Ray and Tom Handley."

Now I don't know about any of you lot, but I've never really gone in for lazy stereotyping. But the prospect of a few hands of Montana Red Dog with a trio of Scouse comics? Do me a favour, Wack! In fact I can honestly say that the only time I've ever been part of a Liverpool card school, before or since, was in that guard's van during A Hard Day's Night when I was Wilfrid Brambell's body double. *(A crack squad of lawyers, film technicians and bullshit spotters is checking this unlikely assertion, frame by frame).*

"Sorry, Robb, old lad," I told him, "but I'll have to turn you down."

"It's a pity," Robb informed me. "There's a spot all ready and waiting for you at our little green baize table."

I decided to move the conversation on.

"Strikes me," I said, "it's a bit risky that you Merseyside merriment merchants are all booked down here at the same time."

"How do you mean?" Robb asked with a look of suspicion.

"Well, we don't want too many Londoners dying of laughter, do we! Especially now there's a war on."

"Very funny," he said, shaking his head in synch with the rest of his floppy body. "You should be on de stage. Besides none of us is playing anywhere. We're just down in de Smoke for a bit of sight-seeing and racing at Kempton on our own without de little women."

"You said you'd just spoken to your missus."

"De cottonwoollybacks where you come from, don't they have phones? Perhaps you all shout very loud. Eh? Eh?"

Fearing that my sides would literally split asunder if I remained in Robb's company a moment longer, I told him I'd consider the kind card school offer and wrote down the name of his hotel on a handy scrap of paper. Then I took my leave and promptly dropped the paper into an even handier litter bin, one of the few in London that hadn't been melted down to build an aircraft carrier.

Frankly, I was already sick of the war and it hadn't been going two hours. I was especially fed up of bumping into people charging around with their stupid faces pointed skywards as if expecting to see Hitler himself straddling a barrage balloon and lobbing incendiaries at them.

The evil axis of Birmingham and Liverpool having completely seen off my appetite, I decided there was nothing for it but to head homewards and endure the inhuman wailing of our sprog. The bugger was only twelve weeks old but already as big as half a house with a voice to match.

And that reminds me, the old fool hasn't been near Cold Tits in weeks and furthermore *(in the interests of brevity Frankie's incessant bleating about family visiting at the Wisteria Home has been censored).*

Anyway, back to the story. On the way back to Earl's Court I reflected that if Goering's Luftwaffe needed guiding towards London they could do a lot worse than follow the screams of young Balthazar as he terrorised our household. And, before you ask, I had nothing to do with the name. It was Nancy's idea – something about a favourite uncle and The Gospel According to St Luke.

When I arrived home, Jennifer the housemaid was waltzing around the sitting room while our wailing offspring vomited with gusto all over her shoulder. Ignoring them both was Nancy, buried deep in my favourite armchair and reading a film script while drawing deeply on a Black Sobranie. I do give my wife credit for stopping smoking while she was carrying the baby, a good 40 years before the practice became fashionable. I also damn her for being stupid enough to start again straight after. However, seeing her glare at me, I kept these views to myself.

"You could have taken the baby out for a walk," she snapped.

"I had no idea he could walk."

"I take it you are capable of pushing a pram?"

"I was the last time I checked."

"Very well, you can take him out for the afternoon," declared Nancy as two-year-old Julia capered across the hearth rug. "Give us all a bit of peace."

I contemplated playing the bereaved son card yet again but I knew it would no longer cut any ice with Nancy. So, instead, I played the Scouse joker.

"Sorry, Nance, but that simply won't be possible. You see, I've got a meeting with Robb Wilton this afternoon."

Nancy gazed at me as though I'd gone potty.

"Robb Wilton!" she spluttered. "What possible business could you have with that dodderer?"

"Bit harsh, Nance. Robb can't help the way he looks ... and talks ... and acts."

"If you say so."

"Anyway, thing is, the old fellow's spruced up his routine - about time too - and he wants to test it out on me."

"Why you of all people?" said Nancy eyeing me suspiciously. "I've never even heard you mention him before."

"Er, I think it's probably ... my expertise in the catchphrase department."

"In that case we'll have to organise a family outing to the catchphrase department."

"Leave the comedy to me, Nance. And to Robb of course."

Tentatively I put my arm around her shoulder and was gratified that she did not draw away.

"Robb's new routine will probably turn out to be rubbish," I told her, "but he needs to show it off. You know how us comics are."

"Yes I know only too well how you are."

I could see Nancy was considering sending me to bed without any milk or ginger biscuits but the spirit suddenly seemed to desert her.

"All right then, go," she said wearily. "But don't forget that Reg and Evie are coming round for tea."

"How could I ever forget something like that," I told her before beating an eager retreat.

In truth, far from remembering that Reg and Evie were coming for tea, I couldn't even bring to mind who Reg and Evie were! A dodgy game of cards against a bunch of Scousers suddenly seemed an enticing prospect and I was relieved that I'd glanced at the piece of paper on which Robb had written where he was staying before throwing it away.

The hotel was in Charing Cross so I decided it would be a splendid notion to get off the District Line at Westminster and have a quiet stroll up Whitehall. Not such a good idea as it turned out! On reaching the top of the Tube station steps, I was reminded that this was no ordinary Sunday by two burly coves – they looked like Press men to me – who dashed round the corner and bowled me up against the sandbag defences. This pair seemed far too excited to notice they'd knocked me aside or even to respond to my shouts of, "It's not a race, you know!"

Pulling myself and my dignity together again, I was surprised to see a fair old throng milling around outside the main entrance to the Palace of Westminster. Then it struck me. Of course, the Commons had been in emergency session, the entire House no doubt still palpitating from Nev's breathless call to arms.

Given that the session had started a couple of hours before, I was surprised to see Winston's hearse-like

Daimler pull up outside the entrance and the man himself bound out, looking anything but someone two months away from collecting his pension. Either he was extremely late for the debate or was returning to the House after another appointment. I watched him exchange smiles and a few words with the crowd as his chauffeur pulled away with Clemmie still in the back of the car.

Even though Winston had disappeared into the building by the time I got there, his new admirers were still buzzing and one of the men he'd spoken to told me excitedly, "Winston's got the Admiralty."

"Well let's hope he puts it back when he's finished with it," I replied to gratifying guffaws. *(It's likely that Frankie saw Churchill returning from Downing Street where he'd accepted Chamberlain's invitation to become First Lord of the Admiralty and take his place in the War Cabinet).*

You had to hand it to Winston; things had come to pass just as he had prescribed three years before. Armaments production had been massively increased; the RAF was in a much stronger state and Winston was now the nation's top sea dog. I resisted the temptation to ask my new and appreciative audience if an elderly peer with only one hand had been found face down in the Thames under Westminster Bridge. *(Edward Frederick Lindley Wood, 1st Earl of Halifax, 1881–1959, known popularly as The Holy Fox, was Foreign Secretary from 1938-40 and firmly associated with the policy of appeasing Germany. He had a withered left arm and no hand).*

My merry banter with the appreciative crowd was interrupted by a terrible wailing. *(The critics?)* This banshee sound was to become all too distressingly familiar a year hence but this afternoon was the first occasion anyone in Britain had heard an air raid siren during wartime. And what an effect it had! The crowd, who seconds before had been chuckling at my midget gems of wit, were drawn at speed, like iron filings to a magnet, towards the Tube station entrance and subterranean sanctuary.

Now I'm no braver than the next fellow and would have been down the stairs like a shot at the first hint of bombs over Blighty. But it seemed to me rather unlikely that Hitler would have been in a position to immediately launch his forces on London, particularly as he was in the middle of mopping up Poland. And it was a Sunday!

So I took a gamble, dodged the remaining few panickers aiming for the Underground and strolled across Bridge Road.

All at once it was a proper Sunday again with nobody around except me and the birds. And this annoying chap! I didn't notice him at first and only gradually realised that someone was matching me step for step up Whitehall.

My new companion, a tall toothy bloke with slicked back sandy hair, grinned at me and said, "Well played for defying the Hun. I fear the general populace will have to develop a bit more steel if we're all going to pull through this little lot."

I studied him a bit more closely. He was casually dressed in a sports jacket over a stained brown pullover and un-ironed light coloured slacks yet there was an air of authority around him that chimed in with our surroundings. This was confirmed a second later when he took hold of my elbow lightly but firmly.

"I think we'll cross here if you don't mind. I'm Donald by the way."

I easily shook free of his grip.

"No thanks, chum. I'm going straight on if it's all the same to you."

Donald smiled again. "Well, of course, you're free to do anything you want, Mr Thirkettle. This is England after all." And he set off alone across Whitehall.

"Hold on, how do you know my name?"

"Carlton Frobisher was most complimentary about you," he said over his shoulder and marched on.

The mention of my Munich rescuer was enough to have me dashing into King Charles Street after this Donald fellow. When I put my hand on his arm, he turned and grinned once again.

"I thought the name Frobisher might do the trick," he said. "Incidentally he's not a man *I'd* ever cross. Now if you don't mind."

Intrigued, I now had little hesitation in following Donald. To our right was a building I vaguely recognised but, instead of heading towards the imposing entrance fifty yards away, he guided me down a small flight of stone steps, unlocked a solid oak door and ushered me into a basement.

"Sunday entrance," Donald told me. "Much more informal."

He led me along a warren of passages before we emerged into a wide corridor at the end of which was a massive rectangular sash window overlooking Whitehall. The funny thing was, I couldn't remember climbing any stairs.

Donald looked at me and smiled again. I began to wonder if he was on something.

"I bet you thought we'd forgotten all about your Munich heroics," he said. "I'll wager you've been smarting like billy-o over our seeming ingratitude."

"Not at all," I lied. "I haven't given it a second thought."

"You're a better man than I would be then," he chuckled before gently pushing me towards an open door. Inside the room I could see a large desk, behind which sat an enormous bald man, nearer sixty than fifty, with tobacco-stained teeth. He too was wearing a pullover and casual shirt but the outfit was topped off incongruously by a rhubarb and custard MCC tie.

I knew it was Lord's colours because of my Denis Compton connection – and due to the fact that they'd been begging me to join for years. I'd refused of course. *(More of Frankie's mendacious nonsense. Anyone nominated to join the Marylebone Cricket Club has to spend years on the waiting list. The current figure is estimated to be eighteen years).*

A lit pipe lay smouldering in a glass ashtray shaped like a cricket bat next to a box of Swan Vestas. Donald eyed the pipe with trepidation.

"Watch he doesn't do his usual trick and stick the pipe in his pocket while it's lit," whispered Donald. "We don't want him - and the FO - going up in flames on the first day. Bad for morale and all that."

"This is the Foreign Office?" I said, surprised.

"Where did you think it was, The London Palladium?"

"Well, obviously not because I know ..."

"In you go," drawled Donald, giving me a gentle shove. As I crossed the threshold the man behind the desk looked up.

"That will be all, MacLean," he told Donald. "And thank you."

"Enchantee, mon chef," replied Donald bowing exaggeratedly as he backed out of the room and closed the door.

The big fellow shook his head. "Cambridge men," he sighed. "They're all crackers. I blame that miasma drifting off the Fens. Take a seat, Mr Howard, I'm Oswald Grosvenor." And he held out his hand.

I shook it and sat opposite him.

"Pleased to meet you, Mr Grosvenor, but my name isn't Howard."

Grosvenor picked up a thick dark red file from his desk and flicked through it.

"It definitely says Leslie Howard here," he mused.

"Do I look like Leslie Howard?"

"I have absolutely no idea. Do you?"

"No because my name's Francis Thirkettle or perhaps you'll know me better as Frankie Funnybone."

Grosvenor's eyes narrowed and he stared at the fat Leslie Howard file in some confusion before lifting it up and pulling out a much thinner one from underneath.

"Ah, forgive me, Mr Thirkettle," said Grosvenor. "You're our man in Munich aren't you."

"If you say so."

"By gum I do say so," he growled. "Our Mr Frobisher was most complimentary about the way you dealt with those murdering Hun scum. The PM hasn't forgotten about it either."

I shrugged as casually as I could.

"As long as old Brummie, er, the Prime Minister remains safe. That's all that matters, isn't it."

"Well said that man," barked Grosvenor, thumping the desk. "We've had our eyes on you ever since then. You'll be joining the forces' entertainment arm of course."

"I hadn't really thought about it."

"That wasn't a question, Mr Thirkettle."

Blimey, the war was three hours old and I was already being conscripted.

"You want me to cheer up the troops?" I asked Grosvenor.

"That's what we'll tell everyone. But I'm sure we can find other uses for you."

And then Oswald Grosvenor, pipe clamped resolutely between his teeth, outlined exactly what those uses could be in the 'upcoming unpleasantness'.

Twenty minutes later, after I'd heard his pitch and signed one or two bits of paper I found myself outside the building wondering what the war had in store for me ... and Leslie Howard for that matter. *(Leslie Howard, 1893-1943, was a British screen actor who died after the passenger aircraft in which he was travelling was shot down by the*

214

Luftwaffe over the Bay of Biscay. A popular theory is that the plane was mistaken for one in which Churchill was travelling but Howard was strongly rumoured to have been working for the British Secret Service and there is a theory that his death was ordered by the Nazi Propaganda Minister Josef Goebbels).

However, if you want to know the details of what Oswald Grosvenor told me you'll have to wait for my wartime memoirs, The Fighting Funnybones. *(Sincere apologies for this rampant outbreak of naked commercialism).*

There was still nobody around when I emerged from the FO but, as I turned onto Whitehall and headed back down towards Parliament Square, the all-clear sounded. By the time I'd reached Westminster Tube, people were emerging from the depths into the sunlight, each trying to look as if it was someone else who had scuttled for cover at the first hint of trouble.

My head was now too full of what had just happened for me to bother with the Liverpudlian card school. I wasn't in any hurry to get home either. It would be far easier to allow Nancy to prattle on to Reg and Evie, whoever they were, while I cooled my heels in the park and slowly digested what Oswald Grosvenor had said.

One thing did strike me, however, but it was well into the 1950s before I saw Robb Wilton again and I clean forgot to ask him whether he was in on luring me towards the Foreign Office that day, at that very hour.

Whatever the truth is, one thing's for sure. If I hadn't been interrupted on my way to a session of Montana Red Dog with a gang of Scouse comics, Hitler would probably have won the war and, more importantly, I'd have lost a packet.

PART TWO – 1945-51

Chapter Twelve: Guy the Gorilla

"Well I voted for your lot," I assured Winston as he subsided even further into one of The Reform Club's voluminous brown studded leather armchairs.

It was 24 hours after the 1945 General Election results had been announced and, needless to say, I'd done no such thing in the privacy of the polling booth. I mean who, with his head on the right way round, would actually demand a return to means testing and cramming small children up chimneys?

But the old boy looked badly in need of a lift and what's a little white lie among politicians? *(Typically, Frankie is mistaken about the location as Churchill resigned from The Reform Club in 1913 over the blackballing of his pal, Count Arnold Maurice de Forest, known to his dearest friends - and quite possibly his bitterest enemies - as 'Tuty'. Frankie and the outgoing Prime Minister were probably in the neighbouring Athenaeum on Pall Mall on that day, July 27th 1945).*

Winston had good reason to look bombed out. The great war leader, saviour of his nation, had been forced into using the tradesman's entrance to flee from Major Attlee and his Socialist hordes rampaging up Downing Street – if you were to believe what the 'quality' newspapers were saying.

For my part, I was finding it mightily difficult to imagine careful Clem storming anything. As far as I could discern, disrupting the village beetle drive would have been well beyond the man. Then again, I knew that he'd managed to see off more than one of the security service's ham-fisted plots to jigger up the Labour Party so he must have had something about him.

Unlike his predecessor at that precise moment! Not for the first time John Duke's heir was well into his cups and the old vicarage clock stood not yet at fourteen fifty hours.

Winston leaned forward with some difficulty, pointed a wavering finger at my right nostril and growled, "The two men who did most to win this war for Britain - myself and your good self - cast aside like a worn and threadbare pair of mittens."

At least the old boy hadn't lost his gift for rhetoric – or exaggeration. After all, it could be fairly pointed out that *I* hadn't been voted into political oblivion in a landslide poll.

But I kept my counsel. Besides, for all his moonshine, Winston was right up to a point. I had been somewhat overlooked after my recent heroics but you'll have to wait for my special wartime memoirs to read about those *(Presumably because he hasn't made them up yet).*

Winston spent the next ten minutes bewailing the easy ride Attlee was about to give Uncle Joe Stalin – when our new leader was not busy putting a flaming torch under the British Empire. To my mind it showed how out of touch Winston had become. Managing to conflate the Utopian ambitions of mild-mannered and consensual Clem with the behaviour of our mad and murderous Soviet ally was a leap of logic far beyond even his usual excesses.

To his credit, Winston appeared to sense this and the tirade ended as suddenly as it had begun, with the old boy slumping forward and marinating his pinstripes in Johnnie Walker's finest. At that point, I did consider sneaking off and leaving him to soak but resisted the temptation as I felt compelled to have one more bash at cheering him up.

"Never mind, Winston," I cried. "Now that you're out of the political front line, you can spend more time with the family."

It was said, in all seriousness, by someone who had recently seen his own brood swelled by another squawker – more of which anon. But, if I'd expected the sentiment to bring comfort and joy to my pal, I was wildly wide of the mark. Winston sat up with a jerk and glared first at me then his empty glass – I think he suspected I'd been snaffling his spirits.

"Family!" he thundered. "You *are* very well acquainted with my only son?"

"Randolph, yes."

"And you are therefore aware of what a confounded ass the man can be."

"Well, yes."

"And yet you persist with this fairy tale that the family is some kind of haven against the world's vicissitudes?"

"Well, now you mention it, no."

Winston nodded forcefully as if to emphasise the total supremacy of his logic over my asininity. The nod was perhaps a touch too forceful as it drove his jowls deep into his chest where they remained.

Maybe I should have left it there but, not wanting the great man to lapse into one of his infamous black dog episodes, I tried one final stratagem to lighten the mood.

"Honestly, Winston," I told him. "What a curmudgeon you are. You're acting like the safety curtain's just dropped on your foot."

Winston raised his head and opened one eye. It was obvious I'd reawakened some of his attention.

"How in heaven's name," he boomed, "would a curtain settling upon my foot incommode me?"

"You've obviously never been backstage in that long and interesting life of yours," I replied. "If you had, you'd know those things weigh a ton. Fire regulations and so on."

Now he opened both eyes. I'd obviously commandeered his full attention.

"Weigh a ton!" he cried. "Weigh a ton! From what material is this so-called *curtain* manufactured?"

Well, it wasn't something to which I'd ever given much thought.

"Oh, er, I dunno exactly. It could be asbestos or maybe metal. Iron I suppose."

Winston exploded out of his armchair like a big baby Kraken awaking and seized me by the lapels.

"An iron curtain," he thundered. "An iron curtain! Whoever heard of such a thing? You are a damned fool, Francis, and I shall listen to you no more."

With that, he released my lapels, subsided back into the armchair and uttered not another word to me until 1953.

Considering myself well and truly admonished, I decided to leave our erstwhile saviour to his own devices. Maybe a game of snakes and ladders with the boy Randolph would pep him up.

Leaving by the club's rear entrance, I dodged across the Mall, down Horse Guards Road and into the top end of Downing Street as a short cut to Westminster Tube. I soon realised my mistake, however, as the street was packed to the gills with bodies and all but impassable. Gawkers, hawkers, snappers, scribblers and the odd copper milled around straining for a glimpse of the new Cabinet's latest member arriving to receive Clem Attlee's blessing. I say 'new' but the first person of note I saw as I elbowed my way to the front of the scrum was old stalwart Ernie Bevin, wheezing and coughing as he struggled to haul himself out of a gleaming new Bentley.

"Anything to say, sir," squawked an eager young reporter, almost thrusting a huge microphone up Ernie's purple nose.

"Yeah," came the reply in that distinctive West Country growl, "bugger off or I'll shove that lollipop where the monkey stores his nuts."

Of course the crowd lapped up this no-nonsense nonsense and responded with gales of mirth. Never knowingly one to ignore an audience this gullible, I proposed three cheers for Mr Bevin and tipped the reporter's trilby over his eyes. This kept the merriment on the boil and I was even treated to a round of applause as I finally broke free of the scrum, to which I bowed low in my finest pantomime manner.

So I was in grand fettle as I turned into Whitehall. And yet within seconds my mood had begun to darken. Maybe it was my knee which, despite the warm weather, was giving me considerable pain again; I swear I could feel the bits of shell tunnelling around in there.

Or perhaps I was unsettled by the annoying waves of celebratory parties, young men and women flowing arm-in-arm up and down the pavements.

However, approaching The Cenotaph, I finally realised what it was - the memory of my pre-war stroll up this very thoroughfare with that treacherous swine, Donald Maclean. What that man had done was beyond the pale.

But for these dark thoughts slowing me down, I would most likely have missed it. Passing Edwin Lutyens' simple but beautiful war memorial, I noticed a flicker of ... well, something familiar. There it was again; a figure trying unsuccessfully to hide behind The Cenotaph.

Intrigued, I tiptoed over to the far side of the memorial and someone quickly disappeared around the other end. I moved around to the far side again ... and you get the picture. Deciding it was time to bring this merry-go-round to a halt, I doubled back suddenly and found myself nose-to-nose with of all people ... Donald Maclean!

"You treacherous hound," I yelled, grabbing him by the scruff of the neck. "You'll pay for what you've done."

Maclean looked absolutely petrified. "Please, Francis, old boy," he whined, "you can't begin to understand my motives."

"Understand! I understand only too well, you two-faced toad," I snapped back. "You've sold me and everyone I love down the river. Now you'll pay the ultimate price."

I must say I've never, before or since, seen anyone look quite as fearful as Maclean at that moment. A cornered sewer rat would have been more relaxed – and less slippery. For, seconds after apparently collapsing into my arms, he gave my left shin such an almighty kick that I dropped to the ground in shock and pain, allowing the double-dealing rodent to make his escape up Whitehall.

Struggling to my feet, I tried to alert a band of juvenile revellers as Maclean tore towards them,

"Stop that traitor," I cried.

Maclean looked at the young people in abject terror as if he fully expected to be grabbed. He needn't have worried as this bunch of morons merely cheered and clapped, believing it yet another jolly jape that marked the ushering in of a new political dawn. There was nothing else for it. I'd have to snare the slug myself.

Even though I had Jerry hardware in one leg and a swelling the size of a duck egg on the other, I was still confident of catching our Cambridge two-timer. For one thing, he'd put on a fair bit of weight and looked badly out of condition. For another, he ran like a constipated granny.

To the boys and girls making merry in and around Westminster that pleasant summer afternoon we must have presented a strange sight. Two grown men, limping and lumbering up Whitehall, one intent on doing the other extreme harm – and slowly gaining on his quarry.

There could be no doubt about it, Maclean was flagging. By the time he reached the entrance to Downing Street he was almost out on his feet and as he tried to stagger in amongst the crowd, now straining and pushing towards Number 10, my right hand landed firmly on his collar.

"Now then, you weasel, you're going to talk," I told him as he cowered with his arm hovering pathetically above his head.

"Please don't torture me," he begged. "I'll tell you everything."

"Damned right you will. So talk."

Maclean stared wildly at the crowd but all were facing the other way, intent on what was happening in front of

Number 10. He suddenly looked resigned and appeared to deflate in my grasp.

"All right. All right. I'll spill the beans," he said bitterly. "If you must know, the whole rotten business was Guy's idea."

"Oh, it's all too easy to blame that oaf," I told him.

"Yes, yes," Maclean eagerly agreed, "isn't it."

"But enlighten me on this, Donald." My face moved to within a few inches of his. "Who was it who foisted the confounded nuisance on my family in the first place, eh? Tell me that, Mr Foreign Office bigwig."

Maclean gazed at me as if I'd asked him to recite the Periodic Table - backwards, and in Greek - so great was his puzzlement. Then he began to nod eagerly and with some relief.

"So all this is merely about Guy Burgess staying at your house?"

"I'll give you merely!" I roared and grabbed him again. "The man's been infesting our place for a fortnight because of you."

An unwelcome memory of waking up to find Nancy hammering in fury on my chest sprang to mind.

Maclean's breathing became gradually more even as he put his hands up in surrender.

"I'm so sorry, Francis. I do realise it is serious and I'm truly repentant for anything I might have done."

"You will be sorry," I replied.

"But let me be clear," he added. "Your accusation of treachery referred to me introducing you to Guy?"

"What else would I have been talking about?"

Maclean's eyes moved shiftily left, right and left again before he replied, "I really have no idea, old boy."

"You seemed to have some idea when you put me in the way of the drunken fool that night in The Nell of Old Drury. Remember?"

A light went on in Maclean's head. "The pub in Covent Garden! Ah yes, now I recall."

"Yes you were quick to dump the damn nuisance on to me. How many times has he set your place on fire, eh?"

"I also remember that we were all rather tipsy, which is no excuse," Maclean added quickly as I raised my fist.

He held up his right forefinger. "Look, I have a solution to this problem. A mutual friend will take Guy off your hands, I guarantee it. Here's his name and telephone number."

Maclean fumbled in his jacket, pulled out a small card and handed it to me. Not convinced, I screwed it up. But he was insistent.

"Just ring that chap and everything will be taken care of. I'd do it myself but I'm going back to Washington tonight."

"That's what you told me two weeks ago," I said, reluctantly shoving the card into my coat pocket. "Remember?"

"Yes, and again I must apologise most profoundly."

I let go of Maclean, who began to rub his neck. He'd recovered a fair measure of equilibrium and glanced slyly at me.

"Did, er, Guy say anything to you?" he asked casually.

"Say anything! The drunken fool never shuts up. Luckily most of it's in Greek and Latin or else he would be an even greater nuisance."

"Ah, calyx meus inebrians," intoned Maclean sonorously. *(My cup making me drunk).*

I glared at him and he smiled in return, no doubt under the impression he was back in total control. Well I'd give him something to mull over while he was conjugating.

"Oh and, Donald," I said off-handedly. "Next time you plan to kick me in the shins, think about this will you."

I reached out and casually pressed my thumb just under Maclean's right ear. It was a wheeze I'd picked up from

224

Carlton Frobisher early on in the war and it never failed to work.

Maclean dropped to the pavement, screaming and clutching his head at precisely the moment the crowd parted to reveal our new Prime Minister, Clement Attlee, in the process of glad-handing his admirers. Clearly puzzled, Clem looked at Maclean rolling around in agony and then at me.

"Your charisma, Clem," I told him. "It's sent him clean off his rocker."

Still bemused, Attlee replied, "The unfortunate fellow. Perhaps he is concerned about our looming struggle against Sir William Beveridge's five giant evils."

"Ah yes, I recall those rascals," I told the PM with some authority. "Let's see, there's want, ignorance, squalor, idleness and what's the other horror we need to see the back of sharpish?"

"Disease," replied Attlee, back on firm ground.

"And here's me thinking it was Tommy Trinder," I shot back immediately to considerable laughter. Even Attlee could not suppress a grin.

"These evils are far from being matters of levity, sir," Clem informed me. "But you do seem to have cheered us all up, which can be no bad thing."

For the second time that day I took my leave of Downing Street with applause ringing in my ears. Bowing to the crowd, I caught a glimpse of Maclean leaning against the wall of the Foreign Office, rubbing his head and breathing heavily. He gave me a look of pure malice which turned to fear as I took a step towards him.

Then I turned, hopped into a waiting taxi just ahead of Sir Stafford Cripps and Bessie Braddock, and left Downing Street with considerably more panache than Winston Churchill had shown.

However, while I was in the back of the cab, I immediately began to have doubts about my harsh treatment of Donald. True, he had foisted a roaring drunken boor on to our family, disrupted the entire household and stretched Nancy's patience to the giddy limit. But when I thought back in detail to that Saturday night in the Nell a fortnight before, I concluded that my own enthusiasm might have been as much to blame.

What had happened was I'd just finished a stint at the Theatre Royal, Drury Lane, providing comic relief in yet another steaming pile of patriotic claptrap put together by Noel Coward. So I was on a high, having wowed the crowd and finally escaped from the marching bands, bunting and young Vera Lynn. *(Wherever Frankie was 'wowing' the audience, it wasn't at the Theatre Royal, Drury Lane, which only reopened in 1946 after being bomb damaged during the war).*

Winding down in true showbiz style, I'd happened upon one or two old wartime pals making merry in the Nell and we had launched into a fine old session, swapping half-truths and drinking ourselves stupid. I was unclear at what exact point Donald Maclean had appeared beside me but his tale of a pal who would have nowhere to go when Donald returned to Washington the following day resonated with me.

For his part, Donald seemed delighted with what he termed my magnanimous gesture and we shook hands on it. The following afternoon Guy Burgess turned up on our doorstep with his belongings in a knotted handkerchief on a stick and the rest, as they might well say, is hysteria.

It was therefore most unfortunate that, by the time my cab pulled up outside our house in The Boltons, I'd temporarily forgotten about Burgess. Instead I was fondly recalling the Tommy Trinder gag which had gone down so well in Downing Street and was wondering how to work it into my act.

So I was grinning like an idiot as I climbed the steps and came face to face with Nancy, leaning against our front door and managing to fold her arms angrily and smoke at the same time. She looked as if she should be wielding a rolling pin.

"You look as if you should be wielding a ..."

"Shut your stupid face, right now," she screamed and I thought it advisable to comply with the request.

"If you don't get that idiot out of our house pronto then I'm divorcing you."

"You usually call me Franco not Pronto," I replied lamely, examining her face for the merest flicker of amusement. None was evident.

"OK, old girl. You're right. Enough's enough. I've got a plan."

"Well it had better work," said Nancy, angrily stamping out her cigarette. "I'm just about fed up to the back teeth of Burgess and his drunken ways. Julia can't bear him either."

We went inside and I was heading for the stairs when Nancy shook her head in exasperation.

"He's not in bed. He's in there," she snapped, pointing to the sitting room before stalking off towards the study.

I put my ear close to the door and listened but all I could hear was the distant wailing of the latest addition to the Thirkettle family, young Jonathan who had debuted two months previously. Then, from the sitting room, a high-pitched voice piped up, "All aboard the train to Burgess Hill. Whoo hoo!"

Intrigued, I crept into the room and was confronted by a most singular sight. Guy Burgess was lying on his back, completely comatose, smelling like a brewery had exploded all over him. Nothing unusual there.

The bizarre aspect of this scene was that he had model railway track criss-crossing his chest. Plus a little station waiting room with toilets. And a field of cows. To top it off, our six-year-old son, Balthazar – henceforward known as Baz – was running his model train by hand across Burgess's sleeping form.

"Look, Daddy," Baz trilled as I entered the room. "Uncle Guy's a hillock."

"Nearly right, son," I told him, ruffling his wispy fair hair. "Now go and get out of that school uniform and then see if Hilda will let you have some milk and biscuits there's a good little chap."

Baz threw his arms tightly around me for a couple of seconds before skipping off happily. Meanwhile I turned my attention to the great steaming hillock which had begun to snore. I considered giving Burgess a good kicking but doubted this would actually rouse him. So I reached into my coat pocket for the card Maclean had given me and dialled the number on it. A male voice, soft and almost diffident, answered.

"H...hello."

"Good afternoon," I said. "Is that Mr Harold Philby?"

There was a long pause at the other end before the voice finally answered, "Y...yes it is. M...may I ask who's calling."

I got straight down to business and informed this Philby about my problem with his roistering pal Burgess. I was ready to issue all sorts of threats so the man would take Guy off my hands but, to my surprise, Philby was immediately sympathetic to our plight. He obviously knew what a pain Burgess could be.

"I ... I do see your p...problem, Mr Thirkettle, and I promise to resolve it. A...at the moment I'm in the m...middle of some rather important work but if you'll allow it, I'll take Guy off your hands p...permanently within two days."

I weighed it up. Two more days of hell and then merciful release. It seemed a worthwhile exchange.

"OK that's a deal, Mr Philby. Can I call you Harold?"

"I'd rather you knew me as Kim like everyone else."

"You're on. But listen, Kim, don't let me down or else Burgess might not be alive when you eventually bowl up here."

There was a further long pause at the other end. "W...what on earth do you mean?" he asked warily.

"I mean that the Missus will have murdered him."

I heard Philby snort with laughter before replying, "And doubtless your good lady would q...qualify for a royal pardon. Have no fear, Mr Thirkettle, I'll be there the day after tomorrow."

After I'd put down the phone I considered booting Burgess awake and telling him that his days chez Funnybone were numbered. But I decided to leave it as a splendid surprise and limited myself to dragging his snoring carcass round the back of the Chesterfield – before carefully replacing the train tracks and little figures on top of him.

When I told Nancy the joyous news we decided to celebrate that evening with a meal at one of her favourite little restaurants in Soho, whose menu ran to a touch more than coley and corned beef, although I do recall that the place was selling something called Mock Tomato Soup.

We got back just before midnight to find Burgess no longer kipping behind the sofa but Baz's track with all the extras laid out neatly there.

When I came into the kitchen early next morning, Guy was already at the breakfast table, playing slapsies with Baz and exuding his usual bonhomie as our housekeeper Hilda deposited a small plate of bacon, mushrooms and greyish powdered egg in front of him.

Immediately Guy broke away from the game and examined the food as if he were about to dine at the Savoy Grill.

To delighted chuckles from Baz and Julia's look of complete loathing, Guy held a forkful of powdered egg above his head and brought it slowly towards his nose, inhaling deeply.

"Ah, Madame 'ilda. Votre Oeufs Brouilles, ils sont magnifique."

"I'll feed it to the dog if I have any more of your old buck," blustered Hilda, making a good-natured grab for the plate.

"You misconstrue me, madam" cried Guy, shielding his breakfast. "De gustibus non est disputandum." (*In matters of taste, there is no argument*). "How can I possibly repay you, my dear old thing?"

Hilda glared at him, trying unsuccessfully to suppress a faint smile. "Well," she said, "you could stop throwing up all over your bedroom floor for a kick-off."

"Ah, mea maxima culpa, dear lady" intoned Guy.

"Or if you must be sick, have the good grace to do it in the same place every time and don't spray it around like a fireman's hose."

Despite being in her early forties, the pocket battleship that was Hilda had already brought up four sons to adulthood and knew whereof she spoke.

Before Guy could show off any more of his erudition he was interrupted by the entrance of Nancy, smartly dressed and ready for work.

"The Americans are arriving at the agency at nine and I need to be there," she told me in reference to a transatlantic deal Eddie Star was setting up.

"Get the children off to school by quarter past eight, Franco."

Then after a quick peck on the head for each of the kids and a barked order for Guy to sit up straight and damn well chew his bacon, she was gone. Truly her father's daughter.

Guy watched Nancy go wearing an expression of extreme fondness. "Au revoir, my dear Lady Nancy," he boomed, craftily waiting until he'd heard the front door slam. "As our good friend Horace was wont to say, 'domus et placens uxor.'" *(A home and a pleasing wife).*

"She won't be so pleasing if she finds you pole-axed in the parlour again," I told Burgess, without mentioning that his stay with us was about to be terminated.

"Those days of wine and roses are far behind me, old boy," Guy declared grandly. "Hilda has shamed me into a life of abstemiousness. Isn't that right, old girl?"

And, jumping up from the breakfast table, he grabbed Hilda round the waist as she washed up.

Now, in certain parts of the East End that sorta caper could land a face in a right old loada Sarf *(Sea Bubble = trouble).* But, instead of belting Guy, Hilda merely wriggled happily, then turned and playfully dotted him on the nose with her dish cloth.

"You saucy blighter," she told him. "I'll give up breathing before you stop drinking."

"Aaaah, that would truly be the end of me, dear heart," replied Guy, finally releasing Hilda from his embrace and turning his attention to me.

"Thought we might visit Lord's today, old boy," he said. "Someone mentioned that our chums from the Antipodes are in town."

I looked suitably shocked. "The Aussies? Are they really? Oh, what a pity. On the very day I have an appointment to see my book-keeper. Come on, kids, hands and face washed."

Fifty minutes later, after ushering Julia and Baz to the school gates, I was strolling down the Wellington Road in St John's Wood. Well, I wasn't having that drunken clown spoil my first appearance in the Lord's pavilion since a grateful nation had conferred MCC membership upon me. I wanted this to be a special occasion – if I could get near the place!

My stroll, as I put it, was soon reduced to a shuffle as about half the capital appeared to have converged on the home of cricket. I had the devil of a job just to fight my way through a heaving multitude to get to the members' entrance and sanctuary among the egg and bacon tie brigade.

Settling as comfortably as I could onto the slatted wooden bench, I made a quick inquiry to be told what I already suspected. My old mate Compo would not be playing as he was still on army service in India.

But there was plenty to look forward to as England had Wally Hammond, Len Hutton and Cyril Washbrook in their ranks and turning out for the Aussies were Lindsay Hassett and a young cavalier called Keith Miller. *(Frankie either has his dates mixed up or he and his family tolerated Guy Burgess for longer than he remembers. He is absolutely correct that England played an Australian Services Eleven at Lord's in the Fourth Victory Test which included all the above mentioned great players. But it was a three-day match, starting on August 6th and not July 28th 1945. Such was the public's renewed appetite for organised sport that ten thousand people were locked out of Lord's on that first day).*

The morning's cricket had much to recommend it as did the lunch and I was settling back into my seat among the post-prandial dozers when disaster struck. My concentration on the fiery batting of Keith Miller was interrupted by a commotion at the end of our row. To my utter dismay, looking as if he'd been run over by the groundsman's heavy roller, Guy Burgess was swaying and staggering towards me.

"Francis," he boomed. "You made it after all, you dog."

How the hell he'd made it, when half of London couldn't get into the ground, defeated me but here he undoubtedly was.

"Coming through," shouted Guy, tripping over an elderly member, swathed in a blanket. "Sorry, Pop, mea maxima culpa and all that."

He took a closer look at the slumbering pensioner and cried, "Stewards, this man appears to be dead. Please ensure his carcass is removed before the commencement of the 1948 season."

From somewhere to the rear of us came a quiet but authoritative voice. "For god's sake, Burgess, sit down and stop making a spectacle of yourself."

Guy slumped down beside me with a sheepish grin. His tie was draped over his shoulder like a noose and he smelled awful – a potent mixture of neat gin and BO.

"You're pissed," I informed him.

"I resent that," he cried. "In fact, I'm honour bound to call you out. But let's have a sherbert first." He handed me a hip flask.

"It's empty," I told him.

"Empty!" thundered Guy, snatching the flask and turning it upside down. "Call the Bow Street Runners. Some rascal's nabbed me grog."

"For Christ's sake, Guy," I urged, "just watch the game. Look, Miller's thrashing Pollard to all parts."

Guy leaned forward and squinted towards the field of play. "Is Miller the tall, dark, handsome young chappy?" he asked with a glint in his eye.

"Er, yes."

"Interesting! I might snatch a word with him afterwards."

"I really wouldn't if I were you."

I could barely envisage the scene moments after a ragingly heterosexual Australian had had his bum tweaked by an English 'aesthete'.

But Guy had already grown tired of events on the field and was starting to look around for further mischief.

"You know what, Francis," he told me. "I reckon this funeral parlour needs livening up. How about a sing-song?"

"For pity's sake, Guy," I pleaded. "Just watch the cricket."

Burgess swung his head round again.

"Who's partial to a bit of music hall then, eh?" he shouted. "Let's have a chorus of 'My Old Man'."

That did it for me. I was out of my seat like a rocket because I already knew that Guy's distinctive version of that particular song was not one its originator, Marie Lloyd, would recognise.

"Come on," I could hear him cry as I headed swiftly out of the members' area. "'My old man said' ... oh do make an effort, you lot. Right then, after three, three, 'My old man said, be a Tottenham fan so I told him' ..."

Mercifully I was able to dodge round the back of the pavilion before I heard any more. All I could make out was a frenzy of boos, catcalls and a shout of, "String him up!" *(Hardly surprising, as the chorus goes, 'I told him, fuck off bollocks you're a c**t').*

On my way over to The Lord's Tavern, I noticed a scrum of people still hanging about hopefully outside the Grace Gates, even though it was mid-afternoon.

"Oi, Frankie," shouted one young fellow with barely a tooth in place, "be a good 'un and unlock these blighters will you."

It doesn't do to ignore your fans so I strolled over to the gates and gave them a theatrical shake.

"It's no good," I told my new pal. "This is a job for Lon Chaney. I think I just spotted him in the Tavern." To laughter and applause, I moved off. *(Lon Chaney, 1906-73, was a 6ft 2in, 220lb US screen actor whose most famous roles were Frankenstein's Monster and the slow-witted giant Lennie Small in Of Mice and Men).*

Typically he saw me before I spotted him. Not Lon Chaney but Carlton Frobisher, who was propped up on a stool, his crutches leaning against the Tavern wall. He beckoned me and I pushed my way through the drinkers to join him.

"You should be fielding at short leg," I said, pointing to the lower part of his right limb which was no longer there. Frobisher turned his one good eye towards me and grinned.

"You comics can be awfully cruel buggers."

"You're lucky I wasn't shouting 'Pieces of Eight.'"

Frobisher smiled again. "Yes at least there is that. Drink?"

I nodded and Frobisher inclined his head ever so slightly. Thirty seconds later we were each cradling a pint of Young's.

"Miller looks rather good," muttered Frobisher as a cut backward of square from the young Aussie sent the ball skittering into the crowd next to us, prompting a good natured scrum.

"Yes I think we'll see more of him."

Frobisher took a deep pull of his pint and, without looking at me, said, "I hear you're having trouble with the lodger."

Crikey, not much escaped this fellow even with his one eye.

"You mean Guy Burgess? Yes, perhaps I should have taken a lead from the Lord's stewards."

"How so?"

"They seem to have no problem evicting him."

I nodded towards the pavilion where, amid some commotion, Guy was being dragged away by two bruisers. He was still singing.

"What's your interest in Burgess anyway?" I asked Frobisher as Guy's lusty tones faded and the boos died down.

"I'm a desk man aren't I," Frobisher reminded me, "with particular responsibility for liaison with our American cousins."

"So what's Uncle Sam's interest in Burgess?"

Frobisher took another long swig of beer and wiped the froth from his lips. I noticed his left hand was trembling ever so slightly.

"It's not Burgess as much as an old Cambridge pal of his," he told me. "Cove named Philby. Kim Philby."

"Philby! What a coincidence. The man's coming round tomorrow night to take Burgess off our hands."

"Is he, by jiminy?"

"Yes, so what's the problem with Philby?"

"No real problem at all. He had a good war - in counter-intelligence. Now he's head of the Russian section at SIS."

"And ...?"

"He was a Communist at Cambridge. Oh splendid shot, sir."

I waited until the applause for Keith Miller's latest blitz through extra cover subsided before whispering, "For goodness sake, Carlton, everybody at Cambridge in the Thirties was a Red. Burgess included."

Frobisher nodded slowly and continued. "Then Philby became a Fascist with direct links to Franco. Of course that was useful during the war. He was a big help in keeping Spain neutral and Gib away from the Nazis."

"There you go then. I repeat, what's the problem?"

Glancing from side to side, Frobisher said in a low voice, "Our pals across the pond are getting a bit jumpy about him. They're worried he may be batting for the other side."

"So he's queer. Big deal."

"You know exactly what I mean, Francis. Oh, magnificent stuff, that man! We've not heard the last of this young chap Miller."

While the applause died down I mulled over what Frobisher had told me.

"Why don't you drag Philby in?" I suggested. "Give him a fright."

Frobisher shook his head impatiently. "It's only suspicions by the Yanks - and that mainly from one source."

"Then you've no real choice but to leave things as they are," I told him. "Just keep your eyes - sorry eye - open."

Trying not to grin, Frobisher nodded and replied, "You too."

"Meaning?"

"Let me know what you make of Philby."

He scribbled his home phone number on a scrap of paper and crammed it into the top pocket of my blazer.

"I suppose I could do that," I said. "And what about Burgess? Is he under suspicion too?"

"Good God no," snorted Frobisher. "There are enough hopeless drunks in Moscow as it is. What would they do with another one?"

"Pity," I replied.

The matter was not mentioned again and we spent the rest of the afternoon session reminiscing over things that had happened during the war. Frobisher finally fell silent and after about a minute I felt compelled to speak.

"Look, Carlton, I've said it before but I'm truly sorry that things ..."

Leaning forward, Frobisher placed his forefinger lightly across my lips and shook his head.

"Absolutely no need, old boy. The problem was entirely of my own manufacture."

He eased himself off the stool and on to his crutches, almost managing to disguise the pain he was in.

"I think I'll leave it there," he muttered. "Scoot off back to Dollis Hill before I get knocked about too much."

This from a man whose life's work it was to knock any number of bad hats into a cocked hat. A man who had saved my bacon more than once. It was simply tragic to see how he was now.

"Take care, old fellow," I sighed and patted him on the shoulder.

"You too," Frobisher replied with a tired smile. "And don't forget to call me about you know who."

I nodded and watched as he manoeuvred his way gingerly through the boisterous Tavern crowd – never imagining that this would be the last time I'd ever see him.

Frobisher's slow and deliberate shuffle towards the exit had upset me profoundly and I wasted no time in taking it out on those around me. There were oaths and threats as I pushed my way aggressively through the scrum to the bar, not caring who I shoved aside. One fellow even told me to get back in the pavilion where I belonged.

However, I'd only swallowed a couple of mouthfuls of a new pint before it was obvious I didn't belong anywhere round here. Furthermore, whether it was due to the sun, the beer or even Keith Miller's assault on our bowlers, I'd developed a thundering headache which didn't lift until I reached home and spent half an hour soaking in the bath.

Feeling several degrees more human, I rang Nancy at work and arranged to meet her later for a film and a bite to eat. We had the evening to ourselves because the children, including the baby, were over at Hilda's in White City – a regular Monday night treat for all of us.

At around eight the doorbell rang and, glancing out of the window, I saw there was a battered cab parked right in front of our house. Damn taxi drivers, I grumbled to myself. Always late, apart from this idiot who's fifteen minutes early. Still in my vest, I threw open the door impatiently ... and was confronted by Guy Burgess. He was with another man.

"M ... Mr Thirkettle," the mystery caller said with some difficulty. "Forgive me. I'm Kim Philby."

So this was the character who was spooking the Yanks. He didn't look much to write home about.

"No need to apologise for the fact, Kim," I told him.

"Indeed, it's just that I find I'm in a p...position to take this young reprobate off your hands a day earlier than planned."

He indicated Guy, who stood slightly behind him, uncharacteristically saying nothing. He didn't even look at me.

"Well come in but I can't gossip as my taxi's here."

I indicated the bashed-up cab and Philby smiled.

"Actually that's my vehicle," he said. "It gets me around at any rate."

I told them to come in and fix themselves drinks while I got dressed. When I came back down, I noticed that, while Guy had poured whisky and sodas for Kim and me, he didn't have one. Most odd! I also noted that he'd tidied himself up after his Lord's pantomime. He'd even combed his hair.

In contrast, Philby wore a scruffy tweed jacket with elbow patches in a manner which strongly suggested a studied and raffish inelegance. This, I thought, was a man who knew exactly what he was doing and the impression he wanted to create. Yet, for all his confidence, I detected a hint of anxiety.

Sitting down in the armchair opposite Philby, I inwardly prayed that my cab would be late.

"What line are you in, Kim?" I asked him as I sipped my Scotch.

His face twitched ever so slightly. "I w...work for the War Office," he replied. "Very h..humdrum. Nothing like these glamour boys in the FO."

He nodded towards Burgess, who looked anything but glamorous.

"Or indeed the m...music hall. Guy tells me you're a f...first-rate comedian. I'll m...maybe take in one of your shows some time."

I looked at Guy who again avoided my gaze. It was hard to believe that this man had been terrorising Lord's a few hours before.

I turned back to Philby and said, "Give me a ring beforehand and I'll get you tickets. Best in the house."

"How k...kind of you."

I took another sip of Scotch and asked, as casually as I could, "So, Kim, what did you get up to during the war?"

"Oh, this and that. What about yourself?"

"I was here and there. And what ..."

We were interrupted by a car honking its horn. A quick glance through the window confirmed this *was* my cab and only ten minutes late.

"I'm awfully sorry but I'll have to leave you fellows," I said, getting up. "Please take all the time you need to get Guy's stuff together. Just slam the door when you go."

Kim jumped to his feet and held out his hand. "Lovely to meet you, Francis," he said warmly. We must talk again. Perhaps after a show."

"I'd be delighted to, Kim," I replied shaking his paw. The grip was light but unyielding.

"Goodbye, Guy," I added. "Don't forget to leave your keys there's a good chap."

Again Burgess nodded but said nothing. What on earth was wrong with the man, I wondered as I left the house?

The taxi hadn't gone fifty yards when I patted my jacket pocket and groaned.

"You'll have to go back," I told the driver. "I've forgotten my wallet."

"No problem, captain," he said, slamming on the brakes and spinning the cab into an alarming U-turn.

"Let me guess," I said as I picked myself off the taxi floor. "Tanks?"

"Field artillery trucks," he replied proudly. "We chased Rommel all the way to Tunis."

I was still dusting myself down as I unlocked our front door. They were obviously still here as Guy's hat was on the stand in the corner of the hall. I couldn't see my wallet so I headed for the sitting room ... and stopped.

There was one hell of an argument going on in there, furious and insistent. I definitely heard someone spit out the word 'Istanbul' and then what sounded like 'Falstaff' screamed in a mixture of fear and desperation. The odd thing was, I couldn't tell whether it was Guy or Kim doing the talking – and the screaming! After a few more heated words that were difficult to make out, there was a loud crash as if something had been kicked over. I decided to join the party.

When I threw open the sitting room doors both men, next to each other by the fireplace, spun round to face me. Guy looked absolutely petrified while Kim regarded me with what I could only describe as a look of fear and loathing. The expression lasted just a fraction of a second but I saw it ... and he knew I'd seen it.

"Francis," said Kim, partially recovering his equilibrium. "What are you d...doing here?"

I'd learned enough about interrogation techniques during the war to put them to good use in this situation. My narrow-eyed stare lasted barely ten seconds but, beneath it, Guy crumbled, and began to take an unlikely interest in his shoelaces. Philby nearly faced me down but in the end coolly averted his gaze and picked up the empty coal scuttle, which had been propelled into the middle of the rug. He set it back on the hearth.

"Doing here?" I replied eventually in an icy, measured tone. "I'll tell you what I'm doing here, Kim. I appear to be justifying myself to a complete stranger – and in my own home too."

Another very brief burst of anger flashed across Philby's eyes before it was superseded by a confused look. It was obvious he wasn't used to being spoken to like that. He managed to force a smile.

"You're right of course, Francis. My phraseology c...could have been a lot clearer. M...many apologies."

I didn't reply but, coming across my wallet on the coffee table, I made a point of examining it closely.

"We haven't snaffled anything out of it, old boy," said Guy, trying unsuccessfully to lighten the mood.

I stared at him but again remained silent. Guy's barely chirpy demeanour was replaced by a look of fear mixed with pity. But pity for who?

Kim took hold of Guy's elbow and manoeuvred him gently towards the door.

"Come on, old fellow let's get your togs together," he said. "We'll b...be out of your hair in two ticks, Francis."

While Guy and Kim were upstairs I signalled the cab driver to hang on and waited until they came back down around five minutes later. Guy was clutching a medium sized hold-all like an overgrown boy on his first day at school. However, he had recovered some of his equilibrium.

"Goodbye, old man, and thanks for the billet," he said as he shook my hand. "My best to Nancy and the kids. Oh and not forgetting the lovely Hilda."

"Goodbye, Guy."

Philby nodded at me and steered Guy down the front steps to his vehicle. It was only when the battered cab was weaving erratically down the street I realised that Guy had not left his keys behind.

"Diabolical liberty," the cab driver spluttered as I got in.

"What is?"

"People like that shouldn't be allowed to have black cabs," he replied before pulling away from the kerb like a drag racer.

"Why ever not?" I said, returning to the vertical.

"He'll give us all a bad name with driving like that."

242

Later in a cafe on Tottenham Court Road, as we munched joylessly on something called Victory Cake, I told Nancy about the strange interlude of the flying coal scuttle. But her only emotion was one of relief that Guy had finally left.

"He could have kicked the parlour to bits for all I care, just as long as I never see him again."

But we did see him again.

A couple of days later to be exact. The baby was asleep, Julia and Baz had just been put to bed and we were already in the middle of an argument about something I'd done – or rather hadn't done. Nancy had been nagging me to take down a long and extremely sharp coat hook from the back of the study door which had been there since we bought the house. Of course, I'd forgotten and my most profuse apologies were apparently not enough.

"You will be sorry when Baz impales himself on the thing," Nancy proclaimed.

"What's he going to do? Climb up a ladder and launch himself at it?"

"Don't be ridiculous! Just get rid of the thing. Use a screwdriver or something."

I clicked my heels together and saluted, adding, "I solemnly promise to shift the coat hook before Baz is twenty-one. And I further pledge not to do it with my teeth."

"Prick!"

The culmination of this fraught, yet exhilarating, exchange was definitely not the most propitious moment for Guy Burgess to arrive on our doorstep. Indeed, when Nancy threw open the front door and saw him with a large canvas bag at his feet, she nearly had a blue fit. Immediately Guy held up his hands in surrender.

"Don't shoot, fair lady," he pleaded in mock supplication. "I come in peace, bringing gifts."

Guy reached down into the bag and pulled out two parcels, wrapped in the type of gaudily coloured paper I hadn't seen for years. He offered both to Nancy in the manner of a small boy in a nativity play.

"Gold, frankincense and ciggies," he told her as she warily accepted the gifts. "Those filthy Turkish objects you favour to be exact. Red hot out of the diplomatic bag."

With a mixture of exasperation and curiosity, Nancy ripped apart the paper on one parcel and recoiled in shock.

"This is Chanel No 5," she spluttered. "My absolute favourite."

"Is that me or the perfume?" said Guy with a nervous grin.

Not for the first time, he had rendered Nancy almost speechless. "Er, thank you very much," was the limit of what she could come up with.

"A pleasure, my dear," replied Guy. "And look, here's a pretty little pen and pencil set for Julia."

He handed Nancy another package and added, "Now she can finally write that essay about how much she misses good old Uncle Guy pinching her oxygen."

By now I could barely suppress a smirk and was relieved to see that Nancy was battling hard not to smile too.

"This is for Baz," Guy said, handing me the largest of the packages. "It's a model train and track and associated whatnot. The thing is, I do feel rather bad about taking away the major part of his railway lay-out." And he tapped his stomach.

"Oh and I've even got something for the baby. He has started smoking hasn't he?"

"Come on in," I told him, trying not to laugh too much. "That is OK, isn't it?" I asked Nancy.

"Unless Santa has any more chimneys to tumble down," she said, beckoning him into the house.

Quickly ushering Guy into the study, I confessed that we only had the merest drop of Scotch in the house.

"Well, I suppose we could always drink this," he said pulling a bottle from the bag. To my amazement it was a 1928 Remy Martin Extra. I hadn't seen its like in more than six years – even after being parachuted into the Cognac region.

"Where did you pinch this?" I asked in wonder.

Guy shrugged. "It was among the treasures of the Washington diplomatic bag. Amazing what you'll find in there."

He handed me the bottle.

"For you."

"I couldn't possibly take this," I replied.

"Tell you what," said Guy, "I'll let you have it on approval. But I suggest you don't delay in testing it out."

Grinning, I poured out a couple of large shots and handed him one. We touched glasses.

"You're looking uncommonly well," I said.

Usually Guy looked as if he had been dressed by a blind man in a sandstorm but today his clothes were neat and tidy and his habitually unkempt hair well-groomed. He looked quite the suave diplomat he was reputed to be.

"Kim must be looking after you," I observed.

"Kim's a bit slapdash himself as you might have noticed. But it's his better half, Aileen, who does the looking after. Actually they don't live too far from here. Carlyle Square, do you know it?"

"Guy, I'm only a provincial," I said with a faint smile. "You did tell me that often enough. Remember?"

In fact he'd never called me a provincial, not to my face anyway, but how was he to know that, the number of times he'd been steaming drunk in my presence. However the admonition, which was made in jest, clearly embarrassed him and he immediately changed the subject.

245

"Oh, Francis," he cried, beating his chest like King Kong., "I've only gone and forgotten those keys again. What a total idiot! I will drop them off, I promise."

As the conversation went on, I began to notice a couple of odd things. Firstly Guy hardly touched his fine brandy, merely moving the glass incessantly round and round in his hand as if mesmerised by the swirling, sparkling patterns left by the drink. Secondly his initial bonhomie gradually dissipated and he began to look more uncomfortable by the minute.

Anxious that my comment about him calling me a provincial may have brought this on, I tried to lighten his mood by telling him, for the first time, about pole-axing Donald Maclean in front of Attlee. But my story did not have the desired effect.

"Good for you!" he said with a surprisingly bitter laugh. "Don could do with taking down a peg or two. And so for that matter could ..."

He just stopped himself but not before I'd become intrigued by his increasingly shifty manner.

"Who else do you reckon is too big for their boots, Guy?"

Ignoring the question, he grabbed me by the shoulders

"Friendship, Francis," Guy said emotionally. "It's the cornerstone of all our lives. Please say you agree."

"You're good friends with Don Maclean but you chuckled when I said I'd walloped him."

"If you can't laugh at your pals who can you laugh at?" he replied emphatically. "Friendship's like that. The most important thing in the world, I can tell you."

And, despite having hardly touched his brandy, he draped his arm around my shoulder."

"What about family?" I said, gently freeing myself from his embrace.

"Oh god, yes! Family life is crucial. So crucial!"

He nodded with such force I feared his head might roll off.

"And what about loyalty to your country?" I asked. "That's got to be pretty important after all we've been through."

Guy gulped and stared so hard at me that I thought he'd misunderstood the question. Then he began to nod again, though less vehemently.

"Yes of course you're right. I vow to thee my country and all that business. Although ..."

"What?"

"Well, we'd never have come through it without the help and sacrifice ... of others."

"You're absolutely right," I cried and held up my glass. "God bless America!"

He looked momentarily stunned before raising his own glass.

"Oh yes, America. Let's drink to Uncle Sam."

Guy sipped the tiniest bit of brandy and fell into deep rumination. I got the impression that he wanted to say something else but couldn't quite bring himself to do so. In the end he contented himself with a banality.

"Governments are so rotten aren't they," he told me. "The whole blinking lot of them."

I couldn't see where that had come from and told him so.

"Besides," I added, "you represent the government - and you do it in other lands."

"Ach," he spat, again with uncharacteristic vehemence. "I'm like you – a performer. We play a part and say the lines we've been given. If we're very fortunate we can take a bow."

Now I'm almost as cynical as the next miserable bugger but this was beginning to get on even my nerves. I found myself yearning for the old drunken Burgess and his many party tricks, the best of which was undoubtedly tumbling down stairs and shattering the wooden spindles one by one like toothpicks. That story always raised a laugh, even among Nancy and the kids.

By now Guy had picked up on my annoyance but, instead of doing the decent thing and making himself scarce, he became even more emotional.

"Take good care of yourself I beg of you, Francis," he urged, embracing me again.

"I came through the war in one piece didn't I?"

Quite suddenly Guy looked old and very tired.

"Undoubtedly," he replied, leaning heavily against the desk, "but at least you knew who your enemies were then."

What was wrong with the man? In just twenty minutes he'd metamorphosed from a suave boulevardier into a fussier version of my Granny Thirkettle. I wouldn't have been at all surprised if he'd spat on his handkerchief, scrubbed my cheeks and pressed a shilling into my palm.

Finally sensing my perplexity, Guy picked up the glass and downed his brandy in one. Wiping his mouth, he forced a smile and said, "Oh and see that you tidy this place up, Francis. It's a pigsty."

That was a bit more like it.

"You should have seen it when our old lodger lived here," I told him, grinning as we shook hands.

Opening the front door for him, I was struck by an odd thought.

"Guy, there's something very rum about all this."

He glanced at me nervously. "W...What would that be, old boy?"

"Well, you've been here half an hour and you haven't thrown a single line of Latin at me. No Horace or Ovid quotations. And not a trace of Virgil. What is going on?"

I expected him to roar with laughter at the observation but he barely smiled.

"Very well," he said, zipping up the empty canvas bag. "Try 'de pilo pendet' for size."

And, before I could reply, he was down the steps and away without a backwards glance.

I suppose it's over 65 years since I watched, puzzled, as Guy Burgess scurried off into the dusk but barely a month goes by when I don't wonder what he meant. Was he warning me of something? Because what Guy had said meant literally, 'it hangs by a hair' or more pertinently, 'we are at a critical stage'.

When I walked slowly back into the sitting room, Nancy pointed to her neck.

"You've still got a tide mark there," I told her.

"No, smell it, you idiot."

I leaned over and took a whiff.

"Christ, that's er ... pongy."

"Coco Chanel's finest is what that is. It must have cost Guy a small fortune."

"I'll bet you're sorry you weren't nicer to him."

"A little bit maybe," she said, dreamily stroking her neck and sniffing the back of her hand. "I suppose he wasn't altogether bad."

"I'm glad you think so because I've invited him to lodge with us again."

Nancy turned a deep shade of puce before realising I was conning her. Then it was my turn to go purple as she covered me in bruises. I didn't mind because I knew we'd make up in the time-honoured fashion of warring lovers. Which we did.

Later, as she lay snoring beside me, I studied Nancy closely and suddenly understood why she'd been so thrilled to receive the perfume from Guy. It represented a small measure of release from the endless physical and spiritual grind that the war had put everyone through.

Even when asleep, Nancy looked tired and washed-out. She never even bothered to use gravy browning on her legs any more! As I gazed at my wife I made a pledge that I'd treat her to our first family holiday since I was demobbed. And sooner rather than later.

As things turned out, it would have to be later because Nancy had planned a small break which didn't include me. She was taking the children, including the baby, to visit her eldest sister Alexandra up near Lancaster. Throughout Nancy's years in family exile, Alex had remained the one sibling in whom she could confide.

I couldn't join them on their northern adventure as I was about to begin my slow re-integration into the showbiz world, otherwise known as playing second spot at Mile End Empire. With that sort of heady activity going on, I hardly gave Guy Burgess and his odd pal a thought. All that changed dramatically the following Monday.

****

Having finished the East End booking two days previously, I was enjoying an early evening drink with Eddie Star to discuss the possibility of more work. Perhaps 'enjoying' was not quite the word.

"Let's not walk before we can run, old son," was the general tenor of Eddie's considered advice. "Things have changed since 1939. There's hundreds of these young ENSA types clamouring for their chance. For instance have you ever heard of Benny Hill?"

"No," I said grumpily, "where is it?"

"You never lose it, do you, Tosh" said Eddie, roaring with laughter.

"If I'm so entertaining why don't you get me spots at ..." but a chuckling Eddie was already disappearing in the direction of the toilets.

It wasn't as if I was some kind of pensioner, I mused grumpily, crunching my way home to Earls Court through the bomb-scarred streets of Notting Hill. Some of these 'new' comics were barely younger than me anyway. I couldn't help it if I'd been a child prodigy.

This darkly reflective mood persisted until I got home around seven and found to my alarm that the front door was off the latch and opened at a touch. Nancy and the children were still away and there was no need for Hilda to be in the house.

I closed the door silently behind me and tiptoed nervously to the dresser in the corner of the hall. If there was an intruder at least I'd be armed. So it came as an awful hammer blow when I opened the bottom drawer – and found my Luger PO8 was missing.

Then came something equally disturbing; the sound of a footstep from the study. It was the faintest of noises but left me in no doubt that someone had broken into my home.

I paused, aware that pearls of sweat were forming on the back of my neck. My stomach had begun to churn too in that horribly familiar way I thought was behind me for ever. Yet, even at this stage, it would have been simple enough to rush from the house and summon the constabulary.

So why didn't I cut and run? Maybe it was an inner voice telling me that this was a problem that I, a seasoned war veteran, needed to sort out myself. As listening to that inner voice nearly cost me my life, I've never paid it much heed since.

The door to the study was slightly ajar so I was able to look in without making a sound. Sure enough somebody was there in the half darkness. Lit only by the small torch he held, a tall, shaven-headed man was rifling through the desk drawers, quickly scanning papers before replacing them and scooping up another sheaf.

I pushed the door open wide and switched on the light. The intruder, who looked Eastern European to me, jumped away from the desk as if he'd been hit by a grenade.

"Perhaps I could be of assistance?" I said, desperately trying to disguise my fear.

Shifty calculation had replaced shock on the man's Slavic features and he watched warily as I walked, heart pounding, into the room and made for the desk drawers. I noted that this fellow looked about my age but more muscular than I could ever hope to be.

As I reached the back of the desk, he stepped round to the other side and drew a gun from inside his jacket.

"So that's where my revolver ended up," I said. "Thank goodness it wasn't stolen."

My lame attempt at humour went unappreciated *(a situation hardly unknown to Frankie)*. Instead the intruder urgently signalled with the Luger for me to move to the far side of the room. Momentarily mystified, I stood my ground before working out what he was up to. He wanted me away from the window so it would not be shattered by any bullet that ripped through me. He signalled again, levelling the pistol at me. Silently saying my prayers, I called his bluff and shook my head.

"Please step away from desk," he said in what sounded like a Russian accent. Again I declined.

The Russian was growing more nervous by the second. He quickly took a couple of steps to the right to change the angle but I countered by moving the same number of paces to my right and one step back, which put me flush up against the window. The man peered around wildly until his glance fell on the Bakelite wireless on a table next to him. He switched it on.

"A fan of Tommy Handley," I said as the radio valves began to warm up slowly. "I knew there must be at least one around."

I was fully aware that he'd switched on the radio to drown out the sound of gunshots but I was intent on disorientating him as much as possible. And I could see it was working.

252

"Move away from window," he almost screamed.

"Do you know," I replied as calmly as I could, "just before I slit his throat, a German who'd served on the Eastern front - the one I took that very gun from - told me what useless fighters you Russians were."

The intruder's eyes nearly bulged out of his head.

"Oh I know you came out top in the end but this Nazi reckoned that it took ten Ivans to beat one Fritz. And then they'd need all the guns and knives they could lay their thieving hands on."

"That is filthy lie," he shouted.

"Why don't you put down the weapon and prove him wrong then?"

Instead he lifted the gun and pointed it straight at my head.

At that precise moment the wireless burst into life. The empty air was suddenly filled with Tommy Handley's unaccountably popular show, It's That Man Again. Plummy voices were repeating the phrases "After you, Claude" "No after you, Cecil" ad infinitum and, despite my terrible situation, I couldn't help snorting with laughter, more at the absurdity than anything else. God only knows what the Russian made of it.

What he did, however, was to throw the gun aside and launch himself at me with fighting moves like nothing I'd encountered before in my bouts with Les or any of the wartime training.

For a start, he flew horizontally across the desk feet-first like some sort of murderous ballerina and I only just managed to avoid being scissor-kicked through the window. He was on his feet in a second, circling me and lashing out with a bewildering flurry of punches and kicks at my head and chest, before stepping back. At first I wondered if he was wary of engaging me full-on but as each of his next two or three shots struck painfully home, I realised with dismay that he was toying with me.

"Can I do you now, sir?" Mrs Mopp's nasal tones burst out of the wireless, followed by a tide of laughter. It wasn't only the ITMA studio audience who were having a good time either. My opponent had become confident enough to grin along, displaying a set of surprisingly well-maintained teeth.

"So, flabby bourgeois pig, teach me all about fighting please," he said shooting out a lightning right to the head, followed by an even quicker left into my guts, which had me staggering back towards the door.

"I don't mind if I do."

You'll probably have guessed that this was not my response to his request but yet another of the brain-dead catch-phrases spewing out of the radio. I just had time to reflect on the bitter irony that Britain's favourite comedian was about to die, to the accompaniment of the Home Service pumping out Handley's feeble gags. However, I could barely hold on even to that thought as the Russian moved in for the kill.

I backed towards the door, wondering if I could make a run for it. But I could hardly move as it felt like he had cracked at least a couple of my ribs. And, even if I had been able to flee, it was too late as he was leaping at me, his huge outstretched paws ready to close around my neck. Staggering back, I realised I would have to do something as I'd be no match for him hand-to-hand.

Painfully summoning my last bit of strength, I half turned, slammed my elbow into his mid-riff and spun him round. He was moving at some lick too because he twisted nearly one hundred and eighty degrees and landed heavily with his back against the study door. But the ploy had not worked and his massive hairy hands tightened around my neck.

"This is it," I remember thinking as I began to lose consciousness. "The final curtain - and so many people left to entertain."

Then, just as I was about to pass out, a miracle happened. His grip around my throat slackened all of a sudden and I was able to breathe again. I glanced up groggily and saw that the Russian was staring at me in utter confusion.

I also noticed the dangerously sharp coat hook that Nancy had been banging on about was protruding from his throat. I don't know who was more surprised, me or him, but as his hands flopped down by his side I broke away and staggered across to the desk where my gun lay. I snatched up the weapon and turned quickly but it was blindingly obvious I would not need it.

The Russian was suspended a couple of inches from the floor like a puppet whose strings had been cut. The hook appeared to have severed or at least terminally damaged his spinal cord and he was clearly incapable of movement. I watched horrified yet fascinated as blood began to bubble from both sides of his mouth. The man was a goner and he knew it too. His chin had come to rest on the hook sticking out of him – as if in final surrender.

I put the gun down on the desk and rubbed my neck, trying desperately not to pant too much as every breath was total agony.

Meanwhile the black Bakelite box continued booming out inanities including, "It's being so cheerful as keeps me going." Whatever damn well happened to proper catchphrases like, "I've come on me bike"? I reached across and switched off the wireless.

By now the Russian's breath was coming in short, jagged bursts accompanied by greater volumes of blood. And, as he gazed at me imploringly, I knew it was no good - I had to do something. I couldn't just leave him hanging there like that, for pity's sake.

So, taking great care not to jar my injured ribs too much, I carefully removed my jacket - and plonked it over his head so I didn't have to watch him die. Well, what did you expect? The sneaky bastard had just tried to murder me!

A glance in the mirror revealed the shocking extent of the damage he'd wrought too. I had a number of deep gashes across my cheeks, the Russian's finger marks were clearly visible all round my throat and my nose looked broken in a couple of places. I could even feel a couple of back teeth rattling. There was also blood all over my shirt and, to this day, I'm unsure how much of it was mine and how much was his.

I badly needed something to take away the pain so I reached into the bottom desk drawer and pulled out Guy's bottle of Remy Martin which had lain there untouched for a week. Trying not to let my hand shake too much, I poured myself a large shot of brandy. Then another. And another.

Ten minutes later, when I was feeling somewhat more human, I picked up the gun, approached the door and carefully removed my coat from the Russian's head. He looked quite dead but I was taking no chances. I pressed the gun barrel firmly against his chest while I checked for vital signs. Thankfully, there were none.

I was speculating on exactly what I would tell the police when there was a sound - a faint click - out in the hall. Someone had opened the front door and surely it could only be one of the dead man's colleagues.

Swiftly moving round to the far side of the desk, I crouched down and levelled the Luger at the door, trying not to breathe too heavily as it began to open very slowly - unsurprisingly really as there was a 12-stone Russian corpse attached to it.

My finger tightened on the trigger; this time I would not be in a fight to the death. But it was lucky that I held off firing as the florid, anxious features which appeared round the door were those of Guy Burgess. His eyes darted round the room before lighting on me and his concerned look changed to a relieved smile. As I stood up Guy came right into the room.

"My word, Francis," he said, surveying the body pinned to the door. "I see you took me at my word and started Spring cleaning with a vengeance."

"This mad bastard tried to kill me," I mumbled. "I'm calling the police."

But, as I began to dial, Guy put his hand on mine.

"Let's hold off for a moment, old cock, before we summon the Peelers," he said and quickly began to go through the dead man's pockets. Fishing out a wallet, he examined the contents and gave a whistle.

"I thought as much," he exclaimed. "This character is – was – a Russian diplomat. Believe me, things could get very messy if you call the police. Let me bring Kim on board, he'll know how to handle the situation. Whoa, watch yourself!"

Guy later revealed that he just about caught me as I staggered and passed out. When I came to, I was sitting in the chair and he was gently bathing my facial wounds with warm water. He smiled and held up a handful of bandages he'd taken from our first aid box.

"Now I'm going to wrap you up like Tutankhamun," he grinned. "If that doesn't work we can always put you on display at the British Museum."

As Guy set about bandaging my ribs, something struck me. "I don't understand why you arrived at that very moment, Guy?" I said.

He shrugged. "Coincidence, dear boy. I was merely bringing your keys back as promised." And he took the set out of his pocket and dropped them on to the desk.

"And that's another thing," I said. "How did this joker get in?"

Guy put down the bandages and went through the dead man's pockets again. He held up a set of keys.

"Skeleton thingies," he said. "Standard issue at the Russian Embassy, I'll be bound."

This was confirmed by Kim Philby when he turned up five minutes later.

"Some of them use diplomatic immunity to p...plunder London, using keys like this," he told me as he went expertly through the dead man's clothes, checking behind lapels and carefully examining the lining of his jacket. "As they're based just up the road it gets particularly b...bad round here."

"Why doesn't the government make a fuss then?" I said rubbing my neck.

Philby glanced at Burgess and turned to me with a faint smile.

"P...Personally I'd kick the whole tribe of them out," he said. "But we have to be practical. We can't c...cause a public hoo-hah with our allies so things like this are generally dealt with quickly and quietly."

"Things like this!" I exclaimed. "Exactly how many dead Russkies are there hanging around London?"

It was the first time I'd seen Philby laugh out loud.

"With you around, I shudder to think," he replied before his features fell back into the prim, schoolmasterly countenance he presented to the world.

"However, I'll tell you this for nothing; there aren't many like your pal here. Most of their burglars are from the b...back of beyondski. But this one's a fully-trained M...Moscow hoodlum. And before you ask how I know, I've seen his file. Name of B...Bilyatov. Yuri Bilyatov."

"Kim has a photographic memory in matters like this," said Guy, hardly able to disguise his pride.

I slumped down into the desk chair and tried my best to absorb what I'd been told. You see, things were puzzling me. Things like why, if Bilyatov was only burgling the place, did he try to kill me?

Again Kim had the answer.

"Any description you gave to the police would certainly have identified him. After all, how many six foot two, shaven-headed Slavs are there k...kicking around this part of town. Then it would have been straight back to Moscow for him."

I shrugged. "So what? He'd be in disgrace."

"No, Francis, not in d...disgrace. In a crate! Just as he will now make that final journey. Now if you d...don't mind. I'll inform Special Branch that a team from my department is dealing with our little problem. The FO will have a quick word with the Soviet ambassador and the problem will cease to exist. Is there anywhere you could possibly be while we g...get on with it?"

A night out was about the last thing I'd planned but reluctantly I let Kim run me the short distance up to a local pub, The Prince of Teck.

On the way he again tried to reassure me that, although Special Branch would be in touch over the next day or two, the matter would then be quietly dropped.

As I climbed out of his cab, Kim grabbed my sleeve and said insistently, "Like I m...mentioned it's in nobody's interest to kick up a fuss. Here, have one or two on me." And, to my amazement, he thrust a fiver into my hand. Before I could throw the note back in his face I was standing on the pavement watching Philby's taxi bring traffic to a halt with a perfect U-turn and roar back down Earls Court Road.

I spent the next couple of hours in the pub chewing the fat with a muscular young hod carrier called Alan who came from Goole. His story was that he'd landed without a scratch in the first wave on D-Day but was wounded in the thigh when his outfit, the East Yorkshires, hit the outskirts of Caen. Alan was particularly fascinated with my own injuries too and didn't appear to accept the explanation that they'd been caused by the top flying off the toothpaste tube and striking me a glancing blow.

259

"If tha' wants, I'll go and sort him out," he told me. "It's no bother."

"Thanks, Alan, but I've a feeling he won't be troubling me again."

Alan sighed in deep disappointment. "Pity," he said. "It's so bloody dull these days, in't it?"

"Yeah, nothing ever happens."

As we parted I slipped Kim's fiver into his hand.

"What's all this about?" he said, fists clenching.

"Keep your hair on," I replied. "You need it more than me. Don't worry it's not funny money."

And with a quick handshake, I left him shaking his head and smiling at his good fortune.

Perhaps I should have used some of that money to hire a cab because by the time I'd walked the few hundred yards home, my ribs were killing me and my nose felt like it was melting all over my face. I could barely breathe.

At least when I finally got back into the house it was empty and silent. I cautiously opened the door to the study but it swung back flush against the wall. Nobody was hanging around there any more. I jumped as the phone rang. It was Kim.

"S...sorry you had to experience the more seamy side of our world tonight," he said.

"Yes, and me having lived all my life in an enchanted palace."

I heard him chuckle down the line. "I f...forgot you were such an experienced - and cynical - old hand," he replied. "Even so, I'd say you've had an extraordinary escape tonight. You're v...very lucky to be alive. Now forget all about it. Goodbye, Francis."

And I was left staring at the receiver.

Whenever the phone rang over the next couple of days I was convinced it would be Special Branch but it never was. Nancy and the kids arrived home on Wednesday and even though I'd been skilfully patched up by medics at St

Stephen's Hospital, it was clear to her that something had gone on.

"You can tell me, I won't be angry," she said. "Unless it's another woman and then I'll kill you."

I assured her that other women were the last things on my mind and that I'd merely stumbled face-first into the hearth while tying my shoelaces. Amazingly the explanation appeared to satisfy her and she forgot about the matter. Unlike yours truly. After three days I'd had enough of following Kim's advice to put the incident behind me so I decided to contact Carlton Frobisher.

I fished out his number from my blazer and, although I let it ring for a couple of minutes to give him a chance to hobble to the phone, my call went unanswered.

Nor was he there when I tried about ten o'clock the next morning after another restless night. Then I recalled that I had his office number in my diary so, after some soul-searching, I rang there asking to speak to Carlton.

There was a long pause before a softly spoken Scottish voice finally said, "I'm afraid he's not here."

"When will he be back?"

There was another hiatus before the voice demanded, "Who's calling, please?"

"Just a friend of his. Jesus Christ, what is this, The Spanish Inquisition?"

I heard a gasp. "Francis, is that you?"

I confirmed the fact.

"This is Kenneth Parlane. You remember, the man with the van in Naples, 1944."

How could I forget! "Kenny boy," I cried. "It's great to speak to you again. We must get together some time. Now stick your boss on there's a good chap."

There was no immediate response from Parlane so I added, "I know he's there, Kenny."

"The thing is," replied Parlane evenly, "Carlton's not here." His voice went even quieter and I struggled to make out the words.

"I can't hear what you're saying, Kenny. What did I tell you about mumbling!"

His voice became crystal clear. "I said Carlton Frobisher was found hanged at his home two days ago."

It took me thirty seconds to realise I'd dropped the receiver which was still swinging from side to side. I picked it up and put it to my ear.

"Thank god," said Parlane. "I thought you'd passed out."

He went on to tell me that, when Frobisher hadn't made contact for 24 hours, a couple of the team had broken into his North London home and found him strung up by his belt from the banister.

"Things must have got too much for the poor fellow," added Parlane.

"Kenny, you surely can't believe that Carlton would take his own life."

"He had been rather depressed recently. You know, not being able to do what once came easily."

This smelled to high heaven.

"What did his note say?" I demanded.

"I ... I don't think there was a note."

"You really imagine Frobisher would do that without so much as an explanation? Pull the other one!"

There was an uncomfortable silence at the other end, so I dug a bit deeper.

"What was he working on, Kenny? Come on, out with it."

The long silence was finally broken when Parlane replied warily, "You know I can't tell you that."

"Let me help you then," I told him. "I'm willing to bet you any money that Carlton - and his cousins - were keeping a very sharp look-out for a small, blind rodent."

"Jesus Christ," Parlane croaked and the line went dead.

It appeared as if I'd indeed had a very lucky escape and, what's more, this was not the end of the matter. I needed to take out some life insurance.

(Phew! I have to confess that was so exciting I was rendered temporarily unavailable to supply notes. So, a tiny bit of background. In 1945, American intelligence officers, particularly James Jesus Angleton, later a high-ranking CIA man, were beginning to harbour suspicions about Kim Philby.

Then in August, Konstantin Volkov, a high-ranking officer in the NKVD – a forerunner of the KGB – told British diplomats in Istanbul that he had the names of three Soviet agents in Britain, two of whom worked for the Foreign Office and the other as head of counter-espionage. When the Volkov information landed on Philby's desk in Section Nine of the Secret Intelligence Service - MI6 - he realised that Burgess, Maclean and himself were about to be exposed.

So he immediately tipped off Moscow and Volkov was shipped back to Russia from Turkey, never to be heard from again. Frankie, who in all likelihood overheard an anguished Philby telling Burgess about the Volkov threat, was indeed a very lucky man to escape assassination.

But Britain's favourite comedian? OK, maybe under the circumstances, we can allow him that one. And raise a glass to his survival).

Chapter Thirteen: Frankie Goes to Slatterwood – and then to Hollywood

All that palaver seemed so far away by October 1948 as I squinted in awe at the wild Pacific rollers bursting against Santa Barbara Pier. Even though I was a mile away, relaxing by Sol Cosminsky's kidney-shaped pool, in the foothills of the Santa Ynez Mountains, I could just make out the sparkling curtains of spray as the waves constantly threatened to turn the pier into matchwood – but never quite managed it. In case you're wondering, I was squinting because the juice from an exceedingly plump red grapefruit had shot into my eyes as I'd gone at it with a dessert spoon minutes earlier. Even the mountain of sugar I'd piled on to it could not entirely take away the sting.

My excuse for this clumsiness was simple. Like most Britons, I had seen little fruit of any kind for the previous ten years and the miserable dried-up odds and sods that had found their way into our home during the war and beyond were as unlike this succulent cannonball as they could be.

Quite simply, I'd forgotten how to eat fruit. However, as I stretched back on the yellow and blue striped sun bed to rest my smarting eyes, I resolved to launch an extensive re-education programme. Mmmmmm.

My citrus-based reverie was curtailed by the appearance of Nancy who stepped out of Sol's Moorish-style white villa and onto the pool terrace, as if about to accept the world's applause. She even had a devoted acolyte in tow; one who pawed her constantly and seemed in the mood to tear her swimsuit right off.

However, even though we were among Hollywood folk, I didn't feel at all threatened as this fervent admirer was our young son Jonathan. And, to be fair to the lad, he was more in thrall to the swimsuit than the mother inside it. This two-piece garment was a thing of wonder to him, made as it was from the very latest rainbow-coloured synthetic material. The boy could not keep his hands off it.

Nancy sashayed towards me as alluringly as she could with a three-year-old welded to her right leg and I encouraged the performance with a prolonged bout of applause. However, it turned out that Nancy was in no mood for my nonsense. She stopped, looked around in annoyance and said, "You utter pig, Franco."

"Why is daddy a piggy, Mummy?" inquired Jonathan.

"Because he's scoffed the lovely green melon, darling. A whole one. All by himself."

Crikey I'd forgotten about that. After all, it was at least half an hour ago. Well before the grapefruit.

"There's plenty more fruit in the refrigerator, dear." I informed Nancy soothingly. "No ration coupons in California, remember!"

"You're still a pig."

"Come on, Jonno, time for our whale ride."

Jonathan screamed in delight as I escaped further interrogation by flinging myself into the pool before resurfacing and holding up my arms up to catch him. Soon I was swimming up and down with Jonathan clinging to my shoulders.

"Daddy's a big whale fish not a little piggy," he whooped.

"A whale is a mammal, darling, not a fish," said Nancy from behind her paperback. "It doesn't alter the fact that Daddy's still behaved like a prize porker but you do need to talk properly ... oh, Franco, you complete arsehole!"

"It's only water, Nance. Sorry about the book."

"What's a horse hole, Daddy?"

"It sounds like a very, very strange kind of mammal. Or perhaps it's a fish."

Soon the pool exertions started to give my injured knee some real pain, yet I couldn't risk getting out of the water in case my wife smashed me across the aching limb with her dripping parasol. My strokes became slower and slower until, thank goodness, Nancy eventually stalked off in search of unforbidden fruit.

Immediately she disappeared inside the villa, I swung Jonathan out of the pool and made for my sun bed, thanking the good lord that at least our other two offspring were still at school in England. Although they would be joining us when the deal Sol had fixed up was finally signed and I became a worldwide movie star. And surely that was just a formality!

But, as usual, I'm stumbling ahead of myself so let's catch ourselves up a little.

Going to the USA and leaving Britain's frozen gloom and desperate post-war rationing behind us was not the insurance I'd mentioned at the end of the last eventful chapter. No, my gilt-edged safety policy was far simpler than that. And extremely effective, as it turned out.

What I'd done was to set down a long and detailed account of everything that had gone on, much as in this memoir in fact. I wrote down every last detail, apart from the bit about Nancy continually nagging me to deal with the coat hook; I didn't want folk thinking I was some sort of idle so-and-so. Oh, and in the time-honoured spirit of never giving publicity to your rivals, I didn't mention Tommy Handley to anyone either.

The next step was to collar Guy Burgess at lunch-time in the Admiral Duncan in Soho before he could drink himself senseless. He was doing some work for an MP around this time but it didn't seem to have affected his leisure pursuits. I told him all that had happened to me was so fascinating that I'd written it down and deposited the manuscript and its various copies in a number of secure locations, including Eddie Star's solicitor's safe. These would be opened and read out only if I were to meet a tragic and untimely end.

"God forbid that should *ever* happen," murmured Burgess, intently scrutinising the county cricket scores in the Daily Telegraph. "But should the worst ensue then it may be some small comfort to remember the words of Tacitus - corpora lente augescent cito extinguuntur." *(Bodies grow slowly and die quickly).*

Despite this show of scholarly claptrap, I knew he'd taken the message on board and would pass it on, very probably in Ionian couplets, to his pals Philby and Maclean.

Of course, I couldn't prove if all or any of them were involved in the Russian's murderous assault on me or the suspicious death of Carlton Frobisher. In the absence of any note, the coroner had recorded an open verdict there. But at least it would give their bulging posh brains pause for thought, if only to wonder why I was addressing the warning to them.

And, watching Burgess appear to casually ignore what I was saying made me resolve to get my own back on him and kick his arse very publicly. Which I did, in rather spectacular fashion, as you'll see in the final chapter. *(For once in his life, Frankie is not gilding the lily).*

Eddie Star, on the other hand, showed extreme interest in my account. We had gone but a few paces down The Strand after leaving the manuscript at his lawyer's office when Eddie began pestering me about its content.

His fascination grew when I told him that the saga involved spies, grisly murders and a cohort of naked, sex-starved Amazonian warriors.

"Are there pictures as well?" he asked as his eyes began to glaze over.

"Most certainly," I replied. "What's more, the girls have all signed them."

Eddie pulled himself together long enough to light a cigar. He put a trembling hand on my shoulder and said seriously, "It sounds a right old tale, Tosh. And, god forbid, should the worst happen, then rest assured your story will be placed with the very best publisher, possibly attracting the interest of a top movie producer and an extremely generous advance for the option."

That cheered me up no end and I told Eddie as much.

"I'm so relieved," I said, "that as I lie cold on a slab you'll still be taking your cut out of me. Thanks so much for putting my mind at rest on that matter."

"Think nothing of it, old son," said Eddie, patting me again with a firmer hand. "After all, haven't I always done my very best for you?"

Well, if we're counting, up to a point! For instance his best hadn't been much to write home about during the months after the fighting ended although to be fair there were mitigating circumstances.

In post-war austerity Britain it wasn't only bread, spuds and sweets that were on the ration; comedy spots at our better theatres were like gold dust too. That's because, as Eddie had correctly predicted, the legions of new boys flooding back into Civvy Street were starting to create a big impression. Most of these kids had used ENSA as a valuable wartime training ground and were now intent on making up for lost time. *(The Entertainments National Service Association or ENSA was an organisation set up in 1939 to provide amusement for British armed forces personnel during the war. Some reckoned the acronym stood for 'Every Night Something Awful').*

Although I wasn't much older than most of these new entertainers, they seemed to come from a different generation with rules I couldn't fathom. Yet the plain truth was that none of them were any good – and I speak from a position of some authority.

For instance, early in 1946, I remember walking off stage into the wings at Plymouth's Theatre Royal slap bang into Max Miller who was too busy shaking his head to get out of the way. As second spot comic, I'd just introduced a young ventriloquist, Norman "Nobby" Norris and his aging pal Monty. Miller, who was topping the bill, appeared unimpressed.

" 'Ere, I've been keepin' an eye on this geezer all week," he said with a sniff. "His mouth moves more than the dummy's."

"How can you tell?" I asked.

"What d'you mean how can I tell? I've got eyes in me head haven't I?"

"I mean how can you tell which is the dummy?"

"What a totally spiteful thing to say, Francis. God forbid that should find its way into my act."

Of much more interest to me were the young comedians who were keeping food off my plate. It was an odd thing but many of them didn't even tell jokes as such; just rambled on and on. And can you believe this? Some did without regular catchphrases as well!

For instance, I recall watching from the wings as young Frankie Howerd performed at the Pier Theatre in Great Yarmouth, during the big winter of 1946-47. Quite frankly he was terrible. He just kept banging on and on about how the cold was shrivelling his potential. He didn't have any as far as I was concerned.

Yet the oddest thing was that, for some reason, the audience seemed to love this young Frankie and laughed their bleedin' heads off at him. The very same mob who couldn't - or wouldn't - even tell me on which particular mode of transport I'd arrived at the theatre. There's no accounting for taste is there?

So, to cut a short story even shorter, by early 1948 my career had gone as cold as the previous winter and if it hadn't been for Nancy, who already represented quite a few of this new comical army, we'd have been on Queer Street.

Noting her success, I'd been planning to ask my dear wife ever so nicely if she'd make it official and be my new agent. From a ringside seat, I'd seen how her acts unfailingly swooned when she addressed them as "my

269

boys" and more particularly when she found them work, which was on a regular basis.

So it was perhaps fortunate for me that, when I stalked into Eddie's office, he immediately cut in before I could give him his marching orders. What he told me was that his latest plan for me involved just two words.

"Yeah, you an' all with knobs on," I told him grumpily.

"No, you chump," said Eddie. "I'm talking about the movies."

"Films? What's the cinema got to do with me?"

"Formby and Randle are already well in there," he explained. "So why not you?"

Well, why not indeed? I was five hundred times better looking than George and a thousand per cent more sober than Frank. And that, dear readers, is how I ended up guzzling grapefruit, high above the Pacific Ocean while listening to the gentle trilling of cicadas in the hot Californian ... hold on, hold on! Cut, rewind, hair in the gate! That was not how things happened! It turned out that Eddie didn't mean Hollywood at all. He was talking about Slatterwood.

"Slatterwood," I exclaimed, totally bemused. "The only Slatterwood I know is a town about five miles from Butterthwaite where they all look like Ben Turpin – if you can imagine Ben Turpin with six fingers on each hand." *(Ben Turpin, 1869–1940, was a cross-eyed American comedian, best remembered for his work in silent films).*

"And that's exactly the Slatterwood where you're bound, old son," said Eddie offering me a cigar as if some sort of celebration was warranted. "Does the Ben Turpin look include women as well?"

"I was referring to the women."

It turned out that Slatterwood Studios had opened with little fanfare the previous year in a line of old weaving sheds and since then had been churning out cheap and cheerful northern comedies at the rate of one a fortnight.

Eddie opened a large folder on his desk and showed me some of the posters. The films had names like 'World Heavyweight Chump', 'He's At It Again' and 'Much Ado About Colin'. They generally starred forgotten names from music hall's alliterative dim and distant past. Names like Saucy Sally Stockingtops, 'Pansy' Pat Masters and Derry Doughballs.

"This is classy stuff," I told Eddie. "Have we got Orson Welles on board yet?"

"Don't come over all Graham Greene with me, Tosh," he frowned, pointing insistently at the posters. "For every 'Citizen Kane', this lot could give you twenty 'Don't Do It, Noshers'."

"That's what I was afraid of."

(Orson Welles, 1915-1985, was an American film director, actor and all-round enfant terrible, who in 1941 made Citizen Kane, which many cinema experts reckon to be the greatest film, ever. Celebrated English novelist Graham Greene, 1904-1991, also worked as an influential film critic for the magazine Night and Day).

Eddie then broke a piece of even more joyous news. Without further ado, I was to star in the film, 'Down Your Trousers', about a precocious young northern lad, Franny, and his pet ferret, Fulton, who - guess what - manage to get themselves into all manner of hilarious scrapes. The movie would also feature those ageing limelight hoggers Teddy Tosspot and Dolly Spicer as my parents, Ted and Dol. Apparently Michael Redgrave and Dame Sybil Thorndyke cocked up their auditions.

I could have ditched the offer and sat on my thumb all summer but I reasoned that I might as well kill a number of birds with this one stone. For instance, here was our chance to finally have that family holiday I'd been promising Nancy since 1945. We'd rent a pretty little cottage up in the hills halfway between Butterthwaite and Slatterwood where the kids could run free without the threat of being mown down by the 211 to Ealing Broadway. Nancy could continue her career, edit scripts and play hostess to Lady Agatha while I tried to sneak into Protheroe Hall without getting shot and see what Les and the rest of them were up to.

I knew Tommy had recovered from the wounds he'd suffered in Normandy and I was keen to catch up on things. On the only previous time we'd met since the war's end, neither of us had felt much like talking.

So that was settled. Eddie made a call to the studio and the following week our entire family sallied northwards in the nearly new Austin 12. And when we rolled up to the cottage late in the evening, bedraggled and irritable, ample compensation awaited us. It was a hamper full of the goodies we weren't used to seeing any more down in London. These included bread that looked and tasted as if it wasn't made largely from wainscot dust, a box of dates and two large tins of boiled sweets which the children fell upon like hyenas.

"Agatha must be keeping Butterthwaite's spiv community going on her own," I mused, munching a large slab of white unsliced with Lancashire Cheese. "I wonder if they give her a dividend."

"She's never got over the guilt she felt about how Daddy treated us," said Nancy, biting enthusiastically into a stick of celery. "Long may it continue!"

I'd have drunk to that sentiment if there had been an opportunity - or any drink. As it was we all fell shattered into bed after the feast.

This meant I was at Slatterwood Studios bright and early the next day for my debut as a matinee idol. Even then I'd worried that arriving at nine would mean I was the last there but when I pulled up in the Austin there was no-one around, apart from a stick-thin cove who wore a cravat and had a cigarette holder permanently clamped between his teeth. This was Robin Bullingdon, the film's producer, who greeted me as I stepped out of the car.

"Frankie, old fellow," he purred as if this were not the first time we'd clapped eyes on each other. "How utterly marvellous to be working with you. Come and meet our poor actors who strut and fret throughout their life on the stage and then are heard of no more."

Well, it sounded like he didn't have much confidence in his cast!

Appropriately the first poor actor I encountered was Teddy Tosspot, an aged, crumpled figure who looked as if he'd been auditioning for the lead in The Guy Burgess Story.

Teddy threw down his newspaper and grabbed my arm. "I knew your Granny Thirkettle, dear boy," he wheezed at me through broken teeth. "We were on the same bill at Llandudno in '96."

"That's nice to hear," I replied, touched that he had fond recollections of a much-missed family member.

"Ah yes, Maud, the Blackburn Barn Owl," intoned Teddy, his eyes glazing over wistfully. "Banged like a shithouse door in a gale force wind. No offence meant."

"Er, none taken."

Well, I could hardly flatten him as he was the wrong side of eighty and I wasn't quite ready for a spell on Devil's Island. And to be fair, he was only repeating a long-established truth. You might just remember old whatshisface mentioning that what she lacked in talent, Granny Thirkettle made up for in raw sexual allure. *(See, right again. Get in!)*

As Teddy returned to his kiddies' crossword puzzle the other member of my screen family shuffled into view. By all accounts, Dolly Spicer had been a fair old warbling beauty up to the 1920s but the ensuing years had exacted a bitterly heavy toll. She now looked more like Elsie

273

Swineford after a particularly energetic crumpet digs evening with a troupe of acrobats.

"Nice to make your hacquaintance, dear," she sighed, continually dismissing wisps of unruly grey hair away from her face. "Don't listen to what that old muffin says either." She glanced at Teddy. "I know for a fact that he never got within hactual spitting distance of your Gran."

"That's good to hear," I said, relieved that family honour had been restored.

"Mind you, I'm reliably hinformed that plenty did," Dolly sniffed as she pulled out a pile of knitting from a large shopping bag.

I decided to forgo further discussion of my lineage and take a peek inside the studio. The sound stage, such as it was, consisted of just two sets; a dining room with table, chairs and a framed picture of Prince Albert on the back wall; and a street corner with one grimy and stained lamp post outside a tobacconist's shop. Neither set looked particularly new. It appeared that all the Slatterwood comedies consisted of families chatting endlessly over dinner before occasionally popping out for a pack of fags with the dog.

There wasn't even any lighting equipment around. Instead the large south-facing skylights in the former weaving shed looked as if they'd be providing all the illumination we were going to get.

A short, glum looking fellow with a shiny bald head approached me and held out his hand.

"Jimmy Bradbury," he said. "I'm the director on this piece of shit."

Ah, now then, I'd done my research and discovered that people in the movie world habitually referred to any film they were involved in as 'a piece of shit' even if it was a masterwork. I told Jimmy as much.

"You have a very impressive knowledge, Frankie," he replied lugubriously. "It is indeed a phrase that we in the business use constantly no matter what the quality of the production. Sadly for all concerned, however, this thing really *is* a colossal piece of shit."

Jimmy went on to outline the catalogue of misfortunes that had already befallen a production barely off the drawing board. Barry Norton, the bloke down to play my feckless yet good-hearted brother Barry, was still in police cells after a punch-up in the town on Saturday night. Someone had broken into the equipment store and pinched all the lighting gear. And, to cap it all, Fulton the ferret had done a bunk.

"Normally that would entail a major script re-write," deadpanned Jimmy, "if there had been a major script in the first place."

Blimey, this was getting worse by the minute. Mind you, now that Fulton had made himself scarce at least it looked as if I'd escape with my nuts un-nibbled. It was a thought which led directly to my next question.

"What are you going to call the film now it appears that a ferret will not be going down my trousers?" I asked.

Jimmy scratched his head. "I suppose the new title could be 'Where's My Bleedin' Ferret Gone?'"

We kicked that one around for a few minutes before deciding it wasn't going to fly. Then I had a brainwave.

"If you have no script then what's to stop us doing what we want? We can make it up as we go along."

Nodding eagerly, Jimmy revealed that this was what usually happened anyway. As long as the actors stood on their correct marks and the two-week shoot produced about seventy minutes of more-or-less watchable material then nobody would much mind what we got up to.

"So, as long as our story includes an aged drunk, a past-it glamour girl and a debonair young rascal whose brother is unavoidably absent, then we're laughing?"

"I suppose so," replied Jimmy. "Even if it's unlikely anyone else will be laughing."

"You're dead right there, Jimmy boy," I replied, "because I'm here to reveal that you'll be directing an espionage thriller."

Jimmy shrugged. "Suits me," he said and gathered the cast and crew together. "This here is Frankie," he shouted. "And Frankie's got something to tell you all."

I spent the next ten minutes outlining how our little adventure might develop. Beyond the fact that it concerned a nest of spies in the highest reaches of government, the murder of the hero's trusted friend and the villain impaled on a coat hook in the final scene, everything else was open to interpretation.

"Spies, murderers, coat hooks, hit hall sounds very hunlikely to me," sniffed Dolly. "Besides who will I play?"

"Elsie the Yorkshire landlady," I replied without hesitation. "The villain's at her place when he meets a very timely end. I haven't quite decided whether it's the coat hook or Elsie's cabbage that finally sees him off."

"Cabbage," she sniffed dismissively, "has hif!" But I could detect in her eyes that the role had already begun to intrigue her.

Even the lack of proper lighting helped. After Robin explained that it would take five days to get in new spots we simply sent Joseph the odd-job man up on to the roof, to cover sections of skylight with bits of old carpet. To everyone's delight this managed to create a surprisingly moody atmosphere, akin to what we now know as 'film noir' but in those days was termed 'just that little bit too dim'.

Our production schedule quickly settled into a routine. Every evening I'd go back to the cottage and write an outline of the next day's scenes. The following morning we'd rehearse for a couple of hours and then begin filming. The only rule I insisted upon was that dialogue was kept to a bare minimum and improvised to make it sound as un-theatrical and natural as possible.

Imagine, I told the cast, that you're talking to the milkman or a pal in the pub. It worked too, especially after we'd persuaded Teddy to stop flinging his arms in all directions and launching into yet another Shakespearean soliloquy. Robin, who was much more savvy than he looked, came up with the solution. He told Teddy that he'd knock a quid off his fee every time he waved his arms around or spoke more than five words at a time. We had no more trouble.

I also encouraged Jimmy to focus closer in on the actors' faces and, with Joseph rolling around on the glass roof and falling through it only once, we produced some interesting effects with half-light and shadows.

However, there was still something missing. Films of this sort needed a femme fatale! Luckily I noticed that in Robin's rather striking young dark-haired production assistant, Jeannie, we had the perfect candidate on our doorstep. And that, let me tell you, is how the cinema career of the late, great Jean Simmons came to be launched. All because of me!

(As usual Frankie is talking through his trilby. The undeniably beautiful Jean Simmons, 1929-2010, had already played young Estella in David Lean's 1946 film Great Expectations, and, at the time, was filming the role of Ophelia in Laurence Olivier's Hamlet. History does not record Jeannie's real identity).

We'd been at it about ten days and had nearly an hour of interesting if rather eccentric footage when catastrophe struck from a completely unexpected direction. As usual Jeannie and I were perfecting our romantic clinches and Barry, hanging by a hidden harness on the back of a door, was proudly drawing everyone's attention to the end of a vicious looking coat hook supposedly protruding from his chest, when Jimmy rushed in.

"The studio owner's here," he blurted breathlessly.

"So what," I replied.

I turned round, still lovingly cradling Jeannie, and came face to face with my father-in-law.

"What the hell are you doing here?"

We'd both said it simultaneously but thereafter it was Joshua who made all the running.

"Stop mauling that chit at once," he barked. "Do you hear me!"

"This chit," I replied calmly, "is a talented actress and we're rehearsing a scene."

"Well you can stop it off at once. It's downright immoral. You're a married man."

I could not believe what I was hearing.

"Yes I'm married to your daughter, the one you haven't shown any interest in for over ten years."

"I'm interested when someone's making a monkey out of a Protheroe," he spat, looking around angrily for something else to beef about. His gaze quickly fell on Barry.

"And that prick with the skewer poking out of his tits. Cut him down from there. What kind of comedy is this anyway?"

"Actually, sir," said Jimmy, "it's not really ..."

I stepped in quickly. "It's not really worth fighting about. Me being here that is. So I'll leave the set right now – if that's what you want."

"Dead right," replied Joshua. "Clear off."

And that looked as if it was that. A promising movie career over in a flash.

Having shattered my celluloid dream in four words, Joshua began laying down the law to Robin. As I packed my small canvas bag I noted that he looked even more prosperous than when I'd last seen him; that suit, if I wasn't mistaken, had come straight out Savile Row. Joshua had piled on weight too while the rest of the country had gone lean and hungry. His jowls flapped around as he made his points to the unfortunate producer before finally stalking off.

Robin walked slowly over to me, rubbing his chest where Joshua's forefinger had repeatedly jabbed into it. I looked up from packing my bag.

"Where's Joshua gone? Setting fire to the cottage hospital?"

"No. He's off to a three-day race meeting at York."

Jimmy, who was just behind Robin, piped up with an excitement I'd not seen in him before, "Then Frankie can stay on ..." He was quickly silenced by the producer.

"That fellow there," whispered Robin, pointing to a gorilla of a man with a flat nose and a trilby pulled down over his forehead, "is Sir Joshua's representative on earth. Left here to look after his interests. In loco parentis."

I took a closer look at Maurice Lake's latest successor, who was loitering menacingly by the door. He might as well be put to good use.

"Get Joseph to pretend to film a scene," I whispered to Jimmy, "and you use the second camera to get shots of that orangutan. Without knowing it, he could add a nice touch of menace to the picture – and you could all share his fee."

Jimmy nodded sadly and hugged me.

"I wish it could have been different, fella," he sniffed. "I don't know how we'll ever manage without you."

"You'll find a way," I replied, patting him on the shoulder. "It won't be easy, mind!"

All that remained was for me to say goodbye to everyone else. Jeannie was particularly distraught so I had to take a little extra time over my farewell to her. Barry was still dangling from the door as the harness had become twisted so I just patted his cheeks and told him not to worry. Joseph, who was still playing with carpet squares on the roof, gave me a farewell salute as I climbed into the Austin and left the film world behind for ever – or so I thought.

****

Pulling up in front of the cottage, the first thing I saw was Julia and Baz by the well vigorously winding the handle. They were chanting "Ding dong bell pussy's in the well."

All of a sudden Jonathan's head popped up out of the well. He was perched on top of the bucket, dripping wet.

"This is fun, Daddy," he shouted.

"That's good to hear, son," I said doubtfully but, as they all seemed to having a whale of a time, I decided not to interfere.

Inside the cottage Nancy was scribbling away furiously on a script at the long wooden kitchen table. All she had on was one of my shirts, tied around the middle with a thin leather belt. As I might have mentioned before, she looked sensational! If only the kids weren't ... but the fact is they were - and getting up to all sorts while mummy did her own thing.

Deciding to tackle the matter of the children head-on, I casually asked her, "Can we be entirely sure that the well is safe?"

Nancy paused in mid-scribble and looked at me uncomprehendingly.

"What well?" she replied.

When I explained what the kids were up to, she merely shrugged and recalled that when she was younger they'd done far more dangerous things up at the hall.

"I can't tell you how many times I fell off Bouncer head-first," she said. "And Robbie winged me with his air rifle when I was six. Look I've still got the mark."

She hauled down the shirt to show me a small round white scar on her shoulder – and in doing so revealed a fair bit more.

"Goodness sake, Nance," I hissed. "Have a thought for desperately deprived husbands everywhere."

She slowly pulled the shirt back over her shoulder and winked seductively at me. "Why do you think I'm letting the kids run themselves daft? So they'll be in bed early. Just like us."

She reached across, ran her forefinger down my shirt front and gave me the most demure smile imaginable.

"Speaking of the hall," I said, desperately trying to re-focus my thoughts, "I ran into your Dad today."

I told her everything that had happened, with great stress on the totally callous manner in which Sir Joshua had shattered my dream of silver screen immortality.

Nancy shook her head dismissively. "The studio will be some kind of tax fiddle. He probably doesn't visit the place from one year to the next. You were unlucky."

"Well, now I'm no longer needed, I was thinking of visiting the hall tomorrow."

"Are you and Daddy going to slug it out on the lawn? I might need to print tickets."

"Daddy won't be around, thank god."

I explained that the unfortunate peasantry of East Yorkshire were shouldering that burden for three days.

"Then we'll all go," said Nancy. "Get the kids in. They'll need baths."

"Apart from Jonathan."

Nancy was dead right as usual. An early bedtime did us all a power of good. The kids slept like logs and so did we – after a long overdue session of energetic, if largely silent, bedroom PT. As a result we were all up by seven and at the hall by half eight. While Lady Agatha and Nancy's sister Imogen fussed over the children I made my way very slowly down to the stable block.

The reason for this reticence? Well, I was apprehensive about how Les and Tommy would greet me as I hadn't shown my famous face around these parts for nearly two years. I felt especially neglectful as Tommy had been in a really bad way at the end of the war, both physically and mentally.

In his regular letters to me, Les was as reticent about describing what my kid brother had been through as he was with own Great War experiences. But, reading between the lines, Tommy had had it rough in northern France.

For instance, Les had ended one of letters in this way, "Tom states as he will never ever walk down a country lane with high hedgerows again. Blinkin' murder! I never much hugged him when a child but have somewhat made up for said in recent times."

In the event I was wrong to worry about my reception as Les and Tommy greeted me like the prodigal son/brother. If Tommy was still battling his Normandy demons then he hid it well. And when Rose, who was passing the stable block, squealed in delight and threw her arms round me, the homecoming was complete.

Rose had her own exciting news too. She was now secretary and head housekeeper at Protheroe Hall. Apparently Mary Cunliffe had fluttered her eyelids at Sir Josh once too often and had departed on the toe of Lady Agatha's boot.

"Well I can't top that," I said, quietly shelving the details of my film debut. "The only news I can give you is that we're off to watch the cricket at Old Trafford. Right now. My treat!"

The reaction was hardly what I'd expected. Les and Tommy glumly shook their heads.

"I wish it was possible, kidder," said Tommy.

"Les nodded. "There's nothing I'd like better than to see this Aussie team, Bradman an' all," he said. "But I'm afraid today's a day of work round these parts."

I told them about Joshua being away in York until Sunday but Les remained doubtful. It was Tommy who came up with the solution.

"Tell you what, Dad," he said, hanging one of his great muscular arms round Les's shoulders. "The Bentley needs a good run out after all the work we've done on it. Where better than down Manchester way? Vital engine maintenance, you understand," he said, winking at me.

Les kept up his severe expression for around five seconds before replacing it with a huge grin and announcing, "If it's work, then why not indeed!" He gave a nod to Rose, who turned away immediately and sprinted back towards the hall.

"What's to do with her?" I asked.

Les didn't answer me. Instead he and Tommy concentrated on dragging off their heavy blue overalls in record time and scrubbing themselves clean of oil and dirt at the large Belfast sink. Within five minutes we were strolling across the lawn to the front of the hall where the Bentley was parked. Rose came rushing out of a side entrance and nodded at Les. He nodded back.

"Right, let's go and watch those Aussies take a beating," he said with relish. "You two in the back."

All the way across the moors and down through a string of grey, smoky mill towns, Tommy and I were like a couple of kids again. In fact, Les threatened to make both of us walk to Manchester if we didn't stop scrapping. Les might have looked cross but I could see that he was actually delighted. Tommy hadn't been this carefree for years.

During the journey we'd passed a good few bomb sites that had either been cleared or were being built on but, as we approached the docks in Salford, the landscape changed dramatically. We saw whole terraces, flattened by the Luftwaffe, that had lain untouched since the war. Pink rose bay willow herb grew thick and luxuriant among the rubble. The docks too had been badly knocked about as the number of builders' cranes testified.

We knew we were getting near the ground when the pavements became slow-moving streams of pale-faced men in shabby suits and ties and excited schoolboys, all carrying snap tins and plastic macs. But, by the time we'd reached Old Trafford and saw the great queues of spectators winding up and down Warwick Road, I was becoming concerned that we might not get in.

"No need to worry, lads," said Les. "Just hold off your scrapping for five minutes and behave."

With a squeal of tyres, Les swung the Bentley into the members' car park and waved a piece of coloured cardboard at the two stewards on the gate. The pair stepped respectfully back to allow us in and another gatekeeper rushed over to the car. I thought we'd been rumbled for sure but all this fellow desired was to personally direct us to our destination among the committee members' parking spaces. When I inquired how he'd managed it, Les shrugged and mentioned he'd brought Joshua here once or twice.

"Don't let 'em fool you that the war's done for the class system," whispered Les as he switched off the engine. "The minute this mob see a Bentley – or a beer mat," he added, showing me the piece of cardboard he'd flashed, "then they can't do enough for you."

He was right too. As we got out of the car the steward was still dancing attendance on us. He ushered us a few yards and rapped on a small blue wooden door set into the wall which opened up like Ali Baba's cave. Hey presto, we were in the ground.

"This way, sirs," said the steward, leading us towards the pavilion. But I stopped him.

"Thanks for that, chief, but we'll take it from here," I said, stuffing a ten bob note into the top pocket of his club blazer. With a salute, the steward wheeled around and marched off.

"What's your game?" asked Tommy in annoyance. "He was probably taking us to the royal box."

"Never mind the royal box," I said, pointing Les and Tommy in the opposite direction. "I want to sit behind the bowler's arm and see what Keith Miller can do with a ball in his hand."

Like the rest of Old Trafford, the Warwick Road End was nearly full but not quite as bursting as it would become later when the thousands still queuing outside finally got in and spilled over the boundary's edge.

With a spot of good natured comic banter from me and one or two menacing glares from Les, the three of us managed to squeeze on to one of the benches together just in time to see my old mate Denis Compton sauntering towards the middle. He'd been on sixty-odd overnight, quite an achievement in itself as earlier the previous day he'd top-edged a short ball from Ray Lindwall straight into his napper and staggered off as the blood flowed. But now he was firmly back in the driving seat and thrilled the crowd with some typical Compo swashbuckling cuts and pulls – although I didn't notice one single reverse sweep.

Twenty minutes before lunch Compo, the off-white bandage clearly visible above his left eye, reached his century with a sweep to the boundary. To acknowledge the huge roar of acclaim, Denis waved his bat around as if swatting flies.

As we stood to applaud, Tommy leaned over to me. "So you reckon you know Compton," he whispered.

"There's no reckon about it. Denis is an old pal."

"Bet you can't fix it so that he has a drink with us later."

"Five bob says I can."

"You're on," replied Tommy, licking his right palm and grabbing mine.

Lunch arrived and, while Compo strolled off triumphant with his young batting partner Bedser, I noticed Tommy staring intently at Keith Miller, who was sportingly applauding his old pal's efforts. It took five seconds before I realised what Tommy was seeing. There was no getting away from it; with his wavy black hair, wide mouth and ship's hooter, Miller was a dead ringer for my enormous little brother. Les too had noticed Tommy's stare and smiled at me.

"You weren't out in Australia during your war by any chance?" I asked Les - and immediately regretted it. Dad had already endured thirty years of folk whispering about my origins without me adding to the complications.

I made an attempt to recover with a stuttering red-faced apology but Les merely smiled and laid his large hairy hand on my arm.

"Time for lunch, son" he said, "We're here to enjoy ourselves."

I anticipated that our lunch would be located in the nearest stall selling meat and potato pies and pasties but instead Les ushered us towards the car park and a surprise.

"Rose packed us a tiny bit of something," he explained as he opened the boot of the Bentley.

A tiny bit! The hamper Les heaved out, with some difficulty, contained four plump chicken legs, a large pork pie with an egg through the middle of it – a real egg, mind you – and two rounds of tongue sandwiches. There were also slices of Battenburg cake, a jumbo bar of chocolate and three pint bottles of light ale. And not a trace of snoek in sight. *(Snoek is a long thin perch-like fish. Large quantities of canned snoek were imported into Britain during the war to feed the hungry population. We didn't much take to it).*

While I couldn't hide my delight that Rose had plundered Sir Joshua's pantry so thoroughly, I was less sure about the wider morality of our actions. As I glanced nervously around, I saw that even the people with posh cars were unfolding sad-looking little packets of sandwiches wrapped in grey, greaseproof paper and pouring weak tea from vacuum flasks. One or two spectators greeted our feast with disapproving looks and I even heard mutterings about black marketers before narrow-eyed stares from Les silenced the grumbles.

However, I could sympathise with the other spectators' feelings that we were taunting them.

"Blimey Dad, the meat allowance has just been cut!" I said in a low voice. "How many coupons did Joshua need for this banquet?"

"Joshua doesn't bother much about ration coupons and he won't miss any of this," replied Les. "Here." And he handed over a beer to shut me up which, as usual, it did.

As we munched and slurped our way through the feast, there was one thing on the minds of myself and Tommy. I'd be delighted to tell you it was Compo's scintillating batting or the new National Health Service launched by Bevan just down the road from Old Trafford the previous Monday. *(Aneurin Bevan inaugurated the NHS at Park Hospital in Davyhulme on July 5th 1948).*

Yet it was none of that! The matter obsessing me and my little brother was simply who would get that fourth chicken leg. I could see it was on Tommy's mind too because he was wolfing down his own at great speed while glancing covetously at the remaining limb. I too wasn't dawdling and it later occurred to me that our shovelling was so brisk that we hardly tasted the food, which must have made us even more popular with our neighbours. The race turned out to be a dead heat but an unseemly bout of tug o'war was prevented by the firm hand of Les who snatched the remaining chicken leg from our greedy grasps.

"I should give you both a thick ear," he growled before calling over the oldest steward around and slipping the chicken leg into his hand like a very slow changeover in a sprint relay. The pensioner gazed at the leg in disbelief before tucking it into his blazer pocket and retreating to a quiet corner.

"Share and share alike, eh?" said Tommy, shaking his head at the steward's deficiency of Socialist ideals.

"You mean, like you were going to?" I replied, cuffing Tommy thereby launching a bout of shadow sparring which was only brought to a halt by Les carrying out his threat and boxing our ears.

During the afternoon session Compo carried his bat to an undefeated 145, a dazzling innings which recalled his golden season, the previous summer. Also completely typical was the slapdash manner in which he managed to run out his eighth wicket partner, young Alec Bedser. But nobody, including Bedser, appeared too bothered as England ended up on 363 before reducing the Aussies to 126 for 3 by close of play. Even sweeter, one of those wickets was that of the great Don Bradman, trapped lbw by local lad Dick Pollard. *(In the summer of 1947, Denis Compton had become a national idol after scoring a staggering 3,816 runs including 18 centuries. It is a record never likely to be beaten. Compton's 145 not out at Old Trafford in July 1948 helped England to avert defeat by the Australians, the only time they managed it in the series, although the draw could easily have been an England victory had not the Manchester rain washed out the whole of the fourth day's play).*

Compo's heroics were now seriously threatening to do me out of five bob as it seemed half the crowd wanted to pay homage to him. I weighed up the scrum around the side entrance to the pavilion in dismay as I could see no way on earth we'd get through to the front.

As ever, I reckoned without Les who gradually poked and prodded his way forward until we were right up against the gate. But here we hit a greater problem. The two stewards guarding this entrance were not the gentle pensioners who had guided drivers, unchecked, into the ground. This pair were burly ex-sergeant majors who suffered no nonsense.

I found this out from a stunning brunette of about twenty, who had also kicked her way to the front of the scrum. This young lady proved interesting on two counts. Firstly she wore a short blue and pink floral dress which ended well above her knees - the New Look with its low hem-lines evidently having failed to make much impression this far north. Secondly the girl insisted she was Compo's sister.

"Those two are pigs," she said with a sniff, indicating the stewards. "They won't let me near my darling brother."

"What's your name?" I asked.

"Er, Denise."

"Denise Compton! You'll have to do better than that."

"It's true," she insisted. "Mum and Dad were severely lacking in imagination."

I edged right up to the gate.

"We've been invited into the pavilion by Denis Compton," I lied to the stewards. "He's a good friend of mine. And this here's his sister."

The taller gateman looked me up and down with complete disdain and gave the girl a similar once-over before responding with, "And I'm Ava Gardner."

"Give us a kiss then." This was Tommy putting his oar in.

"You can kiss this, sonny," replied the other steward showing Tommy a large fist.

A dust-up between this pair and Tommy and Les, who were both rolling up their sleeves, would certainly have been interesting and definitely brutal. It was fortunate, therefore, that just as everyone was squaring up, Compo danced down the pavilion steps to a great ovation. He looked as if he'd dressed without much thought and his normally sleek barnet was all over the show, even flopping over part of his bandage. He acknowledged the waiting crowd with a smile and a wave – then spotted me.

"Frankie," he shouted. "You rascal. Get in here at once."

I shrugged and pointed to the stewards, who were looking a lot less sure of themselves.

"John, Eric, let him through. Please!"

I indicated Les and Tommy.

"His pals as well," insisted Compo. "Come on there's good chaps."

The stewards reluctantly stepped aside allowing me to push Tommy and Les forward. As I was about to follow them, "Denise" tapped me on the shoulder and slipped a piece of paper into my hand.

"Give that to my brother," she pleaded. "I'll be ever so grateful."

I put the scrap of paper into my pocket and left her informing the stewards that it was a disgrace women could not go into the pavilion. *(Females would not be allowed into the Old Trafford pavilion for over forty years either until Lancashire members voted to end this outmoded and embarrassing restriction in 1989).*

Compo rushed up and clapped me heartily on the back.

"My dear old fellow, how tremendous it is to see you. Your father? Delighted to meet you, Les. And your brother? Crikey, you're a big 'un, Tom, and no mistake. Come in all of you and let's catch up."

It was said in such a genuine and friendly manner that Les and Tommy, who had stood open-mouthed as the nation's hero approached, immediately felt at ease. Tommy grinned excitedly at me as he slipped two half-crowns into my pocket.

"I've never been so pleased to lose a bet," he whispered.

It took us around ten minutes to get into the bar, such were the numbers wanting to buttonhole England's star batsman. To each Denis was unfailingly polite and would end the exchange with a trademark "God bless." A further five minutes of greetings passed before we reached a corner table where conversation could go ahead relatively uninterrupted. Pints of bitter appeared as if by magic in front of us.

I indicated the bandage over Compo's left eye which covered his stitches.

"Did you think you were playing for the Arsenal?" I asked. "You're supposed to bat it not head it."

Compo roared with laughter at this even though he must have heard it a hundred times before. I put it down to my innate sense of timing.

"Oh, and your sister out there asked me to give you this."

I pulled the crumpled note from my pocket and handed it to a puzzled Denis. He glanced at the message with a smile and screwed the paper into a ball.

"If I did that to my sister," he mused, "they'd lock me up. Hallo, let me introduce this pair of rascals."

Looking up, I was surprised to see Ray Lindwall and Keith Miller towering above us. Compo presided over the introductions as the Aussie stars sat down at our table. Miller took a long hard look at his dead ringer, Tommy, and said, "Fuck me, sport, you're an oddity - a real good looking Pom. On yer feet, mate."

As Tommy stood up to face Miller I worried that this might be the prelude to a skirmish. But the great all-rounder merely skimmed his hand over both their heads.

"Same height too," said Miller, sitting back down. "What pace do you bowl at, son?"

"I've never bowled a ball in my life," replied Tommy.

"Well see you don't start either," said Miller with a grin. "We already get more than enough grief from that stroppy bastard Edrich." *(Bill Edrich, 1916-1986, was Compton's batting partner for Middlesex and England. In 1947 Edrich nearly matched Denis's achievements by scoring 3,539 runs. He was also a handy fast bowler, adept at putting the wind up opposition batsmen).*

Lindwall was a head shorter and much quieter than his rambunctious bowling partner. As he sat down, I noticed he pointed to the bandage above Denis's eye and whispered, "You sure you're OK, mate?"

"Never better, Raymond" roared Denis. "You'll have to bowl a lot faster than that."

There followed a convivial hour which included generous applause for Les's baritone rendering of The Old Rugged Cross. Only when we started swapping war stories did things get a bit serious. Tommy became very quiet and I began to worry that my little brother was heading for another setback.

So I urged Les to lighten matters by telling his famous tale about how much grimmer things were in the Great War.

I can still picture the scene; three great cricketers leaning forward expectantly, waiting on my dad's words of wisdom.

"Go on, Les," said Compo breathlessly, "tell us what it was really like in the trenches."

Les solemnly cleared his throat and, as Compton, Lindwall and Miller, craned further towards him, said, "Plenty racket and nowhere proper to shit."

The place erupted with laughter – a whole posse of rubberneckers were hanging on to our every word. Miller slapped Les on the back and told him he was a genuine Pommy bastard which, thankfully, Les took as a compliment.

Finally, when I told Compo we'd have to make tracks, he would have none of it.

"The night is yet young," said Denis. "We're just off into Manchester."

"Yes but these two have to work tomorrow." I pointed at Les and Tommy.

Les smiled. "We can stay a while, son," he said. "After all we don't often get to drink with legends like these. Come on we'll travel in style."

All six of us managed to cram into the Bentley and, with Compo directing us, travelled around the city in a totally haphazard fashion, until chancing on a familiar pub or drinking club where we'd be treated like royalty.

A few of these encounters later, however, matters became somewhat indistinct. One thing I do clearly remember is Lindwall quietly excusing himself in the middle of the evening and slipping away in search of a taxi.

Then I'm fairly sure we staged a repeat of our 1936 Royal Grand Hotel match in a back street pub down Ancoats way, with someone's gran standing in for Lady Mountbatten. You may recall on that occasion that bat and ball were a champers bottle and a pomegranate. Now, more in keeping with the times and the location, we used a brown ale bottle and a selection of larger pickled onions.

Predictably the evening became more and more raucous and the last thing I remember is grabbing Keith Miller by the lapels and instructing him that the 1945 Victory Test at Lord's proved to me that his cover drive wasn't much cop at all and could definitely do with a polish.

"Show him the reverse sweep, Frankie," said Compo hooting with laughter as Miller harrumphed about know-all Pommy bastards, "so when he tries it in a match his ugly hooter will be even more out of shape."

The next thing I knew I was drowning in bed at the cottage. In fact I had woken up to discover Nancy pouring water on my head.

"What on earth are you doing, woman?" I complained.

"I've heard it's a good method to stop someone snoring like a hippo," replied Nancy, smiling sweetly.

"You've woken me up."

"And, indeed, it has stopped you snoring."

I groaned and lay back down, my head throbbing as though short balls from Lindwall and Miller had been bouncing off it. Then I sat bolt upright in a panic. Les must have got me back home but what had happened to Compo and Miller? They'd been as sloshed as I was. Christ, Australia's star all-rounder and the finest batsman in England could be dead in a ditch because of me. Well, not really because of me, but I hadn't stopped their binge, had I?

Stumbling across the room to a large radio in a wooden case, I switched it on. After a minute fiddling with the dial I finally found what I wanted to hear – and what reassuring news it was. In his usual bumbling way, Rex Alston was describing how Miller had just been given out lbw to Pollard after adding only eight to his overnight score of 23. A few minutes later I was informed that a particularly alert-looking Compo had caught Arthur Morris off the bowling of Bedser. Whew, I was off the hook.

When I finally staggered downstairs, Nancy was characteristically unsympathetic to my plight.

"Perhaps the children will dunk you in the well if you ask them nicely," she said, tucking into a fine breakfast of scrambled eggs and sausages, ingredients thoughtfully provided by her dear mother.

I, on the other hand, contented myself with a piece of dried toast and coffee which I'd just about managed to finish when we had a visitor. It was Jimmy Bradbury who, pulling no punches, ordered me straight back on to the set.

"I can't," I told him. "Joshua's man would be on the blower immediately and then you'd all be out of work."

Jimmy was insistent, however, revealing that Sir Joshua's gorilla had left the studio.

"When you didn't show yesterday he waited until mid-afternoon then just cleared off. He didn't turn up this morning either so here I am. Are you all right?"

I assured Jimmy that the green tinge across my features owed more to the particular quality of light and shade in the countryside rather than the previous evening's excesses. He didn't seem entirely convinced but went on to say that he reckoned they had nearly enough in the can for a coherent narrative.

"In fact," he added "I was considering using a body double for you but why bother when you can come back yourself."

I couldn't help but be impressed. "Body double for the romantic lead, eh? Who, er, were you considering - Joseph Cotten?"

"Actually," replied Jimmy deadpan. "I was thinking more of Billy Cotton."

This got a predictable guffaw from my dear wife who was just bringing in more coffee and left us with the 'hilarious' shout of, "Wakey, wakey". *(This was the catchphrase of band leader Billy Cotton 1899-1969).*

It didn't take long for Jimmy to persuade me to return to the set. If nothing else, I owed it to Jeannie to oversee the final part of her transformation into a fully-fledged romantic lead.

I'm getting weary now and the matron in this dungeon has just torn a strip off me for disturbing the other prisoners. She reckons that inadvertently yelling "wakey wakey," at the top of your voice isn't advisable in a place like this at half eleven at night. So I'll wrap things up in order to have enough vim and vigour left to tell the final two parts of my story. And what crackers they should be an' all.

We completed the shoot without any more interruptions from Joshua and within a week Jimmy had edited the film down to seventy minutes and given it the evocative title of Fugitive in the Shadows which, I had to admit, beat Where's My Bleedin' Ferret all ends up.

295

In short order, Robin was so impressed with the cut he gave a private screening to some American industry figures down in London. One of them, the influential agent Sol Cosminsky, loved the look and feel of the film, particularly my menacing presence in it. And before I knew what was happening I was in California, about to meet Warner Brothers studio bigwigs and audition for the role of a deranged killer in their forthcoming gangster movie White Heat.

For the rest of the cast and crew of Fugitive in the Shadows, things did not turn out so well. When Joshua saw the cut and clocked that I was still the star, he sacked everyone connected with the film, including his gorilla bodyguard who'd proved quietly impressive in the role of The Watcher.

For good measure my father in law also closed down Slatterwood Studios – which is perhaps why you've never heard of them – and ordered the destruction of every print of Fugitive, plus the negative. So it's lucky that just one copy of my broody, moody noir performance managed to ... but we'll come to that in the next, and penultimate chapter.

A sudden breeze drifted in off The Pacific, cold enough to send Nancy and Jonathan scurrying inside the villa. I was left weighing up whether to peel a grape or get stuck into another tasty water melon when Sol rolled on to the terrace, wheezing like a pervert. Shuffling his two hundred and thirty pounds sweaty bulk over to where I lay, he lit a huge cigar and looked benignly down on me.

"I take it celebrations are in order, Sol?" I said confidently.

Sol nodded slowly. "Dey sure are, Frankie boy."

I jumped up and was about to hug him when he added, "Sadly de celebrations ain't for you."

"What on earth do you mean?" I asked in alarm.

"You're outta luck, kid, dat's what I mean. Dey gave de part to Jimmy Cagney."

Chapter Fourteen: The King's Peach

The instant I jabbed a Hopalong Cassidy six-shooter into Kim Philby's back and growled "stick 'em up," it was apparent that I'd badly misjudged the moment. The unfortunate chap promptly threw up all over the Times Square sidewalk. Then, when he turned round and saw his tormentor was me, complete with toy gun, holster - and sheriff's badge - he burst into tears.

Later, in an Irish bar on West 43rd Street, while the urine stains on his trousers dried and I apologised unreservedly, Kim explained he'd been "a tiny bit on edge"; which, as you'll discover later in this, the penultimate chapter of my memoir, is somewhat akin to Ivan the Terrible confessing that he had occasional anger issues.

Until I noticed him emerging from that alleyway in Manhattan, I have to admit I'd – almost but not quite - consigned Philby, along with Donald Maclean and Guy Burgess, into the section of my memory marked "do not disturb." In part, this had happened because I was finally prepared to accept that none of them had anything to do with the Russian's murderous attack on me in 1945. Furthermore, in the face of overwhelming evidence, I'd reluctantly arrived at the conclusion that Carlton Frobisher had indeed committed suicide.

The present chain of events had started six weeks previously at the end of March 1951 and, like so many things in the Funnybone saga, stemmed from Nancy's relentless desire to promote my career.

You may have the impression from this memoir that my wife and I were constantly at loggerheads but let me tell you, nobody was more protective of me – or my earning power – than Nancy.

And, even though she'd have been hard pressed to fail in a golden age for variety, she was doing more than all right by me. Here's an example. Shrewdly she'd begun to market me as experienced enough to remind people of the pre-war music hall but sufficiently fresh and adaptable to provide a bridge to the post war breed of comics; the Howerds, Hancocks and Milligans who were flooding on to the radio and - what was that new-fangled contraption that would never catch on called? Television, that was it!

All those theatre managers had obviously swallowed Nancy's spiel whole because I'd never been so busy, criss-crossing Britain as the modern heir to the tradition of Tommy Handley, Will Hay and Sid Field, all of whom had taken their sad final curtain in the previous two years.

The only part of my CV that irked Nancy - and me for that matter - was the lack of a decent mainstream film role. Oh, I'd done bits and bobs for Michael Balcon at Ealing but quickly came to realise that unless I did away with dear old Stan Holloway there was no real future there. *(Stanley Holloway, 1890-1982, an actor, comedian and singer, starred in some of Ealing Studios' most celebrated films, including* The Lavender Hill Mob *and* The Titfield Thunderbolt).

"Bloody Holloway," grumbled Nancy one Sunday night as we sat opposite each other. "What's he got that you haven't?"

I looked up from my penny dreadful. "Well, he can sing," I said.

"I didn't hear him doing much singing in Passport to Pimbledon."

"Pimlico, darling. Passport to Pimlico."

"That's what I said," she snapped, grabbing a bottle from the table next to her armchair and draining the remaining wine into her glass.

"Yes, dear."

Nancy swallowed a deep draught and then threw herself back into the armchair in grumpy abandon, all the while managing to spill none of her precious liquid.

"And those bloody, bloody monologues. I tell you, Franco, if I ever hear another line about the little sniveller who got munched in Blackpool Zoo, I'll take that stick with the horse's head handle and shove it right up Stanley Holloway's ..."

"Thank you, darling. I feel you've made your point."

I wasn't entirely comfortable with Nancy's train of thought as I knew Stan Holloway, along with Arthur Askey, to be one of the more pleasant and kinder characters in show-business – a place not exactly overflowing with such types.

Furthermore I often recited Albert and the Lion to our children who never failed to laugh when Mother, hearing that the king of beasts had swallowed her little lad whole, responded with, "Ee I am vexed." Yet, still I couldn't resist the next little dig.

"Having said that, Stanley Holloway's never starred in un film noir."

Nancy exhaled in annoyance before taking in another slug of wine.

"And neither have you, effectively," she replied, "since my dear Daddy bunged every last copy of Fugitive in the Shadows plus the negative on to a large bonfire."

"Not every last one."

"What do you mean?"

Nancy put down her glass. I now had her full attention.

"Well, you see, Nance, Jimmy Bradbury's got a copy."

Now, Nancy was out of her seat, eyes gleaming.

"Tell me more, Franco? She said, sitting on my knee. "Come on, lover, spill the beans."

So I did. I explained that I'd met Jimmy by chance a couple of weeks ago in a pub off Sloane Square. After a few beers, he became bold enough to reveal he'd smuggled a copy of Fugitive out of the studio. Its precious three reels were now in a safe and secret place – in a cake tin on top of his wardrobe.

The news galvanised Nancy and soon she had come up with a simple, yet inspired, plan. She reckoned that we should plant a story in a national newspaper about the discovery of a brilliant 'lost' British thriller now being pursued by more than one Hollywood studio.

This could stimulate interest from other studios determined not to outdone by their rivals. Furthermore, if the publicity was handled skilfully enough, argued Nancy, Joshua might be shamed into agreeing to the film's release. My movie career would be revitalised and this time I wouldn't just settle for playing fourth bumpkin from the back, patronised by someone who could speak 'proper'.

No, I'd be lining up a starring role like the one I thought I had before it was cruelly snatched away by Sol Cosminsky that day in Santa Barbara.

Incidentally, while it's true that James Cagney had done moderately well in White Heat, I reckon I'd have added an extra touch of swivel-eyed menace to the picture. Let's face it, when push came to shove, Jimmy was just too cute. *(In White Heat, nominated for an Academy Award in 1950, James Cagney plays psychopathic gangster Cody Jarrett who's a tiny bit too attached to his mother. The final scene in which Cody screams 'Made it, Ma. Top of the world,'' while standing on a huge petrol storage tank just before it explodes, is part of Hollywood legend. But consider how much more effective the scene would have been if, instead, Cody had informed the pursuing constabulary, "You've no chance, copper, I've come on me bike")*.

We'd have celebrated with a toast – if Nancy hadn't already gargled down the remaining vino, dregs and all. But the heroic alcohol consumption did not hold her back the following day when she carefully selected her prey and made contact with him.

Two days later I was in Ye Olde Cock Tavern happily nattering to The News Chronicle's junior show-business hack, Daventry Murtlock. It was four in the afternoon so naturally the place was full of Fleet Street's finest, yelling and puking up into each others' hats. Through that fearful din I managed to get across to Dav the tantalising story about Hollywood's pursuit of our 'missing' noir masterpiece and, give the youngster credit, he agreed it was a decent tale and might merit a few pars at the bottom of page twenty-two but no promises.

The job done, I was about to make my escape from that bear pit when Dav asked me if I fancied another quick one. Despite the mayhem going on around us – I saw one chap actually set fire to another's shirt tails – something made me sit back down and it's a good job I did. Because, if I hadn't agreed to have that extra drink with young Murtlock, two defining events of mid-twentieth century Britain would not have happened in the way they did.

When Dav finally fought his way back from the bar, he plonked a pint and a whisky chaser down in front of me and sighed.

"What's up," I asked him, "girlfriend trouble?"

"I wish it were that simple," he groaned. "But no, it's this bloody festival, driving us all nuts. And, on top of everything else, we've now got this business with the King."

Before we start to pick the bones out of that particular mess, it's time for a short history lesson – unless old whatshischops has already dived in with some fascinating statistics *(Oh, please, do carry on)*.

Dav, of course, was talking about the Festival of Britain, due to begin in five weeks time. If you can remember that first-hand then you'll very likely be reading this at arm's length under a bright spotlight. And probably struggling to open that tin of Werther's Originals with the business end of your white cane.

There was a programme on the telly a bit back about the Festival's sixtieth anniversary and most enjoyable it was too – until some clown switched over to the Ice Road

Truckers' Christmas Special featuring Petula Clark – another old flame incidentally.

However, before the goggle box was surrendered to the Philistines, we were treated to a bunch of the old familiar images. That gleaming darning needle, Skylon, looking as if it was about to blast off for Mars; the new funfair at Battersea Park and even a ship that transported entertainment and enlightenment around the coast to the provinces. It all looked splendid, as indeed it was.

But the TV programme also reminded us of the fraught preparations for the Festival; particularly the horrendous winter that had left the organising team, led by Gerald Barry, former editor of the News Chronicle, with huge headaches. Constant rain had turned the main site, across the Thames from the Palace of Westminster, into a quagmire. There had also been strikes and other problems with the unions, and building materials had had a habit of not turning up when they should have.

Yet to everyone's credit these problems had been overcome and five weeks before the official opening, scheduled for early May 1951, everything finally seemed to be on schedule. The one thing the telly programme didn't mention, however, was that the King then went and got the collywobbles.

"What do you mean - collywobbles?" I asked Murtlock above the din of the pub.

Dav looked morosely at me. "I mean," he sighed, "that His Majesty is refusing to do the Festival's opening ceremony."

"You are joking!"

"I wish I bloomin' well was," he replied. "Gerald Barry's going spare. Our editor's going spare. The whole thing's a mess. And, as usual, it's us poor bloody infantry who are getting it in the neck"

"Yeah, hard chedd. What's the King's beef?"

Murtlock glanced around conspiratorially before beginning to talk very loudly above the din of sozzled hacks.

"Don't say a thing to anyone about this, it's a state secret," he yelled, "but apparently the King's stammer has come back. He's been recalling a previous bun-fight when he got the yips and the smart set giggled at him behind their hands." *(Prince Albert's stammer reduced his closing address at the British Empire Exhibition at Wembley in October 1925, to one of excruciating embarrassment for all concerned. The incident is accurately portrayed in the 2011 film, The King's Speech).*

It all sounded a bit thin to me and I told Dav there was surely more to it than a stammer.

"Well," he replied, "I expect he's thoroughly fed up with all the sniping at the Festival by Beaverbrook and Churchill. And it's rumoured he's not well."

"I could try to bring Winston onside," I offered.

Murtlock shook his head. "That's not the problem," he said. "We can live with Churchill's carping because the PM's right behind the festival. So, unless you're on speaking terms with the King, then you're not much use to us."

"It's funny you should say that ..."

Now, while it's true I had once talked to the King in his previous guise, 'speaking terms' was laying it on a tiny bit thick. My excuse is that alcohol can be a taxing mistress, demanding ever-wilder flights of fancy.

Accordingly, after another round of drinks, I told Dav the 1936 Balmoral story as if I had been a valued guest of my dear, dear friends Bertie, Liz and their two darling daughters. In doing so, I may have left out one or two minor details such as the date it all happened, the fight between two royal brothers and the final look of utter disdain I received from the future George VI as he and his family took their leave. Oh yes, and the fact that Edward VIII became my best man.

During my tale, Dav's eyes had grown wider and wider so I was fairly sure what his reaction would be to my final words, which were, for the record, "and Liz said 'any time you're in our area, Franny, just bob around. Night or day'."

Yet what transpired next genuinely surprised me. Giving no warning at all, a fifteen stone man crashed on to our table, scattering the drinks to all parts. With a snarl, Dav immediately leapt on top of the intruder and they rolled onto the floor, punching each other. Uncertain if this was everyday Fleet Street horseplay or something a touch more serious, I was considering whether to weigh in, until Dav managed to disentangle himself from the interloper long enough to indicate that he could manage and we'd talk some other time.

Relieved, I staggered out of the pub's smoky, almost impenetrable atmosphere – and straight into an unseasonal London smog. It was so bad I could hardly see my finger in front of my face and, by the time I'd picked my way home, I was breathless and in need of more restorative liquid. But Nancy was having none of it.

"No more pop for you, Franco," she said, snatching the beer bottle from my grasp. "Not with your royal visit tomorrow."

"What royal visit?"

"You're off to see the King so I'm not having you hung over and smelling like Ben Trumann's."

Blimey, Dav must have seen off the flying giant in short order because, before I'd arrived home, he'd phoned his office with news of my idle boasts. They'd immediately contacted an old chum of mine, Herbert Morrison, who'd rung Nancy and told her that I had an appointment to see King George VI at Buckingham Palace the following morning at 11 o'clock. *(Herbert Morrison, 1888-1965, a prominent Labour politician who held various Cabinet posts, including Foreign Secretary, was one of the principal organisers of The Festival of Britain).*

"Apparently Morrison was due at the Palace himself," explained Nancy, "as a final desperate throw of the dice to get the King back onside. But he was more than delighted to let you go in his place when he heard of your 'excellent relations with HRH'. When did they happen, by the way?"

I slumped into the armchair and groaned. Usually it's weeks before the chickens come home to roost in cases like this. But now I'd been caught out by my own stupidity before I could catch a wheezing breath.

"The good thing is," added Nancy, "you're guaranteed a two-page spread in the News Chronicle about the missing film noir. As long as you persuade the King to open the Festival of Britain."

"And if I don't?"

"You will. Now drink your cocoa."

Nancy's utter certainty haunted me over a largely sleepless night during which the only rest I got was interrupted by a recurring dream of Herbert Morrison and me sliding down the outside of the Dome of Discovery while the Queen waited for us at the bottom with Compo's cricket bat. Incidentally, before we leave the subject, I offered to give Morrison's grandson *(Peter Mandelson)* some valuable advice before the other Dome fiasco a decade ago but he and that Cheshire Cat they had in Downing Street didn't want to know. Serves 'em both right.

The following morning, as I approached a discreet side entrance to Buckingham Palace, I was half hoping the huge copper on duty would clip me round the ear with an order to sling my hook. After all, it is the only language people of our generation understand.

But when I told him who I was, the officer respectfully checked his clipboard, unlocked the gate and let me in. I was told to wait by a nondescript door in the main building but as I crossed the small courtyard, the door opened and a tall, upright middle-aged chap with a toothbrush moustache stepped out. He was wearing a dark, well-cut suit and a patterned silk tie.

"Mr Thirkettle," this cove said, scanning me up and down, smiling as he did so, "be so kind as to follow me."

As we walked down a long blue-carpeted corridor there didn't seem to be anyone else around and the only sound I could hear was the distant banging of a workman's hammer. At first I stayed quiet, being largely unfamiliar with how to behave in royal residences. But my companion broke the silence by asking, "How's the world of entertainment?"

I told him it had never been better and added, "I'll bet you don't get many comedians around these parts."

"Only when there's a state visit," he murmured, opening a door and showing me in. As he did so I fancied I glimpsed a familiar figure further down the corridor beyond him but could not bring to mind who it was. Speculation was cut short as the retainer closed the door behind us and I found we were in a room the size of our parlour at home.

"Please wait here for just a moment," he said and disappeared through a door at the far end of the room. I have to admit I was a touch confounded. I'd expected bewigged flunkies and huge ornate chambers but this room was sparsely done out. The only pieces of furniture of any note were a large desk and three dark brown leather chairs, one behind the desk. In the corner was a table on which stood two tumblers and a decanter, half-filled with water.

Correctly surmising this was the King's study, I was about to steal a look at his blotter when the door opened and in stepped the monarch himself, followed by my friend with the walrus soup-strainer.

I heard the King say, "... a matter of the gravest urgency, Tommy. Please expedite it," before the other man bowed slightly and backed out of the room.

I was now alone with the King of jolly old England, who signalled for me to sit down. His pallor matched the light grey colour of the suit he was wearing and there were large bags under his weary eyes. In other words he did not look particularly well.

"Tommy has looked after you I trust," he said as he lit a cigarette from a large silver box on his desk.

"Oh yes," I replied eagerly. "He seems quite an affable chap." *(Sir Alan Frederick "Tommy" Lascelles, 1887-1981, was private secretary to George VI and later to Elizabeth II. His memoirs are highly entertaining and illuminating, mainly because Frankie does not feature in them).*

The King nodded and sat down. Then he jumped up immediately, his pale face reddening slightly.

"Forgive me," he said and pushed the cigarette box towards me.

"No thanks, sir" I responded quickly. "I always take my wife to task for smoking so I can hardly ..."

My voice trailed off as I realised that I was implicitly criticising the King's behaviour. But he merely nodded and replied, "You're right, it is a beastly habit."

I'd hoped we could get straight down to business and, above all, avoid any mention of events in August 1936 but the King quickly scotched that idea.

Taking a long, deep pull on his cigarette, he said, "The lady you were with the last time we met at Balmoral. The one with the insolent papa. Is she your wife?"

"Yes, sir."

"Extremely pretty girl."

"She is, isn't she, sir."

"Were you married at the time?"

"Er, no, but we did tie the knot soon afterwards."

Thank goodness neither his brother nor anyone else had informed Bertie of the ceremony that took place in the Balmoral ballroom the following day. I decided against mentioning it too but did make a mental note to let Joshua know that George VI had him very much in his thoughts. I also noted that the King hadn't once stammered.

He rose from his seat, walked to the window and stared out over the Palace gardens. With his back to me he said, "I suppose you know I've only agreed to see you because of your war record."

"I was unaware of that, sir, but thank you. We all did our bit during wartime – you especially."

The King turned and glared at me. "I was half-sick with fear on that gun turret," he spat. "Nobody knew what the hell was going on, particularly Jellicoe or Beatty. And we lost over six thousand seamen in just two days. I'm not proud to be associated with that damned mess."

It took me a few seconds to work out that he was talking about the Battle of Jutland in 1916 during which he'd served as a junior officer. I had to play this even more carefully than I'd anticipated.

"Er ... yes, sir, I'm aware you served with some distinction on HMS Collingwood in that action. But, with respect, I was referring to your leadership of the nation in the recent war."

All at once the King lapsed into a violent coughing fit and for a few seconds I agonised whether I should risk slapping him hard across the back. Luckily the spasm soon passed.

"I did what I had to," he said breathlessly, stubbing out his cigarette in annoyance. "Anyone would have done the same."

I strolled around to near where he stood.

"The fact is that you and the Missus, pardon my boldness, but you both helped to lift the nation and kept us all going."

The King eyed me closely. "I'm reliably informed that you weren't even here most of the time," he said.

"True enough, sir, but I am still aware of what went on. It's already become, well, part of our island history."

He shook his head and slumped back into the chair. "I'm still n ..n... not opening the Festival and there's an end to it. You can go back and tell M...Morrison as much."

That was that then. I nodded respectfully, turned to go and turned back. Staring pointedly at my shoes, I made a heroic effort to speak.

"Sir, with the greatest respect you're mistaken if you think I'm doing this for Herbert Morrison or Gerald Barry or any other of the Festival crew. I'm actually here as a representative of the people. The ordinary folk. Any one of your subjects in fact."

I glanced up slyly to see what effect this noble drivel was having. The King was gazing vacantly at a waste paper basket in the corner so I pressed on.

"The fact is that we've been at peace now as long as we were at war. And although things are better than they have been, quite frankly they're still not back to how we'd like to see them."

I paused as we both tried to weigh up exactly what I thought I was talking about. The King reached a conclusion ahead of me because he replied, "I suppose I s...see what you mean."

"Then I do wish you'd explain it to me," I thought but added, "therefore why not open the Festival, bring the old era to its close and launch the future. There's no-one who could do it better – unless you fancy leaving things to Gracie Fields." *(Frankie's old amour did indeed play a part in opening the Festival's celebrations).*

Mention of Gracie actually made the King smile fondly for a brief second before his tired features once again fell into a picture of grim misery.

"Do you know, Francis," he confided with a frown, "it was at that exact moment on Balmoral moor that I realised my brother would cut and run. And damned soon too.

That's why I l...l..left the place in such a rage – and I really must apologise for any offence I caused you."

"No apology necessary, sir, I do assure you."

The King did not appear to have heard me because he went on, "I sometimes wish David had succeeded in strangling me that afternoon in the hills. It would have made things a lot s...simpler for everyone."

As I recalled, it wasn't David who was impressing everyone as the star graduate of Dr Throttler's Academy for Young Psychopaths but I remained quiet about that. I also kept my counsel about who it was - quite inadvertently I must remind you - had persuaded Edward VIII to 'follow his heart'. However, the King's defeatist assertion did call for some sort of energetic response.

"Nonsense, sir," I cried, "again if you'll pardon my boldness. Your brother strangling you would have been a disaster for this country – not to mention yourself."

OK, he'd been my best man, but I shudder to imagine how Dapper Dave would have conducted the war against a character he so admired. Especially with Calamity Jane rampaging around, hotly pursuing anything in jackboots.

The King gazed at me wearily and for a moment I thought I'd won him over. That was before he put his startling proposition to me.

"Do you know, Francis," he said finally. "I can't remember the last time I actually laughed out loud. Guffawed. Do you understand what I mean?

I wasn't sure where this was heading at all but I went along with it.

"Of course I do, sir, yes but I'm sure that you've ..."

"No." He shook his head sadly. "I cannot recall a single solitary g...g...giggle."

But for the cigarette he was lighting, the King, mournful stare and all, could easily have been mistaken for a sad small boy.

"Yet here I am on this fine Spring morning standing in front of a comedian. So I'll present you with a deal, Mr Frankie Funnybone."

"A deal, sir?"

"Yes, and the deal is make me laugh out loud and I'll open the Festival of Britain. You have ten seconds."

I gazed horror-struck at the King. My mind had gone totally blank. Apart from ...

"You have five seconds remaining. Four, three ..."

There was nothing for it. "OK, sir, pardon my French but what do you do if a bird shits on your windscreen?"

For a second I was afraid I'd gone too far – until the King's shocked expression turned into one of genuine puzzlement.

"I have absolutely no idea," he said thoughtfully. "What does one do if a bird shits on one's windscreen?"

I took a deep breath and replied, "Don't ask her out again."

For five seconds George VI considered this scenario without moving a facial muscle. Then he nodded and smiled weakly. Then he gave a couple of little laughs, nodding a bit harder before falling ominously silent. Then he exclaimed, "don't ask her out again," and burst into a hurricane of laughter.

I have to say that, in those few brief moments, I'd hardly seen a monarch more merry. Certainly I'd never made his brother laugh anywhere near as much – although I'm told he nearly wet himself watching The Crazy Gang wallop me around The London Palladium. It did last only a few moments, however, because the King's laughter turned all too quickly into that familiar rasping cough.

I already knew there was a decanter of water on the table in the corner of the room. It was simply my bad luck, therefore, that I'd not quite reached the table, but was about as far away from the coughing King as I could be, when the door opened and in marched the Queen.

"What on earth is going on, Bertie?" she demanded, glaring at me.

"Your Royal Highness I was just about to ...

"...ignore my husband while he's about to peg out? Bring me a glass of water at once. It's behind you on that table."

I carried a glass over to the King, who was still coughing mightily, while Elizabeth gently removed the cigarette from between his fingers and stubbed it out. After three deep gulps of water the King's coughing stopped and he sighed in relief. Thankfully some colour, albeit predominantly grey, had returned to his cheeks.

"Dearest, you cannot blame Mr Thirkettle," he whispered. "It is not his fault that I had a coughing fit." The King paused. "Actually, strictly speaking, it is his fault but ..."

The Queen had heard enough. Without looking at me she said glacially, "I think it's time you left, Mr Thirkettle."

Nodding in agreement, I backed slowly away from the royal couple. When I reached the door the King said, "You can tell Morrison and Barry that I will open the Festival. And remember, in future, keep that windscreen spotless."

Success! I put my hands together and bowed appreciatively to both of them. Then I backed out of the doorway into the corridor – and collided with a stunning looking young woman. You could even say there were sparks between us - as the cigarette she was holding burst like a firework across my chest.

"Can't you look where the fuck you're going?"

I'm ever so eager to admit that I was not the one who said this. Doubly so, when the Queen flew out of the study to see what the commotion was about. For a moment I thought she was about to rip into me again but instead she glared at the young woman, who was alternately grinning sardonically and blowing on her cigarette.

"Margaret, you will apologise to Mr Thirkettle at once," ordered the Queen. "And then join your father and I in the study."

The door slammed shut behind her.

Princess Margaret took a long drag on the revived cigarette and looked at me insolently.

"I'm so terribly sorry, Mr Kettlefur," she said in a loud voice before adding under her breath, "that you are such a clodhopping oaf." And she grinned at me.

I smiled back and replied loudly, "I had forgotten the incident already, miss," adding in a whisper, "unlike your mother who is about to give you six of the best."

Margaret stepped back a pace and we weighed each other up. What I saw was a confident and sophisticated 20-year-old in a fashionably cut long dark blue coat and white pill-box hat; the image was as far away from a carefree little girl doing handstands against the wall at Balmoral in 1936 as it could be. She was obviously dressed up for someone and it certainly wasn't on the off chance she'd bump into me.

What Princess Margaret saw as she looked back at a 35-year-old entertainer, who could have passed for ten years younger, *(on a very dark and stormy night)* is uncertain but I must have awakened some interest in her because she narrowed her eyes and asked, "Don't I know you?"

In the spirit of our original exchange, I took a chance and answered, "I believe so. Last time we met, you showed me your knickers."

Margaret blew out a cloud of smoke and once again her brow furrowed.

"I'm afraid that doesn't narrow it down all that much," she replied straight-faced and opened the study door. Then she handed me her cigarette, whispering, "mustn't let matron catch me," and, with a wink, slammed the door in my face.

Seeing nowhere immediately obvious to stub it out, I solved the conundrum of what to do with Princess Margaret's fag end by dropping it into a large empty plant holder, one of many which lined the never-ending corridor.

I waited anxiously for a few moments to make sure the cigarette was out – not wanting to start a fire and finish the work that Adolf had started. *(During the Blitz in 1940, the Palace suffered nine direct hits from German bombs. The worst attack came on September 13th when, with the King and Queen in residence, the Royal Chapel was almost obliterated).*

As I lingered, I realised I was not alone. Next to me, looking more like a footman than Lascelles ever could, had appeared the distinctive, haughty figure of Anthony Blunt, to whom Guy had introduced me at a party about six years earlier. So it was him I'd glimpsed on my way in.

With a feather duster quivering in his right hand, Blunt indicated a picture on the wall in front of us.

"Poussin," he barked.

"Bless you," I replied.

Blunt disdained even to look at me. "This," he intoned loftily, "is a drawing in pen and ink of The Triumph of Pan by the artist Nicolas Poussin. The magnificent original oil painting is in the National Gallery." *(Nicolas Poussin, 1594-1665, was French painter in the classical style. As well as being a Soviet spy, Anthony Blunt, 1907-83, was one of the world's foremost experts on Poussin).*

I studied the picture a bit more closely. It depicted a bunch of old-time drunks – men and women. And they were all over the shop.

"It looks like Billy Cotton's Band after a bad night out," I told Blunt.

He glanced down at me as if I was something he'd just stepped in. Then he staggered back in surprise. Obviously he'd only just recognised me.

"Francis Thirkettle," he squeaked, "what on earth are you doing here?"

"I've just been chatting to the King. What's your story?"

Blunt looked mightily miffed, as if he thought I should damn well know what he was doing, poncing around Buckingham Palace with a feather duster.

"I work here" he replied haughtily. "Supervising the royal pictures."

"Are they very naughty?"

With a sniff, Blunt indicated that my response was unworthy of his attention and began to glide away down the corridor. But I hadn't finished with him.

"So, Tony, tell me about Kim Philby."

I'd expected some sort of reaction but nothing like what happened. Blunt gave a croak and immediately dropped both the feather duster and a large book he was carrying. I watched in fascination as he scrabbled around trying to retrieve the objects in the manner of a baby giraffe who'd wandered on to an ice rink.

"I'm so sorry to have pole-axed you with an innocent query about the health of your dear friend," I said.

"No, no, I was not shocked at all," blurted out Blunt who had finally resumed a vertical position. "I merely felt a trifle faint."

"Then you must sit down," I said, ushering him to a nearby chair. Now I could look down on him. Which I did.

"Kim's all right I take it?"

Blunt gulped and his face reddened. "I ... I have no idea. I hardly know the man."

"That's funny because you and Philby were thick as thieves at that party. In fact I seem to remember you had your arms round each other."

"Mere drunken horseplay, I assure you."

"With someone you hardly know! I wonder where Kim's doing his snogging at the moment."

Breathing heavily, Blunt tried to compose himself. "I had been informed that he is now at our Embassy in Washington."

"Well," I said, lightly patting Blunt's shoulder, "give him all the best from me when you see him. And don't forget to dust right into those corners."

I left him sitting there like one o'Tatlocks *(I've absolutely no idea either)* with little or no anticipation that my message would ever be passed on. As it turned out, however, I was able to convey the greeting to Philby myself and all because of a chain of events set in motion by my successful meeting with the King.

In the first place, I was showered with gratitude by Morrison and Barry. As promised, a centre spread appeared in the News Chronicle about the mysterious but highly rated British film noir - and its enigmatic young star - that all Hollywood was talking about. Directly after this I received an invitation from Sunshine Studios to travel to New York on the Queen Mary and discuss "possible scenarios".

Oh, and to complete my happiness, Joshua went crackers. In fact, he became so utterly unhinged that he turned up on our doorstep one morning and I had to threaten to summon a bobby and get him banged up for a breach of the peace. Perfection!

Luckily Nancy had already gone out at the time but she didn't seem too bothered when I told her about it that evening.

"... and then Joshua started ranting and raving about how his lawyers would stop Fugitive ever being seen at the flicks," I recalled with a satisfied smile.

I glanced at Nancy, who sat in the armchair with a vacant look on her face, making not the slightest pretence of listening to me.

"That was after he threatened to have me horse-whipped." Still no response.

"And finally your dad pulled down his pants in the street, set fire to them and began shoving gobstoppers up ... Nancy, you're not listening to a word I'm saying are you?"

She looked up at me in surprise. "Sorry, Franco, what were you saying?"

I sat down on the side of the chair and put my arm around her. She rubbed her head against my shoulder.

"I know what's bothering you," I said. "Come with me to New York. They'll provide another ticket."

Nancy shook her head. "No, there really is too much on at work at the moment. Besides it's not that. I have been on the Queen Mary before."

"What's bothering you then?"

She pulled my head down to hers and gave me a big beautiful lingering kiss before tenderly stroking my hair.

"Nothing's bothering me," she said, smiling. "You go to America and show those studio bosses what a big star really looks like."

"I'll give it a go but I still don't know what's ..."

Our tender little moment was fractured by Julia, now a 13-year-old tomboy. She ran into the room and flung her arms around my neck.

"When's the New York thingy, Daddy?"

"In a couple of days, flower, but you know you can't come this time. There's the little matter of school."

"School, huh!" She wrinkled her nose. "All right then but you must promise to bring me something back."

"I'll bring myself back. Will that do?"

"It will be a start," she sniffed. "As long as you are accompanied by a genuine Hopalong Cassidy cowboy gun and matching holster. And a sheriff's badge."

"I'll bring you his horse as well, shall I?"

"Daddy, they would never let Topper on The Queen Mary. You are so silly."

Coincidentally, that's exactly how I felt a week later when I made poor Kim Philby throw up, burst into tears

318

and piss himself, using the toy gun I'd just bought for Julia in a store on Sixth Avenue.

I'd been at a loose end after dropping off the three precious reels of Fugitive at Sunshine Studios' executive suite in the Waldorf Astoria and had decided to stroll a few blocks and sample the late afternoon atmosphere in Times Square. I'd been greedily taking it all in – the crowds, the smells and the con artists – when, to my amazement, Philby walked out of the alleyway just ten yards ahead of me and I decided the moment was too good to lose.

Sitting in that bar on West 43rd Street, I was relieved to see that Kim had recovered some of his equilibrium, doubtless aided by the four whisky sours which had disappeared in short order.

Trying to lighten the mood more than anything else, I said, "I thought you worked in Washington."

The ploy was not entirely successful as Kim promptly spilled the drink down his freshly-dried trousers.

"Your cleaning bills must be something else," I said, using my handkerchief to wipe off the excess.

"Just a t...tiny bit on edge, old man," said Kim quickly. "And to answer your question, I do work in Washington but I thought I'd treat myself to a first visit to N...New York. I've always wanted to see this place." *(In fact Philby made regular trips to New York to meet his Russian contact, who he had probably just left when Frankie stumbled across him).*

Kim then revealed that one of the reasons he'd been on edge was that, unbelievably, Guy's drunken buffoonery had become even more erratic.

"I know I'm his friend," Philby confided in me, "but I'm his boss too and the time is rapidly approaching when I may have to send him home."

"What's he been up to?"

"What hasn't he been up to," groaned Kim, who reeled off a series of outrages committed by Burgess, mainly involving the spouting of violently anti-American sentiments. By far the worst of these incidents was his drawing of the FBI chief's wife. I knew to my cost what a savage caricaturist Guy could be, remembering how he kept our family entertained with his quick, acid sketches of yours truly. Even Julia, hardly Guy's greatest fan, loved the one where he made me look like Pinnochio after he'd been turned into a donkey.

So it was no surprise to hear that, at a party thrown by Kim for an FBI bigwig, Guy had outraged the whole guest list by sketching the man's horse-faced Missus in a few devastatingly deft strokes. *(This is the well-documented story of a disastrous drunken evening during which the entire FBI delegation flounced out after Burgess's perceived slight to their chief's wife).*

"I don't know too much about the Yanks, Kim," I said, "but getting the wrong side of Hoover's men can't be sensible."

Philby sighed gloomily. "In fact it's the golden rule over here," he said. "You should never, ever upset J.E.'s boys. However, since when have you known Guy to take the sensible course? Anyway, old man, enough about m...me. Why are you here?"

I told him about the Sunshine execs, Herman and Sherman, who were no doubt enthusiastically devouring my film as we spoke. And he had the good grace to look impressed when I revealed my ambitions to be a movie star, murmuring, "Funnybone and Hepburn, eh?"

But when I told him exactly what the movie was about, Kim's indulgent smile faded and he began to look terribly alarmed. I knew he wasn't feeling right when he lit a cigarette while one of his was still burning in the ash tray. Then he went much too far and actually drank my Scotch as well as his own.

"Sorry about that, old fellow," said Kim, quickly calling the waiter over. "B..b...but it does sound a lot like, you know, what happened to you at your d...delightful house that time. And I thought that was going to remain our little secret."

"I suppose it does sound a bit like that night," I agreed. "But they always say you should write what you know. So I did."

Kim nodded but looked even more ill so I assured him that I'd never harboured thoughts that he and Guy had really been behind the Russian's murderous attack. It was simply a plot device. To help cheer him up I related a few tales of Hollywood duplicity.

"For instance," I revealed, "when they like what you've done, they refer to it as 'a piece of shit'. Can you believe that?"

"Most unusual," agreed Kim.

"And when they reckon your stuff stinks they tell you they like it. Who could live in a world of lies and deceit like that?"

"Nobody I know," replied Philby, nervously mopping his sweaty brow. "Good lord is that the time."

Apparently he was already late for the last train from Penn Station back to DC so we shook hands quickly before Kim stumbled out into the New York evening while I finished my Scotch and wondered what had really made him so jumpy.

The following morning at the Waldorf, I was handed a large brandy and Jimmy's cake tin before one of the two smiling Sunshine Studios execs – I think it was Sherman, or it could have been Herman – told me through his gleaming white teeth, "Freddy, boy, we really, really love what you do."

Ah well!

I suppose there are compensations for becoming mixed up with Hollywood – even if it usually ends in tears. First class travel on the Queen Mary for one, which I was determined to take advantage of on the way home. On the outward journey the sea had been so rough that I spent nearly all the voyage groaning in my well-appointed cabin. You'd think I'd have been used to it, the number of times I was buffeted about on the high seas during the war. *(How on earth would we know?)* But even with its new-fangled stabilisers, the liner bucked around like a mustang.

So, on the calmer homeward leg, I was determined to grab myself a bit of high life on the ocean wave. And, let me tell you, things don't come much higher than the captain's table to which I was summoned on the first evening.

Sadly, the experience was ruined by the wrinkled dowager next to me, who insisted on perpetually squeezing my thigh under the table, while grinning dementedly in what she must have imagined was her come-hither expression. Honestly, she made Elsie the Rotherham landlady look like Lana Turner.

After the meal I fled back to my cabin and locked the door behind me. The following evening, however, the randy fossil was back on the warpath and it was while trying to dodge her that I ran straight into Guy Burgess. It says much for my predicament that the first words I gasped to him were, "Guy, in the name of all that's righteous, please help me."

To give him credit, no-one could accuse Burgess of not being quick on the uptake. As the aged harpy bore down on us, Guy grabbed me around the shoulders and planted a big, lingering smacker on my lips. He then linked my arm and steered me past the horrified granny, to whom he tipped an imaginary hat.

"For god's sake, Guy, you'll get us arrested," I said, glancing around nervously.

"Nonsense," he replied, squeezing my elbow. "These are the high seas, remember. The only thing that's taboo on a boat is leaving a floater in the swimming pool. Now how about that drink you were about to promise me."

(Homosexual activity was illegal in Britain until 1967 and offenders were often pursued ruthlessly through the courts. However, on board ships there was traditionally a much more relaxed and tolerant atmosphere).

In the bar Guy needed no prompting to relate what had been happening to him.

"I've been Blightied," he announced, proudly.

"Really? When do they demolish you?"

"Not blighted, Blightied. You know, sent home in disgrace."

Blimey, it looked as if Philby had already taken action so I decided not to mention our meeting. I noted, however, that Guy looked anything but ashamed.

"Tell me, Guy, what did you do to get sent home?"

"I biffed a rozzer."

I could hardly believe my ears.

"You slugged a cop? Jesus, man, you're lucky to be alive."

"Ah, he was only traffic."

"And that object in his holster. Made of barley sugar was it?"

Guy smiled at the memory. "The cops don't tend to go around plugging diplomats. Even in America. Nice looking boy, as well."

That night, mercifully alone in my bed, I pondered on the essential unfairness of things. I mean, I had to make a *(very)* neglected cinema classic to merit first class travel on the Queen Mary. All Burgess needed to do was strike a policeman and he too was living the Life of Riley.

Luckily the ship was so big and there was more than enough going on that I hardly saw Burgess the rest of the voyage. The few times we met, he usually had a different good-looking young man on his arm who he invariably introduced to me as, "Tom, the cabin boy."

I, on the other hand, swam and read by day and after dinner generally took in a show. One of these, in the liner's

Observation Bar, featured my old pal Jimmy Juggles who I hadn't seen since our Rotherham misadventure. After the show, during which he'd kindly introduced me to the appreciative audience, we reminisced about south Yorkshire and he tried to kid on that Elsie was aboard and hunting for me. If this were true, she'd certainly bring down the average age of my female pursuers.

Apart from that, the days slid by without much incident until a slightly odd occurrence on the penultimate morning. I'd arrived back at my cabin after breakfast to find a steward fumbling with the lock. At first I thought he might have been up to no good but he quickly assured me he was just checking the ship's safety system, which included locking and sealing cabin doors from the outside.

"You mean you could lock someone in their cabin and they wouldn't be able to get out?" I asked him.

"Oh no, sir, we'd only lock and seal the door in an absolute emergency and of course we'd first check there was no-one in there."

"Nice to hear. Why does this only happen on the Queen Mary?"

The steward looked at me oddly. "This system is in place on most passenger ships, sir. It's just that on the Queen Mary it's checked more regularly than most. We take passenger safety extremely seriously."

"That's good to know. Keep an eye out for icebergs won't you!"

On our final evening, while drinking in the Observation Bar, I was joined by Guy, minus any of his Tom, Dick and Harry the cabin boys.

He appeared more reflective than usual, as if something was weighing on his mind and it took two or three large brandies before he began to loosen up. Then he started to boast that, as well as slugging the cop, he'd picked up three speeding tickets in as many hours.

"That was careless," I told him. "You wouldn't catch that happening to me. I'm far too good a driver."

The fact was that I'd driven a car no more than half a dozen times, usually with Nancy screaming things at me. But he wasn't to know that.

"You're a driver?" said Burgess. "I never realised. Anyhow I'm not really that bad behind the wheel. I mean ..." and he leaned towards me across the table in what he imagined was a confidential manner, "I picked up those tickets on purpose."

"Why would you do that?"

"Because I've become sick of the Yanks, the bloody great shitbags!"

I looked around in alarm but luckily no-one appeared to have heard him.

"Steady on, Guy," I whispered, "Americans don't take kindly to being called shitbags. Especially by one of the mouthy Limeys whose ass they saved."

"Well fuck 'em all and the asses they rode into town on," he shouted, knocking over his drink in the process. Thankfully this calamity seemed to calm Guy down and he became reflective once again.

"I've got to keep my head, that's the thing," he said, nodding to himself.

"You certainly do," I told him. "Or some Yankie asshole will knock it off."

Guy looked blearily at me. "You keep your head, don't you Francis? A man for a crisis – that's you, old fellow."

I agreed that I'd encountered enough scrapes to know my way around them.

Guy smiled to himself. "Look at the way you dealt with that Russian who ended up skewered to the back of your study door. I mean," and he started giggling to himself, "you certainly took him down a peg or two!" The last bit was shouted out for effect so I put my hand on his arm.

325

"Guy, we don't really want everyone knowing about that," I said and he winked and tapped the side of his nose.

"Mum's the word, eh?" he said, winking again. "Although I still don't know how you kept a straight face."

"It wasn't exactly funny."

"Oh but it was, old man," said Guy chuckling to himself. "I mean, here you are in a life or death struggle, while on the radio good old Tommy Handley's blathering on ten to the dozen. 'Can I do you now, sir?' Priceless!"

Burgess was right about one thing; I could keep cool in a crisis – as I was proving at that very moment, although my heart was pounding like one of the ship's engines. I told Guy I was going to the toilet and left him ogling the barman.

Bending over the sink, I tried hard to compose myself. You see, although he didn't realise it, Burgess had just announced that he was working for the Russians. I was sure of it because he knew about ITMA being on the radio during my desperate struggle - and I'd never mentioned that fact to a soul, not even Nancy. That meant that he, and quite possibly Philby, must have been waiting outside as I battled for my life.

I splashed cold water all over my face, gazed in the mirror and tried to fit what I'd just heard into some kind of pattern. It was clear that Guy's unscheduled trip home was no accident. He knew exactly what he was doing when he hit that traffic cop – and so too did Philby. Things were coming to a head and, although I didn't yet know how, I made a solemn promise to my dazed reflection that I'd have a hand in the fate of both men.

Chapter Fifteen: A Visit to Your Uncle Joe

What's that phrase really annoying people use these days? A goldfish is not just for Christmas? No that's not it. Ah, I remember, it's 'be careful what you wish for'. In other words, the moment you achieve your heart's desire, it will turn round and bite you on the bum. That's if you've also turned round. Well, in the fortnight that followed my Queen Mary homecoming, I wished passionately for nothing more than a chance to bring Guy Burgess down and my bum could go to the devil – so to speak.

I realised it was no good marauding up and down Whitehall with a loud-hailer, telling the great and good what a treacherous so-and-so he was but I was sure, given the right opportunity, that I could really stick the knife in. Some hope! Burgess seemed to have disappeared off the face of the earth and, remembering Philby's jumpy demeanour in New York, I concluded that the game was already afoot.

So, with Burgess having gone to ground, it appeared that my chance had come and gone. What I didn't find out until much later was that instead of eagerly rushing to carry out Philby's instructions, Burgess typically spent his days tarrying with a new lover – one of the Queen Mary cabin boys for all I knew. Then, when he finally got round to acting, he presented me with what I'd waited for - a gold-plated chance to nail him.

The whole sorry business had preoccupied me since I got home and it showed. More than a fortnight later, for instance, while Nancy and I sat on the back row of the news theatre at Victoria Station, it was still all I could think about. As I brooded, Nancy was getting angry, though mercifully for once not at me. She glowered through a smoky blue haze at the screen in the nearly-empty cinema.

"Honestly what does he look like," she said, appropriately, out of the blue. "Franco, your pal's making a fool of himself again. The big baby."

It's unlikely that I would have responded at all had Nancy not accompanied her comment with a sharp elbow in my ribs.

"Ow, what was that for, Nance?"

"It's Churchill, just look at him."

I peered through the cigarette haze and saw the hero of Omdurman, scourge of the Boer and saviour of our island race grinning like a toddler as he excitedly travelled up and down an escalator.

Mystified, I asked, "Is he doing his Christmas shopping?"

"No, he's at the Dome of Discovery. You'd think he'd never seen an escalator before, the great muffin."

"Someone's probably told him he's on one of those new rides at Battersea Park."

Nancy glared at the cinema screen again.

"I wouldn't mind," she said angrily, "but he's been against the Festival from the start. Now look at him – the hypocrite." *(Churchill, along with Beaverbrook, had been among the siren voices which opposed the Festival of Britain at every turn. And when he became Prime Minister again in October 1951 he gave an order to demolish everything on the South Bank site except the Festival Hall which still stands. Churchill reportedly described the architecture of the Festival as 'too Socialist').*

"Maybe Winston should try climbing the Skylon next," I mused. "Now I would pay to see him stuck on top of that like a big fat cocktail cherry. Blimey, are we having an earthquake?"

"We aren't but they are," said Nancy indicating with her eyes along the row of bouncing seats to where a not-so-young man and woman were going at it hammer and tongs.

"I hope he's got some protection," I told Nancy.

"Looks like he might need it," she replied as the fleapit fancy man's thoroughly modern missy swung her bulk on top of him before they resumed relations.

"Let's get out of here," I said.

The warmth of the Spring evening immediately cheered us up and, on a whim, we decided to catch the 44 down to Battersea and see if the new funfair had more to offer than bouncing cinema seats. It would be the first time we'd been to anything Festival-related since the King, dutiful monarch that he turned out to be, had opened proceedings three weeks before.

And what a spectacle it was. The excited crowds, unusually garish colours and smells of candy floss, toffee apples and fried potatoes mingled to give us both an immediate lift. For the first time in a fortnight, I began to relax as Nancy shunted me excitedly from one ride to the next, cheerfully admitting that she'd never been to a funfair before.

"We'll bring the children here at the weekend," shouted Nancy as we rode on the Big Dipper, but could not resist adding, "whereas all these youngsters should be in bed as it's school tomorrow."

Luckily nobody could hear her admonishment through the screams and clattering of cars on the rails.

"Relax," I said, squeezing Nancy's arm, "it is Thursday and they're all having a really smashing time."

We got home around ten o'clock thoroughly relaxed and happy, to be greeted by Hilda, who had been babysitting. She informed us that Guy Burgess had rung three or four times.

"He's not changed a bit the saucy blighter," she said, stroking her hair and smiling as she put on her coat. "Always had an eye for the ladies did Mr Guy."

I didn't have the heart to enlighten her about Guy's retinue of cabin boys and she disappeared into the night still twittering about "that naughty boy." Hilda had little idea just how naughty Guy Burgess had actually been.

When Guy rang again a few minutes later, I detected an uncharacteristic edge to his voice, the Old Etonian certainty undermined by events outside his control. I knew at once that this could be the chance I'd been waiting for. But I had to play it very cool and see how events unravelled.

"Thing is, old boy," he said after the usual pleasantries, "I've gone and turned my confounded ankle over."

"And you want me to come round and kick the cat?"

"Certainly not! I'd have to go and buy a cat for a start. No, I ... I'd like you to drive me somewhere."

Hell's bells, I hadn't driven anywhere since the war but I wasn't telling him that – especially as this sounded like my big chance. And I had been boasting to him about it just three weeks before.

Guy must have sensed my mounting excitement but, luckily, put it down to something else entirely.

"Don't fret about your petrol coupons," he said. "We'll go in my jalopy."

"I didn't know you had a jalopy."

"Just a little run-around I've hired."

"Why on earth would you hire a car, Guy? Are you planning fisticuffs with more policemen?"

He paused for a second and I became aware of his rapid breathing.

"Of course not. The thing is, a pal of mine is going on holiday - to France - and I'd like to see him off in style."

"Do I know this pal of yours?"

There was another longer pause before Guy revealed who our third man would be.

"It's Don Maclean, old thing. I know you two have had your moments but I was kind of hoping you'd let bygones be bygones and all that."

Well, one thing was certain. I would not be instrumental in allowing this pair to flee the country and escape what

330

was coming to them. But for the moment I had to play a slightly cannier game.

"If Don's pardoned me for the pasting I gave him in front of Clem Attlee," I told Guy, "then I'm big enough not to remember what he did." Which, of course, was foisting Burgess, BO and all, on to our family.

"Splendid chap!" replied Guy. "Come round to where I'm staying at about four tomorrow and we'll set off from there."

He gave me an address in Wandsworth and, after an uncharacteristically brief observation about the weather, rung off. I walked thoughtfully into the sitting room where Nancy was cradling a mug of cocoa, her legs tucked up underneath her. Huddled up on the settee like that, she looked vulnerable – not a word I'd normally use to describe my wife. I sat down and put my arm around her.

"What's the matter?"

"Nothing. What did he want?"

"He's keen to come back and live here."

I was ready for a tongue-lashing and a fist fight, not necessarily in that order either. But no attack came. Instead Nancy looked bleakly at me and said, "Come on, Francis, what did Guy Burgess want?"

I don't think she'd ever used the name Francis before and it threw me.

"Oh, er, he and Don Maclean are off to France for a hol. I'm just driving them there."

"Where are you driving them?"

"I didn't ask. Dover I suppose. You're sure you're OK, Nance?"

Her lip was trembling and I could swear there were tears in her eyes.

"You won't be in any danger, will you?" she asked, trying to control her voice.

"Of course not. Unless lynch mobs are roaming the A23 through Crawley."

Nancy attempted a weak smile before lighting a cigarette and picking up a script from the coffee table. I reckoned I needed something a bit stronger than cocoa but, as I stood up, Nancy took hold of my arm.

"Please be careful," she said simply.

"Have you ever known me to spill whisky?"

She gave me another faint smile before returning to her script. Meanwhile I poured a Scotch and water and watched her. She was still in the simple white blouse she wore for work, her blond hair was tied back in a ponytail and she had no shoes on. My mind leapt back sixteen years to the day I came across her torturing the ivories at Protheroe. She still looked every bit as stunning.

Nancy noticed me eyeballing her but didn't say anything. She merely grinned again and half-closed her eyes.

I sat in an armchair next to the hearth and tried to absorb what Guy had told me. It was obvious that he and Maclean were intent on going further than Boulogne or wherever – a lot further. And I had to find a way of stopping them. But how?

The solution was no more apparent the following afternoon when I stood on the top step of a handsome three-storey Victorian terrace facing Wandsworth Common. A couple of hundred yards away I could just glimpse the tallest turrets of the prison – surely a good omen if things went my way.

I had barely taken my finger off the bell button when the front door flew open. A tall, not quite handsome young man - hardly more than a big boy really - stood there with an expression that suggested he might well try to murder me. The youth smoothed back his wavy fair hair and glared down a long thin nose.

"What d'you want?"

The accent was a bit of an affected mess – pitched somewhere between Mill Hill and Millwall.

I glared back at him without speaking until he took a deep breath and turned away.

"A civil tongue would do for a start, sonny," I said sharply.

"Oh."

He stepped back, much less confident now, and watched me carefully.

"I suppose you're here to see Guy?"

"I suppose I am," I said, brushing past him into the cramped hallway in which a bicycle leant against the wall amidst a pile of clutter.

"What do you want with Guy?"

Evidently this was not someone to whom small talk came naturally.

"We're off down to Brighton," I told him, "For a dirty weekend ..."

The young man's face instantly became a mask of tearful fury and he couldn't help clenching and unclenching his fists.

"... of motorbike scrambling."

Now thoroughly confused and miserable, he started picking at a loose thread on his sleeveless pullover.

"Types like you have never had any time for the likes of us," he said bitterly.

I leaned over to him. "If you mean miserable whining little bastards then no I haven't. Now go and tell your lord and master that I'm here."

There was no need for that, however, as Guy appeared at the top of the stairs and began to limp slowly down. He indicated the youth.

"Ah, Francis, I see you've met Ross. He's a dish isn't he?"

"He's a little darling all right."

Ross looked at me with loathing.

"In fact he was overjoyed to hear about our dirty weekend in Brighton."

Burgess looked puzzled for a moment before breaking into a grin. He stepped off the bottom step and held his arms out to the pouting Ross.

"Come here, lover," he said and embraced the man, adding, "Quis separabit?" *(Who shall separate us?)*

Ross stared moodily back at Guy who pointed at me.

"Don't take any notice of old Frankie," he said. "He's a well-known comedian. We're forever laughing in his company."

"You won't be laughing soon, you traitorous shit," I thought but limited myself to the observation, "Laugh and the world laughs with you, eh?"

"Francis, it is as if Aristotle had never left us," said Guy, who spun Ross away from me and whispered something to him. I wasn't meant to hear it but I caught, "keep the bed warm, I'll be back later tonight."

He was obviously deceiving poor old Ross as well as everyone else but I hadn't the time or inclination to start grieving over that. After all, I still hadn't worked out my strategy.

Guy released Ross with a kiss, snatched his jacket from the peg and went carefully down the front steps leaning heavily on my arm. I could imagine the look on Ross's face.

"Think you can drive this?" said Guy pointing to a small cream-coloured car parked in front of the house.

"Be serious. I practically grew up driving Ford Pops."

"Pity this is an Austin A40 then. Here's the key."

While helping Guy into the passenger seat, I wondered for a moment where his bag was before realising he'd probably put it in the boot already so as not to alarm Ross. I climbed into the driver's seat and after a couple of comedy false starts – one of which propelled us backwards ten yards – I managed to get her going.

"Not working tonight?" Guy asked as I eased us into the homeward bound Friday traffic on the A214 towards Streatham.

"I'm resting this week," I told him, "But it's back to The Palladium on Monday. You must come. Bring Ross too; he looks like he could do with a laugh."

Even though it was rush hour, the 20-mile journey to where Maclean lived should have taken us no more than an hour. However, with Guy's woeful map reading and my even more hopeless driving, it took us twice as long.

My lack of skill was so marked that at one point in the journey, after frenzied attempts at double de-clutching, I felt obliged to apologise to Guy for half wrecking his gearbox.

"No worries, old thing," he said uncertainly. "Just get us there in one piece."

Finally, just after six we bounced into the picture postcard village of Tatsfield, high up on the North Downs. The magnificent view across the Weald reminded me of being at Churchill's home, Chartwell, in 1936 – with good reason as you'll see shortly.

I slowed down as we passed a large red-brick pub festooned with hanging baskets bursting with anemonies and primulas. The scene looked so inviting that I had half a mind to join the shirt-sleeved crowd putting away warm beer at their leisure in the early evening sun. However, Guy gently urged me on and, round the next corner, ordered me to swing sharp left. We were on a long drive which ended in front of a huge Victorian house, set in considerable grounds.

"Bloody hell," I exclaimed. "Don must be loaded."

"It's only a semi," Guy sniffed.

While I was helping him out of the car I heard the front door open and close followed by the crunching of footsteps on gravel. I looked up expecting to see Maclean but, of all people, who should be approaching but Anthony Blunt. On seeing me, his mouth fell open in total shock and dismay before he glared at Guy and marched off down the drive without a word.

"What's Dandini doing here?" I said.

"I ... I ... really have no idea," Guy replied.

When Maclean answered the door, he struggled not to look as staggered as Blunt had been when he saw me. Evidently Guy hadn't seen fit to mention who their chauffeur would be.

"You'd both better come in," he snapped.

Maclean was still wearing his Foreign Office tie but that was the only smart thing about him. He looked about ten times worse than when we last met, which took some doing as, at the time, he'd been writhing around on the Downing Street pavement. He was even more overweight, there was an ordnance map of prominent blood vessels across his sagging, wax-like features and his teeth were discoloured.

"You're looking extremely well, Donald," I told him as I stepped inside. "Had a good day at the office?"

Maclean glanced in exasperation at Burgess who mumbled, "I went over on my ankle. Francis has kindly offered to drive us to Southampton."

Maclean turned to me and I noticed his light hair was streaked with grey.

"In which case," he said, "thanks are in order. Please come in."

He ushered us into the sitting room, quickly poured out three large Scotches and handed them round.

"King and Country," I said raising my glass.

"King and Country," mumbled Burgess and Maclean in unison.

I noted that Maclean was trying to avoid my gaze.

"How's my old sparring partner Oswald Grosvenor?" I asked him. "I hope you'll pass on my regards."

"That would be difficult," replied Maclean, "Grosvenor died three years ago."

"We'll miss him," I said. "He was a great patriot."

Maclean nodded but said nothing. He was deep in thought.

"Three years ago, eh," I mused. "That would be just about the time Carlton Frobisher passed away too. You remember Carlton of course, Don."

The mention of Frobisher snapped Maclean brutally out of the reverie. His mouth twisted in an expression of distaste.

"I do remember Frobisher," he said. "He was a vicious thug. A psychopath."

"I doubt that," I snapped back, "but at any rate his kind of thuggery helped us win the war. And kept the world safe for people like you to go about your business."

Maclean's eyes flashed and for a moment I reckoned he was about to fly at me. It would have been an interesting bout too as he had bulked up a couple of weights from middle to cruiser since 1945.

However, speculation was rendered academic when Maclean glanced over my shoulder and took a step back. I turned to face a tired, heavily-pregnant dark-haired woman in her thirties. She gazed at me like I was something the dog had fetched in before asking in a surprisingly refined accent straight out of the American mid-West, "Don, who's our friend?"

In the event it was Guy who did the introductions. "Ah, Mel," he said, kissing her hand. "It's been far too long. Allow me to present my good friend Francis Thirkettle. Francis this is Don's wife Melinda."

We shook hands but she continued to eye me warily so I made an attempt to break the ice.

"I'm driving your husband to the boat tonight as Guy has turned his ankle over. You really must stop chasing those ladies, Guy."

Evidently irony was not Melinda Maclean's long suit because my whimsical salvo made absolutely no impression on her. This didn't bother me at all but I made a final attempt for form's sake.

"Nice place you have here, Melinda. I just love the wallpaper."

It was hideous actually, the sort of flowery nonsense with twigs and budgerigars that Nancy dismissed as 'chocolate box chic'. But then I had to admit, my wife did have genuine style.

I expected little reaction from my lame compliment but all at once Melinda's features softened and she gave me what must have passed in her circles as a smile.

"Well I thank you, Mr Thirkettle," she said. "It's kinda pleasing that you like our humble home."

"It's absolutely enchanting," I told her. "And please call me Francis, Frankie or just Funnybone. I'll come running when you shout any of them."

"And you must call me Mel. Come and join us for the party."

She linked my arm and we stepped across the hall into the dining room where the table was laid out festively. In the middle was a small sponge cake with "Happy Birthday Daddy" iced in pink on to the top.

I turned to Maclean who'd followed us in.

"Don, you didn't tell us it was your birthday," I said and shook his hand warmly. "Best wishes, old fellow. How old are you. Fifty-two?"

Maclean's eyes went back into danger mode. "I'm thirty-eight," he hissed.

"Oops," I replied, "it must be the light in here."

I'd love to report that Donald Maclean's birthday meal, the last he would ever eat in England, was a joyous affair. Sadly this was not the case and the whole shebang was shrouded in gloom.

Yet it was not without its touching aspects. Maclean's two sons – around five and six years old - sat down with us at the table and I could not help but notice the sad and poignant looks that flashed between Melinda and Don when they were not stealing glances at their best-behaved boys. Moreover, seeing the pride Maclean obviously felt surrounded by his family, present and future, began to make me uncomfortable. After all, I had three children who I could not bear to be without. Plus a wife who worshipped the good earth upon which I walked – please stay with me on this one. Neither had Maclean been involved in the Russian Bilyatov's attack upon me.

Maybe, if all things were considered equally, Donald Maclean should be allowed an escape route, a chance to disappear into the night. Along with Guy Burgess? No, definitely not. I was unsure how to accomplish it but Burgess would face justice for what he had done – and was about to do.

And then, quite unexpectedly, there came a moment that made everything clear as crystal. The meal was over and Guy had helped Mel clear the pots away while Donald took his boys into the sitting room for a private word. I got up from the dining table with the intention of looking round for some kind of map to steer us towards Southampton.

A small bookshelf by the kitchen door had just the thing - The English Countrygoer. However, as I bent down to pick up the book, I caught a snatch of urgent conversation from within the kitchen.

Unaware I was ear-holing, Burgess said, "I shall leave it a week or two."

In a whisper, Mel replied, "You're right. We must wait until things have died down. Then you can come and bring me any news you have."

"There'll be a tremendous fuss, Mel, but I promise I'll do my best to shield you from it ... and then maybe in a few months ..."

From the sitting room I heard Maclean say, "Now run along, there's good chaps."

I quickly stepped back to the dining table and sat down with The English Countrygoer open in front of me.

My brain was turning somersaults. That was it! Guy Burgess was never supposed to flee! He'd been deputed to get his pal safely out of the country before Maclean was unmasked as a traitor. Then Guy could brazen out what - if anything - was thrown at him. It all fitted! After all, Moscow would not suit Guy one bit. He may still have been in thrall to a romantic concept of furthering the cause - like a lot of his posh Cambridge pals - but clearly that meant travelling no further east than the Channel ports and certainly nowhere near Uncle Joe Stalin's palace of varieties. It was now perfectly obvious what I must do.

Guy limped into the dining room and saw me apparently perusing the map.

"Good man, Francis," he said, "'dimidium facti qui coepit habet - he who has begun has the work half done' - that's Horace by the way."

I looked up from my supposed labours and replied as coolly as I could, "Hold Your Hand Out, You Naughty Boy. That's Florrie Forde by the way."

Guy grinned and said, "What a card you are, Francis. I really must catch one of your shows some time."

"You'll have to be sharp, buster," I thought but contented myself with checking the time.

"Shouldn't we be moving?" I asked.

"I suppose so," replied Guy. "Just let Don finish saying his goodbyes to Mel."

"He's going to San Malo not San Francisco, for goodness sake."

"Er, true, but they are very close."

Within ten minutes, Maclean had completed his farewells and we were on the road just as dusk was falling and the drinkers in front of the Old Ship had begun to disperse.

While I drove, Burgess and Maclean sat in the back and whispered like naughty schoolboys. My thoughts turned to the boisterous Old Trafford trip in 1948 when Tommy and I happily punched out each other's lights to Les's annoyance. This pair in the back were much less raucous but equally as conspiratorial. And it was because I was straining so hard to hear what they were whispering about that we ended up where we did.

Maclean was the first to notice that something was amiss. He stared out of the side window into the gloom and said, "This doesn't look like the A25 at all. Where are you taking us, Francis?"

I stopped the car and got out to see if there were any signs around. We were in a lane lined with beech trees which, even in this half light, looked vaguely familiar to me. Across the road and beyond a high outer wall I could see the silhouette of a large house and it was only as I approached the gate I realised with a jolt that I'd been there before, albeit fifteen years ago.

I rushed breathlessly back to the car.

"You'll never guess," I eagerly told my passengers, "where we are."

"I'm hoping you'll say halfway to Southampton," replied Burgess.

"No. We're right outside Chartwell Manor, you know Winston Churchill's place."

In the driving mirror I saw Maclean grab Burgess's arm in total terror.

"What on earth do you m...mean by this," said Maclean, his voice rising and falling in blind panic.

"What do you mean what do I mean?"

"He means," spat Burgess, "what could have possessed you to bring us to see Winston Churchill?"

"Nothing possessed me. I just got lost and we ended up here. Or maybe an invisible hand guided me towards Winston's."

Maclean slumped back into his seat, breathing heavily and irregularly. Sweat was cascading off his forehead. Burgess leaned forward, grabbed The English Countrygoer from the front seat and examined it by the beam of a small torch he pulled out of his jacket.

"Jesus and Mary," he said shaking his head, "we're way off track. Turn the car round, Francis."

In my view it's unwise to ask an inexperienced driver to do a three-point turn at any time but particularly in the dark. It took five minutes of jerking, gear-crunching and expletives from the back seat before we were finally on our way to the A25.

"That wasn't too bad, was it?" I told them cheerily. "Actually, I don't expect Winston was in. He's probably still going up and down the escalators at the Dome of Discovery."

From that point Burgess took charge of the journey with considerably more skill than he'd displayed on the trip from London and we were soon on the A25 bound for Dorking.

The shock of pitching up outside the home of the Soviet Union's most implacable enemy had truly shaken Maclean and, once Burgess could be certain we were heading the right way, he put his arm around his shivering, tearful pal.

They hardly spoke again on the entire journey, apart from when we passed a sign saying Southampton was ten miles away.

"Don't worry," I heard Burgess whisper, "you'll soon be on that boat and away."

This confirmed what I'd suspected. Wherever Maclean was heading, Burgess was not planning on going with him.

Although the words were supposed to soothe Maclean, they had the opposite effect.

"Have you got my ticket?" he snapped.

Burgess confidently tapped his coat pocket.

"Let me see it."

"Jesus Christ, Don."

"Show me. Now!"

Reluctantly, Burgess pulled the ticket from his inside pocket and handed it to Maclean who breathed a sigh of relief. Then he examined it more closely.

"For god's sake," he whispered desperately, "hand me your flashlight."

Burgess gave him the torch and Maclean urgently scanned the ticket before turning to his friend in despair.

"You dolt, it's for the wrong bloody date!" he wailed. "This says the 26th. The SS Falaise sails at 11.45 on the 25th. My birthday, remember?"

Burgess snatched the ticket, scanned it and raised his eyebrows. It was his turn to be flustered.

"Don't worry, Don," he panted. "I'll make everything right at the docks, I promise. There'll ... there'll be an office."

"Nobody works at this time of night!" By now Maclean was almost screaming.

"Don, please stay strong," urged Burgess, indicating my back with his eyes. I could see it was taking great effort but Maclean managed to remain silent for the rest of the journey.

At around eleven-fifteen we pulled into Southampton's western dock and cruised along the cobbled road at the harbour side until we came upon a small but brightly lit office. It was no more than a large shed, set against the dock wall.

My passengers alighted and Burgess made a decent attempt at limping rather quickly after the rushing Maclean. I got out of the car and sniffed the air which smelled of tar and salt. Even by the dockside's dim lamps I could see there were few people around. Either the passengers were already on board or there wasn't much demand for a midnight trip to France.

As I leaned on the car door, a police constable approached and indicated the vehicle.

"Is this yours, sir?"

"Yes, officer. Well it's a hired car actually. Is there a problem?"

The constable rubbed his chin. "Not at all, sir. It's just that I'd advise you not to leave it there any length of time."

"Don't worry. We're just seeing a friend onto the SS Falaise."

The policeman nodded. "That's about two hundred yards further on," he said pointing down the dock road.

As he spoke, I saw over his shoulder that Burgess had appeared in the doorway of the office. The moment he realised I was talking to an officer of the law he turned and desperately shoved Maclean back into the shed before dodging after him.

"Yes," I told the constable, "my friend is in there clearing up a problem with his ticket." I indicated the office and the policeman looked round briefly before turning back. "We'll be gone before you know it," I said.

"Well take care you don't leave the car up there for long either," he advised. "We get a good few lorries along here and you wouldn't want to take it back scratched would you?"

"Absolutely not. Thanks for the gen, constable."

The officer saluted and moved off. When he was fifty yards away Burgess and Maclean emerged from the office like a pair of miscreants from the head's study. I got back into the car and they followed me.

"What did he want?"

"Who do you mean, Guy? Oh, the policeman? He was giving me a sharp warning."

"What about?"

"Apparently there's a maniac on the loose. This fellow sneaks on to boats and, when they're in the middle of the Channel, he starts throwing passengers into the sea one by

344

one. I should keep an eye out for him, Don. Or walk around in a lifebelt."

Maclean, deep in his own thoughts, barely registered what I'd said. Burgess's radar, on the other hand, had picked up my frivolous tone.

"Very funny, I'm sure," he sneered.

"And, Guy, be careful he doesn't toss you off as well. Oh, I forgot you're not going, are you."

I started the car and we rolled along the dock-side, passing the police constable who saluted again. As the SS Falaise loomed above us, I could hear its engines turning over and noticed black smoke beginning to pour from its single funnel.

I stopped the car, got out and took Maclean's case from the boot. By now Burgess was out of the vehicle, leaning on Maclean's arm.

For his part, Maclean was gazing sadly round the docks. It was ironic - and maybe fitting - that a man born into the bosom of the British upper class would take away proletarian symbols such as dim street lights, cobbles and the pungent smell of smoke as final memories of the country he'd betrayed.

"Time to go, Don," said Burgess with a regretful smile and Maclean held out his free hand to me.

"Thank you for the ride, Francis. I do hope there are no hard feelings between us."

"None whatsoever, Don. Apart from the fact I'm really jealous about where you're going."

Maclean shot Burgess a look of alarm.

"I mean just don't drink too much of that fine French wine. And see you in a couple of weeks."

Burgess tugged gently at his friend's sleeve and they turned away from me. Burgess said over his shoulder, "I'll just see him to his cabin. I'll be back in a few minutes, Francis."

"Take your time," I replied. "I'll be here until acta est fibula." *(The drama has been acted out).*

For a second Burgess looked bemused and then he nodded. "Good man," he said.

The pair of them went slowly arm-in-arm up the gangplank like an old married couple. At the top Burgess showed the boarding officer the ticket and after a few words, the officer nodded and indicated the way to go. The moment they were out of sight, I tore off my jacket, draped it over my arm and sprinted up the gangplank.

The boarding officer could not have been more helpful when I told him I had to get the coat to one of the two gentlemen who had just come aboard. He even gave me detailed directions to Maclean's cabin.

"But don't linger, sir," the officer warned. "The ship sails in ten minutes."

"That's plenty of time," I replied with a smile.

I sprinted off so eagerly that I nearly caught them up, skidding to a halt just in time to see Burgess and Maclean being ushered into a cabin. Moments later the steward came out, staring at a sixpence in his palm and shaking his head.

"Not great tippers, eh?" I said as he walked past.

The steward, a small stocky lad with dark curly hair and washed-in stains on his off-white uniform, shook his head.

"How would you like to earn a lot more than that?"

Clenching his fists, the steward stood in front of me. Although the top of his head barely reached my chin, I could see by the way he carried himself that he was a fighter.

"And what would you mean by that, sir?"

I smiled and held my hands up.

"Relax, I don't mean what you think I mean."

Then I outlined exactly what I wanted him to do. Listening intently, he grew more and more alarmed.

"I can't do that," he protested. "Besides it's impossible anyway."

346

"They can lock cabin doors from the outside on the Queen Mary so I'm guessing they can do it on this tub as well."

The steward glanced around nervously before whispering, "We can't possibly do it with people inside the cabin. It could be dangerous."

I took a ten pound note out of my wallet and stuck into the lad's top pocket.

"It would only be until the boat has left the dock and then you can unlock the door. In fact I insist you do it then. And nobody's hurt – or any the wiser."

Although he was still unsure, I could sense the possibility of easy money was working its spell. I provided further stimulus.

"Tell you what, er ..."

"William."

"Tell you what, William. If I see the boat has sailed without my two pals getting off there's another tenner in it for you."

"How do I know you'll deliver?"

He was hooked.

"Write down your address and I'll do just that. Straight away. Scout's honour."

The steward nodded and added, "OK but it's another ten and twenty to my house. I only live round the corner in Woolston."

He wrote down the address on his pad and tore off the sheet. Time was now of the essence and I was in no position to bargain.

"It's a deal. Do they call you Billy the Kid?"

I stuffed another tenner into his pocket and told him, "Now get to it."

William paused. "This is all a prank, isn't it?" he said uncertainly.

"That's right, Will," I said, patting him on the shoulder. "The whole thing is just one great game."

As I turned to walk away, the ship's public address system spluttered into life with the announcement that non-passengers should leave the boat. I looked back and saw William had already made himself scarce.

Approaching the gangplank, it occurred to me that the boarding officer might notice Guy Burgess had not left the boat but luckily he was deep in conversation with a colleague. Besides, Guy could easily have gone unnoticed among the number of non-passengers disembarking all at once.

I chose my position carefully while the ship's propellers whined and bumped, gently easing the craft away from the dock side. I was under the strongest light I could find along that section of the harbour road and watched intently as the boat slowly swung its bow round towards The Solent. There was no way back now.

The SS Falaise had made the middle of Southampton Water when I noticed two figures had appeared by the stern rail. One stood as still as a statue but the other appeared extraordinarily animated. I signalled energetically to him, hoping he'd seen me under the light and it seemed he had because he waved frantically back. Only he wasn't waving as such. It appeared that Guy Burgess was trying, very successfully I had to admit, to convey a mixture of fear, anger and the threat of retribution in his flailing arm movements. So I decided to send him a message of my own.

Bathed in the yellow sodium light, I mimed a large spike sticking out of my throat and pointed back accusingly at Burgess. In a flash his flailing arm movements stopped. I had a further two tableaux for him to consider. The first was mimicking a phone call while again pointing directly at him; the final part of this impromptu pantomime saw me point at Burgess again, tilt my head to one side and move a clenched fist up and down above my neck – as if tightening a noose.

Now Burgess was as statuesque as Maclean next to him. I could see he was staring hard but I was unsure if his gaze was focused on me or at the very last glimpse of England he'd ever have before the Lord - or whoever - claimed him. Burgess's chin then dropped on to his chest and his hands went slowly up to his head. He can't possibly have seen me wave goodbye to him for the final time.

Of course, had he been thinking straight, Burgess might usefully have wondered who the hell I was going to phone and with exactly what evidence? The fact was that I had no idea to whom I could have passed on my suspicions. The service had changed fundamentally since I was involved with it during wartime. Maybe Winston would have appreciated a call.

I walked slowly back towards the dock gates past the hire car, taking care to check that the policeman was not around. Approaching the gates, I took the Austin's key out of my pocket and threw it as far as I could into the harbour. I did not hear the splash.

I thought I'd have to walk to Woolston, wherever that was, but luckily there was a taxi idling just outside the gates and within five minutes I was in front of William's house on a cramped terrace, pushing an envelope, provided by the cabbie, through the letterbox. The twenty quid inside the envelope was the final part of my thanks for the steward's invaluable help in ridding Britain of not just one but two dirty rotten scoundrels. I reached the station with five minutes to spare before the final train to London pulled out.

(This bizarre episode finally clears up the mystery of why Guy Burgess joined Donald Maclean as he fled to Moscow. This outcome was the one least desired by Kim Philby because his close links with Burgess shone an unwelcome light on him and ended his career in MI6. Unlike Maclean, Guy Francis De Moncy Burgess never

came to terms with life in Moscow and died there twelve years later, a 52-year-old alcoholic).

It was nearly two o'clock when a cab dropped me off in front of our house – and I realised there were no door keys in any of my pockets. I agonised for a few moments but there was nothing for it; short of breaking a window I would have to wake Nancy with all that entailed.

But when I rapped softly on the front door, it swung open. I was enough on edge after the events earlier on and this development, with its echoes of the Russian's assault on me, put the tin lid on it.

The hall was in complete darkness but I could see a faint light under one of the doors, this time to the sitting room and not the study. I reflected I had never told Nancy the full story of what had happened with Bilyatov. I had eventually explained away my wounds and evidence of chaos in the study with the story that I'd interrupted a burglar, we had fought and I ended up slinging him out on to the street.

Whatever the story, I was relieved when, on opening the sitting room door, I saw Nancy dozing in the armchair. Almost panting with joy, I shook her gently and she opened her eyes and smiled. Then she jumped to her feet and flung her arms around me.

"Oh, Franco," she cried. "I didn't think you were coming back."

"Why?" I asked in amazement.

She turned her head away from me. "You looked so determined when you went out. Like you did during the war. Oh, Franco, I was so afraid I'd lose you."

And then, most un-Nancy-like, she burst into tears. I managed to soothe her and over a mug of coffee told her the full story of the Russian's attack, Guy's involvement in it and his unscheduled flight to the continent with his treacherous pal.

"So it's highly unlikely you'll be tearing a strip off Guy Burgess again. Not unless you intend visiting Moscow."

Strangely enough, Nancy didn't look as delighted about Burgess's disappearance as I thought she would. Instead, she wanted to know if I was absolutely sure he was a traitor.

I shrugged. "We'll find out soon enough when their disappearance is discovered but my strong feeling is that Carlton Frobisher was right all along."

Nancy bit her lip. "But how can you be so certain?"

"Because it was Guy, along with Kim, who set the Russian on me in the first place."

And I told her about Burgess and Philby arguing in this very room – a dispute I was never meant to see or hear – followed by the murderous attack on me a few days later. Finally I related my drunken conversation with Guy on the Queen Mary in which he let slip information only I knew about.

"What was it?" asked Nancy breathlessly.

"The name of the programme on the radio as I struggled to survive."

Nancy's eyes widened so much I wondered if she was going to have some kind of seizure but I decided to plough on.

"You see, I've never told another living soul that the show on the radio that awful night was ..."

"ITMA, starring Tommy Handley."

Nancy said this in a strange deadpan manner but she might as well have hit me over the head with a shovel such was the shock it gave me. I leapt away from her aghast. My own wife had involvement in this horror. I was in complete turmoil.

"Nancy, how in heaven's name can you know information that no-one else is party to?" I screamed. "Tell me now, woman!"

"Because you announced it to the whole room at Reg and Evie's."

351

Now, I don't recall this at all but, according to Nancy, I arrived home early one evening much the worse for wear; so sozzled in fact that Guy Burgess was supporting me. He helped Nancy sober me up enough to attend the party and then he came along for support - and the free booze. It was after I'd had a quick nap that I began to relate to an appreciative audience the sanitised version of what happened the night I caught an intruder in our house.

Nancy added, "You said, and it got a great laugh, that you kicked this burglar down the street to the background of Mrs Mopp saying, 'Can I do you now, sir?' So that's how Guy Burgess knew about ITMA."

"Oh bloody hell!"

I'd cocked things up good and proper ... and I still hadn't a clue who Reg and Evie were!

(Editor's final footnote: Frankie should not unduly 'beat himself up' – as the unpaid interns in our publishing house would doubtless have it. Guy Burgess may or may not have been involved in setting the Russian on to Frankie but there was no doubt he had been spying for the Soviet Union since the mid-Thirties. So he got what was coming to him – and was thus spared the experience of watching Frankie's early television career, which might get the odd mention in Volume Two).

THE END
(For now, chums!)